Jet Trails
Looking for Blue Skies

by

M. H. Sullivan

Romagnoli Publications

RP

This book was printed in the United States of America.

First Edition

To order additional copies of this book, contact: www.romagnoli-publications.com

ISBN-13: 978-1-891486-01-2

Edited by Elizabeth A. Romagnoli
Cover designed by Lisa M. Romagnoli
Cover photography by Maureen S. Romagnoli

Romagnoli Publications
Manchester, NH, USA
email: romagnoli.publications@gmail.com
website: www.romagnoli-publications.com

To Overseas Brats

You may not always end up where you thought you were going,
but you'll always end up where you were meant to be.

- Unknown

Table of Contents

Chapter 1   Yesterday

When Meara climbed into Jill's car back in Boston, she had no idea that her trip to the Oregon Coast to plan her future would snowball into an unplanned jaunt across northern Italy and Switzerland with a man she barely knew.

As she sat on the Oregon beach staring out at the ocean, she thought about the past weeks. Maybe if she could go back to the beginning, she could figure out how her life had veered so off-course.

Just a couple of weeks ago, she was in Boston, heading to the airport for her flight to Oregon. She settled herself into the passenger seat of her friend, Jill's car. She remembered she sighed and said, "Oregon or bust."

"What?" Jill said as she started the car.

"Don't mind me. I'm just really looking forward to my trip and I'm glad you came up from D.C. before I left," Meara answered.

Jill turned her head to check for traffic up the street, but paused and glanced over at Meara instead, studying her for a second. "You sure about this trip to Oregon, Mere? I mean, if you wait a month, I could go out there with you. Keep you company. I'd finally get to see why you like the coast out there so much better than what you have right here."

Meara smiled again and reached over to touch her friend's arm. "Thanks, Jill. But yes, I'm sure. I want to be alone for a while." She shook her head dramatically, "Believe me, I need a break from this family."

Jill nodded with a chuckle. "No question that families can be complicated."

"You haven't been here with Tony's family for the past year."

"Bad, huh?" she asked sympathetically.

Meara breathed out. "Yeah. His death turned his whole family upside down."

"Did a number on you, too," Jill added lightly. "So, what do you hope to find out there in Oregon that you can't find here?"

"Honestly? I'm hoping to figure out how to get unmarried."

Jill grinned. "Unmarried? You mean like divorced?"

Meara shook her head. "No, I'm talking about what to do about this?" She lifted her left hand and fluttered her finger with her wedding ring in the air between them. "If I listen to Tony's family, I should build a memorial altar in the living room and just wait to join him."

Jill chuckled. "And what do you want to do?"

"That's the problem, Jill. I don't know. I've been a part of a couple for over thirty years. I can't remember what it is I want just for me anymore."

"Wow, that doesn't sound like the Meara I know."

Meara's shoulders fell and she sighed. "It's not like me, is it? I had no idea I was this tied into Tony's plans, Tony's future. Now that he's gone I realize that none of it works without him. I need a new plan, a solo plan."

Jill looked at Meara for a long second, and then backed the car into the street. "OK, you're right. I can see that you need to go and do this. But promise me that you won't just hole up in a condo out there, brooding."

Meara nodded, "I won't brood. Promise," she smiled.

After a pause, Jill's eyebrows lifted. "Unmarried, huh?"

Meara glanced down at her wedding ring and sighed. "Yeah. I'm making that my first goal."

Chapter 2 Up, Up and Away

Cade sat in the gate area at Logan waiting for his flight back home to San Francisco. He had his laptop balanced on his thighs and could feel the heat emanating from the bottom of it. He wondered if it was the heat, the radiation, or the electronic pulses that would eventually make him sterile? He smiled wryly.

He had wanted to get through the last of the emails in his inbox but he was only halfway through them. He glanced up to admire the view as a shapely redheaded flight attendant moved through the door to the jetway, pulling her small wheeled luggage behind her. Good, the arrival of the crew meant the flight would probably be leaving soon. Maybe they'd take off on time, he thought with satisfaction.

Cade had taken this flight many times. His law office was in San Francisco, but the firm had clients on the East Coast, primarily in Boston and New York, and a few down in DC. They also had a few European clients, too, and he especially enjoyed dealing with them. His language skills gave him an edge. He was raised speaking Italian, thanks to his mother and her close ties to her family in northern Italy, where he'd lived for several years. He had also picked up French and German as a teenager when his father, an Air Force pilot, was stationed in Europe.

He heard the swish of movement around him as the announcement came over the PA system that the flight would be boarding shortly. He shut the lid of the laptop and lowered it into his briefcase. He'd finish up his email when he got on board.

He caught the whiff of a light sexy perfume and he glanced up with interest. He couldn't see her face but he definitely admired the view from behind. She was wearing dark slacks beneath a short jacket. The slacks were cut just right, he noticed — not skin-tight, but just close-fitting enough to outline her shapely legs. Now, there was a lady who knew how to wear her clothes, he thought with appreciation.

He rose and gathered up his luggage and sauntered over to the counter to see if the middle seat in his row had been filled. It would be a lot more comfortable on a long flight to have an empty middle seat, but empty seats were getting more rare as the airlines strived to put more passengers on each flight. He would've paid for an upgrade to first class but there hadn't been any seats available up front when he booked.

He pulled out his boarding pass and waited for the agent to look up. He gave her his most charming smile, showing his dimples. He saw the agent respond with a provocative smile of her own.

"May I help you, sir?" she asked, her eyes looking directly into his.

He smiled wider. "I'm on the aisle, and I was wondering if the middle seat next to me has been taken?"

She smiled seductively as she glanced down at his boarding pass. "Let me check, Mr. Chandler." She looked at her screen and after a second, shook her head, "No, not yet. But I can't guarantee it will stay empty."

"Understood." He nodded. "Just wondered is all. Thanks..." he glanced at her name tag, "Suzanne."

"My pleasure," she purred. She handed back his boarding pass. "Do you come to Boston often, Mr. Chandler?" she asked, ignoring the throat clearing from the man behind him.

Cade looked at her speculatively and nodded. "Pretty often. Please call me 'Cade,'" he added with a smile.

"Cade," she repeated. "That's an interesting name."

The man behind Cade stepped forward. "Miss, could you check my boarding pass, please?" he said as he slapped the piece of paper onto the counter.

Cade smiled and shrugged. He turned around. "Sorry," he said to the man. He nodded to Suzanne, "I'll be back in Boston in a few weeks." He picked up his bag and headed towards the gate agent with his boarding pass at the ready.

Chapter 3   Leaving on a Jet Plane

Meara let out a long breath as she plopped down in the window seat on the plane. She used her foot to scoot her dark leather backpack further under the seat in front of her. Could they make this space any tighter, she wondered? Her knees were almost touching the closed tray of the seat in front of her.

This would be a long flight — Boston to San Francisco – so she hoped whoever sat in front of her wouldn't recline the seat into her lap. She watched the passengers streaming by and then saw a happy young couple step into the row of seats in front of her. Their heads were nearly touching as they whispered and looked adoringly at each other. She nearly rolled her eyes, but then decided on second thought that it might be a good sign; the young lovers might not sleep on the flight.

Meara glanced out the window and could see the line of boarding passengers in the jetway. It was probably too much to ask that she'd have the row to herself. And almost in response to her thoughts, a man in a business suit stopped at the aisle seat. He dropped his briefcase into the center seat next to her, then in one fluid motion he lifted his suitcase into the overhead compartment and smoothly slid it into place. He had his back turned to her and Meara noticed how well the suit jacket fit him. It looked expensive and tailored. His hair was brown threaded with grey and was well cut. When he turned, she saw that his sideburns were completely grey but even so, dark boyish tendrils of hair fell across his forehead. Not looking like a psycho is good, but being good-looking is even better, she thought with relief.

It really was no fair, though, that men ended up looking better as they aged. Women just seemed to slowly shrivel up like rotten fruit. Yeah, and she was getting close to the expiration date on her fruit, she thought sourly. Damn, she never thought she'd ever be this old. It would've been nice to stop aging at around thirty-five.

She was sure she still looked pretty good back then. She smiled at the thought.

She twirled her wedding ring idly around her finger while her thumb rubbed the smooth gold band softly. She caught herself and glanced down at the ring. She ought to just take it off and put it away somewhere. After all, Tony had been dead now for over a year so technically she wasn't really married to him anymore, was she? At any rate, she wasn't his wife now; she was his widow.

Widow. The word made her think of huge black Halloween spiders, dark and sort of creepy. Did people still wear black in mourning these days? And if so, how long was that supposed to go on for? Not that she minded that tradition. She looked good in black. It was very slimming. But there was so much she didn't know about death and dying.

It was funny how you could get so caught up in it all: the accident, the hospital, calling the kids to come home quickly, first praying that he'd make it, then when it was clear he'd end up on life support forever, praying that he wouldn't; then the wake, his huge crazy family, the funeral, and finally the burial. It was like a runaway train that you just hung onto until it finally slowed down and you could get off. But then what? She asked herself for the millionth time. What would she do with the rest of her life?

Life is like a roller coaster ride. Youth is the ride up with everything still ahead filling you with anticipation and excitement. Then you reach the top, but of course, you don't know it's the top until the bottom drops out and you are careening downhill towards old age and death at ever accelerating speeds. Youth is about everything being open to you, where time is plentiful and seems never-ending. Getting old, on the other hand, is the sound of ticking clocks and all those open doors shutting with a bang, whether you're ready or not. That's when you realize that there is only a finite amount of time, and unfortunately, you've already used most of it up.

The man in the business suit glanced briefly at her with a perfunctory smile and settled himself into the aisle seat. He leaned over and pushed his briefcase under the center seat. When he noticed that she was watching him, he shrugged, "If anyone sits in the middle seat, I'll move it."

Did he think she was the carry-on baggage police?

She shrugged, smiled and said, "That's OK. I just wondered if you were waiting for someone, or if the middle seat would be empty for the flight."

He grinned and suddenly his whole demeanor changed. He had a wonderful smile — great teeth, with slight dimples in his cheeks and creases of smile lines around his light brown eyes. "I checked at the counter at the gate," he said conspiratorially, "and it was still an empty seat as of a few minutes ago. Keep your fingers crossed that they don't find some standby or deadheading pilot that needs the seat." He held up his crossed fingers.

Meara smiled back. She crossed her fingers and held them up, too, and nodded. "Good idea."

She turned and buckled her seatbelt, and as she pulled the belt to cinch it in, she marveled at how thin she'd gotten. Geez, how much weight had she lost in the past couple of months? Well, she thought grimly, if someone you love has to die, it's nice to lose some weight in the bargain.

She saw that her seatmate had been watching her and she felt her cheeks turn pink, as if he was reading her thoughts. Great. She must look like some nutty old lady. She let out a long breath. She shouldn't be thinking about Tony right now at the beginning of this solo trip to the Oregon coast. She could almost see the dark clouds of melancholy laying in wait at the edge of her peripheral vision. She glanced over at her seatmate and saw that he was still looking at her. Jesus, how embarrassing! She cleared her throat when their eyes met and asked, "Do you travel a lot for your business?"

"My business?" he repeated with a slight frown, as if she wasn't speaking English.

Immediately, she felt stupid to have started up a conversation. "Oh," she sputtered, "I just assumed...you know, your business suit...you look so...uh...professional is all...." God, she felt like a tongue-tied teenager. How humiliating. She wished she could climb out the window and spend the rest of the flight on the wing.

He looked down at his suit and smiled again. "Oh, do you like the suit? It's new. And 'professional' is definitely the look I was going for." He laughed easily. "I'm a lawyer so suits are pretty much our uniform. And, my firm does a lot of work on the East Coast, so, you're right, I do a lot of flying."

He clicked off his cell phone and slid it into his inside coat pocket. Then he glanced down at his watch, a fancy expensive one, Meara noticed. She also saw that he was wearing a heavy ring with a large yellow stone on the ring finger of his right hand. Married? Or was it just his college ring? Oh, geez, Meara, get real, she admonished herself. Wait until she told Jill that she had been checking out whether a guy on the plane was married. They would have a good laugh over that.

Then the flight attendant – an energetic redhead in her late thirties, maybe early forties – was standing in the aisle. She smiled a little more widely when she caught the businessman's eye. Meara watched the interplay between them. Was he one of those road warriors always on the prowl, she wondered? Hmmm, he was certainly good-looking enough, and he was obviously very well off with his nice suit and fancy watch. No doubt he garnered a lot of flight attendant interest. Heck, if Meara were a flight attendant, she would find him interesting, too. She wondered at what age one stopped being interested? Apparently, she hadn't reached it yet.

She turned and glanced out the window again and saw an airport worker wearing huge headphones walking alongside the plane. She never got tired of airports, big jets and flying. Maybe it was because of her childhood. Her father had been a diplomat in the Foreign Service and growing up overseas meant that she had spent a lot of time in airports around the world.

During college she took a part-time job at a travel company across the Charles River in Boston. By the time she had her degree, she also had a career of sorts as a specialized tour guide running a concierge travel service for some very unique and demanding clients. She had organized theme wedding trips, like the one on Lake Maggiore in southeastern Switzerland that involved renting multiple villas and chartering a boat for the ceremony, or the couple who wanted to say their vows against the backdrop of the Northern Lights in Iceland. There were cycling trips across Europe, river cruises on private barges, and in one case, the rental of a private tropical island in the Pacific for two week where the guests lived a Gilligan's Island fantasy in huts along the beachfront.

Her parents thought she was wasting her education as a glorified travel agent. And maybe she was. But the only thing she felt she was really good at was traveling. Meara could see now that her confusion and the missteps that she went through during and after college weren't all that different from everyone else's transitions to adulthood. But it had always seemed especially hard for her. And it wasn't just the culture shock of living back in the States again; it was also learning to live without a diplomatic passport, paid air tickets and the freedom to travel all over the world. The truth was, when she left home, she hadn't been homesick for her family; she had been homesick for a whole lifestyle.

A few years later, the chance to even revisit that lifestyle ended with her father's untimely death. He had been killed in a horrific suicide bombing at the Embassy in Beirut. Not only was her world turned upside down but the door to her childhood had been slammed shut.

Still, things eventually worked out. If you bide your time, they usually do. She moved up the ranks at the travel company in Cambridge, met Tony, and her life was soon on a totally different track. After a couple of years of dating, they got married. Then as soon as Tony earned his CPA with a large accounting firm, he quit to go into his family's business, a bakery in Boston's North End.

She never told Tony, but for her, getting married and him entering the family business felt more like an end than a beginning. She thanked God that she worked in the travel business because at least she still was able to get on a plane and travel occasionally to lead customized tours for groups that needed lots of pampering.

She and Tony made trips to Italy on bakery business every couple of years. But, living overseas? That was one option that was no longer on the table.

If her father had lived, who knew what choices she might have made? Would she even have met and married Tony? Life was strange. Every moment builds upon the next and the next. You can't see the patterns or where they will lead until much later.

Meara was jolted out of her revelry when the pilot asked the flight attendants to be seated for departure. She relaxed back into the seat, and soon they were in the air. She could see clouds rushing along below them. This was Meara's favorite part of flying, this in-between world when you were neither here nor there. Flying gave you a sort of suspended existence. For the duration, you didn't have to worry about all the responsibilities that were waiting for you below, neither the ones you were leaving behind, nor the ones that were waiting for you up ahead. In this brief bubble of time, you could just live in the moment.

"Would you like anything to drink, Ma'am?"

Meara blinked at the interruption, but was also glad for the distraction. The flight attendant was leaning in, nearly onto the businessman's lap, not that he seemed to mind much. "Oh, yes, sure," Meara answered hoarsely. She cleared her throat. "Uh, wine...a glass of white wine, please," she said with a cheery smile to the flight attendant.

"Do you want to put it on your credit card?" the woman asked. "Or perhaps, your husband will get this?" she eyed the businessman with a flirty smile.

Meara's heart sank. "Oh, no, he's...Oh! Wait, I have a drink coupon!" Meara grinned, amazed that she remembered. She fumbled for her purse and after a moment or two of digging through her billfold she found the folded frequent flyer drink coupons. "Here!"

The businessman blinked, and then smiled broadly. "Excellent!" he said. "Thanks for reminding me. I have a couple of those, too." He pulled out his wallet and thumbed through a few business cards until he found his coupons. He glanced at Meara, "Thanks, I would've forgotten that I even had these."

She smiled and nodded at him. "Glad to help out." Then she laughed, feeling oddly pleased with herself. Suddenly she realized that he'd pulled her back from the brink of some very dark thoughts. She studied him for a long moment.

He squinted at her. "You know, I've been sitting here thinking that you look very familiar. Have we met somewhere before?"

She chuckled. "Well, if I didn't know better, I'd say that sounds like a very old line." She shook her head. "Anyway, when you're traveling, everyone starts reminding you of people you once knew, don't you think?"

He grinned. "True, but I'm serious! You really do look like someone I've met before. Do you live in San Francisco?"

She smiled ruefully, "Not even close, sorry to say. I've been living in Boston since college."

He studied her for several moments. "Hmmm." And he shook his head. "I'm good at remembering faces."

When the drinks arrived, he reached over and dropped the tray from the middle seat so they could share the table between them, a luxury on an otherwise full plane.

He soon had his laptop out and was typing away, pausing occasionally to sip from his scotch and water to savor the drink. She noticed when he was thinking, that he'd unconsciously thread his fingers through his hair pushing it back off his forehead. It was such a boyish gesture, she thought warmly.

After a moment he set the drink down and glanced over at Meara as if he knew she had been watching him. He smiled at her before turning back to the computer screen.

"Excuse me." The flight attendant leaned in close again. "Would it be alright if you moved over next to your wife while I borrow your aisle seat for a little while?"

The businessman looked up at her quizzically. "My wife..." He looked over at Meara then back at the flight attendant, "What's up?"

Meara's heart was beating more quickly as she realized the businessman was once again mistaken for her husband. What was that all about anyway? And why didn't he correct the flight attendant?

The flight attendant leaned in very close, and so Meara leaned over, too. "The couple sitting in front of you folks?" She pointed and nodded to the seats in front of them. "The boy is going to propose to his girlfriend on this flight!" She grinned in excitement. She lowered her voice. "We have confetti for you folks to throw over them when she says 'yes' to his proposal, OK?"

The businessman nodded and smiled. "Sweet."

"I know, isn't it?" the flight attendant said lingering a moment to look speculatively at him while batting her gorgeous long lashes.

Meara nearly laughed out loud, it seemed such a caricature of flirting but she covered it with a cough instead.

The flight attendant ducked in close to the businessman, she whispered in a very sexy voice (that again made Meara want to scream with laughter), "I'll need your seat because they want me to film the proposal." Her tongue licked her bottom lip.

The businessman watched her and her tongue, interested. "Sure. I can move over."

"Good. Because it's going to happen very soon."

The businessman leaned over to Meara, "Did you hear that?"

Meara nodded. "Crazy, huh?"

He looked at her, then paused and studied her for several long seconds. "Yes, it IS crazy, isn't it? Who does this sort of thing on a plane full of strangers?" He closed the table in the center seat, and holding his drink, he plopped down in the seat next to her. He looked at Meara, "Hi. I guess we're going to become closer friends." He grinned. "By the way, my name is Cade...Cade Chandler." He held out his hand.

She grinned. "Hi Cade Chandler, my name is Meara Cellini."

"Cellini?" he said. "Mira Cellini?"

"Where...." she began to ask, but she never got to finish the question because the flight attendant was back, and was now sitting in the seat next to Cade.

"OK," the flight attendant whispered, as she fumbled for the camera in her lap. "It's going to happen any time now...." she smiled warmly at Cade.

Cade Chandler. Hmmm, that name did sound vaguely familiar to Meara, but she couldn't for the life of her remember why. A lawyer from San Francisco? What are the odds she'd ever met him before? Maybe he went to law school in Boston perhaps?

There was a kind of collective holding of the breath as the young man in the seat in front of Meara stood up. He had an uncertain smile on his face as he pushed his glasses up on the bridge of his nose. He glanced out over the seats of passengers and Meara thought that they must've seemed like a huge audience from his vantage point. He smiled a crooked sort of smile before glancing down. The expression on his face changed then and Meara could see the deep emotion playing across his features.

"Oh my God," Meara whispered as she watched the young man. She felt tears well in her eyes. What a baby she'd become lately. Sentimental commercials, babies on Internet videos, geez, any little mawkish thing and she'd want to bawl. She squeezed the edge of the seat and then realized Cade's thigh was right there next to her knuckles.

She glanced at him just as he looked down at her hand then he looked up and their eyes met. "Sorry," he said and he moved his thigh away, as if he were at fault.

She laughed, embarrassed, and then quickly released her grip on the seat. "No, really, I'm sorry," she apologized.

He reached down and took her hand and squeezed it softly. "Don't worry about him." He nodded at the young man. "He'll be fine." Cade whispered into her ear, "Look."

She glanced up and saw the young man lean over, his face aglow. Probably going in for the kiss after the momentous "Yes."

The flight attendant jumped up with the camera out in front of her as she smiled and waved the happy couple together. She was now in charge, the director of the happy tableaux.

Cade looked at Meara, then down at their hands clasped together. "Oh," he said and released her hand. "Sorry." He smiled and the dimple in his cheek showed for a second. "Got carried away in the moment, I guess."

She felt herself blush. Jesus, was she really blushing again? What was that all about? She could still feel the warmth of his hand on hers. When was the last time a guy – any guy – even Tony, for God's sakes – had held her hand? On second thought, she decided, that admission was sort of sad.

He handed her a small bag of confetti and she reached in and grabbed a handful. When the flight attendant nodded, they and the people in the row opposite threw handfuls of confetti into the air above the newly engaged couple.

"Mazel tov," someone yelled from a row or two behind and everyone laughed.

A few minutes later, the flight attendant was back, thrusting small plastic cups of champagne at them from her tray. Meara laughed and took a cup. She and Cade toasted one another and then turned to the young man and his new fiancé who were now standing at their seats in the row ahead, like the host and hostess of a party. Cade caught the boy's eye and then he and Meara raised their plastic cups and toasted the couple together saying, "Congratulations!" in unison.

Meara and Cade turned and toasted one another. He stared for a long second at her, his light brown eyes studying her face again. Then he smiled, "Cheers," he said, raising his glass slightly.

"Cheers," she replied lifting her plastic cup and then downing the contents.

It wasn't bad champagne, considering they were sharing it with about a hundred-and-fifty other passengers. Sure, she'd had better. But then, let's face it; she'd had a lot worse, too.

A minute later, the flight attendant seemed to fall into the seat next to Cade and she reached out for his arm to pull him close. God, was she drunk? Meara wondered in amazement. Wasn't that illegal or something? She studied the woman. No, she decided, not drunk; the woman was just flirting once again.

"Wasn't that positively brilliant?" the flight attendant barely cooed at Cade.

He smiled crookedly and nodded. Meara saw that the flight attendant had pushed her bosom up against his arm and then she crooked her finger to indicate he should come in closer for a secret. Meara stared as if mesmerized. This was better than a movie, she thought with glee.

Wait a minute. She was supposed to be his wife, right? Didn't the flight attendant think she was, at least? Well, then...what would a WIFE do in this situation?

She reached over and tucked her hand into the crook of Cade's other arm, and leaned over, pulling him closer. Surprised by the attention he leaned towards her to hear what she had to say. In a low whisper she said, "Cade? Could you ask the flight attendant for another glass of champagne for me?"

He glanced at her and it was as if he could read her mind. He smiled broadly and nodded. He turned to the flight attendant who was now looking confused, "Miss? Could you get...uh...my wife another glass of champagne, please? And heck, another one for me, as well."

The flight attendant got up and looked in confusion from Cade to Meara and back again. "Sure...sure."

When she'd gone, Cade turned to Meara, and said, "I think we're alone now...."

She immediately sang the rejoinder from the Sixties song.

He blinked and she smiled and they both laughed. "Tommy James and the Shondells, right?" he asked and she nodded with a chuckle.

God, it was great when someone was on your wavelength, Meara thought.

Chapter 4   Homeward Bound

The flight time was five hours and twenty minutes but seemed to go by so much faster to Cade. Usually on these long coast-to-coast flights, he'd catch up on his email and office work. But by the time he'd had a second drink, he would look down at his watch and be dismayed to find that he still had three hours to go. It made him fidgety. But this flight had been different. He was actually stunned when he heard the pilot come on the PA and say that they would be landing in San Francisco in less than thirty minutes.

"Wow," he turned to Meara. "I can't believe we're almost home."

"Time flies, right?" she chuckled. "I'm envious of you, though. I still have another flight tomorrow, so my trip isn't nearly over."

Her eyes lit up when she smiled and it made him want to make her smile at him again.

"So you're spending the night in San Francisco?"

Meara nodded. "Well, out near the airport actually. It didn't make sense to book a room in the city when I have to get back out to the airport tomorrow morning for my flight to Brookings."

Cade nodded. "I can see your reasoning, but you're missing a great city."

"Well, I suppose so, but what's the point of going out for a fun evening by myself? Besides, I've been to Fisherman's Wharf and all that before."

"Fisherman's Wharf?" Cade repeated with a laugh. "No, no, no. I'm talking about the REAL San Francisco. There are a lot of really wonderful little places to eat, drink, listen to music or even dance, if you want to."

Meara smiled and picked up the plastic cup of her second white wine to drain the last sip when the little cocktail napkin fluttered to the floor by her feet. As she leaned over to retrieve it her hair fell over her cheek and hid her face. Cade got a whiff of something herbal and wonderful and he found himself leaning in slightly to smell it again. Boy, she smelled good. As he was enjoying the scent, Meara's head came up and nearly smacked into Cade's face.

"Oh! Sorry," she exclaimed. Then she pointed to the napkin still on the floor, "I couldn't reach it."

"Here, let me get it for you." Cade said unbuckling his seatbelt. He reached down but soon found himself twisted with his head wedged tightly up against her leg as he stretched his arm down to snag the napkin between his fingers. When he sat back up and realized the awkward position he'd been in, he made a face and shrugged, "Sorry about that. Not much room to maneuver in these seats, is there?"

Meara blushed and then laughed. She lowered her voice, "I think they want to discourage any sort of maneuvering among passengers," she teased lightly. "If you know what I mean."

He grinned. "Oh, so THAT explains the tighter and tighter space between the rows. Just trying to keep everyone honest, eh?"

"All hands on deck, as it were," Meara added, and they both laughed.

"You really ought to consider going into the city, you know," Cade said without thinking and then immediately found himself warming to the idea.

"I know, but even if you gave me your insider's list of the best places, I can't imagine hitting the town by myself," Meara smiled. "I mean, don't get me wrong, I'm pretty independent, but checking out the nightlife on my own would be a little outside my comfort zone." She shrugged. "It'll have to wait for another trip. I'll come back with a friend some time."

"It's never good to put things off," Cade said with a small shake of his head. He studied her face for a second. Yeah, he would definitely enjoy spending a few more hours with this woman, he decided. She was interesting and funny and he was intrigued by the way she had handled that flight attendant. "Listen, Mira, why don't you let me show you a little of the real San Francisco? I mean, you're going to need to eat dinner at some point anyway, so why not go to dinner with me?"

"That's really a nice offer, Cade, but I couldn't do that to you. After all, you're just getting home from a business trip. I'm sure you must want to unpack and kick back at home. I know I would if I were you."

He eyed her for a second. Had she just turned him down? He couldn't remember the last time that had happened. He shook his head and smiled ruefully, "No, come on, I've just finished selling you on my city. I feel like I need to back it up with the real experience to prove it to you."

She laughed, her eyes sparkling again. "Are you sure?" she asked doubtfully. "If you really mean it, then I'd love to see your city, Cade. Thanks for offering to be my guide."

"I promise to feed you a great dinner and show you a few of my favorite haunts. I guarantee you'll have fun."

The pilot's voice came over the PA telling them to prepare for landing. Cade watched as Meara stared down at the lights below, a slight smile on her lips. She turned and saw that he was looking at her. "I love the way cities look from the sky. I never get tired of it."

"I'm the same way," Cade agreed leaning in to look over her shoulder; again he could smell her hair and something else; maybe the lingering scent of her perfume? Geez, he loved the way women smelled, especially this woman. He nodded out the window to the airport lights coming into view. "I really like the blue lights on the runways at night. I've always thought they look amazing."

Meara nodded her head, "Oh, I know what you mean. It's like the ground is covered in twinkling blue stars." She looked right into his eyes. "Funny, most people don't seem to notice them."

He smiled. Come to think of it, he couldn't remember ever talking about runway lights to anyone in his life.

Chapter 5   Hotel California

Meara was in her room at the Embassy Suites, looking at her reflection in the bathroom mirror. She'd taken a quick shower and she was glad she did because it had made her feel more awake and alive. And she wanted, no, she needed to feel alive because she was going out to dinner in San Francisco with a very nice looking man. She could feel the excitement bubbling up in her belly. She scanned her face, hair, and body critically. She didn't look half bad for a middle-aged woman. She'd always taken care of herself – exercise, organic food, and vitamins – but more importantly, she was blessed with good genes. Heck, her mother used to brag about snagging the interest of the older gents in her assisted living facility. Like mother; like daughter.

But going on a date? Was she really going to go on a date? she wondered in amazement. She eyed herself in the mirror. "Seriously, Meara, what are you doing?" she asked her reflection out loud. She shook her head. It was unbelievable. She hadn't been on a date in decades, for chrissakes. The sheer enormity of it suddenly struck her. Oh my God, she thought, closing her eyes for a second. Was she nuts or what?

Cade was a good-looking man, though. She laughed and relaxed. He was a nice guy and she would have a decent time. They'd eat dinner, have some interesting conversation, and then he'd drop her off back here at the hotel afterwards. Why was she making such a big deal of it? It'd make a nice memory and a good story, plus, she had to admit, it was doing wonders for her ego. After all, she never thought she'd be dating again in this lifetime. Here she was middle-aged and a widow, and she was going out to dinner in San Francisco with a really nice looking man. Amazing.

Meara thought about Cade waiting for her downstairs. She had left him in the lobby. He said he'd hang out in the atrium bar area. "Take your time," he'd said, and added, "There's no hurry."

"Thanks, but I'll try to be quick." She looked down at the keys she'd just received from the registration desk. "Here," she said, handing one of the keys to him. "They gave me two room keys."

His eyebrows shot up questioningly as he took the key.

She blushed as she realized what he was thinking. "Oh my God, I'm not suggesting anything, Cade." She laughed with a shake of her head. "It's just that you can get a free drink at the hotel's manager's reception if they think you're a guest here. I just figured if I set you up with a free drink, you might not notice how long it takes me to pull myself together."

Meara recalled the conversation now and her cheeks turned pink at the memory. Oh my God, I am so pathetic at this stuff, she thought ruefully. And I've blushed more in the past couple hours than I've blushed in the past couple of decades. What is with me?

She took her toothbrush and toothpaste from her toiletries bag hanging from the towel rack nearby and turned on the water. She glanced up and met her own eyes in the mirror. You can do this, she told herself. You can SO do this!

A little while later, Meara had changed into a skirt with a shimmery silk blouse. She carried a sweater over her arm, knowing that it would probably cool off during the evening in the city with the sea breezes. She boarded the glass elevator and turned to look down at the atrium tables surrounded by foliage, and the koi fishpond with its little waterfall and bubbling fountain. She quickly scanned the tables for Cade and then she suddenly caught sight of him at one of the small tables near the bar but secluded slightly from the rest. Her heart leapt a bit in her chest as she realized that that guy was actually waiting for her, Meara O'Connell Cellini. Her stomach felt hollow and tight. She swallowed nervously then turned as the elevator doors opened and she stepped out at the lobby level.

Here goes nothing, she thought. It made her pause and realize that throughout her life she had faced so many situations like this – interviews, marketing presentations, greeting her husband's employees at the annual Christmas party at Faneuil Hall in Boston, speaking at her father's memorial service in Washington, DC. These were the times when all eyes would be on her — or so it had always seemed to her — and she had to steel herself, put on her best smile, and just go ahead and do it. That was what she needed to do now. She took a deep breath and let it out slowly, counting out the seconds in her head. She visualized the way Cade had looked when he leaned towards her to look out the airplane window. She felt her body relax a bit. It was going to be fine.

Chapter 6   San Francisco Nights

Cade had been completely nonplussed when Meara had handed him the room key earlier. He had felt a charge that went straight to his groin. As his sister, Terry, would've said while rolling her eyes, "Cade, you are such a guy!" He smiled and shook his head. But where had that feeling come from, he wondered? She certainly wasn't his usual type.

She was something else, this Mira Cellini. How old was she, he wondered? Forty-five? Older? He wasn't sure. He'd never been good at guessing people's ages, particularly women. What with makeup and hair dye and all the rest, it was hard to tell. Heck, if a woman kept herself up, she could be any age really. Just look at Diane Sawyer or Jane Fonda – Jesus! They were damn attractive and they were in their late-sixties and mid-seventies, for chrissakes. He grinned, not able to imagine a scenario where he would ever even meet women like that.

His phone rang, and he tapped it and saw that the caller was Vanessa, his stepdaughter. "Hey!" he said into the phone a smile spreading across his face.

"You back home yet, Dad?" Vanessa asked.

"Sort of. I'm at the Embassy Suites by the airport at the moment, but I'll be in the city soon. Why? What's up?"

"Nothing much. Just checking on you," Vanessa said with a laugh. "How was Boston?"

"Great. Got all my business taken care of, but will have to go back next month to get the final papers signed. What about you? How are things in Silicon Valley?"

"I can't speak for the rest of the Valley, but my company is having the usual start-up problems. You know — the cash flow doesn't always match our ambitions — but we'll get it figured out eventually," she said with a laugh. "Beyond that, everything is going well and I still love the job."

"That's worth more than money. Believe me, honey."

"Hey, wait a minute! Did you say that you're at the Embassy Suites hotel by the airport? How come?"

This was the daughter that he knew. She didn't miss anything and wanted to know everything. He smiled. "Met a nice lady on the plane and I'm taking her to dinner and showing her a bit of San Francisco. I'm just sitting at the bar waiting for her to change."

"Into what?" Vanessa said with a laugh.

"Funny," Cade responded dryly, with a shake of his head.

"No, seriously, who's the new woman? Another flight attendant?"

"Actually, she's not a flight attendant; she's just a nice lady from Boston. I sat next to her on the plane and she was interesting. We talked for about four hours straight."

Vanessa was silent for a second. "Wait. So this lady isn't some Barbie-thin young thing with big boobs? I mean, did you say you find her 'interesting'? Whoa! Look out, Dad," Vanessa said with a chuckle.

Cade frowned, but still smiling he asked, "What do you mean by 'Look out'?"

"Well, I've been around for a number of your conquests, and this is the first one that you mentioned 'talking' to, or described as 'interesting.' I think I might want to meet her," Vanessa said with a laugh.

"You probably won't unless you're out prowling the city tonight."

"No, JJ and I have plans to go to a movie over near the Stanford campus tonight."

"OK, well, maybe I'll see you on the weekend then. Any plans?"

"Would love to see you. I'll call you later in the week, OK?"

"Sure, sounds good. Talk to you then."

"Ciao, Dad. Good talking to you. Glad you're home."

Cade nodded, "Hmmm. Me, too."

He clicked off and looked around. He noticed several of the men at a large table by the bar had turned their attention to the path near the koi pond. He turned his head and followed their gaze, and saw what had caught their attention – it was Mira heading his way. He smiled. Damn, she did look pretty good.

As she approached, he stood up and opened his arms slightly. She leaned in and gave him a friendly hug. She smelled wonderful, as he knew she would; clean, like soap, but with the lingering scent of her perfume or maybe it was her shampoo that was making him crazy. If her handing him the key had gone straight to his groin, her scent was definitely revving him up all over again.

"You look great," he said with a smile.

"Good," she nodded with a laugh, "That must mean that you've had enough to drink to befuddle your judgment." She added, "My plan has worked!"

He grinned and laughed. "I love a woman who plans ahead."

"I imagine that would depend on what she has planned..." Meara said softly.

He knew she was flirting with him and he realized he was really enjoying the interplay. He leaned in close, "And what has this woman got planned for the evening, pray tell?"

She paused and with a twinkle in her eye whispered, "Murder!" Then she laughed and linked her arm in his. "You know, Cade Chandler, I think this is going to be a lot of fun."

"Hang on and I'll call the driver and have him bring the car around."

She blinked. "The car? I thought that was just an airport limo earlier."

"No, actually the firm has a car and driver under contract. It's definitely one of the better perks of the job." He dialed the number and put the phone to his ear and smiled at her while he waited for the driver, Peter, to answer.

"Geez, I'm impressed," Meara said. And she certainly was.

He took her to Campton Place Restaurant on Stockton Street and afterwards they stopped at a small dance club near Union Square. Meara had paused when she saw the large flyer next to the door announcing that the club had a cover band that evening playing old Eric Burdon & the Animals hits.

"Want to go in?" Cade asked. "I've been here many times. It's a great little club."

"Are you kidding?" Meara laughed, "It's the Animals!" She sang along to the music drifting out as the door swung open. "That song was practically my anthem when I was a teenager."

Cade grinned. "They definitely had a few classics."

She nodded in agreement. "Hmmm, like 'House of the Rising Sun!' Seriously."

Cade pulled open the door for her, and Meara saw that there was a bouncer sitting on a stool just inside. It was a weeknight so the place wasn't too busy.

"Cade, my man. Good to see you again," the bouncer nodded with a grin and shook Cade's hand. "Been awhile, huh?"

"I've been out of town on business," Cade replied. He turned to Meara, "Meet Nixon, the bouncer."

She grinned, "Nixon?"

The bouncer nodded and grinned back, "Obviously, my mother had a dark sense of humor. She says she thought I'd have to turn out tough with a name like that." He chuckled. "That or dead, I expect."

Meara laughed. Cade watched the interchange with a smile and realized that few of his dates ever made conversation with the bouncers or servers.

Nixon nodded at Meara and Cade and they entered the dimly lit club. To their left was a small dance floor and just behind it was the raised platform for the band. There was a scattering of tables around the edge of the dance area. To the right of the door was a long bar that ran the whole length of the room with some stools, that were currently filled, surrounded by knots of people standing.

"There's a table back there," Meara pointed.

"Good. Why don't you grab it and I'll get us something to drink. Wine? Mixed drink?"

Meara glanced around, "A place like this with great old music? I'm thinking a beer would be more appropriate."

He grinned. "I know just the one. They serve a really good local craft beer. I think you'll like it."

She smiled and headed towards the small table. Cade watched her from behind for several seconds. He rarely brought any of his normal dates to this club. He smiled and nodded at Meara when she waved to let him know she'd found a table for them.

He turned and headed to the bar humming along to the song 'Monterey' that had just started up. He glanced over at the band. They were really good. The lead singer sounded just like Eric Burdon. Cade lip-synced the song along with him. Geez, he felt like a teenager again. He remembered how the excitement would build in him when he listened to his rock albums on his stereo when he was a kid and his family had lived in Bangkok.

Cade's father had been career military – a colonel in the Air Force when he retired. It was a crazy life, moving from base to base around the US and then overseas. Cade had two brothers and a younger sister. Overseas, just as in the States, they mostly lived on base – Clark Air Force Base when they were in the Philippines and South Post in Seoul, Korea; but in Thailand, there wasn't a base, so they lived among the locals.

He found there was an incredible amount of freedom for a teenager not living on a base. On base, everyone around you was military and reported everything you did or said to your father, or worse, to his superior officer. Nothing worse than having your dad come home and tell you that his commanding officer read him the riot act for something you did last Friday night.

He looked back on his teenage anger and angst and it seemed silly now. He spent much of his childhood resenting the fact that he was held back in the first grade so that he ended up in the same grade as his brother, Curt, who had a September birthday and just made the cut-off for first grade. Cade's birthday, on the other hand, was in October and he had missed the cut-off the year he started school, so he was already older than the other kids in his grade. Then when he was held back because he had trouble with reading, not only was he nearly two years older than the other kids, but he had his little brother in the class, too. And, by contrast, Curt was naturally smart and schoolwork came easily to him while it was always a struggle for Cade. Curt had been a great brother, though. He always helped Cade with his homework, especially any papers he had to write.

Cade was better at mechanical things. He once went into his parents' bedroom and took his father's wind-up alarm clock apart just to see how it worked. He was fascinated by the tiny inner workings. When his father came home and saw all the tiny pieces laid out across the bedspread, he had exploded, nearly smacking Cade in his anger and frustration. Cade's mom had talked him down and finally Cade was told to take all that junk and go to his room. He did and two hours later when his father had come to talk to him, he had the clock put back together and ticking away. He'd never forget the look of wonder on his father's face. "You did that?" he'd asked incredulously. Cade had nodded somberly. From then on, he often heard his father tell the story, and he always ended it by saying, "and by God, if the clock didn't keep better time!"

Cade carried the two beers to the table. Meara was tapping her hand on the table to the song. "Don't Let Me Be Misunderstood." She looked up at him, "Hey, they're playing your song, Cade."

He laughed. "Want to dance?"

She bit her lip in hesitation. "Geez, it's been years..." Then she shrugged and nodded. "You know, I'd love to!" And they got up with several other couples and soon they were happily dancing the way kids from the Sixties used to dance – touching hands occasionally, facing each other, moving to the music, and lip-syncing to the songs.

After two fast songs, "The House of the Rising Sun" started up.

"God, this one was a classic for slow dancing," Meara said, as Cade pulled her into his arms.

"Kids today just don't know what they're missing, huh?" Cade whispered in her ear.

"I know. They don't seem to dance WITH each other anymore, do they?"

He loved the feeling of her body moving against his. He'd forgotten how much he had always liked slow dancing. He had his hand on her back and he gently pressed her closer to him, while his other hand covered hers against his chest. His head was leaning gently against hers and he could hear her singing along to the song. She spread her fingers over the back of his neck along the edge of his shirt collar and he could feel her gently touching his hair. God, he realized he was getting turned on. When was the last time that had happened while dancing with a woman? Should he try and think about work to distract himself, he wondered? He felt her hips press into him and he glanced down at her.

She smiled mischievously.

He looked at her with longing then he chuckled and pulled her close, in a hug. He whispered, "It's been a long time since that's happened on a dance floor. Thanks for the memory."

"Nice to be appreciated," she chuckled and tightened her hand against his neck.

It was like being a teenager again, listening to the old music and dancing close with a woman who knew the lyrics and music as well as he did. It'd been so long since he'd felt that kind of synchronicity between the music and his date. Sure, he'd danced with plenty of twenty- and thirty-somethings to music from "his" era, but to dance to it with someone who actually knew the music and understood what it meant? This felt different.

After dancing, they returned to their table and he realized they were holding hands as they threaded their way through the tables. They sat on chairs side-by-side facing the band and he didn't release her hand. They drank their beers and listened to the music, smiling at each other when a song started that either of them especially liked.

He looked at Mira and could see that she was transported to a different time. It was funny to see that faraway look when neither of them was stoned. It was just the music's effect on them, he guessed, making them feel like they had gone back several decades. He saw that she mouthed the lyrics to nearly every song, just as he found himself doing. He had never felt closer to anyone as he did to her at that moment.

When "San Francisco Nights" started, she was already getting up and he knew they were going to dance another slow dance together. He held her hand and twirled her playfully into place when they got to the dance floor. She grinned and fell into his arms leaning her head against his chest. "God, I love this song," she breathed.

"Me, too," he whispered, softly kissing the top of her head and breathing in her scent. He pulled her a little closer.

Afterwards, he called for his car and it arrived out in front of the club about ten minutes later. They got in and he leaned over to Mira.

"This was has been an incredible night for me, I hope you enjoyed it," he said in a low voice.

"Cade, it was perfect — the dinner, the club, the dancing. Thank you so much! I loved every minute. You are right. It's an incredible city!"

He smiled, and leaned in to kiss her lightly before draping his arm around her shoulders. He felt sixteen again; like it was prom night and the dance and date were all but over and now he could relax.

Chapter 7   We Gotta Get Out of This Place

Peter drove them south out of the city and back to the Embassy Suites. It was late; after midnight. Geez, that would make it early morning on the East Coast, Meara thought. And yet she didn't feel exhausted at all; maybe a little tired, but pleasantly so.

They got out of the car in silence and Cade guided her in, his hand gently touching her lower back. She reached back and linked her fingers in his and they were once again holding hands as they walked through the lobby.

As they stood in front of the elevator doors, Meara had no idea what would happen next and she didn't care. She felt happy just to be standing there holding this man's hand while they waited for the elevator to arrive. "I'll walk you to your room," Cade finally said as the door opened. She smiled and leaned her head against his shoulder. He touched his lips to the top of her head.

The elevator stopped at her floor and they walked slowly to her door, not talking. She stopped in front of the door to her room and he pulled his key from his pocket and unlocked the door, pushing it open for her to walk through. He followed her in and the door clunked shut behind them.

Cade looked down at her and she looked up at him. Then she stepped nearer and put her arms around his neck and pulled him close and they kissed again. She could hear his breathing as the kiss continued. She could feel his hands moving slowly up and down her back. It wasn't long before his breath began to quicken and so did hers.

"Cade?" she whispered.

"I can leave if you want me to..." he said softly against her lips.

"No, it's not that. I think I'd...I'd like you to stay, but...uh, what about your car and driver downstairs?"

He grinned and relaxed. "Not a problem. I'll call down to Peter and let him know he can leave. Is that OK with you?"

"Perfect," she said and smiled.

She headed for the bathroom while he pulled out his cell phone to make the call.

She closed the bathroom door with a click and leaned against it for a second. She couldn't believe she had just agreed to let him stay the night. Oh, my God! She was going to sleep with him. She shut her eyes in disbelief.

The truth was that she hadn't thought she'd ever have sex again. It'd been long before Tony's death that she'd resigned herself to an all but sexless marriage, and when Tony died, she assumed she was too old to get back into the dating scene, whatever that was these days. Besides, who'd want an older woman when they could have any number of nubile younger ones? She smiled and hugged herself, feeling giddy. Apparently, she was going to get one more chance.

When she came out of the bathroom, he was in the bedroom and had already pulled the bedspread down and opened the sheets. She saw that he'd also unbuttoned his shirt and removed his shoes.

He stood up and she went directly into his arms. He kissed her deeply and suddenly her body responded with a familiar gush of warmth and excitement. God, she'd missed this.

The anticipation was killing her. It'd been so long and she missed lovemaking. But for as much as she wanted it all, she also didn't want it to be over too soon either. They had all the time in the world, she reminded herself, as she reached out for him.

His hands and mouth were all over her. Finally, he reached down and slid his fingers up the outside of her leg, under her skirt, until he reached her bottom. She had removed her panties in the bathroom.

He chuckled softly, "I like a woman who plans ahead," he said.

"I do have a few good ideas," she joked breathlessly. "Cade, could you touch me right there," she whispered, "Oh God, yes, there..." her breath came in short gasps.

"Like that?" he asked softly. She could feel his breath on her as he spoke and that seemed to turn her on even more.

"Oh my God, yes!" she said laughing. "Again...there. Oh yes, there!" she gasped. And then the orgasm enveloped her.

When she opened her eyes, she saw that he was putting a condom on. "I wondered..." she said and smiled.

"I love a woman who knows what she wants," he said leaning in and kissing her. His hand caressed her lightly. "You are a surprising woman," he added, grinning happily.

He moved over her and she could feel his muscles straining as he hovered above her. She closed her eyes and with a smile said, "It's been a while for me. You have no idea how much I've missed this."

It didn't take her long to reach a second orgasm and was surprised at the intensity of it, not to mention the intensity of his.

Afterwards, they cuddled and talked lazily. Eventually, she got up and went into the bathroom to take out her contacts, wash her face and brush her teeth. When she came out, he was in the front room holding a little plastic bag.

"What's that?" she asked.

She noticed he had put on his slacks and t-shirt, but no socks or shirt. He put his arm around her and ran his hand along her back down to her buttocks. "You look good in that outfit," he said with a laugh.

"Partial to nudes, are you?"

"Yes, I am. How'd you know?" he grinned and kissed her lightly. He held up the bag, "This is a toothbrush, toothpaste, shaving lotion and a razor for the morning. Compliments of the hotel."

"You asked them for all that stuff?" she laughed, putting her hand over her mouth.

"Sure. It's their job to accommodate guests; apparently, even non-paying ones."

She laughed again and shook her head. "I'm the wanton woman in this scenario, you know."

"Nah, they think I'm your husband."

"Hmmm, just like the flight attendant on the plane, huh? Why do you suppose that is, anyway?" she asked with a slight frown.

Then she glanced down at her left hand. The ring. Of course. He followed her look. "Yeah, I wondered why you still wear that."

She shrugged one shoulder. "Old times' sake, I guess. It's just been there for so many years...you know?"

He nodded. "I get it. It doesn't bother me, by the way," he added.

"I don't know if that says something good about you or not," she chuckled. "I mean, what if I was still married?"

"It'd still be up to you," Cade responded and smiled.

Chapter 8   In My Life

When they got back into bed, he pulled her up against him, spoon-style. He liked this position because it meant her whole body was within the reach of his hands.

"So I'm wondering something, Mira," Cade said, running his hand down the side of her torso to her thigh.

She sighed with pleasure. "Hmmm, what?"

"You said it'd been a while, right?"

"Uh huh, a couple of years, but who's counting," she chuckled.

His hand stopped moving. "Years? But I thought you said your husband just passed away a year ago."

"He did. But he had prostate problems, surgery, and geez, I don't know, maybe we were just married too long." She sighed again, but not with pleasure.

"But you stayed with him, anyway, huh?" Cade said, thinking about that.

"Well, we had two kids, and a pretty good life together. Sex isn't everything. And besides, I still loved him." She chuckled a bit, "I guess you could say I loved him like a brother."

He smiled. "You could've had an affair if you got really horny, though, huh?"

She snorted, "I'm not sure that's in my DNA." She grinned and added, "Well, maybe if you had come along back then..."

He pulled her closer. "Hmmm," he agreed breathing in her hair scent. "If I'd known about your need, I'd have definitely come running."

She was quiet for a moment and then she sighed. "Life doesn't always turn out the way we thought it would, does it? For me, I just decided to focus on being grateful for what I had. Maybe it's from living overseas and being exposed to people who really got dealt a lousy hand in life. I've been so lucky. I just couldn't wallow in self-pity for too long; not without feeling like a self-absorbed bitch."

He chuckled.

The room grew quiet and Cade wondered if she had fallen asleep.

"On the plane you said you were married before?" Meara said sleepily.

"Two times, actually," he replied. "I'm apparently not as good at it as you are."

"Lord knows it isn't always easy, that's for sure," she agreed. "Geez, two times, though. That must've been expensive. Alimony and all."

"I was lucky there. Both of them remarried pretty quickly. I paid child support for my stepdaughter – from my second marriage — but she's all grown up now, too."

"You had to pay child support for a stepchild? I didn't know that was required."

"Her real father was out of the picture before she was even born. When I met Jan, she was a paralegal trying to support herself and her baby. At any rate, I was the only father Vanessa ever knew. When Jan and I got married, I adopted Vanessa." He settled himself a bit, then added, "I suspect now that being financially supported was really all my wife ever wanted from me. In all other respects, our marriage was pretty shabby."

"But what happened to Vanessa when you divorced?"

"Since I had adopted her, she was legally still my responsibility. I paid child support, got visiting rights, and all the rest. Heck, even if she weren't my responsibility, I'd have taken care of her. She was a great kid and is now an incredible young woman. We're still close."

Meara smiled. "OK, so you were married twice, did you have any other children besides Vanessa?"

"No. But I have a nephew, Nate, whom I've also pretty much adopted. My brother, Curt, died from a heart attack and Nate's mother remarried. Nate didn't get along too well with his new stepdad so I took him in for a while. He's in college now back East. I see him every month or so."

She lay on her back next to him and looked at him thoughtfully. She reached over and pushed the lock of hair off his forehead, but it quickly fell back again. She smiled. "You are a surprising man, Cade Chandler."

He blinked. "Surprising? How's that?"

"Well, being married two times sounds like you might have lots of commitment issues," she said, raising her eyebrows to see if he would disagree. Then she continued, "But stepping in to help raise two kids, well, that's an even bigger commitment than marriage, in my book."

"What about you? You have kids, right?"

She nodded and smiled happily. "I have the greatest kids," she gushed. "A daughter who's thirty and a son who's twenty-seven. And who knows? Maybe some grandchildren soon, if these kids figure out how it's supposed to work." She laughed.

"I take it they're both married?" Cade asked.

She nodded. "Yes, my daughter's been married for a couple of years and my son and his wife have been married about a year. He met Tina right after he got back from Afghanistan three years ago."

"Your son was in the service?"

"Yes. It was an awful time having him over there and knowing how much danger he was in. He lost several close friends," she said solemnly, then shook her head and sighed. "He was a mess when he came home."

Cade's eyes clouded over for a second. "I know the feeling."

She frowned. "You do?"

"Vietnam. I joined up after high school and was sent over right out of boot camp."

"No college deferment?"

"My grades weren't that good. Plus, in my family, we all knew that Curt was the one who deserved to go to college and my parents couldn't afford to help both of us. He was the smart one in the bunch. And besides, my older brother had gone into the Air Force like my old man, so it felt like something I should do, too. Don't get me wrong, I was glad to join up. At the time, I couldn't imagine being confined to a classroom after I got out of high school."

"But, Cade, Vietnam…"

"I know. Well, I know now, but back then? I was a dumb kid raised on old war movies where the hero never dies." He smiled, but it didn't reach his eyes. "Anyway, for me, Vietnam was just one long haze of drugs, interrupted periodically by stark raving terror." He tried to make his voice light, but he hadn't forgotten any of it. He would never forget. But after some group therapy with a bunch of other vets, and working with his hands as an airline mechanic at Minneapolis/St. Paul airport afterwards, the darkness eventually receded. Vietnam wasn't the crippling presence overshadowing his life like it had been when he first got back to the States.

She reached over and put her hand on his chest. "Oh, Cade, I'm sorry you had to go through that. It must've been awful."

"No, ironically, the part that was awful was coming home. Having people call me 'Baby-killer,' and practically spitting on me in the streets. THAT was the awful part." He shook his head. "Back then long hair was in vogue, so grunts like me stuck out like targets with our skinhead haircuts. Believe me, my hair couldn't grow fast enough." He could hear the tinge of anger in his voice even now after all these years.

Meara looked thoughtful. "Funny, it's not like that for the vets today, is it? When Paul came back, he was welcomed — celebrated even — and got all sorts of recognition. Heck, even today, people walk up to him and shake his hand and thank him for his service; they tell him he's a hero." She shook her head. "We've certainly made the word 'hero' become pretty meaningless in the last ten years, haven't we?" She sighed. "But, if I had lost him, Cade, no amount of thanking could've filled that hole."

He saw the hollow look in her eyes and knew that she had faced that possibility and lived and relived it in her imagination while her son had been overseas in harm's way. He knew it was time to change the subject. "His name is Paul, huh? Not a very Italian name…wouldn't Paolo be more like it?"

She giggled, "Maybe, but I named him 'Paul' because Paul was my favorite name. In my husband's family, all the boys are named either Anthony or John – boring, right? So I talked Tony into the name Paul Anthony Cellini. He was fine with it; he never liked the idea of a "Big Tony" and "Little Tony." You know what I mean?"

Cade laughed. "Yeah, that would've sounded very Mafiosi. Probably would've been hard on a kid, especially after *The Godfather* movies came out."

"Not to mention *The Sopranos*!" she added.

He grinned. "Oh, wait a minute....Paul....Let me guess. You were a Beatles' fan and Paul was your favorite Beatle, right?" He eyed her, then seeing the guilty look on her face, he laughed out loud.

She laughed, too. "Of course, Paul was my favorite Beatle. I knew when I was fourteen that I would name my son Paul, if I had one. I still love the name and I still love Paul McCartney, by the way."

"Yeah, well, that worked out...I mean, Ringo Cellini would've sounded completely ridiculous."

They both laughed. He reached out then and pulled her in towards him and kissed her. At first, it was going to be a simple peck, a goodnight kiss, but once she was in his arms the kiss got deeper and more urgent. How does someone not have desire for this woman he wondered?

She pulled away for a second, "Uh, Cade, do you have another condom?"

He chuckled. "All taken care of." His hand moved slowly up and down the side of her body.

She kissed his chin. "Geez, I hate to ask, but now I'm curious. How many condoms do you normally carry around with you?" she asked.

"Just one. But I had the front desk put some in that package of toiletries earlier."

"Oh my God! You're kidding! I am going to be so embarrassed checking out of this hotel tomorrow." She laughed and actually blushed.

He pulled her to him again. "They must've figured you were a marathoner, too, because they gave us six packets of them."

"Oh my God!" she said again, covering her eyes, but a few minutes later when she repeated the phrase, he was certain it had nothing to do with the hotel front desk.

Chapter 9   Good Morning Starshine

It was especially dark in the room because of the black-out curtains, but Meara was certain it was morning outside. She stretched languidly and felt the warmth of Cade's body next to her. God, she loved sleeping next to someone again. Even without sex, as it had been with Tony, she still had felt comforted by his physical presence, and in the winter, by the heat his body seemed to radiate.

Cade was the same way, toasty warm. She curled into him. His arm came around her and he made an unintelligible sound in his sleep. His hand rested next to her breast. She moved a little and after a minute she was sure he was waking up because she could feel the hardness nudging the back of her thigh.

"Someone's waking up," Meara said softly. She turned over and reached out for him.

"Oh, yeah, that's definitely how I want to be woken up," he mumbled with a smile, as he reached out and caressed her. "Come here," he said.

"No, you've had your fun. Now it's my turn to be on top."

His eyes opened in a squint. "OK, woman, you've got my full attention," he said in a husky morning voice and smiled widely, his dimple showing.

"I should hope so," Meara said with a laugh.

Cade started to roll over but she held him back. He grinned. "Oh, you can be on top, babe, but I was going to get a condom on."

Cade reached over to the side table and got another of the little packets. "We should open all of these, even if we don't use them, don't you think? Really get the maid's imagination going."

Meara leaned in and kissed him deeply. She could feel his heart racing beneath the palms of her hands as she lifted herself and straddled him. She saw that he was watching her, totally mesmerized. She couldn't remember the last time she'd felt so sexy and bold. She had wanted to feel this kind of intimacy with a man again and now that it had happened, she didn't want it to end.

She began slowly, but as the excitement and anticipation began to build, her body took control. Soon the world was just the two of them and they seemed to be in perfect synchronicity.

Afterwards, when she collapsed on him, he rolled on top of her. He stared down at her with a crooked smile, "So 'woman-on-top,' huh?" He let his breath out in a whoosh of appreciation.

Her eyes closed and she nodded, "Hmmm, and I'd definitely like to try that again."

He snorted in her ear as he whispered, "I don't think I'll be up for a replay for a while. But, you're right. I'd definitely be interested in trying that position again. Absolutely!"

Chapter 10   Please Don't Let Me Be Misunderstood

Cade was waiting for Mira in the atrium where breakfast was being served. After a quick shower and shave, he headed downstairs to give her some time alone to pack her luggage and pull herself together – hair, makeup, and whatever the hell else women did to get ready.

He'd had an incredible night with her, one that was so unexpected, he was sure he would be thinking about it for days. He sipped his coffee and stared at the newspaper in front of him, but didn't really see it. His mind was still upstairs thinking about, well, yeah, thinking about woman-on-top, of course. Boy, that had taken him by surprise. It wasn't the first time that he'd been with a woman with lots of self-confidence who was fun in bed. But Mira was self-confident and more. She knew what she wanted and she was willing to tell him — heck, show him – what she wanted. He found that incredibly erotic. Sexy and funny and smart; the perfect bedmate, he thought with a smile. And, he realized with a jolt, that he really liked her.

That could be problematic. When would he tell her about the Witness Protection program, he asked himself? Or about his name change, or about Italy, or about any of his past? He hadn't lied to her yet, but he'd certainly left a lot out of his biography.

As if just thinking could conjure her, he looked up and saw her waving from the glass elevator. He smiled and waved back. She was wearing tight black jeans today, with a deep purple blouse. Her face was bright and almost glowing. Her hair was brown and now straightened and shiny. It came down to just above her shoulders and bounced as she walked towards him. He couldn't wait to get a whiff of that scent again.

"Hi there," she said as she walked up to him.

Cade stood up and gave her a hug and kissed her. "You look great. Not a bit like you've been up half the night," he said in a low voice that only she could hear.

"Thanks, you look pretty awake yourself." She smiled conspiratorially back at him, and then turned to the buffet, "I must say that I am starving now, though. You?" she glanced down at his coffee cup.

"I was waiting for you."

They went over to the breakfast buffet and filled their plates and returned to the table. After several minutes of silent eating, he looked over at her. "You said your son's name is Paul ... so then, what's your daughter's name?" Cade asked with interest.

"Donna," Meara replied. "I wanted to choose a name where there wouldn't be fourteen other girls with the same name in her class at school."

"Hmmm, not Madonna? Wouldn't that have been more Italian?"

She smiled and shrugged. "My husband didn't care whether his daughter had an Italian name – if it wasn't going to be Marie or Theresa, he was fine with whatever I wanted."

"What about your own family names?"

"Oh, my family is Irish, through and through. But I wasn't going to go all Gaelic or Celtic and have her go through life like I have with an ethnically mismatched name."

He looked questioningly. "What do you mean mismatched?"

"Come on, Meara Colleen O'Connell Cellini? You don't think that clashes a bit?"

"Wait a minute. You're maiden name is O'Connell?" Cade sat up with interest. "Geez, I knew a girl named Meara O'Connell when I was a kid. I had a big time crush on her."

Meara smiled. "Really? Do you know that I've never met a single other person with my first name. I mean, I knew a Maureen once and a Meaghan, but never a Meara."

"Hold on. How do you spell your first name?" Cade asked with a frown creasing his forehead.

"M-e-a-r-a. Why?"

Cade's mouth hung open. "I thought it was "M-i-r-a" – which would've been the Italian version of it, I guess." He was speaking slowly, as if what he was saying had little to do with what he was thinking. Because what he was thinking was: Could it be her? Oh, my God, Meara O'Connell from high school in Bangkok? As he stared at her, it was like a thin veil had parted and he could suddenly see the resemblance. Jesus. Then his next thought was: Damn! I've actually slept with Meara O'Connell, and he broke out in a huge grin.

She looked at him quizzically. "Hey! What's going on in that mind of yours, Cade? Why the big smile?"

"Did you live in Bangkok when you were in high school?" he asked, already knowing the answer.

She nodded slowly, looking mystified, "Yes, for two years. I lived there during my junior and senior years of high school. I graduated from..."

"ISB – the International School in Bangkok," he finished for her.

She blinked. "But, how did you know?" she raised her eyebrows.

"Because I went there, too. I had a huge crush on you in Bangkok. I was a lowly sophomore when you were a senior. I used to see you around school, or down the *soi* (road) at the Chavalet restaurant after school, and at the Teen Club on weekend nights."

"Oh my God!" Meara said, a smile growing across her face. "This is so bizarre, Cade! How did we not make this connection sooner?"

He shook his head. "I don't know. We must've had other things on our minds."

She smiled with a nod of appreciation. "So, your dad was... what? Military or embassy? Or missionary perhaps?" she asked with interest.

"Military. Air Force. He was a pilot and flew all over Southeast Asia."

"My dad was Foreign Service. He worked for USAID in Bangkok."

Cade stared at her for several seconds, but his mind was jumping ahead, calculating and figuring. Then he looked at her again and focused, "If you are the same Meara, then you and I are about the same age, but that can't be...I mean, you look..."

"Thank you for what I hope is a compliment about how I don't look my age. You don't look too bad yourself, by the way."

He swallowed and shook his head. "I still can't believe it."

Meara chuckled. "Want to see my driver's license?" She took a sip of her coffee. "Age is funny, isn't it? Just a number, but then again, not just a number." She looked thoughtful.

Cade's mind was spinning. It was her, Meara O'Connell. The more he looked at her, the more the resemblance was obvious. But Jesus, if she was his age, she was the oldest person he'd ever gone out with, the oldest woman he'd ever...well, yeah, ever went to bed with. He couldn't get his head around it. And even though he knew it was incredibly small-minded of him, he wasn't sure how he felt about getting seriously involved with an older woman.

For the past ten or fifteen years, all his girlfriends had been a lot younger than he was. That kept him young, right? When he was with them, he could fool himself into believing that he was fifteen to twenty years younger, too. There would be no fooling himself if he dated Meara. Was he ready for that? But, Christ, it was Meara O'Connell! He needed some time to think.

Chapter 11   When I Was Young

Meara ate in silence, her mind going back to Bangkok and her last year of high school. Did she remember Cade? She glanced over at him again. He did seem familiar, especially his smile with that dimple. But it was high school. She had been a senior, after all, and probably wouldn't have considered going out with a guy two years behind her in school, even had she known he was nearly her age.

She had lots of friends in the other classes. The school just wasn't big enough that anyone could remain anonymous for long. Still, she didn't recall a Chandler family. When she got the chance she would make a point of looking online at the school's yearbook and find out what he looked like back then. Maybe it would jolt her memory.

She had lived in Bangkok for two years and had graduated from high school there before returning to the US for college. That same summer her family had been transferred to Nairobi, so she never got the chance to go back to Bangkok and reconnect with her friends there.

Her first year of college, living away from her family, and then having her family move to a new post in Africa, had made her feel dislocated for the first time in her life. It was as if suddenly she didn't belong anywhere. For sure, she didn't belong in the States. Half the time, she felt like a foreign exchange student among the other freshmen in her dorm. She was homesick, of course, but it was more than that. It was the first time she'd realized that her life overseas had given her perspective on the world that none of her peers shared. The knowledge had made her feel more alone and out of sync than she'd ever felt.

Meara looked up and saw a faraway look in Cade's eyes and figured he must be remembering his own overseas days.

"Did you miss living overseas when you came back to the States after high school?" she asked.

He blinked, coming back from his daze and focusing on her. He shrugged. "Well, keep in mind that I went into the service right away and I was only in the States for a few months before I was sent to Vietnam, so I guess I didn't really get the chance to miss it too much."

"Oh, I forgot about that...that you went right back overseas."

He nodded. "I know what you're talking about, though. I felt like that when I came back to the States after Vietnam," he admitted. "That was a tough time for me."

She smiled wistfully. "I had a terrible time adjusting to the States those first couple of years back. I just couldn't relate to people my own age."

"Really? I thought it was just me. After all, I was a mixed up Nam vet and all. I hadn't thought it might be my whole childhood that had screwed me up," Cade gave a laugh although it was apparent he didn't find the thought humorous.

Meara smiled. "It took me a long time to get over it, to start to feel comfortable here, to feel like I belonged. Which is so odd, since the whole time we were living overseas, we were these gung-ho super-patriotic Americans. Heck, we were uber-Americans, I think." Meara shook her head with a laugh.

Cade nodded and grinned, "Yeah, I know what you mean. Don't forget my father was a full-bird colonel in the Air Force. They don't get much more patriotic than that! It was all 'Yes, Sir!' 'No, Sir!' 'God Bless America, Sir' around my house, believe me."

Meara chuckled. She glanced down at her watch and suddenly raised her eyebrows. "Oh, geez, Cade, I've got to get moving. My flight is at eleven and I still need to get over to the airport. Who knows how long the security lines will be." She stood up.

Cade stood as well. "Do you need any help with your suitcases or anything?"

Meara shook her head, "No, thanks, I already brought them down and the desk said they'd keep an eye on them until the airport shuttle comes." She paused and reached out to touch Cade's arm. "Thanks for everything, Cade. You turned out to be a good tour guide, after all, and you were right about your city. It was really fun last night."

Cade opened his arms and gave her a hug. "We'll have to do it again some time, huh?"

Meara smiled and nodded. "If you get the urge to see the Oregon Coast, give me a call. I'll be up there until the middle of October."

"Sure, I'll let you know."

He leaned down and kissed her, and while the kiss was fine, Meara felt...well, that something had changed between them, that he seemed somehow distant. She looked up at him and studied his face. But she couldn't think of anything more to say, so she turned and started towards the lobby.

"Brookings, right?" Cade said after her.

She stopped and turned back. "Yeah," she nodded. "Brookings, Oregon." She waited but he didn't say anything more. So to cover the awkward moment, she waved and he nodded with a smile. And that was it.

"Huh," she thought as she made her way to the airport shuttle bus. What just happened? But then she shrugged; maybe she was over-thinking an awkward moment is all.

Chapter 12   Hey Jude

Cade sat at the table in the atrium long after Meara's airport bus had departed. In a little while, she would be on her way northward. He felt a little dazed by the sudden veer his life had taken in the past hour, not to mention in the past twenty-four hours.

First, he still couldn't believe he'd ended up on the flight from Boston sitting next to a woman he had been infatuated with as a young teenager. What were the odds? And then although she had looked vaguely familiar, he hadn't recognized her. He shook his head in disbelief.

Still, there was obviously a strong attraction between them because even though she wasn't the usual type of woman that he dated or even flirted with, he had not wanted the connection to be broken after the flight and he had invited her to dinner. And for her part, even though she was hesitant, she had accepted.

They had gone into the city and had one of the best nights that he could remember. She was fun and interesting and — OK, he'd admit it — she was damn sexy.

But then she laid the bombshell on him that she was Meara O'Connell. And that meant that she was his age. She didn't look old, of course, but then some women can deceive you with the dyed hair and makeup and – God, he didn't know what else – girdles? No, wait. She didn't wear a girdle. He smiled at the sudden warm memory. At least, her body hadn't tried to trick him; he felt sure of that.

But had she tried to deceive him? No. She hadn't pretended to be anything other than who she was.

He looked around and saw that the service staff was cleaning up and closing down the breakfast area. He should go. He stood up, feeling a bone-weary tiredness for the first time. He took a deep breath and then pulled out his phone. He needed to get to his apartment to change before going into the office. He dialed Peter, his driver.

After chatting with him, Cade clicked off. He studied the cell phone in his hand. He should call her; common courtesy, wasn't it? He paused and looked around the atrium and then up at the ten-storied ring of rooms. He sighed and shook his head. If he called, she would make assumptions about his intentions. But what were his intentions? What did he want? He sighed again. He shouldn't call until he knew. Besides, it was time to get back to real life. He turned and headed towards the lobby.

Chapter 13   For Once in My Life

Meara arrived in Crescent City, California, rented a car and drove the twenty minutes north across the state border to Brookings, Oregon. It was nice to arrive at the familiar condominium overlooking the ocean. She and Tony had spent many vacations at this condo. A friend owned the condo and let them rent it whenever they wanted. They had even talked about buying a unit in the development themselves, but Tony could never make the final commitment. He kept saying that maybe they ought to find a place closer to home, out on Cape Cod, perhaps, or up in the White Mountains of New Hampshire. As for Oregon? Sure, it was a nice place to visit, but it was just so far from home, you know? And he'd leave it at that, assuming that she agreed with him.

Meara understood what he meant, but it made no difference. She'd arrive and look out at the sea stacks and the waves breaking against them, and she'd always feel something primordial. Heck, maybe it was a past life thing. Maybe she'd been on that beach down there ten thousand years ago as a cavewoman or something. But regardless, she felt at home and at one with the sun, the sea and the surf here. It was an exhilarating sense of belonging. She was not one to take that feeling lightly, so rarely had she felt she truly belonged in most of the places she'd lived throughout her life.

So now she had been at the familiar condo for a few days. Her suitcases were unpacked and she had settled in. With not much else to do, she began to wonder: Will he call?

But Cade hadn't called. On the first day, she thought he must be busy, what with being back at work after his trip. But on the second and then the third day, she ran out of excuses for him and it slowly dawned on her that he wasn't going to call. Still, she couldn't help herself. She thought about him and wallowed in erotic memories of their night in San Francisco.

She knew what the problem was, of course. She shouldn't have slept with him. How could she have been so dumb? How could she not have known that she wasn't a one-night stand kind of woman? Far from it; she was the kind that bonded with a man when she slept with him. Not very modern of her, she would admit, and particularly unfortunate now to discover this facet of herself after the fact. Thoughts of him were going bother her for some time to come; he'd be an itch that she couldn't scratch.

Women are just so bad at this sort of thing. Well, she was, anyway. She took sex way too seriously. Oh, yeah, at the time she would have said she was on board with the whole "no strings" attitude. But really? When she decided to sleep with a guy, she felt committed and wanted him to feel that way, too. And, now...well, that didn't appear to be in the cards, right?

I should not have gone to bed with him, Meara told herself again. Even though it was a perfectly rational admission, it was quickly followed by a second, plainly irrational thought. She was glad she did it!

After all, he might be the last guy she ever had sex with for the rest of her life. Even so, where did that leave her now? She sighed at her lack of answers.

She had come to Oregon to spend some time alone to decide what she wanted to do with the rest of her life. Obviously, she needed to stop wasting her time thinking about Cade. But how?

She needed to distract herself. She decided to hike down the cliff trail to the beach below. Maybe a long walk in the sand would get rid of all the second-guessing she was doing. Before she could talk herself out of it, she put on some flip-flops and grabbed a rolled up beach mat from the hall closet.

She knew the way down to the beach. There was a pretty decent trail that started at the other end of the building. She started down being careful to watch her step.

"Hey, how ya doing?" an old man called out genially, taking out his handkerchief and moping at his brow. He was leaning on a weathered hoe just below her on the trail.

She smiled. "Hello, there. You look like you've been doing some work here," she said brightly. She wondered if he was one of those old guys who've been alone a lot and who needed to hear a friendly voice once in a while.

"Just putting in some gravel along here where the rain has gouged out the path a bit," he said, pointing to the ground and then up the path a little ways to a small wheelbarrow full of dirt and gravel. "Name's Pierson. You own one of these places?"

Meara smiled and shook her head. "No, a friend lent me a place for a while. My name's Meara, by the way. I think I remember you from the last time we were here."

"Probably. I've been here a long time."

"So do you live here year-round then?" she asked curiously.

He nodded and grinned and she could see there was a gap where one of his eye teeth was missing. "Yup. I live in the first building. Been here since the place was built."

Meara looked down the trail with its small trees lending shade to the path. "The trail looks good."

"I've been taking care of it for the past few years," he'd replied proudly. "I don't have much else to do with my time, you see, so I'm glad for the chance to help out when I can."

Meara smiled, "Nice job." She was going to use his name, but wasn't certain if Pierson was his first or last name.

"Well," he said apologetically. "I've got to get back to work. Have a nice time down on the beach. It's a bit windy today, but still nice."

"Thanks. Nice to meet you."

He nodded and turned back to his hoe carefully smoothing the gravel onto the trail.

Meara headed down the switchbacks among the white and silver pampas grass and under the trees that provided much-needed shade. She wondered if Pierson was lonely? God, was she going to end up like him, stopping people in order to have a human conversation when things got too quiet in her life? She shuddered.

She made it all the way down to the driftwood piles along the edge of the sand without seeing anyone else. Luckily, her life wasn't too quiet yet and she liked the solitude of this place. The surf was gentle today with the tide out nearly to the first of the several sea stacks, the tall rocky islands that jutted up out of the ocean along this stretch of beach.

She walked down the beach a short distance to a rocky ridgeline that stretched out into the water, and then picked a spot to roll out her mat to sit on. It was breezy on the beach, as Pierson had warned, but still warm. The sun beat down on her and then just when it started feeling uncomfortable, a puffy cumulus cloud drifted in front of the sun and it was like moving into the cool shade.

Meara stared out at the ocean, mesmerized by the seagulls circling the closest sea stack. Several were perched on it and seemed to be peering at her. She looked at the birds and they looked back at her. She smiled at the thought.

She glanced up and down the beach. She was all by herself, alone on a beach in Oregon. Waiting for no one — no Tony, no Cade, no one. Damn. Meara leaned her head down and rested it on her crossed arms. It was tiring learning how to be alone.

Meara sat there for a while, then got up and walked slowly further down the beach, kicking at shells and small stones in the shallow tidal waters. A cooler breeze kicked up from the sea and soon Meara turned and walked back to her mat and flip-flops. She decided it was time to go up to the condo and have some dinner. The thought suddenly made her feel lonely; heading up to the two-bedroom condo all by herself. Get used to it, lady, she thought as she gathered her things together.

When she got back to the condo, she clicked on her laptop as she went past the dining room table. Cade Chandler, the name, popped into her mind. She stopped, returned and stood in front of the laptop waiting for it to boot up. She had forgotten about checking her high school yearbook. Oh yeah, she was definitely going to check out Cade Chandler in the online yearbook. She felt a kind of warm thrill go through her. It was as if looking him up online gave her a connection to him, an acceptable reason to be thinking about him.

She spent about twenty minutes getting to the right alumni website for her old high school, putting in her username and password and searching for the right web page for the yearbook from so many years ago. She spent some time going through her own senior class, seeing once again the young faces of her friends as well as a few faces she hardly recognized. Geez, were THEY in her class too? Maybe her memory wasn't as sharp as she thought. Soon she reached the junior class and then scrolled further to the sophomore class; that would've been Cade's class. She went through each of the names in the section of C's but there wasn't a last name of Chandler. No Chandlers.

Well, that was odd. He and his brother should both be in the yearbook in that class, but neither was listed. She went back through the sophomores and the juniors again more slowly, and then went even further back through the freshman class. No Chandlers in any of the classes. Not a one. Had she heard Cade wrong when he talked about living in Bangkok? Could he have been there different years? But what about his story about having a crush on her back then?

She clicked off and headed towards the kitchen to see what she could rustle up for dinner.

"He wasn't in the yearbook," she said, first in her head, and then out loud. All his talk about his crush on her? His seeing her at the Teen Club at the weekend dances? Did he make it up? If he did, how could he have gotten so many details right? But if it were true, why wasn't he in the yearbook?

Chapter 14   She's Not There

Cade hadn't slept well since saying goodbye to Meara at the hotel. He wondered if it was jet lag from all the traveling he'd been doing over the past weeks? But, in his gut he knew it wasn't jet lag; it was Meara. He couldn't stop thinking about her.

He tried to distract himself, of course. He debated for a day or two, but then finally called Emily, the flight attendant from Hawaiian Airlines. They'd had an on-again-off-again relationship for the past six months; well, a sort of relationship. Basically, she was a friend-with-benefits, as the younger generation called it now; and at times, the term "friend" was stretching it. But they'd lasted this long because she'd never been interested in dragging him to the altar, and maybe that was as friendly as he could hope for and still get a roll in the hay occasionally.

They didn't have a lot in common except for a mutual need for sex on a semi-regular basis, and she liked to dine at the nicer restaurants in the city when they went out and she knew he could afford it. When she wasn't otherwise in a relationship or wasn't using her flight passes to go to Paris or Singapore or Athens with her girlfriends, she'd normally be happy to let him take her to dinner and there was an unspoken agreement that there would be sex afterwards.

"Cade!" Emily said excitedly when she answered the phone.

He relaxed. It was nice having someone so excited to hear from him. "Hey," he said in reply. "I'm back in town and wondered what your flight schedule looks like this week?"

Emily laughed. "Well, you're in luck, because I'm available tonight. My next flight is tomorrow afternoon. I have a long layover coming up and my friend, Becky and I are going either to New York or Hong Kong, we haven't decided."

"Tonight it is, then," Cade said easily, not wanting to get into a discussion of the merits of picking up men in New York versus Hong Kong. "How about seven-thirty?"

"Hmmm," Emily said and countered, "How about eight? Or actually eight-thirty might be even better for me."

He groaned inwardly. That meant it would be dinner at nine-thirty or ten and a very late night. But, he really wanted to see her. "How about eight? I've got work tomorrow morning, don't forget," he added.

"Oh, pooh, you can go in whenever you want. You keep forgetting that you're a partner at the firm, love," she said. "But, if I must, I'll rush around and see you at eight."

"Good," he replied. "See you then, Babe." He heard her click off and he thumbed the End button on his phone. He knew that she wouldn't be ready at eight, but it would've been worse if he'd agreed to eight-thirty and then had to cool his heels until nine. He sighed.

Emily was a good-looking woman, twenty-five or twenty-six years old, with the dark black hair and eyes that helped her blend in with the other Hawaiian attendants. The truth was that she was as *haole* as they came; she had been born and raised in Chicago, in fact. She played up having dated a big Hawaiian football tight-end in college, and she probably got the job with the airlines thanks to that connection. The guy went pro after college and even though he was married and had a couple of kids now, Emily still saw him occasionally. Cade never asked to know the details.

When Cade arrived at Emily's apartment, he wasn't surprised to discover that she wasn't ready. Emily lived with several other flight attendants, and he glimpsed two of them going in and out of the bedrooms down the long hallway off the living room area. Cade assumed they were new roommates because he didn't recognize either of them. But he could never keep track of who belonged and who was just visiting at that place.

One of the roommates was a female who looked to be about Emily's age, the other was a guy and Cade guessed he was probably gay. Emily wouldn't like the complication of living with a straight guy.

If he had to make a sweeping generalization based on the two gays he'd known pretty well during his life so far – one, a gay associate lawyer at the firm and the other, a guy in his platoon in Vietnam — then he'd have to say that he found gay men to be pretty good company overall. The gay guy in his platoon in Nam, a kid named Jerome, was one of the funniest characters he'd ever met. Back then, Jerome could have gotten out of serving just by coming out of the closet, but he used to say that gays had to be twice as macho as other guys, the same way woman had to be twice as good to get the same recognition as men. That had stuck with Cade, mostly because he didn't believe it to be true. He believed that the only people who kept score were people who didn't measure up themselves. And, conversely, if you felt you had to be twice as good, it was probably because you yourself didn't think you were good enough. He wondered where Jerome was now.

He could've used Jerome tonight actually, because the evening was already getting off track. Here he sat on the couch in the living room of the apartment with these people coming in and out, speaking in short sound bites of dialog, as if they were all in some funny sitcom.

"Hi, there, I'm Raphael. Can I get you something to drink?" the male flight attendant roommate said as he swept dramatically into the room.

Cade grinned. Raphael? Seriously? "I'm Cade Chandler. Nice to meet you. Uh, no, thanks on the drink. I'm fine. Emily should be nearly ready."

Raphael stopped and put his finger to his chin. "You, my friend, are an optimist. A real half-full-not-half-empty fellow!" He chuckled at his little joke.

Cade nodded. "Actually, I think of myself as a hopeful man," he said, getting into the spirit of the dialog.

Raphael pointed at him and smiled broadly, "You are just perfect for this apartment." He spoke as if Cade were a piece of furniture that fit the layout, and who stayed on-script, of course. Was it possible to out-stereotype the stereotype? Perhaps someone was keeping score, after all.

The other roommate breezed in, just then, wearing a sliver of panties and a revealing bra that left nothing, including her dark nipples, to the imagination. She started to say something to Raphael, saw Cade and her eyes grew round, but then she giggled. "Oh, my! And me without a stitch on," she said and winked at Cade. "You must be waiting on Emily, right?"

"Waiting is what dudes do for Emily," Raphael interjected.

She smiled but didn't look at Raphael. She focused on Cade. "Hi," the bra model said as she came towards Cade her hand outstretched, "I'm Brooke, Emily's other roommate. I just started working at Korean Air about a week and a half ago."

Cade shook her hand. "Cade," he said by way of introduction. "Korean Air?" he added, "Really?"

"Sure, I speak fluent Korean, you know," she giggled again. "However, I think I got the job for some of my other attributes," she said and winked at Cade again. She leaned towards him, so that he was within arm's reach of her cleavage – maybe even hand's reach? "Honey, if she don't come through tonight, give me a call, 'kay? You look like you might know a thing or two about having fun in this town. And besides, you're at least a head taller than any of my Korean admirers." She laughed and turned. "I'll let Em know you're waiting on her. Can't say that'll speed her up, though." She waved vaguely over her shoulder and disappeared into the first bedroom on the left.

"Brooke definitely has her attributes, I'll have to give her that," Raphael said, letting his breath out and fanning his face comically.

Cade grinned and said, "I'd have to agree with you there."

When Emily finally came out in a cloud of perfume and perfectly coifed hair, wearing skinny jeans and a black shimmery blouse, Raphael disappeared into the kitchen. Cade glanced down at his watch and saw that it was a quarter after nine; an hour to put on a pair of jeans, he thought, but didn't say aloud. He had been a hopeful man, but now he was just a hungry one. After a lot of discussion back and forth in the elevator going down to the lobby, they finally decided to walk down the hill and over a few blocks to Union Square. Emily pointed out a pizza place that she'd been meaning to try.

"I'm really not all that hungry, Cade. Plus, I've been eating like a pig for the past week – went to a luau with a group of executives from a convention flight to Maui — so I really need to watch my weight."

"OK, pizza it is," Cade said agreeably. He was starving and actually pizza that would be served hot and quick sounded perfect.

He felt better after they got inside and although it was packed, they were able to get a table and the food was, indeed, served fast and hot.

"Where shall we go after we eat," Emily asked, wiping her mouth delicately after putting away three large slices of a vegetable and pepperoni thin crust.

He thought about the Cover Club and how much Meara had loved the place the other night. Emily didn't like going to the same place twice, unless it was a celebrity magnet and uber expensive, so maybe the club would be different enough for her.

"I know just the place. It's not far from here," Cade said. He drained the last of his beer and while he paid for dinner, Emily trotted off to fix her makeup in the ladies room. He assumed that was her way of saying she had to pee, without actually having to say those crass words. He shook his head.

She came out with a huge satisfied smile on her face, which he hoped didn't mean she'd just thrown up her dinner. He squinted looking at her, but he couldn't tell. He knew she'd done it before, though, because she told him all about it one drunken weepy night. She certainly looked more together than he knew she actually was. She took his arm and pulled herself close as they walked out onto the street. It was September and although the air was still warm, there was an ocean breeze that stirred up the leaves in the trees and could cause a few goose bumps on a young lady who never thought to bring a wrap with her. He sighed and put his arm around her shoulder and rubbed at her arm. "Cold?" he asked.

She shook her head. "Nope, I just like your arm around me is all," she cooed.

He could feel the goose bumps.

When they got close to the club, they saw the line snaking out the door and continuing down in front of the building next door.

"Looks pretty busy," she commented.

"Let me talk to my friend, Nixon," Cade said and he craned his neck to see over the people at the front of the line.

"Hey, Mr. C.," Nixon said, waving him in when he recognized Cade. "Come on in. Let the man and his date through there," he admonished the people pressing close at the front of the line.

Cade guided Emily through and saw that she was enjoying the special attention. It probably made her feel like a celebrity, Cade thought with a smile. Cade didn't mind the feeling himself.

He tucked two twenties into Nixon's hand as he shook it when he passed him.

Nixon nodded. "Have a good night, sir."

"You, too, buddy," Cade said patting the shoulder of the larger man.

Nixon broke into a grin. "Yup, I'm having a good night so far."

"Want to see if you can find us a table while I grab some beers?" Cade asked Emily. He had to lean down and talk directly into her ear because the music and crowd noise was so loud.

Cade looked over at the band. "Cover band for the Rolling Stones," he said nodding at the stage.

Emily rolled her eyes and shook her head. "Wow, this is a flash from the ancient past, huh?"

Cade looked at her and noticed that she was scanning the room, he hoped she was looking for a table. He headed towards the bar, but it was a good fifteen to twenty minutes before he was back and it took him a while to locate her. She hadn't found a table. Instead, she was standing just a few feet from where he'd left her.

"No tables, huh?" he asked, handing her one of the beers.

She shook her head and sighed. "Pretty loud, too," she added. She took the beer but didn't take a sip.

Was beer fattening? Cade wondered as he took a long swallow of his own beer. He hummed to a Stones' song that the band had just started up.

He felt the music seep into his nervous system, and it was as if he was plugged into the band. The beat thrummed through him. He tapped his foot and clicked his ring against the glass bottle in time to the music.

Emily put her hand on his ring finger and stopped him, "Don't do that. It's annoying," she said. "Geez, you know all the words to this song, huh?" she commented.

He looked at her and could see the frown on her brow. "What's up?" he asked.

She sighed. Even though the music was loud and people were beginning to sing along with the band, he could hear that sigh.

"What?" he asked, leaning closer to her so she could tell him.

Emily spread her arm, gesturing towards the crowd, and said, "Bad Karma, I think. This is like a senior citizen revival meeting." She rolled her eyes and smirked. "Come on, let's go someplace fun," she said, pulling on his arm. She leaned over and set her full beer on the table nearest them. The two guys at the table glanced up and when they saw beautiful sexy Emily, they grinned.

"For you guys," she said with her sexiest smile. "It's just too much for me."

With that she took Cade's hand and led him, weaving in and out of the crowd, towards the door. He stopped for a second and set down his half-empty bottle of beer pushing it up against the wall near the door where he hoped it wouldn't get knocked over.

Nixon gave him a quizzical look when he saw Cade coming out. Cade shook his head slowly and shrugged. Nixon just nodded slowly as if he understood.

When they got out to the street, Emily smiled with relief and took his arm possessively. Then she giggled as she led him down the crowded street, "God, the lead singer looked almost as old as Mick Jaggers himself."

"Jagger," Cade corrected.

"What?"

"His name is 'Mick Jagger,' not 'Mick Jaggers,' there's no 's,' that's all," Cade said.

Emily rolled her eyes again, "Sorry, it was before my time, I guess," she added dryly.

They walked back to her apartment, about a twenty-minute hike all up hill. He was feeling out of sorts by the time they got there, but he could see that she was exhilarated by the exercise, and being a night owl, she was apparently starting to wake up.

"Let's have some fun," Emily said with a gleeful grin on her face.

He grimaced and hoped she didn't notice. He furtively glanced at his watch and saw that it as already nearly midnight. The thought of it nearly brought a yawn on. "What'd you have in mind?" he asked, quelling another urge to yawn.

"I'm thinking wild sex, the hot tub bubbling away on the outdoor deck, you and me naked, and...oh, I don't know...maybe a bottle of cab..." her eyes were lit from within.

Cade gave a half-smile. He was tired. No, he was beat. Sure, he could go upstairs and try to conjure up an erection, not that sex wasn't always fun, no question about that, but...well, the cool crisp white sheets on his king-sized bed back at his apartment were calling to him, he couldn't deny it.

"Cade?"

Cade looked down at Emily's upturned face and realized that they were stopped and Emily was staring up at him. "Are you OK, Cade?"

Suddenly, he saw his out. He grimaced. "Em, I'm feeling kind of funky, to be honest..."

She took a step away from him. "Uh, funky...funky how?"

"You know, I think I'd better head back to my place. You have a flight tomorrow, and I don't know...I might be coming down with something...." he said finally. "Hon, I'm really sorry to mess up the evening."

She touched his cheek. "Aw, it's OK, baby. Next time, maybe. I have to admit; I really, really can't get sick right now. I have a trip to take with my BFF, and I don't want to disappoint, you know," she said with a small laugh.

Cade nodded. "I know. You always look out for your friends. It's something I've always admired about you," he said, sounding almost as if he meant it sincerely.

She leaned up and pressed her cheek against his cheek, not even taking the chance of kissing him, he noticed. "It was great seeing you again, Cade. I hope we can get together next time we're both in town. Looking forward to it, you know?"

He nodded. "Me, too, babe. I'll call my car to come get me," he said and turned to make the call. He almost couldn't stop the edge of his mouth from turning up into a smile of relief.

Chapter 15   You Can't Always Get What You Want

By the end of the week, Meara was going stir-crazy. She decided to get out and drive around a bit. She headed south on Highway 101 towards downtown Brookings, noting the blue skies and the surf rolling in on her right. The ocean was strewn with sea stacks; little rocky islands some with barely enough space for the birds to roost on. She loved the crazy scenery; it seemed so prehistoric and yet new and fresh at the same time.

On the spur of the moment, she pulled off when she saw the sign for Harris Beach State Park. She drove down to the parking lot along the beach. She sat in her car for several minutes, before smiling and deciding, what the hell, she was on vacation, she could give herself permission to just mosey around if she wanted to.

She got out of the car and walked to the edge of the pavement, where the rocky parking lot turned into sandy beach. Walking on the sand, her sandals flipped sand up the back of her calves so she reached down and unlatched them and slid them off. The sand was hot under her feet, but it was only a few steps to the tidal area that was damp with seawater and another step or two before the small waves were gently swirling around her ankles. Suddenly she felt like a five year old wanting to splash and play in the water. She grinned and closed her eyes.

She read somewhere that moving water actually had a physiological effect on our bodies, not to mention our moods. It didn't matter whether it was rushing water in lofty waterfalls, churning rivers, or the pounding of ocean surf. She didn't know the science of it, but she had always felt better near water.

This trip was the first real break she'd had since Tony's death. She had needed to get away from Tony's family and Boston. Although she didn't know what she wanted for her future, one thing she was sure of was that she didn't want to end up one of those widows who memorialized her husband and remained in his shadow long after he was gone. Of course, she understood the impulse to remain safely locked in old routines, to pretend he wasn't really dead but was only away on an extended trip. She didn't want that for herself. She looked up at the sky and thought, "You have to let me go, Tony."

She played with her wedding ring, twirling it round and round her finger. She glanced down and realized what a nervous habit it had become – another bad habit to break. She sighed and stopped twirling the ring and calmly rested her thumb against the gold band.

Her phone rang and the sound jolted her for a second. She saw that the call was from her daughter, Donna. She smiled warmly as she said "Hi, sweetie!"

"Hi Mom," Donna said with a tired sigh. Meara immediately thought, oh great, it's going to be one of THOSE calls. Donna had a way of starting a conversation with a long sigh that let you know she wanted to share her current bad mood with you.

"What's up? Want to talk?" Meara asked encouragingly.

"No, just wondered where you are and how things are going. I thought you'd call as soon as you got to San Francisco to let me know you arrived safe and sound..."

Meara laughed in surprise. "Why? You never used to call me to let me know when YOU had arrived safe and sound when you traveled."

"Mom," Donna said in a bit of a whine. "This is different. Besides, you're not getting any younger."

Meara felt like she'd been slapped. "Really?" she responded in a voice she knew her daughter wouldn't mistake.

"Sorry, I didn't mean it like that. I just meant that Dad died and I'm worried about you, too. I don't want to lose both of my parents...." Donna's voice carried a sob that she tried to swallow.

"I know, honey," Meara said soothingly. "But don't worry about me. I'm not going anywhere. Besides, women live longer than men and besides I'm in great shape."

"So what did you do in San Francisco by yourself? Was it very awful?" Meara could hear the sympathy in Donna's voice, and she found that it grated on her a little.

Meara immediately thought of Cade and she smiled to herself and wondered how much to tell her daughter about him. Was there anything to tell? She hadn't talked to him since she left him that morning at the hotel. Maybe it was just one of those interludes that she would have to chalk up to experience.

"Mom?" Donna's voice interrupted her thoughts. "Are you still there?"

"Oh, sorry, sweetie, I was just checking to see how much battery is left before I have to recharge this thing," she lied.

"So what did you do in San Fran?" Donna asked again.

"Oh, you know, just had a look around. I was only there overnight, after all."

"Did you go into the city then? Your hotel was out by the airport, right?"

"Yes it was. But I met a local on the flight and we had dinner together."

There was silence on the other end of the line. "You went out to dinner?" Donna repeated. "Was the woman in Boston on business or something? Did you have a lot in common?"

"He," Meara corrected. She had no intention of lying to her daughter even though she would edit the version she told her. "He is a lawyer in San Francisco. We sat next to each other on the plane and got to talking. I think he felt sorry for me," Meara chuckled. "Here I was this poor old lady traveling by herself. And you know how I hate to eat alone."

"Well, you could've ordered room service."

"Sure, but I thought I should force myself to be more sociable. I don't want to end up a recluse, after all."

"But, it's understandable. I mean, your husband's only been dead for a few months."

Meara didn't know what to say to that. "Well, I suppose. But it was a nice dinner and good company. I liked San Francisco," she said, realizing as she said it that she did feel fondly about the city.

She had thoroughly enjoyed her evening on the town with Cade, dancing to old music, singing along to songs from bands that were big when she was a teenager. It had been lots of fun.

"So? A lawyer. That must've been kind of boring, huh?" Donna said.

Meara grinned, but kept her voice light. "Not so boring. We had a lot in common." Suddenly, she really wanted to tell someone about her evening. How much fun it had been to forget that she was middle-aged and a recent widow, to dance to old tunes that were popular before her children were born. She almost sighed wistfully, but stopped herself. There was no explaining it to her daughter, Donna; it was too much of a breech in Daddy-worship and way too soon after Tony's death. If she wanted to talk to someone about Cade, she'd have to call her friend, Jill, who would enjoy the discussion and didn't have anything invested in Meara remaining faithful to Tony.

"Well, you haven't heard from him, have you?" Donna asked.

Meara thought it was a rather brazen question, but she sighed, a sigh of regret. "No, honey, it was just a dinner with someone interesting, that's all."

"Oh, well, I'm...I'm glad you had a good time, then," Donna added. "Listen, I've got to go into a meeting with my boss in a couple of minutes, so I'd better sign off. I'll call later in the week, OK?"

"Sure, honey, that sounds great. Have a good week!" she added.

"You, too, Mom. I miss you," Donna said.

"Love you, too, sweetie. Bye now," Meara said and ended the call. She sighed as she held the cell phone for a second or two before sliding it into her pocket. Kids. She felt badly for the hurt Donna was still feeling over her father's death. She'd have to check in with Paul soon, too, to see how he was doing. A parent's job is never done, no matter how old the kids get, she realized.

Had she been a concern for her mother after her own father had died, she wondered? Probably, but she didn't really remember. She wished she could talk to her mom about it, but her mother's memory was a broken thing now. She had been moved to a nursing home from her assisted living place about three years ago and every time that Meara visited she was appalled at how her mother had degenerated. Sometimes she'd visit and she wasn't sure if her mother recognized her. Once her mother had called her by her aunt's name, thinking that Meara was her sister, not her daughter.

It made Meara feel very strange not to be recognized by her own mother, almost like she was a ghost, an orphan. At one time she remembered hoping she'd live to be a hundred, but after watching her mother slowly disappear mentally before her eyes, she no longer wanted to live that long; now she hoped that she would drop dead the second her mind started going. She did not want to be a burden to her own children; but more than that, she did not want her children to see her mentally incapacitated and to pity her. Because the truth was, she did pity her mother. Her mother wasn't a financial burden, thank goodness; her father had left her well off and able to live comfortably. But the mental burden could be as awful as any financial one. Every time Meara went to visit her, she had to face what remained of a once-vibrant woman, and it was pitiable.

Meara stretched and stood up. It was time to go. She smiled into the sunny sky and felt the warmth of the September sun envelope her. She was glad to be alive today; she was grateful for her children and grateful they were alive and healthy; and she was even hopeful for her own tomorrows.

But, now to check a few things off today's to-do list.

Chapter 16   You Really Got a Hold on Me

Cade woke up early the morning after his date with Emily. He called Vanessa before he left for work.

"Hi, Dad!" she said. He loved that she was always happy to hear from him.

"How about lunch tomorrow, honey?" he asked.

"Love to. You buying or am I?" she responded with a laugh.

"Me, since I'm asking," he said. "No, wait a minute, come over to my place. We'll eat here."

"Your place?" she asked.

"Sure, I'll make you a sandwich and we'll sit on the deck and watch the light shimmer off the Golden Gate Bridge. OK?"

"You have a way with descriptions," she laughed. "Sounds like a plan. I'll be there around twelve-thirty, OK?"

"I'll have the tuna salad ready," he said. He clicked off and let out a breath. He was looking forward to seeing Vanessa, but sad that the older she got the harder he had to work to keep her in his life.

The next day she arrived closer to one. "Traffic was a bitch," she said mildly, by way of explanation. "Must be a convention in town or something."

"Figures," he responded. "Luckily, tuna will keep."

She followed him through the apartment. It was a spacious place and Vanessa always had the urge to take a deep breath when she entered. The living room had a soaring ceiling, with a spiral staircase going between the lower floor and the upper. There was a bedroom on each floor, each with its own bathroom suite.

Downstairs was the kitchen and living room area, with only a long oak bar separating the two. Several cushioned stools were in front of the bar and that's where Vanessa sat watching Cade as he pulled together the tuna salad and Italian bread for sandwiches.

He laid everything out but then he stopped, as he seemed to wonder what he was missing. She sighed and went around the bar to help him out. She got out the pickles, and some ice tea, ice cubes and tall glasses.

She found a tray leaning against the side of the refrigerator and put everything on it and carried it out to the outdoor deck. The September sun was beating down and it felt wonderfully warm and cozy out there on his cushioned deck chairs.

When they had made their sandwiches, poured the ice tea, and sat in side-by-side deck chairs, she sighed and looked over at him. "So, Dad, what's going on with you? You seem...I don't know...kind of distracted?"

Cade looked at her and smiled, almost grimly. "Yeah. I need someone to talk to. I'm glad you could come over today, Vanessa."

She rolled her eyes, but smiled, "Great."

They both chuckled.

"First, tell me about the lady from the plane. I think that might jumpstart this whole conversation," Vanessa said, biting into her tuna sandwich.

Cade eyed her. "What did I tell you about her already?"

"Um, I don't know...that you were in love with her and couldn't live without her...I think that was the gist of it, no?" Vanessa smiled and took a long sip of her ice tea through the straw.

"Jesus," he said, covering his eyes dramatically. "I obviously said too much."

"Yeah, you do seem to be drifting into off-the-wall territory right now. What happened?" she leaned forward because actually she really wanted to find out what was going on with him. It had been so long since anyone had connected with him at all, she was fascinated by the change. It was like seeing a whole new side of him.

"First of all, her name is Meara. I met her on the plane from Boston to San Fran – I don't know how to explain it, but we connected somehow on the flight. It's hard to describe now, but I felt like I knew her, you know?" He looked at Vanessa, and then he shrugged. "OK, truth? I DID know her. I mean, I didn't realize it then, but later, it turns out she's a girl that I had a mad crush on when I was a sophomore in high school back in Bangkok." He stopped and looked meaningfully at Vanessa who stopped chewing. "Yeah," he said nodding his head. "Seriously."

"Wait! Wait, you KNEW her? You actually knew her when you were in high school?"

He nodded. "Yeah. Unbelievable, right?"

She stared at him. "Oh my God, Dad, that is an amazing coincidence! What are the odds? I'm thinking...the Wheel of Fate...you know?"

"Well, I don't know about 'amazing', but it was definitely weird as shit. I mean we had a great time together. We went out to dinner and then to the Club and the band was playing Eric Burdon and The Animals, and God, she knew all the words," he said in an excited rush and when he glanced at Vanessa he saw by the look on her face that he had gone way off-course. He paused and cleared his throat. "Anyway, we went to bed together but at the time, I didn't realize that she was the same girl...woman...girl, that I knew in Bangkok until the next day."

Vanessa looked confused. "So?"

"Don't you see?" Cade said. "I knew her when I was a kid in Bangkok! That means she's my age, for chrissakes! Vanessa, she's old. I've never...well, you know, I've never been to bed with anyone that old in my life." He stopped and nodded, like that was all that could be said about it.

"Wow!" Vanessa leaned forward and started to grin. "Dad? Are you kidding me?" She giggled into her hand.

"What?" he said.

"Oh my God, I can't believe it! You are in love with an older woman," Vanessa said drawing the words out to needle him.

"What older woman? She's the same age as me, or nearly!" he said defensively.

"Ah? So you admit it, then? That you're old?" Vanessa cackled.

"Would you be friggin' serious?" Cade said.

Vanessa shook her head, still grinning. "OK, OK, what do you want from me here? You don't seem to realize how you've just denigrated older women...like somehow men don't age, but women do? Is that what you're saying?"

"Jesus! Don't get off topic, would you? I want to know what I should do?"

Vanessa looked at him blankly for a long moment. He was serious. "So, do you like her or not? Wait. You don't have to answer that. You wouldn't be asking if you didn't like her. So, next question is, where is she now?" Vanessa asked.

"Brookings, Oregon," Cade answered, glad that he could answer something simple and straightforward for a change.

Vanessa nodded sagely. "Well, then, I think, Dad, that you should go to Brookings, Oregon and figure out why this woman has you all in a tangle. Go see her, take her to dinner, take her to bed again, if you aren't put off by her age, that is," Vanessa said, her eyes twinkling, "but find out why she has such power over you. I think you need to see this through."

Cade eyed her. That was exactly what he thought he should do, but he wasn't sure if Vanessa was just being dramatic. "You really think so?" he asked.

Vanessa nodded and smiled, "Yes, Dad, I do. I think you should go to Oregon."

Chapter 17   I Am A Rock

Meara was tired of pretending that she wasn't growing lonely and bored in the gorgeous condo overlooking the Pacific Ocean. She should be happy. She was where she wanted to be, she had a million dollar view, and she'd gotten away from the dark grief clouds that draped Tony's family. They hadn't dealt with his passing very well; the shock of a death in the family that had thought itself invulnerable is the most difficult part of getting beyond a loss. Meara had unfortunately learned that lesson young in life. Family was the tie that binds. (And, Oh boy, at times, did it bind!)

She told everyone that she wanted to be alone for a while, to have time to think about the future and to get her life together. And probably if she hadn't met Cade she would've quietly enjoyed this time alone just like she'd planned. Sure, maybe she'd have become a little depressed and moody, but it was only a month. She'd have managed, and maybe been relieved to get back to Boston; she might even have felt rejuvenated.

But, instead, she felt unsettled. Yes, she admitted it, Cade had unsettled her by suddenly making her realize that the person she thought she was might not be as set in stone as she believed. Up until the night in San Francisco with Cade, she had been pretty certain that she knew what her life would be like without Tony. She wasn't in her thirties or forties where a whole new life might magically open up for her. She was a middle-aged widow and she had accepted it, dammit. Truly, she had.

What future did she see? She'd be an involved grandmother, she'd have lunch and drinks every few weeks with her girlfriends, she'd take on the occasional travel consulting project to keep her hand in it and to keep her mind sharp, and for a few weeks each fall she'd travel to places she hadn't been. Yes, that had been her vision of the future. And she planned to get started on it just as soon as her kids gave her a few grandchildren to begin spoiling.

She sighed as she turned to gaze out towards the horizon. The sea was churning softly against the cliffs below, but she was staring straight out to the blue horizon, where the sky met the edge of the darkening sea. That quiet tidy vision of her future life was drifting away from her. It no longer seemed a certainty, or in truth, something that sounded very interesting to her anymore. She knew why.

Cade. Boy, she liked thinking about him. She liked recalling every detail of being with him that night in San Francisco. She hated that as every day went by she grew further and further away from the experience, and it felt less and less real. One day she'd wake up and wonder if it had ever really happened to her, if maybe she had made it up, or exaggerated it until it was more fantasy than reality. She should write it all down, every last moment of it, every feeling, every look, every emotion. She wanted to remember how perfect that night had been for her, because, dammit, it might be the last time she would ever have such a night.

What she would remember most is that he'd wanted her. Her skin tingled at the thought of it. It was the truth and she knew it down to her toes. But now, here she was in Brookings, Oregon, all by herself. Would she be by herself for the rest of her life? Damn, she didn't want to face that thought.

And, by the way, where the heck was he anyway? Still in San Francisco? Did he go back to Boston? Geez, some knight in shining armor he turned out to be! She shrugged. Well, OK, she knew that storybook romances were just that...storybook-bound.

But, oh, man! She had wanted him, too. She really and truly had wanted him. And now that she'd lost him, she wanted him even more. What a twit she was, and what a twit she'd been. She'd lost the guy for one simple reason: because she'd turned and walked away too soon. A freshman mistake. Truly, a freshman mistake.

Chapter 18   To Sir, With Love

This was the craziest thing he'd ever done, Cade thought, as he rolled his wheeled suitcase over to the car rental office, just a stone's throw from the tiny air terminal in Crescent City, California. He went in and there were two young men lounging back on stools on the other side of the counter tossing pennies against the edge of the counter. He watched for a second or two and when they glanced up with a "caught-in-the-act" look on their faces, he smiled.

"Name's Chandler. Got a car for me, boys?"

They scurried around suddenly looking very busy, and probably feeling a bit sheepish, Cade figured. "Sure do, Mr. Chandler. We have your paperwork right here. All you need to do is to sign here and then initial there at the bottom. These are the keys and the car's the silver one just outside."

Cade smiled again, "Thanks. Is there GPS in the car?"

"Sure, that car is loaded! It has a pretty sweet navigation system."

"Great," Cade said and slid the paperwork back across the counter. He took the keys and headed out of the small office. He paused and then popped his head back in to the office, "Brookings? Just north of here, right? About how long a drive would you say?"

"Oh, it's nothing, Sir. Probably only twenty minutes straight up 101."

Cade nodded. "Thanks, again." He nearly ran into a guy coming in when he'd turned suddenly to head towards the car. "Sorry," he apologized.

Instead of accepting his apology, the guy looked furtively away and mumbled something as he spun on his heel and started walking quickly back towards the terminal.

It was such an odd interaction that Cade stopped and watched his receding back for a second. He felt something wasn't quite right about the guy, but couldn't place the feeling. He searched his memory and thought he remembered the guy on the plane sitting in the very back of the small jet. He shrugged. Strange dude is all, he reassured himself.

He started the car and turned on the navigation system to enter the address of the condo that Meara was renting. It took a bit of sleuthing to find out where she was staying, but Brookings luckily wasn't that big of a town, and she'd described the condo building as sitting on a cliff overlooking the ocean. All he had to do was to call a real estate agent in Brookings and describe the condo development just as Meara had, and the guy knew exactly which one it was. Cade wrote down the address, and after a little bit of chitchat, thanked him and said he'd let him know when he'd be in Brookings to look at the place.

Of course, he could've called Meara and gotten the address from her. But he was afraid to let her know he was coming. She might try to talk him out of it, and he didn't want to take that chance. So he'd come, just as Vanessa had advised. Just do it.

He felt considerably less self-assured by the time he got to the condo, though. First of all, there was a security gate he hadn't counted on. How did one get through a gate that required a passcode? Maybe he could park the car down the highway a bit and walk back and just go around the gate? But he thought that would look a little suspicious. So instead he waited and after about ten minutes the answer arrived in the form of a large SUV that stopped at the gate. The elderly driver leaned out and typed something into the security box and after a second the gates swung open. Cade pulled in right behind the vehicle and waved genially at the older couple in the front, just as if he belonged there. He was relieved to see them return the wave.

He drove down to the end, and found the condo building that Meara had described as the last one. There were only two floors and he knew she was on an upper floor. Here goes nothing, he thought, as he got out of the car. He decided against bringing the suitcase with him. After all, he wasn't even sure she'd invite him in. It would be presumptuous to show up with a suitcase. The thought made him smile. He could hope, couldn't he?

He climbed the two flights of stairs and found the recessed doorway. He knew it was the right one because he recognized the coral seagull hanging on the wall next to the front door; it was just as she'd described it. He took a deep breath and rang the doorbell. He could hear the chime sounding muffled on the other side of the door. Geez, he hoped she was home. He hadn't considered that contingency.

A minute went by, and then the door swished open and Meara was standing before him. Seeing her again nearly took Cade's breath away.

"Hi," he said.

She stared at him for one or two very long seconds, and then she blinked. Finally, a smile spread across her face. "Cade. It's you! This is so strange! I've been thinking about you."

He grinned and his dimple showed. "Well, you said if I got the urge to see the Oregon coast to stop by…"

"I think I said to call, but this is even better." She shook her head with a laugh. "Come on in. I can't wait for you to see the view I told you about."

Chapter 19   Bad Moon Rising

Just before Cade had arrived, Meara had been in the kitchen standing in front of the open refrigerator trying to decide about dinner – chicken? Or maybe just soup and a sandwich? She closed the refrigerator door, not wanting to let all the cold air out while she made up her mind. She turned and noticed the laptop screen as it blinked and switched to her screensaver photos. The photos silently floated across the screen. They were mostly family shots — of Paul and his wife on the Coast Guard Beach on Cape Cod, Donna and her husband laughing as they pointed off to something behind the photographer, another one with Tony his arms wrapped around the shoulders of his younger brother, John, in front of the family bakery in Boston. Lots of memories were loaded into those two or three second passages across her computer screen. She sighed.

Then there was a knock at the door. She couldn't imagine who it could be. Maybe a neighbor? She wondered. She glanced around and noticed for the first time that it was nearly dusk and was growing dark in the condo, the only light coming from the gas fireplace in the living room. She flipped on a light as she passed the living room wall that separated the living room from the bedrooms on her way to the front door.

She pulled open the door and was dumbfounded to see Cade standing there. For a second or two she wondered if she had conjured him up, having been thinking about him so much these past couple of days. She blinked but he was still there, smiling at her, the dimple creasing his cheek and did she see relief showing in his eyes?

"It's good to see you," she said leading him inside and then she stopped, making him stop too. "No, the truth is, Cade, it's a shock to see you here."

He glanced down a little sheepishly then looked at her, "Sorry. I know I should've called first. But...I was afraid you might not want to see me and I really wanted to see you again."

She could sense the truth in his voice, but thinking about what he said, she looked confused, "Why wouldn't I want to see you?"

He shuffled a bit, "Because I should've called you right after you left San Francisco. You know, to thank you for the other night, to see if you got up here safely, to follow up..." he stopped, and then shrugged. "Not calling makes me a bit of a jerk, and I'm sorry."

She smiled, "Well, it would've been nice if you'd called, of course. But you know, I wasn't really expecting it, so I don't think you're a jerk." She paused. "Still, I am glad you're sorry."

"You are? Why?"

"Because it puts you at a disadvantage, I think," she said lightly, then took his hand, "Come and see." She pulled him out to the deck off the dining area. "Look," she said spreading her arm out so he could take in the sun setting in glorious purples and pinks across the sky behind the sea stacks and the whitecaps bouncing on the top of the churning ocean below.

He looked out towards the horizon and took a deep breath, "Wow." He stared for a second or two longer, and then pulled her hand so that she stepped closer to him. He leaned down to kiss her. "You're right, this place has an unbelievable view," he whispered then his lips covered hers and she folded into him.

Later, they decided on chicken for dinner. "Do you want wine, beer or a drink?" she asked as she got the chicken out of the refrigerator.

"What do you have?" he asked, reaching out and turning the bottle of scotch around to see the label. "You're a scotch drinker?" he asked his brows rose. "I didn't know that about you."

"Scotch and water...lots of water...and never mixed with soda." She made a sour face.

He chuckled, "A woman after my own heart." He opened the bottle of scotch. "Let's have a drink now while we get dinner ready, then wine with dinner, OK?"

She nodded, "Perfect." She saw him looking around, and then added, "Drink glasses are in the cabinet over there by the stove." She frowned, "Not where I would've put them if this were my kitchen, but I didn't have a say in the matter."

"Pretty far from the refrigerator," he commented.

She smiled and nodded, "Exactly what I thought."

"Great minds..." he said with a laugh.

She began mixing a sesame seed marinade for the chicken as he added the water to the drinks. He set her glass on the counter beside her. "That smells great," he said. "Anything I can do?"

"There's a rice cooker in one of the lower cabinets, although I can't remember which cabinet. Could you find it and get the rice going?"

They worked companionably, making a salad to go with the sesame chicken and rice, and chatted about the weather, about Cade's flight, and this and that. He set the table as she pulled the chicken from the oven. Then he poured them each a glass of white wine.

Looking around, he commented, half in jest, "Aw...no candles for the table?"

She went to the light switch and dimmed the light over the table. "Better?" she asked.

"Better," he agreed. He went over to the living room and turned off the light in there. "Even better, what do you think?" he asked. There was just the dim light over the table and the gas fireplace lighting up the room.

Meara nodded. "Perfect."

When she brought the chicken dish over to the table Cade stood behind her chair and held it for her. For a second she was a little taken aback. She couldn't remember the last time any man had held a chair for her. Tony had stopped doing so many years ago even when they went out to dinner. She thought it was an understandable casualty of a long marriage and familiarity.

Meara put one hand dramatically over her heart, "Wow, holding my chair for me is so gallant, Cade."

"Thank my mother for raising young men with manners," he answered with a laugh. "And you can thank my military father for enforcing her rules."

Meara grinned, "I'd love to. Are your parents still around?" she asked as she sat.

He paused, and then sat in his own chair. "Well, my dad passed on – massive heart attack – years ago. He was sixty-two at the time."

"I'm sorry," she said. "Sixty-two is pretty young for a massive heart attack."

"Yeah, but he was a heavy smoker most of his life. Started trying to quit a few years before the end. I think maybe he was beginning to feel something wasn't quite right. But every time he tried to quit, he went back to it. Some people just can't let it go."

"Did you ever smoke?" she asked.

"In 'Nam, yeah, and for a while afterwards. But it was a no-brainer when I started working as an aviation mechanic. There were too many flammable things around the hangars. It was just easier to quit than to worry about blowing everything up. What about you?"

"I did in high school and college, but once I started working, I didn't want to be known as "the smoker." Besides, I worked in the travel industry and you can't have habits that might offend the clients."

They ate in silence for several minutes.

"Travel industry, huh?" Cade said as he picked up his glass of wine. "Do you still work in travel?"

She shrugged. "Occasionally, I take on projects for particular clients, but I was down to working part-time even before Tony died. I haven't decided what I want to do now. That's one of the things I am supposed to come to a decision about while I'm out here. It's the whole 'What's Next' question." She looked out towards the ocean, but the sun was down and it was black beyond the lights at the edge of the deck. The moon hadn't risen yet, and she couldn't make out any stars through the sliding glass door.

She changed her focus to the glass in the sliding door itself and she could see herself and Cade in the reflection. They were sitting nearly side-by-side, she saw. His head was tilted slightly as he was looking at her, while he held his glass of wine in the hand farthest from her. They looked like a couple, she thought, not just two people, but a set. She smiled at the odd thought.

She looked over at him and she saw that he was still watching her. "So, how do you like my Brookings, Oregon?" she asked.

"I can see why you like it here so much. Your view is truly astounding, for one thing." He raised his eyes towards the deck and seeing the black night outside. "Well, OK, not quite so astounding at the moment, maybe."

"Wait until the moon comes up...well, if it's a clear night, that is. There was nearly a full moon last night and it just hung out there over the ocean." She shook her head. "I am such a sucker for an ocean view."

He smiled, squinting his eyes slightly as he took a sip of his wine and looked at her over the edge of the glass. "I'd like to see that full moon over the ocean."

"Stick around, then, and you'll get your chance," she said as she stood up to clear the dishes.

He immediately stood up too, and she grinned. "Is that your manners training or are you getting ready to help with the dishes?" she asked, teasing him.

He smiled back at her. "Both. My mother also made sure we all knew our way around a kitchen from an early age."

"Do you cook?" she asked with interest.

He nodded. "You'd be surprised at how good I am." And he smiled, to see if she got his double meaning.

She smiled, too, "Ah, I was referring to your skills as a chef." Her eyes sparkled.

He laughed. "You haven't had Italian food until you've had my lasagna. Old family recipe."

"You forget that I was married to an Italian. Believe me, I've had some incredible lasagna." She frowned, "Hey, since when is Chandler an Italian surname?"

He paused and blinked. "You're right, it's not. But my mother's name was Maria Giordano. Is that Italian enough for you?" he asked, arching an eyebrow.

"You're mother was Italian?" she responded with interest.

"Is...She's still alive," Cade said, picking up his plate and bringing it into the kitchen.

"Really? Does she live around San Francisco near you?"

He shook his head, "Italy."

Meara looked at him in surprise. "Your mother lives in Italy? You're kidding!"

He shook his head again, "Nope. When my dad dropped dead, she was practically on the next plane back to Milano. Couldn't get out of the States fast enough," he said with a laugh. "She moved back and lives with her sister and has all her cousins and extended family living close by, happy as any vecchia signora could be."

"Vecchia signora? Wait...that means... uh, something – lady, right?"

He looked at her in mock disgust. "It means 'old lady'. How long did you say you were married to an Italian? How is it you never picked up any of the language?"

"It's sad, I know," Meara said. "Worse, I spent my entire childhood overseas and I have pitifully little to show for it. I can count to ten in about nine languages, say 'hello' and 'goodbye' in maybe six or seven; and 'fuck you' in three."

Cade laughed. "You learned to say 'Fuck you' in three languages?"

"Well, the curse, not the come-on," she added wiggling her eyebrows.

He burst out laughing again. "What come-on would that be? A question? Like "Fuck you?"

She laughed along with him. "God! How did we get into this discussion anyway?" she finally asked, shaking her head.

He stopped and pulled her into his arms. "You are a surprising woman, Meara O'Connell!"

"Meara O'Connell? Geez, no one has called me that since I was in college, I think."

"Well, that's who you'll always be to me," he said as he leaned down to kiss her.

She stopped him, putting her hand on his chest. "Wait! That reminds me. I've got a question for you, Cade Chandler...if that's your real name."

Cade face went a little slack with surprise. "My...real name?"

She blinked seeing his strange reaction and also noted that she had his complete attention. "I looked you up online in our high school yearbook and guess what?"

His eyes narrowed. "Uh...I'm not there?"

She looked at him, completely nonplussed, and nodded her head. "Yeah. Exactly. You are not there. No Chandlers there at all, in fact."

Chapter 20   Daydream Believer

Cade had heard about people choking when someone took them by surprise, and he really didn't know what to say for several long moments. When he should be telling her the whole truth (and nothing but the truth) he found himself falling back into the story that he'd been telling people for the past twenty-something years.

"We didn't get to Bangkok until late the first semester of that year, after the pictures had been taken for the yearbook. None of us – my brothers and sister and me – got our pictures in that yearbook." He shrugged and smiled.

"But..." Meara frowned.

"I remember you, though. I remember how you looked back then. The time I first realized I had a huge crush on you was at the Teen Club on a Saturday night. There was a big dance...I don't remember what it was called, although it probably had a name, they all did back then, didn't they?" he smiled, moving close to Meara, reaching out and putting his arms around her waist and looking deeply into her eyes. "I was in the Smoker's Lounge – do you remember that place in the back of the Teen Club? It was the walled-in patio area in the back. It was outside, but protected, and they let us smoke back there. We were supposed to have our parents' permission to even go out there to smoke, but the chaperones – Jesus, what were their names? I can't remember now, but they were a married couple who ran the Teen Club, do you remember them?"

Meara stared at him and suddenly the memories came flooding back to her. "God, yes, I DO remember them, Cade! The wife had dark brown hair and this great hairdo, cut so that it flipped under and came down just to her chin...." She looked at Cade and saw the lost look on his face, "OK, never mind her hair, but yes, I remember her and her husband. He was a nice guy, sort of quiet, but really friendly and caring...came across like a missionary, I always thought." She looked up at Cade for confirmation.

He gazed at her and then nodded, 'Yeah, you know, that's a pretty good description. Suits him to a 't'."

They were quiet for a moment lost in their own thoughts.

"Anyway," Cade said, "I was hanging out in the Smoker's Lounge and the music was playing inside. 'Wild Thing,' I think the song was. Do you remember that song?" She nodded and laughed in recognition.

Cade grinned and said, "People were dancing, and suddenly you burst through the door. You looked upset. Geez, I was mesmerized by you. You looked so... God, I don't know...you looked hot!" he grinned. "OK, back then I probably would've said you looked...'groovy'...right?"

Meara chuckled and nodded. Her arms were around his waist and she realized they were sharing in this memory together, remembering something from a long time ago, together. It was an amazing feeling of communion.

"Anyway, you came outside, sort of pissed off, and I watched as you pulled a pack of Marlboro's from your purse and started packing them against the palm of your other hand. Then you let one cigarette come out and you pulled it out, put it between your lips and lit it. When the match flamed I could see your face clearly in the dark and you were looking right at me."

Chapter 21   You Can't Hurry Love

Meara froze, looking up at Cade. One hand flew to her open mouth. "Oh, my God!" she said. Because suddenly she remembered it all — the Teen Club, the dance, and that evening so many years before — just as Cade described it.

She had been upset and had come out to the Smoker's Lounge and lit the cigarette and looked out to see a guy watching her. She had felt confused because the look he was giving her just then was the look she had wanted from Steve. Steve — the guy whom she'd had a crush on since the beginning of the school year, the guy whom she chatted and flirted with every day at lunch, whom she had even cajoled into attending the dance at the Teen Club that weekend — had arrived just moments before, with a date on his arm. Meara had been devastated. She had thought he liked her. She thought he would come to the Teen Club dance that weekend to be with her. In her fantasy, he would ask her to dance and at that moment, he would realize that she was his true love, his soul mate, or...something like that. Meara no longer believed in that crap now, but she knew she had believed it back then.

Cade was watching her face. "You remember?" he asked softly.

She nodded. "I do. I remember." She looked up into Cade's eyes now and the two Cades – the kid from high school who had so badly wanted the senior girl, and the man standing before her who obviously wanted her now — were the same person.

"Cade?"

His mouth was inches from hers. "Hmmm?"

"Let's go to bed, OK?"

"Now?"

She nodded and leaned in and kissed him. When she broke away, she said insistently, "I want you...now."

Meara had been incredibly turned on by Cade's description of his crush on her back in high school. She pulled him down the hallway to the bedroom and might have ripped off his clothes if he hadn't already started unbuttoning his shirt and unfastening his belt as they headed in that direction. She'd never felt this way about a man, and in some rational part of her brain she was even then questioning how she could become so wanton so quickly now. Sure, she'd certainly enjoyed him back in San Francisco, but it wasn't magic, after all; it was just sex.

They fell on the large bed and Meara heard his ragged breathing. All her attention was focused on him now, his mouth and his hands. She wanted him with a sole focus.

Then slowly, with a growing sureness and sense of delight, she realized that he was just as focused on her.

Chapter 22   You Keep Me Hanging On

This was exactly the way he'd hoped it would go when he came to Brookings to find her. Even so, he almost couldn't believe that she had been so welcoming and then a couple hours later that he'd be in bed with her again.

Meara was curled up against him. She was breathing normally now, but he didn't think she'd fallen asleep. He caressed her waist and felt the soft smoothness of her skin and could still feel its heat. She moved and sighed, stretching out as she turned over. She lay on her back and held his hand just under her breasts. Her fingers were linked through his.

"I was hoping you might come to Brookings, Cade," she said in a soft voice.

He smiled. "I was hoping that you wouldn't slam the door in my face if I did."

"Not in my nature. Besides, I'd have been too curious about why and how...no, I AM curious about why and how." She turned to look at him. "Why did you decide to come up here?"

"Hmmm. Well, let's see. I had lunch with my daughter, Vanessa, over the weekend and I told her about you and about showing you San Francisco last week. She said that if I was still thinking about you several days after the fact that I ought to follow up. See where this goes."

"So I have Vanessa to thank?"

"Yes, but I'm not sure I want her to get all the credit." He laughed. "Hate to give her a big head. And I like to think it was my idea, too. I mean, I really did want to see you again."

Meara smiled happily. "Good. So how long can you stay?"

"Well, I have my suitcase down in the car. I can stay for a few days. Is that OK?"

She nodded, "Longer, if you want."

He smiled. "I want."

The next day Meara said she would like to show Cade a little of the area. It was obvious that she wanted him to love it the way she did. After some thought, she settled on taking him to Stout Grove, a small park-like area of giant redwoods, that she said was just on the other side of the Oregon/California border.

Meara told him she had been there twice before with her husband and once with her daughter and she was looking forward to showing him the place. Of course, Cade had seen giant redwood trees before. There were some just outside of San Francisco at Muir Woods National Monument, but he'd never been to the Redwood National Park area where the truly giant redwoods were found and he was looking forward to seeing them.

They took his rental car and he drove while Meara gave directions from her map confirming the navigation system's specific driving instructions. He could tell from how talkative she'd become that she was excited for him to see this special place.

They turned off the highway that would've taken them to Grant's Pass in the south central part of Oregon, and soon they were weaving down a smaller road among residential houses and cabins. Soon they were in the forest, but as they proceeded the trunks of the trees became larger and larger and the heights taller and taller. They were in the big trees, or at least, that's how he thought of it. The first time he came around a corner and saw the circumference of the tree on his right, he knew he was among the giant redwoods.

Meara kept exclaiming, "Oh, Cade, look at that one! Look how big! Oh my God!"

And he was as astounded and impressed as she was. She'd seen these same trees before, but she was just as amazed this time, and probably would exclaim as much the tenth or twentieth trip out to the grove.

As they drove closer, the trees were larger and instinctively they became more subdued and quiet. There was an unspoken sense that the trees were a presence that needed to be acknowledged.

Finally Cade saw the sign for Stout Grove and turned into the small parking lot. There was only a single other car parked there. Cade pulled his car in and parked.

"Wow," he said turning to look at Meara.

She smiled at him, "I know, Cade. Aren't they just amazing?" she reached out and touched his hand.

They got out of the car and walked side-by-side to the trailhead. The trail was a circuitous path through the trees eventually returning to the parking lot, probably only a half-mile of walking, at most.

"Ready?" Cade asked.

Meara smiled and nodded, reaching her hand out and he took it. It felt right to be holding hands among the solemnity of these grand old giants.

Cade was amazed as he looked up and followed the trunks soaring into the sky. There just didn't seem to be words for the wonder he felt. Momentarily, it reminded him of Treebeard, the Ent in the "Lord of the Rings" – the Ents were massive tree creatures – and Cade realized that redwood trees must have been the basis of what Tolkien had in mind. "Wow," he said again and again, squeezing Meara's hand. "This is incredible. Thanks for bringing me here to see them."

"It's not just the sight of them, is it?" Meara asked, marveling at the trees around her. "Every time I walk through these types of groves, I think that it's almost a spiritual feeling – like they are live creatures looking down on us. Do you feel it, too?"

Cade nodded with a slight smile. He was amazed by how alike they seemed to think. "I know what you mean," he said squeezing her fingers. "They are the 'old ones', no doubt about it."

They were quiet for a while as they walked along the path through the giant trees, but he noticed that she didn't let go of his hand. He loved that she felt safe and secure with him. It'd been a long time since he'd felt like a protector, someone who could be relied on for safety and well-being.

It was after about fifteen or twenty minutes of walking that he started getting the sensation that they were being watched, maybe followed. It wasn't the strangeness of the trees that he was sensing this time. This was human. He was sure of it.

It began as one of those creepy tickling feelings at the back of his neck. He'd initially shrugged it off, but then slowly he became conscious that something didn't feel right.

He looked around and occasionally felt that someone or something was just slipping into the shadows when he turned to have a look. Being among these huge trees that cast the dark shadows of dusk even in the midday sunshine, made the feeling that much eerier.

Finally, he decided to slow down, maybe get off the main trail and see whether someone came along. He didn't want to scare Meara in case he was wrong. He knew it would sound bewildering to her and he would sound paranoid. So instead, he pulled on her hand and nodded at a hollowed-out shell of a tree a short walk off the trail and in a protected circle of trees.

When they got to the tree, Meara stepped all the way inside the hollowed-out trunk. "Hey, I can see right up to the sky from in here," she said in awe. Her words were muffled slightly and echoed.

Cade smiled but just then off to his right he saw movement on the path. In another second, a guy stepped around the corner along the main path. However, the instant he saw Cade, he spun away and disappeared behind a huge tree. Cade realized with a jolt that he recognized the guy. It was the same guy he'd run into at the airport, the one who had been on his flight.

Meara stepped out of the tree with a huge smile on her face, and Cade returned the smile but a little distractedly as he glanced past her to the path beyond. Suddenly, the guy stepped out and Cade saw plainly that he wasn't looking at Cade, he was looking at Meara.

"Jesus," he thought. It'd been a while — years — since he had worried about being followed, about anyone finding out who he was. Now it was all coming back to him. He really didn't miss the paranoia of always wondering if he was being watched or being followed. But now it was worse, because it wasn't just him this time; the guy had seen him with Meara. If that guy was connected to the criminals that forced him into the Witness Protection program two decades ago then Meara might be in danger.

He had to know. He had to find out. In an instant he made up his mind. "Meara, a guy's been following us. I've got to find out why. Stay here, OK?"

Without waiting for an answer, Cade took off running towards the main path.

Chapter 23   Time of the Season

"Wha...What...?" was all Meara got the chance to sputter as Cade took off running. She stood stock-still and stunned. Cade thought they were being followed? He was going to chase down the guy? It was a guy, right? She spun around scanning the trees and low-growing ferns. She hadn't seen anyone.

"Cade?" she called. She could see his receding back as he raced down the path. She knew he hadn't heard her.

It was fairly open through the grove. The grove contained lots of huge trees but there was a fair amount of space between. Because the trees were so tall, they also blocked much of the sunlight from reaching the ground, so that meant there wasn't the thick foliage and undergrowth that one would find back in the forests of New England. She was surprised to realize that she could actually see quite a distance. She could see Cade, but she didn't see anyone in front of him.

"Tell him..." a taunting voice said from behind her.

Meara spun around and the guy seemed startled by her sudden movement. He cleared his throat and narrowed his eyes for effect. and said, "Tell him I'm looking for him."

The guy was leaning awkwardly against one of the trees close by. He was young – maybe in his mid-thirties – and a little overweight and stocky. He was wearing a denim jacket and it struck Meara that he looked uncomfortable in it, as if it was just a pose and that he'd never worn such a thing before.

She took a step back. "Who are you?" she asked, hearing a strained note in her voice but she wasn't sure if it was fear or just surprise. She squeezed her fists tight hoping to steel herself to gain control.

His mouth twitched as if he was going to smile, but instead said in a low gravelly voice, "Never mind that. You just tell him that it's not over. Not by a long shot."

"Meara?"

She heard Cade calling for her and she turned in relief towards the sound of his voice. When she looked back, though, the guy was gone.

She fell back against the tree and wrapped her arms around her body, as if she were cold. She closed her eyes for a moment. And then Cade was there, pulling her into his arms.

"Are you OK?" he asked. "You look like you've seen a ghost."

"He was here," she croaked out, beginning to shake a little.

"Who was?" Cade asked holding her away from him so he could better see her face.

"The guy...the guy you tried to chase...he must've circled around because he came up right behind me. Scared the shit out of me..." she choked out a laugh that turned into a cough.

"He was here?"

She nodded and swallowed. She looked up at him, "Cade, he gave me a message for you." She paused, remembering, "He said 'tell him I'm looking for him and that it's not over, not by a long shot.'" She watched his face. "What does that mean, Cade? What's not over?"

He shook his head, but he was thinking, taking it in. He wondered who the guy was? What was his connection to Minneapolis?

"Cade?" she said, breaking into his thoughts.

He looked at her, finally focusing on the here-and-now. "Huh?"

"Let's go home, OK?" she said softly.

He reached out and pulled her into a hug. It struck him that this was so much harder for her because she had no idea what was going on. But then, did he? He had been informed when Reston had died in prison and he assumed that that was it. He'd even waited another year in Italy, just to let bygones be bygones. Then he'd returned to the U.S., got his American law degree, worked at Curt's law firm, and his life had moved on. That was what? Twelve, fifteen years ago? So who was this guy? What did he have to do with any of it? The truth was that Cade had no idea.

He pulled Meara close and kissed the top of her head, a comforting gesture he remembered using with his daughter, Vanessa, when she was younger. "Yeah, let's go home," he said.

Chapter 24   Get Back

When they got back to the condo, Cade told Meara he needed to think and maybe a walk on the beach might help.

As soon as he made his way down the cliff, though, he pulled out his cell phone. He dialed the number he hadn't had to dial in a decade. Funny, that he hadn't deleted it from his cell phone contacts list. Even after he had upgraded phones several times over the years, he continued to keep the contact listing updated: WitSec, with a phone number in DC.

He dialed and after only a couple of rings, a man answered. The voice was gruff but not unfriendly, "Yeah?"

"This is Cade..." and he paused..."Cade Chandler" – he'd always paused, never feeling entirely at peace with the fake name they'd given him, so close in sound to the Chambers name he'd been born and raised with.

"Well, Cade Chandler. I didn't think we'd ever be speaking to you again," the voice at the other end responded cheerily. "What can we do for you?"

"Yeah," Cade replied. "I've got a guy following me. He says 'It's not over.' You guys told me it was over."

There was a silence on the other end of the line. "The guy says 'It's not over' to you? You know Reston's dead, right? He died in the prison hospital. Ten years now."

"Yeah, I know. So who is this guy? I know it's not Reston. And I thought the rest of his gang was put away at the same time. So who is this guy?" Cade repeated.

"Dunno, but we'll check it out. Sit tight. We'll get back to you on this line, OK?"

"When?" Cade asked suspiciously.

"Soon." And there was a click and then the line was dead.

Chapter 25   Paint it Black

Meara didn't know what to think; first the scare in the Stout Grove with the guy appearing and disappearing like an apparition, and then Cade acting so oddly on the way back. He was down on the beach now. He said he needed to walk and to think. Heck, SHE needed to walk and to think, that was for certain. Her muscles were tense and balled up with stress. She needed to do something physical.

She pulled out her yoga mat and went to her laptop to turn on in her Pilates video. She decided her regular exercise routine would restore some normalcy. She'd been doing this workout for the past six months, twice a week. She'd do it now and it would ease her mind to be doing something familiar. She was sure of it.

"Sit in a cross legged position and take a deep breath. Take it in through your nose and then slowly let it out through your mouth...."

Meara sat on her green yoga mat. She listened to the Pilates instructor, but part of her mind was all but yelling at her to figure out what was going on. She took a deep breath and slowly released it. 'Just let it gooooo.....'

She breathed out in a whoosh. Then she lay back on the mat and did "the hundred" – one, two, three, four.... She was starting to get into the groove. Next was 'The Teaser...oh God, she hated this one. Her legs always felt like lead weights on this one. Damn, when would she get the hang of it? she wondered.

"Sorry," Cade said from the front hall, like he'd caught her doing something unmentionable. He paused, and then with a quizzical look on his face he asked, "What are you doing?"

"Pilates," she snapped. "Do you mind?"

He smiled. "Mind? Are you kidding?" He got a lascivious grin on his face. "You look sexy as hell."

She glanced down at her bike shorts and tank top. God. "Cade..."

He put his hands up, "No, really, go ahead. I'll just go out on the deck until you're done. Really, I won't bother you." He ducked out the door to the deck.

She sighed and rolled her eyes. This felt awkward, but why shouldn't she go ahead with her normal activities? He hadn't bothered to tell her who that guy was in the redwoods and he'd been acting pretty strangely ever since. What was she supposed to think? She didn't know him THAT well. He might turn out to be a psychopath; who knows these days? And apparently, Cade had enemies after him. She didn't like any of this. She pulled her mind back to the Pilates instructor on the video. Pay attention. Focus on the now, for chrissakes. What good was exercising if she stressed herself out the whole time?

She sat on the floor with her knees tucked in and held her ankles as instructed for 'rolling like a ball'. She glanced over to the doorway and saw that Cade was watching her reflection in the mirror-like finish of the sliding glass door. 'Really?' she thought. How could this be sexy to someone? She rolled her eyes. Then she looked again and he was still watching her. For a second she realized that it was sort of charming that he might actually think this was sexy. I mean, it's not, but it's cute that he might think it is, she guessed. She smiled. Yeah, it was sort of charming. She was a middle-aged woman sitting on a yoga mat in a condo on the Oregon coast doing Pilates while a guy she'd known a little over a week was watching her. She smiled again as she rolled back and then back up and balanced. OK, there were worse ways to spend a life.

When she was done he came in and watched her roll up her mat and put away the laptop. When she glanced up at him he had the smirking smile on his face. She shook her head. "What's with you?"

"Sue me. I think you looked hot as hell doing all that...what's it called? Pilates?"

"You're kidding, right?" she said with a snort.

He pulled her into an embrace and nuzzled her neck.

She pushed him away saying, "Cade, I'm sweaty and gross. What in the world could you find sexy about this?" she asked and then chuckled. "You are nuts."

He leaned in and kissed her. "No sense in taking a shower if you're just going to get sweaty all over again..."

She smiled and looked up at him with interest. "Am I going to get all sweaty again?"

"I'm thinking yes," he said and he kissed her long and hard. A minute later they were both out of breath.

"OK, I see what you mean," she said with a laugh. "Let's go." And she dragged him by the hand towards the bedroom.

A few minutes later they were lying on the bed. He reached for the bedside table and she heard the drawer being pulled out. "Damn," he said.

"What?" she asked.

"No more condoms. I think I have some in my suitcase. Hold on."

"It's alright," she said, holding his arm. " I mean... I'm not at risk of getting pregnant or anything."

"But you want to be protected from STD's, don't you?"

She nodded and then looked at him curiously for several long moments. "So? Have you been with someone else in the last week?"

He sat back down on the edge of the bed and looked at her in surprise. "How did you get from protection to my being with someone else?"

"Answering a question with a question? Now I know you're guilty," she said, sitting up.

He sighed and shrugged. "I have an on-again-off-again thing with a flight attendant back in San Francisco....but..."

She interrupted, "Oh God, not the one from the plane!" Meara said with a gasp, her hand over her mouth.

He smiled, "No, not her. This one – Emily – flies for Hawaiian Airlines."

"Oh well, Hawaiian Airlines...that's a relief," Meara said with some sarcasm.

"Look, I'd only just met you...I wasn't sure I'd ever see you again..."

She watched him, and she was angry, even though, logically she knew she didn't have a right to be. They were a one-night stand. He hadn't cheated on her. But, boy, she felt like he had. Damn it. Then a thought occurred to her. Two could play this game.

"Well, if we are confessing here, I guess I should tell you that I...uh...have been with someone else, too."

He smiled and that totally pissed her off. "No, I mean it," she continued, "I shouldn't be saying anything, but I feel guilty now that you've come clean with me. You see, there's a widower in the first building who's been flirting with me for years. He came over right after I got here at the beginning of the week. He'd heard about Tony, of course."

Cade was eyeing her suspiciously. "So, what's this widower's name?"

Meara blinked then looked down at her hands. "Pierson." Meara realized with horror that she only knew him by one name, "Pierson." Was that his first or last name?

"Pierson? Pierson what?" Cade asked.

"Pierson's his last name," she said. "His first name is...Carl."

Cade stopped smiling and eyed her. "Seriously? You slept with this Carl Pierson guy? I mean, just like that?"

Meara shrugged, amazed that he believed her. She raised her eyebrows slightly. "I slept with you just like that, didn't I?"

Cade closed his eyes and rubbed them a little. He opened them and looked at Meara, letting out a long breath. "Sorry. I know it's none of my business."

"And what you do is your own business, so I'm sorry if I sounded...uh, proprietary," she added.

He smiled, "Proprietary? Huh."

Meara reached out and put her hand on his forearm. "Cade, do you want to tell me who that guy in the redwoods was? Shouldn't we be calling the police or something?"

He put his hand over hers and patted it. "No, it's not a police matter. Just a guy who's stalking me, I think."

"Stalking IS a police matter."

"Look, if I think I can't handle it, I'll call the police, OK?"

He leaned over and kissed her. "My suitcase is in the closet. I'll be right back."

Chapter 26   Like a Rolling Stone

Cade had wakened seconds before from a chase dream. God, he hadn't had one of those dreams in ages. In the dream someone or something was chasing him. It was always the same — it would get close, almost touching his back, even pulling at his shirt sometimes, and he would feel his heart pounding in his ears. He'd wake up and for long seconds would not be certain if it had been real or not. It took a while for his heart to stop racing, and to talk himself back down again.

Cade was wide awake now, staring at the ceiling in Meara's bedroom and thinking about her, about the guy in the redwoods, about what a weird turn his life seemed to be taking. He knew it was that guy that was causing the dream to return. The guy in the redwoods was bringing it all back. He had months of sleepless nights back then, before he testified, and for months after Reston was finally safely behind bars.

The Witness Protection program was great, but it took a long, long time before he felt secure, even with them. In fact, after the first couple of years of being moved three times, he finally gave up the protection and got on a plane to Italy, feeling that he would feel more protected and safer among his mother's kin outside of Milano than he'd ever feel in Wisconsin or North Carolina or whatever out of the way spot they found to hide him.

Plus, it never seemed fair. Who was the criminal, after all? It was Reston and his gang who were shipping cocaine all over the country in the lavatory systems of jetliners. He was the whistleblower; the dupe that discovered what was going on. Of course, they had tried to buy his silence, offering to cut him in on the action, but in the end, he just couldn't. Sure, part of the reason was his dad – the very thought of that proud military aviator made him cower at the idea of him finding something like that out about his middle son. But he couldn't do it for himself either. He'd gone to Vietnam, he'd fought for his country, and even though he had mixed feelings about that whole adventure, he knew that he did believe in America, even now. How could he end up part of a drug smuggling ring?

So, he had become a federal witness and after three years of trials and hiding out, Reston and his gang had been sent away to prison on drug charges. The Witness Security program offered him a new identity to protect him and he had reluctantly accepted.

It should be over. Reston was dead. But now this. All the old feelings washed over him — the fear, the paranoia, and all the insecurity. Cade had no idea what to do. Should he run? Take Meara with him? Run alone to lead the guy – whoever he was – to follow him far away from her? He just didn't know. He'd already called his contact at WitSec – his Witness Protection program.

Cade thought about the call and wondered when he would hear back from them. He didn't know if they'd call him back in fifteen minutes or fifteen days. He looked over at Meara, sleeping so serenely next to him.

He didn't want to run again. He'd spent so many years running. He was done with that life. They'd promised him that it was over.

So who was this guy?

The one thing he was certain of was that WitSec couldn't protect him now and he doubted they would even offer to protect Meara. Not now, not after the guy they were protecting him from had been dead for years.

Italy. It came to him in a flash. He could go back to Italy again. He felt safe there. He'd been safe there. And he knew he could keep Meara safe there, too. He glanced over at her sleeping form. But how would he convince her to go with him?

Chapter 27   Night Train

The next morning after a leisurely breakfast, Meara was taken by surprise when Cade asked her to go to Italy with him.

"Italy? You want me to go to Italy? Now?" Meara replied, flabbergasted.

Cade nodded. "I've got a client in Milan. He wants to meet with me right away. I thought...well, I thought you could come with me. A sort of vacation for you, a working vacation for me," he smiled encouragingly.

"But I have this condo rented for the whole month. I mean it's crazy for me to leave..."

"We'll be back...in a week...I promise," Cade said holding up his hand as if he was swearing the truth of the statement.

"But..." Meara looked at him helplessly. Sure, she wanted to go. Heck, Italy! She loved Italy. She hadn't been in two years, and the last time wasn't all that much fun. Tony had been hassling about every little thing on that trip; nothing pleased him. A typical Italian, she'd thought at the time, the food wasn't as good as his family's, the native Italians didn't respect him enough, and on and on. To make matters worse, every city's services, it seemed, had been on strike or were about to go on strike. It was awful. But still she loved Italy. She loved the craziness and the unpredictability of the place and she especially loved the people.

A part of her really wanted to be spontaneous and just say 'yes' and 'why not?' to Cade's invitation but the other part of her...well, it was hard to overcome a lifetime of being the responsible one, the parent figure to not only her children, but to her husband, as well. She sighed.

"Please, come," Cade said, holding her hands in his, as if they were praying together. "It will be so great to have someone to have dinner with in the evenings, and I'll show you some of my favorite sights. I know some amazing places that you'll love. It'll be great." He looked at her meaningfully. "Really," he said softly.

Meara looked into his eyes. Yeah, OK, it wouldn't take much to talk her into a trip to Italy with him. Even though he hadn't yet explained the whole stalker in the redwoods to her satisfaction, she might appreciate getting away from that situation, too. "I don't have my passport here. It's back in Boston." That was the last of her resistance; the walls were tumbling down.

"No problem," he responded instantly. "We'll schedule a long connection layover through Boston. We'll go to your place, pick up your passport and get the next flight out. OK?" he nearly pleaded.

She smiled tentatively. "God, Cade, I'd love to go back to Italy! It's just that this is so sudden, and oh my God, what about clothes?" she asked in exasperation. She shook her head. "Could we spend a couple of hours at my house in Boston so I can pack properly for the trip?"

He'd have agreed to anything. He nodded and smiled. "Sure, not a problem."

She shook her head in amazement. Italy! And her mind began swirling with her personal to-do list. What clothes she should bring, for one. They'd have to discuss what the expectations would be. Dinners out? How dressy? And shoes, of course. And what would she be doing during the days while he was working? Touring probably, maybe visiting the magnificent Duomo again and some of the museums at the Sforza Castle that Tony had never been interested in spending time in. There would be plenty for her to do. And Milan had a wonderful underground metro so she could get around easily enough on her own.

"Hey," Cade said, breaking into her revelry. "I'm going to call my office to get the arrangements made. I was thinking we could fly down to San Francisco tomorrow, spend the night at my place while I get my gear together, then we'll head to Boston the day after. Sound good to you?"

"Sounds great. Will I get to meet your stepdaughter while we're there?"

Cade's head jerked up. "Vanessa?" He thought about it for a second, and then nodded. "Actually, that's a great idea. I'll invite her to come into the city. I'm sure she's plenty curious about you." He grinned.

"I'm curious about her, too. I'd like to meet her."

"I'll call her and set it up."

Meara stood up and bustled back to the bedroom. Cade followed her. She pulled out her suitcase from the walk-in closet and laid it on the bed.

She looked up at him as if he'd asked her what she was doing, "I'll just take the things I want for San Francisco and Milan, then add the rest when we get to Boston."

He leaned back against the door frame and crossed his arms lazily as he watched her pulling open dresser drawers and stopping to think for a second or two, then putting something back into the drawer, and exchanging it for something else which she then took over to the open suitcase and laid it inside. He shook his head in amusement. "OK, I'll leave you to it, then. I'll be out on the deck making a few phone calls to get things arranged."

"Huh?" Meara said as she watched him turn and leave. "Oh, OK," she agreed, although she hadn't really been listening to him.

She had so much to do, but it was fun stuff and exciting. Traveling – now that was worth looking forward to. And traveling with Cade? Yeah, that was even better. They'd be a real couple out in public for other people to see for the first time; well, the second time if one counted the night in San Francisco. But she didn't, because for her, that had been a one-night stand. Heck, when she was out with him that night she had fully expected to be dropped off at her hotel at the end of the evening. She smiled.

This, on the other hand, was the beginning of a deepening relationship. Sure, it'd only been a week, barely, but she already felt like she was part of something, maybe a couple. She smiled happily. This was working out even better than she'd ever expected. She touched her wedding ring and twirled it idly around her finger. Then she looked up at the ceiling, Tony, she thought fervently, if this is you manipulating things for me, then I thank you. Bless you, and thank you. But, if it's not you; then let it go, OK? She put her hand over her heart and closed her eyes for a second.

She glanced down and realized she had one of her panties in the hand covering her heart. "Oh!" she said and giggled. "Yeah, well...good to see you still have your sense of humor."

Chapter 28   I Put a Spell on You

Cade paced slowly back and forth on the deck with his cell phone pressed to his ear. He stared unseeingly out at the sea stacks and ocean, which was calm today. Angie, the administrative assistant in his law office, answered the phone with her normal chirpy good humor.

When he told her what he needed her to do, he could hear the grin in her voice, "OK, boss. No problem." Then she asked, "Hmmm, can I ask? If Emily, the hula princess, isn't going with you, who's the new lady?"

"For a change, I think you'll approve. She's not a flight attendant," he replied dryly.

He heard her laugh, "I know, Vanessa called me yesterday to see if you'd checked in yet. Sounds like she's all for this one, even though she hasn't met her yet."

Cade sighed, "Vanessa's getting to be a gossip hound. What am I going to do with her?"

"She just wants you to be happy, and you know it. Be glad you have a child who cares so much."

Cade smiled, "I know, Angie, and you know I'm thankful. But sometimes I'd like to get her out of my pockets."

Angie chuckled, "Out of your pockets? I'm going to remember that one."

They chatted about the office and what was on the upcoming schedule before signing off. "I'll email you the travel confirmations, boss, and I'll text you if I hit any snags or have questions."

"Thanks, Angie. Much appreciated. See you tomorrow."

"Bring her into the office, OK?" Angie added with a laugh. "I want to meet her, too."

"We'll see," Cade said before hanging up. He had no intention of bringing Meara near the office.

Next, he dialed Vanessa's cell. She answered on the second ring. "Hey, you!" she said breathlessly. He figured she was probably at the gym, or out walking.

"I figured I should give you a call," Cade said, smiling despite himself.

"I've been thinking about you like crazy these past couple of days! So, Dad, how's it going up there in Oregon?"

The stalker flashed through his mind, but he shook the thought away. "Fine, honey. But, a couple of things: Meara and I are going to Milan for a couple of days."

He heard the silence on the other end. Milan was almost a code word between them and it usually meant he was going away for a while. The past had been hard on Vanessa, Cade knew.

"Is...is everything all right?" Vanessa asked.

"Don't worry, OK? We'll probably only be gone about a week. Anyway, I have some stuff to talk to you about. I'm not sure what's going on really." He paused. "How about coming for dinner with Meara and me tomorrow night?"

"You're coming back to San Francisco tomorrow?"

"Yup. Angie's making the arrangements."

"And Meara is coming with you?"

"Yes."

"Well, I definitely want to meet this lady, Dad. So just tell me where and when and I'll be there."

"I think we'll have dinner at my place. Something quiet. I've asked Angie to get Carter's to cater it so we can relax and not have to do any shopping or cooking."

"Hmmm, that's a good idea. I get dibs on any leftovers, OK?" Vanessa added with a laugh. "Yum!"

"We're heading out the next day for Italy, so the leftovers are all yours."

"Only here for an overnight?" Vanessa asked, troubled again.

"I want to get over there as soon as possible."

He heard the silence on the other end as Vanessa undoubtedly was trying to work out what was up. She was too smart to ask for details over an open phone line. Cade was sorry that he'd forced her to become so secretive and paranoid.

"Does Maria know you're coming?" Vanessa asked.

Vanessa had always called his mother – her grandmother – Maria, although he could no longer remember how it had started. Vanessa had met her grandmother at the age of four and he thought perhaps his mother may have introduced herself that way, 'Hi, Vanessa, I'm Maria.' And the name had stuck.

"No, I'm going to surprise her," Cade said. As he said it, he imagined his mother meeting Meara for the first time. He knew that his mother would make some very big assumptions. He never brought the women he dated to meet his mother. But he'd have to deal with that when the time came, he decided.

"Oh, well, she definitely will be surprised," Vanessa said cheerily. "What time do you want me at your place then?"

"Six or six-thirty, OK? We'll plan dinner for seven or so, I think."

"Sounds good. FYI, JJ won't be able to make it. He has classes tomorrow night. But I'll definitely be there."

"Good. See you then," Cade said smiling again at the thought of seeing her.

"Looking forward to it. Love you, Dad," Vanessa said.

"Love you, too, honey," Cade said more softly. "See you tomorrow night."

"See you," Vanessa said, hanging up.

Cade looked out at the ocean for several minutes thinking about Vanessa and wondering how much he could tell her. Not much, he decided, considering he hadn't really told Meara much. But even so, he wanted Vanessa to know something was up, so she could prepare herself, just in case.

The phone in his hand rang and it startled him. He glanced at the screen and saw that it was his nephew, Nate. Nate was his brother Curt's son. Curt had died five years before of a coronary, and Cade had stepped in to be a substitute father figure for Nate. It was the least he could do. Then when Curt's wife, Laurie, had remarried a year or so later, and Nate didn't get along with his new stepfather, Cade had pretty much taken over the father role. He knew Curt would've done the same for him. Heck, he had done the same for him. He'd watched out for Vanessa when Cade was living in Italy, and gave Cade a job in the law firm when he'd finally returned to the U.S. He'd been more than a brother; he'd been a support, a protector, a mentor and a friend. Cade missed him and there wasn't a day that went by that he didn't think about him. How could Fate be so fickle? The older he got the more he was sure there was no grand plan. Any plans are made right here on earth, as far as he was concerned.

"Nate, I haven't heard from you for a while," Cade said into the phone with a grin. "How's school going?"

"Hi, Uncle Cade, just wanted to check in and when I talked to Angie, she said you were up in Oregon! What's up there?" Nate asked good-naturedly.

Cade squinted, "Don't tell me Angie didn't do a little gossiping to fill you in?"

Nate laughed, "OK, you got me. But don't let on to her that I told on her. She said you were up there with a new lady friend and that this one might be serious..."

"Really," Cade said with a snort. "Angie needs to get a life, then maybe she'd stay out of mine."

"Good luck with that. You ARE her life," Nate laughed. "So, tell me about the lady friend," Nate prodded.

Cade shook his head slightly. "Not much to tell yet. Her name is Meara and I knew her back when I was in high school."

"Seriously? High school? Holy Smokes, Uncle Cade, that was like a half-century ago, wasn't it? Hmmm, I'm picturing a little grey-haired lady, glasses, with a little paunch around the middle... Not your usual type, I must say," Nate teased.

Cade laughed, "Stop fishing. You can call Vanessa after she meets her tomorrow night. Better to get the gory details from her, because you're not getting anything from me."

"Wait! Vanessa is going to meet the new lady friend? Hey, when do I get to meet her then?"

"Who knows? Maybe never," Cade commented dryly.

"Well that's not fair," Nate replied. He paused for a second or two, and then continued, "So, you're taking her to Milano. You never do that with your other girlfriends. Nonna Maria is going to go crazy," Nate teased.

Cade rolled his eyes. "Don't say anything to her, OK? No texts, no emails, no Facebook. I haven't told her we're coming yet."

"Oh, ho, boy!" Nate added with glee. "Damn I wish I could be there when you introduce the two of them. You know, you'll have to marry her, right?" Nate said in mock seriousness.

"How do you figure?" Cade replied.

"Nonna Maria will expect it. Heck, she'll probably call up the village priest as soon as you walk in the door with this lady."

Cade had to smile at Nate's laughter, even at his expense.

"Don't count on it..." Cade said finally.

"Well, many happy returns, Uncle Cade, that's all I can say. You've made my week."

"It takes so little," Cade rejoined.

"Ha! I'd love to keep this conversation going, but I've got a class, so I'm off," Nate said. "Call me when you get back, OK? I definitely want to hear how it went."

"I'll call you, but not to give you any details," Cade replied.

"Aw," Nate said. "Bye!"

"Bye, Nate," Cade said a smile on his face.

"Nate?" Meara asked. She'd just stepped through the doorway from the dining room.

Cade looked at her and smiled. "My nephew. Did I tell you about him?"

"You mentioned you had a nephew and that he's going to school back east," Meara nodded. "How old is he?"

"He'll be turning twenty in a couple of months. He's a sophomore at Brown."

"So he's in Providence? Wow, that's a good school," she said. "A friend of my daughter's went there and she used to visit the campus a lot."

"Where did your kids go to college?" he asked, curious.

"Donna went to the University of Colorado in Boulder. She wanted to make sure she got as far away from the family as she could for a while," Meara smiled. "It was a good move for her. Skiing, camping, hiking, all those outdoorsy things; they were always important to her. She married right after college to a guy she met at school, Gerald Tomlin. They've settled in Denver; for now, anyway."

"And what about your son?"

"Paul went to B.U. – Boston University. He had an apartment in the North End near the bakery and worked there part-time and summers throughout his college years. My husband was grooming him to go into the family business," Meara said with a sigh. She glanced out at the ocean. "I think that's why he joined the Army and went to Afghanistan. He needed a break to decide for himself if the family business is what he wanted." She shook her head. "What a horrible way to make a decision. You know what I mean?"

Cade turned and looked out at the ocean next to her. "So does he work for the bakery now?" Cade asked.

"Well, up to now, he hasn't," Meara said. "He started grad school when he got back from Afghanistan, and he graduates later this year. But, after Tony died, Paul started talking to his Uncle John, Tony's brother, about it. It looks like he may end up there, after all."

"How do you feel about that?" Cade asked turning to watch her face.

She shrugged. "I think it should be his choice. If he thinks he'll be happy there, I'm all for it; but he shouldn't work there just because it's a family business. Heck, he's got two cousins working there already, so it's not like it'll be out of the family or is in danger of being sold off to strangers."

He nodded. "Family is important to Italians."

"Tell me about it," Meara agreed with a laugh. "And I thought the Irish were family-obsessed!"

Cade laughed. "I hadn't thought about how similar the traditions are between the Irish and the Italians."

Meara nodded, and counted off on her fingers. "Both are Catholic, send their kids to parochial schools, have big families and the whole 'blood is thicker than water' ethic, holidays are spent with the extended family, I could go on and on," she smiled.

"Don't forget that both also have their own organized crime," Cade added.

Meara glanced at him quizzically, "Yeah, that's true. But, Tony's family wasn't from Sicily, you know. They were from the Pistoia, inland from Pisa."

Cade paused and then nodded, "I know the area."

"You do?" Meara said with surprise. "You're the first person I've met who has heard of it."

"Sure, it's a town just up the road from Florence."

"You're right, it is!" Meara nodded.

"My mother's family is from just north of Milan, so I've been all over northern Italy and Tuscany."

"Oh, I'd forgotten you're mother is Italian! Humph, I can't seem to get away from Italian men, I guess," Meara added with a laugh.

Cade smiled. "I can be Italian when I want to be and English when I need to be."

"Chandler is an English name, huh?"

He looked at her for a long second, "Yeah, English."

"Why the look?" she asked confused.

He thought for a second, wondering how he'd cover up the fact that he was thinking about his real last name of Chambers, not Chandler. "Oh, I was just thinking about the Irish and the English – the two have been intertwined since way back when but there's a lot of animosity."

She nodded. "True. My grandfather never forgave the British for occupying Ireland, and you have to realize he never even stepped foot on Irish soil his entire life," she said with a bittersweet smile. "Just goes to show you how deep these sentiments are."

"What about your father? Did he feel the same way about the British as your grandfather?"

"My dad? Oh, no, not at all. He was a diplomat in the best sense of the word. He trusted everyone unless there was some reason not to, and even then he'd give them a second or third, or nineteenth chance, if necessary," she laughed.

"Sounds like a good man," Cade said quietly.

"The best."

"I take it he's no longer living?" Cade said.

Meara looked away and shook her head. "He was killed in the Embassy bombing in Beirut in 1983."

"Oh God! I had no idea! I'm sorry, Meara," Cade said reaching out to console her. "That's awful."

Meara took a deep breath. "At the time, we knew that Beirut was unstable, of course. Rockets hit the Embassy every so often. And they were just beginning to put in better defenses for the embassies overseas. They took precautions, you know?" Meara asked; a rhetorical question. She continued, "In Beirut, the Embassy was located on a busy roadway. They felt this was a kind of protection because a vehicle couldn't be left in front of the building without it being noticed." She shrugged. "But, as it turned out, it was a suicide bombing – the first one I think — the driver never left the vehicle; he stopped in front of the building and blew himself up with a van full of nine-hundred kilos of explosives."

They were silent for several long moments, contemplating the horror of it.

"Sixty-three people were killed, seventeen of them American." She was quiet for a minute, but then felt compelled to continue. "They didn't find much left of my father. His office was on the second floor right above the blast. In his coffin, we buried his glasses, a shoe and his wallet." Meara shrugged again and looked over at Cade. "You're the first person I've shared that gory detail with. For me, it's always been the most horrifying thing about it... that he just disappeared from the Earth."

"Oh my God, that's..." Cade stopped and just held her hand, shaking his head. "There are no words, Meara."

"I know," Meara nodded. "I know." She felt her eyes well up; probably from the sympathy he was giving her. She squeezed her eyes closed for a second. "Anyway, I'm glad I told you about it. It's one of those personal tragedies that I want to share with people I care about, but well...it's awful and I hate to burden other people with it."

"I'm glad you told me," Cade said, squeezing her hand again.

He knew now was the moment to unload his own secrets on her. He wanted to tell her about his past. He cleared his throat. "Meara," he began. But then his phone rang.

He pulled the cell phone from his pocket and glanced at it. "It's from my office," he said to Meara.

She pulled away from the rail. "I'll give you some privacy," she said over her shoulder as she headed towards the slider to go into the condo.

Cade was going to tell her to wait that it was fine, but she was already gone, so put the phone back up to his ear instead, "Hello, Angie?"

He looked out at the sea and saw that the clouds were banking in and the sun would be setting soon. He knew the moment was lost. Maybe it was just as well, but still he felt disappointed in himself.

Chapter 29   Different Drum

Their trip back to San Francisco was uneventful. For some reason, Cade thought they should take her rental car back to the airport and leave it parked in Crescent City. She thought it was wasteful not to turn it in and rebook another car for the following week when she came back, but he thought it best to just leave it in the parking lot for the week and so she acquiesced, not feeling strongly one way or the other. She wasn't certain if it was true, but he said that her rate would come out higher to rent for a shorter period. He might have a point.

Cade was very quiet on the trip to Crescent City, too. Thinking back, she realized they'd had a pretty quiet evening the night before, as well. After asking her to accompany him to Milan, she had expected...well, something more. She wasn't exactly sure more of what, but maybe a little more attention or a little more interest in her?

Something had changed in their relationship. It was as if the air had been let out. It's not as if they were old friends or lovers that were so used to each other that they were naturally moving into the next comfortable stage in the relationship. Heck, she felt like she still knew next to nothing about what Cade had been doing for most of his life. She knew bits and pieces – that he had a stepdaughter named Vanessa and a nephew named Nate, that his mother was living in Italy, that his brother, Curt, had died several years ago of a heart attack. It seemed paltry. It was odd, too, because usually she was one of those people who would practically drain information from the people around her. She loved hearing people's life stories and couldn't get enough of hearing the details. So how is it that she knew so little about Cade?

He seemed nervous in the terminal before the flight, too. He kept glancing around, studying each of the other passengers. There weren't many of them since it was a small airport, and the plane only held maybe fifty or sixty people. But even so, he seemed to be paying more attention to the conversations around him than to her. OK, maybe she was feeling a little stung by that, she thought. After all, out of the blue he'd asked her to come with him to Milan, but once she agreed, he didn't act like he particularly cared that she was next to him right now. Was he changing his mind?

She stood close to him, "Cade?"

He looked down at her, "Huh?"

"Look, I don't have to go to Milan if you're having a change of heart..." she started.

He looked genuinely surprised, "A change of heart? Of course, I want you to go with me," he reassured her.

She shook her head, "But...why?" she asked plaintively. She wasn't one to dance around a subject when it was bothering her.

"Why?" he repeated. Answering a question with a question was not a good sign, she thought. He continued, "It's just like I told you. It'd be great to have you there so we can have dinners together, and you know, I could show you a bit of Milan. There's a lot I would like you to see. I lived there for a while."

She glanced up at him in surprise, "You did?"

He realized now that he must not have mentioned that to her yet. "Sure, I thought I told you about it on the plane when we first met. Didn't I?"

She squinted at him. "I'd have remembered if you said you'd lived in Italy," she said dryly. "When was this? How long did you live there?"

He looked up at the ceiling as if thinking, then smiled reassuringly at her. "Geez, I came back to the States about ten years ago, so it was a while ago," he answered.

She looked at him speculatively. "But how long did you live there?" she asked again.

"A few years," he answered vaguely. He nodded for her to notice that people were starting to move towards the TSA area for the baggage search. "Must be time to go," he added helpfully.

She nodded and followed him. Why was he being so vague about living in Italy? He was about the same age as she was, so ten years ago, he would've been mid-career, and if he'd lived there for a few years...well, who suddenly moved to Italy in the middle of a career?

They were on the small plane about a half-hour later and flying towards San Francisco. The flight would take less than two hours.

"So what did you do in Milan while you were living there?" she asked conversationally. Like a tenacious puppy, she couldn't let go of this story.

He glanced at her in surprise, and said, "Milan?" as if he had forgotten all about it. "Oh, well," he shrugged, "Actually, I went to law school there, among other things." He grinned and his dimples creased.

"You went to law school in Italy?" Meara repeated. She couldn't have been more surprised by his answer. "Really?" she asked, not able to keep the shock out of her voice.

He chuckled. "Yes. I had been working at a small airport in Como, as a kind of all-round small plane mechanic, and I guess I finally just got tired of it. So my brother came for a visit and talked me into the idea of getting my law degree. They had this five-year program that would give me an undergraduate and a law degree, so that's what I did."

"So law is sort of a second career?" she asked.

He nodded and smiled, "Exactly. I never thought of it like that, but yeah, it has been a second career for me."

Meara looked out the window for several minutes thinking about what Cade had just told her. She was still confused. Who made being an attorney a second career? And why had he gone to Milan in the first place? There was more to this story, she was certain of it. But how to get him to tell her and if he did, how would she know whether it was the truth?

Chapter 30   Don't Think Twice, It's Alright

It had been a whirlwind trip to San Francisco. He dropped Meara off at his apartment while he went to the law firm offices to pick up the travel confirmations for Milan. He figured he could be in and out in a half-hour, but despite his best efforts it took a good bit longer.

When he arrived, he went directly to his office, sat down at his desk and started reading through the flagged email in his inbox to make sure there wasn't anything that needed his immediate attention. Then he stopped in and talked to each of the other partners as well as a couple of key associates who would be filling in for him. The entire time he had Angie trailing behind him like the wag in the tail of a dog. She smiled and nodded as they made their way through from office to office, clipboard in hand, glasses poised on the tip of her nose, as she reminded him of appointments that must be postponed or turned over to one of the other partners, asked him questions about tasks on a brief he had been working on, scheduled his travel to Boston to finish up on the final papers he needed to get signed by a client there, and generally kept him on task. He had no idea how he could manage without her.

Afterwards, he felt good, like he'd accomplished some gargantuan task and once it was over, he could finally relax. Well, if not relax, then at least turn his mind to other things. Just as he stepped out of the elevator at the ground floor, he saw his car and Peter, his driver, slowly coming around the corner and stopping just in front of the building. He didn't know how the guy did it, but he was always there, just at the moment Cade needed him, whether he was stepping out of his office building, coming out of a restaurant after dinner, or dragging his suitcase out of an airport terminal. Bloody psychic, he figured.

"Hi Peter," Cade greeted him as he climbed into the back seat.

"Hey, Mr. Chandler. Where to now?"

"Back to the apartment. Then I won't need you until tomorrow morning for an airport run. Flight leaves at ten a.m., so plan to pick us up at about seven-thirty, OK?"

"Sure, Mr. Chandler. I'll be waiting out front. Give me a call if you need me to come up and bring down your luggage."

"Thanks, Peter. I don't think it'll be necessary, but I'll call you if I need you."

Cade was silent as Peter made his way through the heavy end of the day traffic. He leaned back and took a deep breath. Now to get back to the apartment, have dinner with Meara and Vanessa and then start preparing for Milan.

He still wasn't exactly sure what he would say to either of them about Milan, but he had to admit that he felt a growing excitement about taking Meara there and showing her some of his favorite places. He smiled at the thought. Of course, there were some flies in the ointment – the stalker, for one; and his mother, for another. It would be a great trip if he could catch the stalker and at the same time, keep Meara away from his mother. Would that even be possible?

Handling Vanessa tonight might be a bit tricky, as well. She had been around when he was dodging trouble and hiding out. To her, Milan meant secrecy and danger, unfortunately. He needed to ease her mind about all that now. Once he figured out who this stalker was, figured out what his relationship to Reston was, then maybe he could figure out what to do about him. He still hadn't heard from the WitSec after his call the other day. He wondered how much they'd actually be able to help? Were they able to find out anything about this guy?

Of course, he knew he couldn't rely on them to solve this problem for him. But, it'd be great if they could pass along some relevant info, at least. Beyond that, he had to assume that he was on his own.

He entered the apartment and immediately sensed a difference. He wasn't certain if it was the smell – light, airy, and fresh – or something else? He heard music coming from the living room, and saw that the sliders were open to the deck. He smiled. He was always amazed at the difference a woman made to a place.

"Hi," Meara said when he peeked his head out the sliders to see if she was on the deck.

"Hey," he replied, stepping out when he saw her. "You certainly look relaxed."

She was sitting on one of his cushioned lounge chairs.

She sighed, "I am relaxed. I think I even fell asleep for a few minutes." She laughed softly. "Cade, this place is wonderful." She stood up and stretched languidly, looking out at the bay and noticing the hovering bank of clouds on the horizon.

He came up behind her and pulled her close to him. "Best view in the city, do you agree?" he asked as he looked out at the city and the bay beyond from over her shoulder.

Meara turned in his arms and leaned up to kiss him. She circled her arms around his neck and touched the hair along his shirt collar and slowly ran her fingers through it. "So? How did the office go?"

"I'm good for a week away, I think. All my projects have been divvied up among the partners and associates, and Angie has taken over as my second in command."

"That sounds good. Are you actually going to have time to relax over there or is it going to just be work, work, work?' Meara asked.

"A little of both, I would imagine," he looked down at her keeping his hands around her waist. "I've got a couple of places I want to take you, but you'll have plenty of time to wander around on your own and shop if you want to."

She smiled.

Just then the doorbell chimed. "Vanessa," Cade said, letting go of Meara.

Meara followed him into the living room and stood a few paces back as he opened the door.

Vanessa stood in the open doorway with a huge grin on her face. "Hey, Dad," she said and paused only for a second or two before falling into Cade's arms for a hug.

Meara could see immediately how much they cared about each other. She smiled warmly. It spoke volumes about him, as far as she was concerned. You could tell a lot about a person by the relationships they forged with their children.

He turned to her. "Meara, this is my daughter, Vanessa. Honey, this is Meara O'Connell."

Meara laughed and corrected him, "Meara O'Connell Cellini… he doesn't seem to want to acknowledge my life for the past thirty-plus years."

He nodded, "Sorry, but she's right. I still think of her as Meara O'Connell, the senior in high school when I was a mere sophomore."

Vanessa came forward with her hand outstretched to shake Meara's hand, but as she got closer she shrugged and pulled Meara into a hug instead. "My dad is a pretty good judge of people. If he likes you, then I do, too."

Meara smiled, "That is so sweet. Thanks, Vanessa. You know, I've really been looking forward to meeting you."

"And I, you," Vanessa said, leading Meara into the living room and steering her towards the kitchen bar. "Dad tells me you have a daughter?"

"And a son," Meara nodded. "Donna is thirty, a graphic designer at a computer company in Denver; and Paul is twenty-seven, and will be graduating in the spring with an MBA from Tufts. Both are married to wonderful people, but no grandkids yet. Now, tell me about you? Your dad says you do some kind of marketing in Silicon Valley."

Vanessa chuckled, "Well, actually I do social media marketing for a small start-up. They have a little niche that's generating lots of interest from the venture capitalists. So either I'll have a steady job for the next ten years or who knows? Maybe we'll all be cashing in on our stock options when some big company buys us or someone takes the company public."

"That'd be amazing," Meara said with a laugh. "I hope it happens. Then you can turn around and do whatever the heck you really want to do with your life."

Vanessa paused and smiled. She looked at Meara with new interest. "My sentiments exactly," she agreed. "It always comes down to time and money, doesn't it?"

Meara nodded, "It seems you can have one or the other, but rarely both at the same time," she added and laughed knowingly. "So that's always the dream, to manage to have both time and money at the same time."

They both smiled and nodded to each other.

"Wine?" Vanessa asked. "I think Dad has some white in the refrigerator, and there's always plenty of red on the rack."

"Hmmm, you choose for me. I like either one."

"Then, red it'll be. I know there's a great cab in here, right, Dad?" Vanessa said looking over her shoulder at Cade.

Cade just nodded, a bemused expression on his face. He hadn't expected the two of them to bond quite so spontaneously. Something had happened between them in the past five minutes and he felt bewildered, not knowing what exactly had been said or not said that had tipped the balance between a guarded acquaintanceship and a deeper friendship. Women were a mystery to him at times like this. He wasn't sure if they spoke in code or if they were just psychically intuitive when it came to other females.

There was a knock at the front door and Cade was relieved to have something to do. He went to the door and when he opened it he found it was the people from Carter's, the caterers.

"Good evening, Mr. Chandler. Ready for us?" Stefan, the chef from Carter's, asked as he led the way into the apartment, followed by two of his staff – a young man wearing a chef hat, and a young woman wearing an apron; a server, Cade assumed.

"Sure, you know the way to the kitchen, Stefan, right?" Cade asked.

Stefan was obviously pleased the Cade remembered him by name. He puffed up for a second, relishing the limelight. Then he nodded. "Yes, sir! Come along, Joseph, Carrie. Let's get that food to the kitchen and start preparing something fantastic for Mr. Chandler and his guests."

Cade closed the door behind them with a smile. He always loved the banter and elaborate tableaux that got played out with people in the competitive and celebrity world of the culinary arts, particularly in a city the size and stature of San Francisco. He knew that to be really good here, was to have excelled far beyond pedestrian dreams of success. People like Stefan made serious money, and they worked for and earned every penny.

"Stefan!" Vanessa said with pleasure. "Good to see you again!"

"Vanessa! Oh! I had no idea you were dining with your father tonight. This will be a real pleasure for me and my staff!"

Vanessa grinned. "That's very sweet. Let me introduce you to Meara O'Connell Cellini, a friend of my Dad's." She turned to Meara, "This is Stefan, the head chef at Carter's in the Mission district."

Meara put out her hand, "I'm honored to meet you, Stefan. And I am really looking forward to your dinner."

Stefan glowed as he took her hand and bowed slightly. "I'm hoping you'll be impressed. So you're not from San Francisco, I take it?"

Meara shook her head, "No, Boston."

"Ah, then I have some work to do to impress you. You have some talent back east, I know!"

Chapter 31   White Rabbit

Meara laughed and marveled at how Stefan made her feel like she was royalty, a person who was supposedly used to dining at the best restaurants. Sure, she'd been to some nice places to eat, and not just in Boston, but in New York and Paris, and Rome even, but she knew she wasn't in that four-star class of people who could afford collecting exquisite dining experiences the way her grandmother used to collect green stamps at the grocery store.

But it made her wonder about Cade and what he was used to? Was he a four-star diner? Another facet of him she didn't know.

Meara studied him from across the room. He and Vanessa had followed Stefan and his crew into the kitchen and were chatting with them amiably. It was obvious they all shared a warm relationship. But was it personal or business? Was it because Cade was doing well at his law firm and could afford the luxury of caters from an exclusive restaurant providing dinner in his apartment? It made her realize how little she really knew about him.

She watched more closely as he grinned and joked with the chef and turned easily to bring Vanessa into the conversation. He was such a warm and sociable person. She could see that. But did she know really know him?

They'd known each other for a little over a week and although they'd certainly spent hours talking, she felt like she'd barely scratched the surface of all she wanted to know about him. She'd also been plagued with the sensation that he was keeping something from her. It was like a small bird loose inside a house when it unexpectedly flutters down trying to find its way out and you run to the doors and windows to fling them open to help the bird get out, but then it flies back to roost at some nook at the top of the house and you have to patiently wait for it to come out again.

She looked at Vanessa, who had just leaned against Cade and nudged him gently at something Stefan had said and they both laughed at some private joke. Cade must have sensed Meara's gaze because just then he glanced over at her and caught her looking at him. He smiled and tilted his head indicating that she should come closer. She smiled and quietly came up next to him and he very naturally took her hand and squeezed it as he listened to something Stefan was saying. The gesture made her feel included and happy. It took so little when you really thought about it.

Tony could've taken lessons from a guy like Cade, she thought. Tony didn't ever reach out to hold her hand, not even back when they were first dating. If there was any handholding to be done, it had always been her taking his hand, not the other way around. It wasn't that he'd pull his hand away, of course, but just once wouldn't it have been nice if he'd reached out for her?

This was probably not a good train of thought to be on, she scolded herself. She knew she'd just end up feeling disloyal and melancholy and she didn't want to feel that way the night before a big trip to Milan with a new man. She moved her fingers and interlaced them with Cade's and he immediately responded by softly rubbing his thumb against the back of her hand. After a second, his thumb touched her wedding ring and he idly played with it scratching it with his thumbnail.

She'd forgotten about the ring until now. She should've taken it off. It felt wrong to be wearing a wedding ring when you were starting to date someone new. But she hadn't taken it off because somehow it seemed a betrayal of Tony to remove it even though she could see that it might be a betrayal of her new relationship with Cade to leave it on. Still, if she took it off, what would she DO with it? She didn't want to lose it, but she couldn't think of what the right thing to do might be. Maybe this is one for Ann Landers? What DID widows do with their wedding rings anyway?

Her mother had worn hers for a couple of years, Meara remembered, but when she started looking for a new husband – and yes, she had been just that explicit about her determination to marry again because she had no intention of living alone forever – she quietly put her wedding band into her jewelry box and there it sat like a treasured museum piece. It's probably still there, Meara thought. Hmmm, maybe she should send hers to her mother to put into the jewelry box, too. She smiled at the thought. Her mother would've been appalled that she would joke about something so personal. Ah well. She glanced up and saw the Cade was now watching her.

"What's up?" he asked.

She shook her head. She wouldn't know how to explain her thoughts. "Just wondering what happened to my glass of wine?" she said instead.

He glanced around and Vanessa, having overheard the question, pointed to the granite bar. He smiled and reached for Meara's glass and handed it to her.

"Thanks," she said.

For Cade, Meara, and Vanessa, Stefan and his people were the evening's entertainment. Watching them set up and cook the dinner was mesmerizing. Of course, Stefan knew a thing or two about these catering affairs and he made sure to add a flourish if he could. He was directing his people in setting the dining table with linens and a fresh flower centerpiece with pencil-thin candles jutting out in a sort of spray. When each candle end was lit, the centerpiece was a sparkling ball of twinkling light. He delighted in their sudden intact of breath.

The rolling cart the caterers brought with them was like Mary Poppins' carpet bag, filled with marvelous delights. There was sterling silver flatware that flashed in the candlelight, crystal water goblets that they filled with ice and water and topped with a thin slice of fresh lemon, and finally the fine china in a delicate ivory-on-white embossed pattern placed just so around the table.

Meara sighed. "It's beautiful," she breathed.

Vanessa nodded. "Well done, Stefan. It's almost too beautiful to sit at!"

Cade laughed, "Yes, but...hunger trumps beauty."

He pulled a chair out for Meara and she thanked him and sat. She noticed that Stefan held Vanessa's seat. Cade took the seat between them.

Stefan was a master of his craft, and part of that craft was to choreograph the meal without drawing attention to himself. He blended easily into the background, making certain that every need was met even before it was felt, so that Cade, Meara and Vanessa could enjoy the food and ambiance. And little by little, Meara and Vanessa started to get to know each other.

"So you're off to Milan tomorrow," Vanessa said. "I'm a little envious. It's such a wonderful area of Italy. Have you been there before?"

Meara nodded. "My husband's family was from Pistoia, near Florence. We'd visit the area every couple of years. Mostly, though, we spent our time in Rome. You see, my husband's family owns an Italian bakery in Boston. He handled the accounting and purchasing so he would go over to meet with suppliers and that sort of thing."

"Oh, an Italian bakery! That sounds yummy!" Vanessa said, her eyes lighting up.

Meara laughed, "Yes, it can be a very fattening line of work, if you don't watch it. I'm convinced that I gained weight just by breathing in the aroma of the cookies and pastries!"

Vanessa nodded. "So hard to resist!"

"Yes. But you would think that you'd get used to it all and after a while one would be able to take them or leave them, wouldn't you? Believe me, that never happened to me!"

Vanessa chuckled. "I'd be the same way. Just as well that I work with electronics and computers."

"I know. I was in the travel business. I was too busy to sit around eating bon-bons."

"Oh? Really? Are you still working in the travel business?"

"Part-time. I take on the more complicated clients. Theme weddings, river barge family reunions, that sort of thing. It takes a lot of organization, but is really satisfying when a trip comes together. You can't give a better gift to a client than a great memory."

"That's so true. I'm envious of you being able to control your work schedule. That's what I'd really like. Right now, my job is 24/7 – I'll get text messages and emails in the middle of the night. It's insane."

"Work is like that now, don't you think? We all thought that the twenty-first century would be a wonderland with plenty of relaxation, peace and tranquility. You know... the hungry would be fed, the naked clothed, and the sick cured. Not sure how or where we got off the path."

"Or if we were ever on it," Cade interjected with a chuckle. "There was maybe a moment back in the Sixties – probably when everyone was stoned and happily playing in the mud at Woodstock – when we thought love might actually be the answer, but sadly, it's been a long time since I've heard that sentiment from anyone."

Meara smiled and nodded, "We were pretty innocent, huh?"

Cade shook his head, "Nope. We were stoned," he quipped dryly.

The three of them laughed together.

"So, do you think your generation was that much more innocent than mine?" Vanessa asked Meara.

"Absolutely! I think your generation has been bombarded with media almost from birth. Every moment of your lives have been recorded – your first sounds were broadcast over a baby monitor, you casually Skype across town or across countries, you play video games against unknown international competitors, you text your friends constantly, keep in touch online, and when you drive there's a camera at every toll booth and intersection snapping pictures. Security cameras are literally everywhere, and now every cell phone has a camera so if it's not someone taking pictures or videos of you, then you are snapping pictures of yourself and posting them for everyone to see." Meara paused and took a breath. "Life really WAS simpler when Cade and I were kids; it's absolutely a fact. Personally, I cherish what we had because who knew that we'd be the last generation that had that kind of freedom and privacy?"

"You don't think we have freedom and privacy now?" Vanessa asked.

Meara shook her head. "No, I don't. It's not just your generation; it's happening to all of us. Our freedom is slowly being eroded by the excuse that it's better to be safe than sorry. We give a little away every time we succumb to a TSA search at the airport, or let a guard paw through our purses to get into a sporting event. If a guy in a uniform yells, "Jump!" We all are trained now to answer "How high?"

"But it is better to give up a little inconvenience in exchange for knowing that no one is getting on your plane with a gun or a bomb, isn't it?"

"Sure, it would be if that was a reasonable guarantee. But it's not. Because if people are really intent on blowing up a plane, there's very little anyone can do to stop them. When we do stop them, it's nearly always by a fortuitous accident — someone notices something and speaks up or takes action on their own." Meara paused to take a sip of wine. She looked at Vanessa again. "I think that the real purpose of TSA is to keep people buying plane tickets and flying. It's a magic act – it looks like they are doing something and everyone feels safer, whether they really are or not. Personally, I think they are an annoyance and a huge waste of money and resources, but you know, the real harm that they do is psychological. They are gradually getting Americans used to the idea that we are guilty until proven innocent, and that it's OK to be ordered around by uniformed police, military men with submachine guns, and special operations guys with jack boots and camouflage. There was a time when all of us would've immediately recognized the similarity to Hitler's Nazi Germany. Now it's just another day at JFK..." Meara sing-songed.

"You've really thought about this, huh?" Cade said admiringly. "I would not have figured you for a left-wing freedom loving hippie." He laughed and shook his head. "Amazing."

Meara grinned. "I know. Once you get involved, it's hard to let it go. I think I've been an undercover hippie for years."

Vanessa shook her head. "Wow! I hadn't really thought about the TSA as a panacea to make us think we're safe. Like handing a baby a pacifier, huh?"

Meara smiled and nodded. "Pretty much."

The evening was a little shorter than any of them would've liked because Cade needed to pack and Vanessa needed to meet up with JJ at nine. After Stefan cleaned up and left, Vanessa packed up the leftovers in her satchel and said goodbye.

She hugged Meara for a second longer than necessary and pulled back to look her in the eye. "I've really enjoyed meeting you, Meara. You are a vast improvement to my dad's usual companion choices." She chuckled. "I hope we can be friends, whether you and my dad figure things out or not."

Meara nodded and smiled. "I'd like that, Vanessa. You are a special kind of woman and I'd like to become better friends, too."

"Good. Then it's settled. Here's my cell phone and email address. Call, text, or email me any time," she said with a laugh. Then paused, and added, "Please."

Meara nodded and took the card. "Done." And she reached out and hugged the younger woman one more time.

Cade watched the two women in bemusement. He was happy and relieved that they liked each other and seemed to get along so well, but he was also mystified by half of what was said. He felt like he wasn't really hearing most of the conversation between them, that there had been another parallel conversation going on but he was only privy to the one he could hear. He shrugged as he hugged his daughter and kissed her goodnight.

It was good seeing Vanessa, it was true, but he couldn't help looking forward to holding the other woman in his bed later that night.

He turned towards Meara after closing the door. "I need to throw a few things into my suitcase for the trip. It shouldn't take me long. Have another glass of wine and switch on the gas fireplace in the living room. That should be cozy."

She smiled. "OK, but don't be too long or the wine and fire will end up putting me to sleep."

He grinned. "Promise I'll be quick."

Meara wandered back into the living room and found the switch for the gas fireplace. Within seconds she had a nice little fire in the fireplace. Boy, she loved these things. She then headed to the kitchen and saw the corked bottle of wine on the counter. She poured herself a glass then carried the glass over to the wall of windows that overlooked the lights of the city. She could see the outline of the bridge with its lights twinkling in the dark. He definitely had good taste, she thought as she stared out into the darkness.

Chapter 32   California Dreaming

Cade whistled as he pulled his mid-sized suitcase from the back of the walk-in closet. It should be more than big enough, he thought, as he laid it open on the bed. What to bring, though, that was the question? Certainly a suit or two since he'd told Meara he was going to Milan for business. However, he suspected he'd need a whole range of clothes from casual right down to rough and ready, because the truth was he really had no idea what to expect.

He hadn't seen the stalker since Stout Grove. Did that mean he wasn't going to turn up? Cade hadn't noticed him on the flight down from Crescent City, and he'd been hyper-aware of everyone on that flight. But upon reflection, it stood to reason that the guy knew a lot about Cade already; no doubt he knew where he worked, and where he lived here in San Francisco, for instance. Was he watching the apartment now? Would he follow them to Milan? Cade had purposefully been very open in his office about flying to Milan tomorrow. He didn't know exactly how or where the guy was keeping tabs on his whereabouts, so it was hard to leak the Milan trip with any kind of assurance that the word would get to him.

Heck, if worse came to worse, maybe he'd just have a really nice vacation with Meara. He smiled at the thought. But then, he quickly admonished himself. He needed to be ready, just in case.

He was done with his packing in about fifteen or twenty minutes. After years of business travel, he pretty much had his travel packing routine down pat. He knew what to pack and how much, and where to place it in his suitcase so everything was accessible when the need arose. He was actually pretty proud of his expertise.

He walked out to the living room and paused at the entrance to look at Meara who was sitting on the love seat in front of the fireplace. Her feet were tucked up under her and she had her glass of wine in her left hand, with her right arm relaxed and draped over the back of the couch. She was staring into the fire, obviously deep in thought. He could see the reflection of the flicking fire on her face, especially in her eyes.

Meara O'Connell. He still couldn't believe he'd found her again. He had spent an inordinate number of hours in high school mooning over her, figuring out where she would be after school or on a weekend night and then making sure he would be there, too, just so he could run into her, somehow to make her see him. He probably didn't say more than a half dozen sentences to her in the year that he knew her, but it didn't matter. She had become his go-to fantasy. He couldn't begin to guess the number of times he'd masturbated to the image he had of her in his mind. Well, to be fair, it was more the image of a Playboy centerfold with Meara's face attached. And when he went into Witness Security and was hidden away for the first two years after he'd stepped forward and become a whistleblower, Meara had been his salvation. He wondered if he'd ever tell her about that. Thank her, even. Because he had thought about her, fantasized about her, and even created elaborate scenarios of how he would meet her again some day. She filled so many otherwise boring hours of waiting through all the not knowing what the next day would bring.

How odd then that when he did see her again, he hadn't recognized her. When he saw her sitting in the window seat on the plane to San Francisco, she had looked familiar, but she didn't look like the teenage girl he remembered, nor did she resemble the image that he had carried around in his head for the past three or four decades. Geez, thirty-five years! His entire adulthood, really. And here he was with the real Meara, and the truth was, he didn't really know her. He was so enamored with the Meara in his head, he wasn't certain if he was letting the real Meara in or not.

He desperately wanted her to be that person, though. He wished he were better at relationships. He always wanted the woman he was with to become the idealized woman he'd constructed in his head. It wasn't fair, he supposed, and unfortunately, it sometimes took quite a bit of time for him to sort out what part of the woman was real and what part he'd made up.

Jan, Vanessa's mother, was a perfect case in point. Probably the worst case, because he ended up marrying her without really knowing who she really was. Now he could look back and see that he had painted this image of a perfect family of the three of them in his mind – himself, the proud father and husband; Jan, the mother and sexy wife; and little Vanessa, the perfect little girl. It wasn't all fantasy, because he was a proud father – that part was true. And Vanessa was a perfect little girl. He had loved her from the first time he'd held her in his arms. He smiled remembering the incident with a strange clarity.

She had been about three when she started waking up in the middle of the night with nightmares. Apparently, that's normal developmental behavior for a young child, but it had scared the heck out of him and tugged at his heart, all at the same time. That first time he'd heard her crying out in her sleep, he'd gotten up, pulled on a pair of jeans and stumbled groggily into her room. When he opened the door, she'd looked up at him with teary eyes and lifted her arms to him to be picked up. He pulled her into his arms and held her and swayed with her cradled against him until she fell back to sleep. He'd never felt so needed by and protective of another person in his life.

Jan was an indifferent mother, who had always been resentful of the unexpected pregnancy that she had discovered long after the boyfriend had moved on. She couldn't seem to let it go, that her life had ricocheted into some mommy orbit that she hadn't wanted to be on. Cade had known even back then that Vanessa was aware of her mother's ambivalence towards her. But still Vanessa tried to be the perfect child for her mother, even though Jan had never seemed to notice.

The marriage wasn't good from the beginning, but Cade always thought that if he tried a little harder to be a better husband and father, it would all work out. They just needed time; or so he thought. He wasn't sure now if more time would've eventually worked. He didn't think so. But they never had the chance to see it through. It was just around then that he'd discovered the group of mechanics, led by his new supervisor, Joe Reston, was helping to distribute Columbian cocaine throughout the continental US in the waste system of the passenger jetliners. He was confused and scared and he hadn't been sure what to do.

He had tried to talk to Jan about what was going on at work, but she had immediately advised him to keep quiet about it. He could be killed or they might come after her and Vanessa; then she began asking whether he thought they might pay him for his silence. When he saw that she wouldn't support his decision to become a federal whistleblower, it was like being sucker-punched in the stomach. He'd never felt so alone in his life. It was soon painfully clear that their marriage wasn't going to survive, but all he could think about was the tragedy that he might lose Vanessa.

Lucky for him, his brother, Curt, was a phenomenal lawyer. He couldn't perform miracles, but he had managed to assert Cade's adoptive parental rights, and he made himself Vanessa's legal protector while Cade was in the Witness Protection program. Curt had made certain that Cade would have continued contact with Vanessa, no matter what. That meant more to Cade than the alimony, or child support, and all the other nitpicking issues. It was a debt of love and loyalty from his brother that Cade could never repay.

The Witness Protection program eventually provided him with a new identity and sent him to one god-awful little town on the edge of nowhere after another. It might not have been so bad, if he'd been able to settle in a place, but something would always go wrong and his cover would be blown and they'd move him, as a preventive measure. One time, Reston's second in command actually tracked him down by following his brother. That's when Cade decided it was time to take his protection into his own hands and he'd moved to Milan.

Milan was perfect for his purposes, and looking back, it's a wonder it took him three years to finally make the move. After his father died, his mother had immediately moved in with her sister back in Italy, and he had dozens of cousins, aunts and uncles, all of whom believed that above all else, family came first. They welcomed him — their American cousin – and called him Nico Giordano. He became nearly as Italian as they were.

He came by his name naturally – "Nico" had been his mother's pet name for him when he was growing up; Nicolo was his middle name, after all. And Giordano was his mother's maiden name. He still had his Italian passport under that name. In fact, he planned to bring it along to Milan, just in case he might need an Italian identity again this time around.

He came out of his revelry when Meara stood up and came over to him. She smiled and leaned up to kiss his chin. "You've been a million miles away," she commented.

He glanced down at her and smiled. "Well, thousands, anyway. I was thinking about Milan, actually."

"Excited about going back?"

He chuckled, "Actually, I'm wondering how to introduce you to my mother and family over there without them calling in the village priest."

She laughed. "Well, my advice would be for you to tell her I'm a recent widow and play up the fact that we knew each other in high school. That may give her hesitation from pushing too hard."

"What's the matter? You afraid of village priests, too?"

"You betcha," Meara replied with a nod. "Been around a lot of very pushy padres in my time. But, mostly what I find is there's usually someone behind HIM doing all the real pushing..."

"Ah, and that would be my mother. Let me warn you, she is a handful."

"You say that with such warmth, I think I like her already. You'll find that I can be a bit of a handful myself." Meara said, arching an eyebrow.

"Point received," Cade nodded. "I don't doubt it for a moment." He pulled her into his arms then and said more quietly, "So a handful, eh? I think it's time we headed off to the bedroom to investigate this handful thing."

She laughed and took his hand. "I thought you'd never ask."

Chapter 33   If I Were a Carpenter

Meara loved that Cade was so spontaneous and open about sex. He didn't seem to have any inhibitions when it came to what he felt and what he wanted. She liked that. She'd spent too many years guessing with her husband. Part of it was probably Tony's Catholic upbringing, she assumed; but the rest was just the person he was. Sex and love weren't the most important things in his life. Boy, even saying that seemed somehow un-American, Meara thought with a smile.

She preferred someone like Cade who accepted what he felt, and when he wanted something, he went after it; much the way she approached sex herself. She couldn't see the point in making things more complicated than they needed to be. You want sex? Then have sex, for God's sakes, and stop blathering about it. On the other hand, she couldn't fathom folks who never thought about sex at all, who truly seemed uninterested.

And that, unfortunately, described her husband in the last years of their marriage. Oh, he'd laugh along with his friends about a woman's butt or her big boobs, but when it came to lust? No, she was sure it had been years since he had felt that emotion truly. Certainly, he hadn't felt it towards her.

And what she knew about herself was that she needed lust. It had taken her a long time to finally realize that lust was what was missing from her marriage.

Was that true of all long-term marriages? She didn't know, but she guessed it might be true for many.

Sure, it was easy to blame the prostate surgery or the aging process, but now she wasn't certain. Sure, he had made a few half-hearted attempts to please her. But they'd get all the way to the bedroom and she'd excuse herself to go to the bathroom and five minutes later she'd return to find him sound asleep. No, he was not a guy who cared very much about sex – or was it just with her? She didn't know.

She frowned. Had he never lusted for her? Now that he was gone, it made her feel sad – sad for him not to have felt lust for his wife, and sad for herself not to have generated it in him. She realized that's she wanted from a man; to be lusted after occasionally. She just hoped her chance for it wasn't entirely gone.

She looked at Cade as they turned the corner to the doorway to his bedroom. Did he lust for her? She stopped to consider the thought, to really look at him.

He jerked to a stop, "Hey, what's up?" he asked with a grin, pulling her into his arms as naturally as holding her hand had been.

"Do you feel lust for me, Cade?" she asked, her eyes narrowing slightly. She wanted to see the truth, even if it was hard to take.

"What?" he asked. "Did you just ask me if I LUST for you?" he repeated with a laugh. "Is that a Biblical question or is this for real?"

"For real," she nodded solemnly. "I need to know if you feel lust for me."

"And...Why would you need to ask that?" he asked gently, reaching out to smooth a strand of hair behind her ear.

"Because, Cade, my husband stopped lusting after me and I'm realizing now that I feel a bit resentful about that. I wondered if maybe the fault lies with me."

"Jesus, Meara! Are you kidding me?" Cade laughed out loud. "I've lusted after you since high school! Think about that. I've masturbated more times than I care to admit to, to an image I had of you in my head. Oh, yeah, baby, I most definitely feel a lot of lust..." he leaned down and pulled her into a deep, very long kiss. He pulled away, still holding her in the circle of his arms and swaying with her slightly. "You know something, Meara? I've thought of you the past week as this incredibly self-confident, self-righteous woman, and now you seem to be going all weak and wobbly...wondering about my lust? Aww, come on, honey, I know that can't be something you seriously wonder about. You can't have already forgotten our woman-on-top moment? Jesus. We rocked the world. Well, you rocked MY world. Is that answer enough for you?"

She grinned at him. "Perfect. You are perfect, Cade," she said, pulling him close and kissing him soundly. "So? How about you show me some of that lust then?"

Chapter 34   Sky Pilot

Cade stood in the TSA line right behind Meara. She was wearing a tan suede jacket over tight black jeans and a light blue silky blouse. She looked amazing. If she'd put on a pair of big sunglasses he was sure she'd be mistaken for some celebrity. Yeah, she looked that good.

He grinned, as he glanced around. It was a sunny day with blue skies and soft puffy clouds in the sky, cut across by a series of jet entrails. He almost regretted leaving San Francisco when the weather was this good. It was going to be an incredible fall, if the weather patterns didn't change too much.

Meara leaned back against him and he loved that she felt so comfortable with him. "Hey," he said over her head. "You falling asleep?"

She turned towards him and yawned, sighing with a big smile, "I blame you, trying to prove the existence of lust and all that. Kept me up half the night." Her eyes blazed and he grinned.

"Yeah, such a sucker's bet, too," he chuckled.

For just a second, there was a flicker of a black coat at the edge of his peripheral vision that caught his attention. He turned as the man disappeared around the corner and he instantly realized why it had caught his attention. It was meant to. He was sure it was the stalker letting him know that he was still paying attention. Cade felt suddenly jolted awake. He pulled Meara towards him embracing her from behind. He'd tuck her into his pocket if he could, just to keep her safe.

He took a deep breath and breathed in her scent and the lingering aroma of her shampoo and perfume.

'You OK?" she asked, sensing a change in him.

"Hmmm, yeah," he said. "Must be that lust thing," he added with a laugh and heard her answering chuckle.

She turned back to the TSA line and pulled her driver's license out, holding it together with her boarding pass. It was nearly her turn.

"See you at the other end of security then," she said over her shoulder.

He nodded and was waved over to another agent at another desk.

It was five minutes or so before they were both out at the other end, shoes back on, belts buckled, and gear restored to their hand-carries.

Meara shook her head, "What a waste of time," she muttered under her breath.

"Best if you don't give them a reason to pull you back through again, my love," Cade whispered.

"True," Meara said with a sigh. "True enough."

The flight was uneventful and quiet. Morning flights from San Francisco to Boston were always extraordinarily quiet. Cade wasn't sure why that should be true. Was it the nature of the cities themselves or of their inhabitants? Or more likely just the hour of the day? They both dozed on and off throughout the five or so hours of flying time.

They arrived in Boston in the late afternoon. The time change made the hours seem like water pouring through a sieve as they slipped away. They would need to hurry to her house to pack her things and then quickly return to Logan Airport for the late evening departure to Milan. No time to linger.

Cade hadn't known quite what to expect of the house that Meara and Tony had lived in. He thought perhaps it would be in some rich New England neighborhood that Massachusetts is noted for, but as it turned out he was surprised to discover that they had lived halfway to Cape Cod on the South Shore. The house was on a cul-de-sac in a quiet development. Sure the area looked well-off, but not a flaunting gated-development of mini-mansions that he had expected. By contrast, the house seemed tame, maybe "mid-rich" if that were a term, the house you'd buy if you weren't sure whether you were going to keep your wealth over the long haul. It was a two story contemporary, but conventional enough to be saleable if things suddenly went south.

Cade hated that he felt so judgmental. He realized that what he really felt was envy towards Meara's deceased husband. After all, Tony knew that when he married Meara he would have children with her and would live for the next forty or fifty years with her, God willing. Cade had never felt that same sense of entitlement with any woman he'd known not even with either of the two women he'd married. Was a man born with that confidence or did he earn it? Or was it granted to him by some unseen Fate?

The car pulled into the driveway. Cade looked over at Meara and he saw that she was studying the outline of the house. When she realized the car had stopped she glanced over at him.

"Sorry," she said. "It just looks like such a sad place now. I hadn't noticed it looking quite that way before."

He paused then asked, "Want me to come in and help?"

She smiled. "Come in, yeah. Help? No need."

Cade gave a nod. "Let's do this, then."

The driver nodded, indicating that he knew he would be cooling his heels for a while. Cade and Meara got out of the car and headed for the side entrance.

She entered, flicking on lights from room to room. "Geez, it's as if I never lived here," she said almost under her breath. "This is so weird."

Cade walked around glancing at the family collage of photos on the wall along the stairway going up to the second floor. Portraits of Meara's two children were paired year after year from pre-school through high school graduation. He could see the maturity in their faces change from year to year. Suddenly he had a vision of what a modern child would be subjected to. Not these few yearly portraits; no, future generations viewing family photos of a child born today would be overwhelmed with digital pictures and videos, sometimes multiple shots in a day. It would begin with birth and continue straight through youth and young adulthood – thousands upon thousands of snapshots. Perhaps it would be like early flip book animation. As you strummed through the shots, the image would become animated with growth and life. The child would become alive before your eyes.

"I'll just be a few minutes while I find some things to throw into a suitcase, Cade, OK?" Meara said.

He nodded, but was still enthralled with the strangeness of being in someone else's house, in the center of someone else's life. He wandered from room to room, found Paul's teenage bedroom with its posters and desk computer, turned off and silent. Donna's room was slightly more retro, she'd left a few years before Paul, but there was a museum feel to the room. It was like she'd been there one day, and simply not returned. It made him wonder if Meara had thought that Donna might return after graduation from college? It made him sad to think that she might've been disappointed in her daughter's choice not to return home, not even to clean out her childhood bedroom.

Was he reading the signals all-wrong, though, he wondered? He had nothing to go on. Meara had never mentioned whether she had wished Donna would return to Boston after college. Did parents always have expectations for their children, even after the child took control of his or her own lives?

He thought about Vanessa, but he believed she was different. He'd never felt that he had a say in what she did or didn't do. It left him feeling inordinately lucky when she chose to stay close to him, that she wanted to see him and be around him often. He'd wanted that, to be sure, but had never felt he had the right to assume or even to cajole her.

He thought it was better to feel lucky to be chosen, than to feel the sting of disappointment at being rejected by your child, even if your child was now a grown-up.

Chapter 35   96 Tears

"Cade?" Meara called.

She was in the master bedroom. She saw that he hesitated before entering. Obviously, he knew this had been their bedroom – hers and Tony's.

"Are you OK?" Meara asked looking at him with concern.

He nodded and smiled wanly. He took a deep breath. "Ah, the truth is Meara...I feel very weird being here," Cade said glancing around the large master bedroom.

Meara's suitcases were open and lying on the huge king-sized bed.

She came around and reached out for his hand. "He's been gone a while now, you know." She paused. "But, if it's any consolation it's weird for me, too." She watched his face for a reaction, but she didn't notice any.

"When I came in here," she continued, looking from the windows to the double chest of drawers and then to the bed, "I almost expected Tony to be here...waiting." There was a moment or two of silence. "But you see, that's the thing about the death of someone you cared about, you can't help but wonder if they will hang around to make things right before they move on...."

"You believe that?" Cade asked in surprise.

She sighed, and shook her head, "No, I don't actually. I believe he was gone from us the moment he died. I like to think he cared enough to want me to be happy without him, but honestly? I'm pretty sure he just left without a backward glance."

"You think he didn't love you?" Cade asked.

"Oh, no, it's not that. In fact, I know that he did; it just wasn't THAT kind of love...you know?"

He shook his head.

Meara took a deep breath. "He loved me, Cade, but I wasn't his be-all, end-all...I wasn't his soul mate, if you know what I mean.

He never expected or believed in that kind of love relationship, so of course, he never looked for it. He married me because I was there just at the moment he was ready to be married, or more likely, just at the moment everyone around him expected him to be married. I could've been anyone. The truth is that it wasn't ME that he was in love with, it was what I could give him – children, a home, a family life, a place in the community."

"Meara, I don't believe that..." Cade said.

"You're being kind, but I've known for a very long time what the nature of my marriage was. I've accepted it. Tony was a very good man, and I was glad to know him, and I'm happy my kids had him for a father, because he was a really terrific father to them. The best. So I'm not unhappy with the way it all worked out for them; it's just that I wanted more for myself."

"Like what?"

"Well, for one thing," Meara said, "I wanted more passion." She smiled. "And I wanted a life partner who really knew me, who wanted me and who would settle for nothing less than me." She paused and shrugged, "I honestly think it's what all women really want." She shrugged again to hide the emotion she was feeling at the admission. "Funny, isn't it? Because I settled in a way, didn't I? Just like he did." She chuckled mirthlessly. "But don't get me wrong, I don't regret my kids or my marriage, I just wish it had been...I don't know...more. I wanted more."

She carried a dress on a hanger out of the walk-in closet and tucked it into the garment bag, smoothing it out thoughtfully. "What about you? What did you hope for in a life partner?"

Cade shrugged automatically, the way he'd always answered those kind of unanswerable deeply personal questions. Then he paused and looked into her eyes. "Truth?" he asked. "I always wanted you."

She chuckled and relaxed, "Good answer, Lancelot." Meara grinned but when he didn't return the smile she paused and frowned slightly. "Really?"

"You were all I wanted in high school. I thought if I could have Meara O'Connell, I would be a happy man."

"Cade, you were a kid with a crush."

"Sure, and I was a kid beginning to see what love could be for the first time. First love sets the standard. Didn't you know that?" he asked, half in jest.

"It wasn't love that you were seeing..." Meara started to say.

But Cade interrupted, "No, you're right. It was probably lust. But that is what I wanted: a life full of lust and passion at its core. For me, it had to begin there. I knew I could do anything with those things at the center of my life."

Meara grinned. "That's what I wanted, too. Lust and passion! And not just in a love relationship, but in every aspect of my life."

"I know," he nodded. "I probably learned to seek them out from you."

Meara knew it was just a game of words, of saying the right things, matching up what you were saying to the other's intent. It was a form of flirting, but he was saying all the right things and she was enjoying the sense of communion they created, of being on the same wavelength with someone, of connecting at a deep level. The truth is she didn't care if he was manipulating her and saying just what she was desperate to hear. Because she so appreciated him in that moment that he cared enough to actually say the words to her.

Meara had been hesitant about returning to the house she had shared with Tony, especially bringing Cade with her. But now she realized that coming back and facing the silent house was the right thing to do, whether she needed the clothes or not. She felt like she now had persmission to go to Milan with Cade.

Chapter 36   Wouldn't It Be Nice

It was an overnight flight to Milan. Well, not exactly overnight since it took ten and a half hours to get to Milan with a plane change and two-hour layover in London. It was mid-afternoon in Milan by the time they arrived, but back in Boston it would've been seven-thirty in the morning and in San Francisco it would've only been four-thirty a.m. Yeah, Cade thought, they would be suffering some jet lag, no doubt about that.

The car met them just outside of Customs at Malpensa International Airport on the outskirts of Milan. It would be a forty-five minute drive into the city to the company's apartment. He'd debated about whether to instead head north to his mother's village and get the introductions out of the way. But he knew his mother would've worn even Meara down and made them stay at the family home. Cade wasn't ready for that yet. Sure, Meara might be safer there, but he wanted her to enjoy a bit of Milan first and he selfishly wanted to spend more time with her, without family. Plus, he thought it might be better to talk with his cousins privately first to discuss the situation he was in, and he wanted to do that before Meara became embroiled with the Giordano hospitality.

Another concern was to make certain that the stalker, whoever he was, would be able to find them. They must look like they were fleeing, but be obvious enough to leave a trail; otherwise, the plan he was formulating in his head couldn't work.

He glanced over at Meara who had her eyes closed and her head resting against his shoulder. She was gamely soldiering on but he could see she was beat. Heck, the thought of the shower and crisp sheets in the apartment were calling to him, too; he had to admit it. The driver pulled up to the apartment building a block from the Piazza del Duomo. He turned and grinned as he noticed Meara's head on Cade's shoulder, now sound asleep. Cade smiled, too.

"Hey, sleepy head, we're here," Cade said softly as he kissed the side of her head.

Meara smiled, her eyes still closed. She sighed and breathed out. "OK," she said as she opened her eyes and looked around. The ancient buildings crowded in, interspersed with the occasional modern structure pushing between the hundred-year-old tenement on one side and the possibly thousand-year-old structure next door. There were crowds of people passing by on the sidewalk, veering gamely around the tiny cafe tables of the restaurant that sat right up next to the doorway of the refurbished apartment building. The sun was shining and everyone looked rested and unnaturally happy to Meara.

"Is this the place?" Meara asked, as Cade opened the car door and she looked curiously at the buildings along the street.

"This is it," Cade said with a smile. He nodded to the driver, who set their suitcases on the steps next to the front doors to the building.

Cade felt around in his pocket for the keys to the place. He was certain that Angie had given him a set of keys – one to the garage on the next street over where a company car was parked, one to the penthouse apartment, and one to the front door and elevator. He pulled out his wallet at the same time to find a tip for the driver. The driver, Arturo, didn't expect a tip, of course, because he was paid well by the firm. But Cade felt the last minute nature of the trip and the fact that he'd need Arturo's assistance in the next couple of days meant a tip would definitely pay dividends.

Arturo was genuinely surprised and pleased by the unexpected bonus when Cade handed it to him and closed Arturo's fingers around the wad of cash to make his point. Cade was certain that he'd be able to ask Arturo for favors and that, in turn, he would work hard for him. Cade took him aside and asked for his mobile number so that he could contact him when he needed him. Then he told him to take the rest of the day off to enjoy himself. He only requested that he be waiting outside the apartment building at nine the next morning, ostensibly to take him to his business meetings, but actually to take him for a ride to a meeting with his cousins and Uncle Vincente.

"A domani, Signore; e la Signora," Arturo said with a slight bow.

"Grazie," Cade thanked him.

Meara nodded and echoed, *"Grazie,"* in a low voice. Cade smiled as he saw her silently mouthing the phrase as if to get a grip on the language again.

Cade extended the pull handles from the two suitcases and began to drag them to the door. Meara came up beside him and took the garment bag pull handle from him and smiled. "Very macho of you taking over and all, but I don't mind pulling my own suitcase."

He unlocked the door and held it for her. "I thought I'd try to make you owe me. Then I'd get to think up lots of ways for you to pay me back."

Meara grinned. "Or you could owe me...either way could be 'win-win'," she added with a laugh.

"The elevator is back here," he led the way through the building. It was an older elevator, balky and slow, but serviceable. They squeezed on with their suitcases pushed up against their legs.

When they got to the top floor, Cade clambered over the suitcases and held the elevator door for her. "It's to the left," he said nodding the way.

The hallway was dark, as the electric lights were only on in the evenings. During the day, the sun shone through the windows at either end of the hall. .

Cade stopped at the last door on the left. "This is it," he said, and unlocked the heavy door and pushed it open.

Meara stepped into the foyer. There were high ceilings, perhaps eleven or twelve feet, with plaster archways between the rooms. The living room area was in the center of the apartment with a wide hallway around it. The design seemed to be based on the courtyards in old Mediterranean style homes. All the rooms were off the hallway – several bedrooms, a kitchen, a powder room with a toilet and sink. The two full baths were off the master bedrooms at either end of the main hallway.

"We'll take the master bedroom at the other end of the hallway," Cade said, nodding the way again.

"What's the difference?" Meara asked with curiosity.

"The views," Cade replied. "You'll see."

They went into the bedroom with its queen-sized bed and two armoires and a matching lady's dressing table. On the other side of the room was a wall of curtains. Cade went to a panel of switches near the door and pushed a button, which caused the sheer outer curtains to slowly gather and slide open. A second button caused a second set of heavy blackout curtains beneath to also open. Soon the late afternoon sunlight began to fill the room.

"Oh, my," Meara said, her hand going to her mouth.

As the curtains swept back out of the way, she went over to the windows and looked out. She could see over the building across the street and beyond that took her breath away. She was looking at the top of the Duomo looming in the near distance, like the top of a Gothic layered cake. The cathedral was magnificent, caught in the full afternoon sunlight.

"Oh, my God, Cade! It's the Duomo! Right there!" Meara said with excitement.

Cade nodded. "Awesome view, huh?"

"This apartment building is just high enough...." Meara said with satisfaction. "This is spectacular, Cade! I love it."

"I knew you would," he said with satisfaction.

"I've got to call my kids," Meara said.

Cade stared at her, the nonsequitur took him completely by surprise. "What?"

"Seeing the Duomo made me realize that I am actually in Milan. And that made me think that if our plane had crashed coming over or been blown up by a terrorist, my kids would've had no idea in the world that I was even on the flight. They think I'm happily vegetating on the southern coast of Oregon."

Cade grinned. "Jesus. You're right. You are one terrible mother."

She scowled but knew he was teasing. "Will my cell phone work from here?" she asked with a frown of concern.

Cade shook his head, "I doubt Italy is part of your cell plan. They'll charge you roaming fees and you'll be paying for that pleasure for months." He went to his suitcase and pulled a slim briefcase from the side pocket. He opened it and pulled out a small phone. "Here, use my company mobile. It's got an international plan and you can talk as long as you want."

"Thanks," Meara said taking the phone from him.

"And shut off your phone completely. Those roaming charges happen even when you're not using it, like when your email account is set to periodically update your mailbox."

She nodded and smiled as she sat on the edge of the bed and began dialing.

Chapter 37   Season of the Witch

It should be mid-morning in Denver now. OK to call, Meara thought as she dialed. "Donna? It's Mom," she said as she heard her daughter's voice.

"Mom? Hey! How's Oregon?"

"Still there, I would imagine," Meara answered sheepishly. "Honey, guess what? I'm in Milan, Italy!"

There was silence on the other end of the line. "You're joking, right?" Donna asked, her voice gravelly.

"Nope. It's a bit of a long story, which I won't bore you with right now. But, I got the chance to come over here for a week and I took it," Meara said with a nervous smile. How odd that she should feel so uncomfortable about her daughter's reaction to her life. When did that happen?

"Milan, ITALY?" Donna repeated. "Mom? Are you OK?" she asked, sounding motherly and concerned.

The role reversal took Meara completely by surprise. "Of course, I'm OK. Why wouldn't I be?" she asked in disbelief.

"Well, Dad hasn't been gone that long..." Donna reminded her quietly.

"Donna, your dad has been gone for more than a year," Meara corrected.

"Oh, I see," Donna snapped back. "And you're over him, is that it?"

"What?" Meara responded. "Of course not. I thought maybe you'd be happy to know that I'm not wallowing in self-pity anymore though."

"You've been anxious to get away from home for a while now," Donna said testily. "First to Oregon and now, geez, now to Italy?"

Meara sat up and took a deep breath. She'd had enough.

"Donna, let's get something straight. I'm calling to let you know where I am, not to seek your permission, OK?"

They were both silent for a full half-minute. She could hear Donna's breathing but wasn't certain if she was holding back tears or fighting the urge to hang up. "Sorry," Meara said finally with a sigh of regret. "But I just wanted you to know that I'm here and am going to be here for about a week, and then I'll be back in Brookings for the rest of the month, as planned. OK?"

"OK," Donna replied in a softer voice. "I'm sorry, too, Mom. It's just that I miss Dad so much, and sometimes I forget that we're all dealing with his passing in our own ways."

Or not dealing with it, Meara mentally supplied. Or are done dealing with it and have moved on, she allowed herself to complete the thought. "Well, I want to give a call to Paul, too, so I'll let you get back to work," Meara said, trying to finish the call.

"Thanks, Mom. I'm glad that you called me. Really."

Meara remembered a time when they were close – mother and daughter. She wondered if that would ever happen again for them? She said goodbye with a perfunctory "I love you" and clicked off and sighed. Well, that didn't go the way she'd hoped.

She dialed Paul quickly, before she could talk herself out of it. One thing about Paul, she reminded herself, is that he was never as judgmental as Donna.

"Hi, Mom!" Paul answered. She was relieved that he sounded quite happy to hear from her.

Meara breathed out. "Hi, honey," she said and smiled. She always remembered Paul as a ten-year-old boy, barely stumbling through one growth spurt after another. He was always so earnest and adorable, she thought fondly. "I'm calling to let you know that I'm not in Oregon this week, I'm in Milan, Italy, OK?"

"Wait...what?" he asked with a laugh. "Slow down, lady, and explain." She could hear him sipping his coffee and could almost imagine him leaning back in his chair.

"You're not in classes today?" she asked, following a hunch.

"Not until later. I'm studying for a test right now and you're a welcome break. Now explain, please."

"Well, I don't know if I can," she said with a chuckle. "The truth is, Paul, I met a guy on a plane a week ago and went to dinner with him in San Francisco, and one thing has led to another, and he had business in Milan, so I came here with him."

There was silence on the phone. "Seriously?" Paul asked. "Oh my God, Mom, do I have to come out and babysit you to keep you from making bad choices?"

Meara was momentarily speechless. "What?" she barely choked out.

Paul burst out laughing. "Sorry, Mom, I have always wanted to use some of your infamous threats back on you. You used to always accuse me of making bad choices and threatening to come and guide me through life if I didn't straighten up." He chuckled some more. "But, you...YOU making bad decisions? Nah, that can't happen."

"Of course, it can't, and I haven't, by the way," Meara replied primly. She wasn't sure how she felt about her son giving her a comeuppance. Although she liked that he accepted her and wasn't judgmental like his sister. "So how are things at school? And how's Tina? Please say hello to her for me, won't you?"

"Tina's great. She was asking about you last night and suggesting that I go out and see you in Oregon when I have a break at the end of the month."

"You're going to come and visit me?" Meara grinned. "I'd love that, Paul! Will Tina come too?"

"No, she's got to work to support us until I finish school. But I'll let you know if I can swing it when we get a little closer to the dates. I don't know yet whether I'll have to teach an undergraduate workshop that week or not."

"OK. I'll try not to be too disappointed then if you can't swing it. But, I'd love to see you; you know that." Meara smiled at how sweet Paul still was. His two years in Afghanistan and all the problems he brought home with him, and now it seemed he had miraculously returned to himself again. She was so relieved.

Chapter 38 It's Your Thing

Cade watched as Meara sat on the edge of the bed after clicking off from talking with her son, Paul. He could tell she had been emotionally touched by the calls to her son and daughter. It was good for her to reconnect with them, he decided.

"Hey," he said from the doorway.

Meara lifted her head and smiled. "What's up?" she asked softly.

"Time for bed," he said lifting his eyebrows suggestively.

"Really?" she replied looking a little confused.

"Yes. I figure we've been up for basically two days, and the only way we're going to get back on track is to go to bed now, and stay there until tomorrow morning."

Meara looked at him in disbelief. "Tomorrow?"

"Seriously," he said more gently. He came in and pulled her up to standing. "First, we get into the shower together and soak off all the travel." He smiled broadly. "Then, we get naked under the crisp sheets of this rather large bed. Sound good to you?" He waited, watching her.

Meara smiled and nodded. "OK, I'm on board with all that," she agreed with a laugh. She started unbuttoning her silk blouse. It billowed out revealing a very sexy black lace bra underneath. Cade took a breath as she stood before him.

He looked down at her. He could not have imagined a more perfect beginning to a week's vacation with Meara in Milan. He quickly unbuttoned his own shirt and pulled it off. He reached down and wrapped his arm around her waist. "To the shower then."

Meara put her arm around his waist and smiled as, together, they headed into the bathroom off the master bedroom.

This was one of his fantasies, Cade thought with a lopsided grin. Who knew that you could actually make a fantasy come true?

Heck, if he'd known it was possible, he'd have come up with more of them, that was for sure.

Cade had had the rather grandiose idea that there would be multiple hours of making love to Meara after the shower, but by the time they'd emerged, glowing from the steam as well as the steaminess of the foreplay, they barely made it to the bed for one long orgasm followed soon after by both of them falling sound asleep as if they'd been knocked out.

Waking after ten straight hours of deep sleep Cade blurrily glanced over at the digital clock on the side table and saw with dismay that it was only three a.m. He wasn't wide awake, to be sure, but he wasn't sure he'd be able to get back to sleep easily either.

So he lay there, his eyes closed, but his mind awake and thinking. He was thinking about Meara, first of all – how could he not think about her with her warm body an electric presence next to him as she was tucked up close to him, her body touching him from thigh to waist? He opened his eyes and looked over at her. Her hands were curled in around her face and neck, reminding him of the way children looked when they slept. He pulled up the duvet to cover her shoulders and she visibly seemed to relax and sigh in her sleep. Maybe she had been feeling cold, he thought.

He wondered where this relationship was heading. To be honest, he really hadn't stopped to consider where he might want it to go. Up to now he hadn't felt that he had much control over its course at all. He enjoyed her company and sometimes out of the blue it'd come back to him that this was THE Meara O'Connell that he'd had such a huge crush on in high school, and he'd feel the excitement roiling up in him all over again. Even now, he could easily get hard just thinking about her.

It was crazy that she could still have this kind of effect on him, considering that they were both nearly forty years older than they had been back in Bangkok. He hadn't forgotten, although he wasn't certain she had any recollection of him back then at all. It didn't matter since he was sure he had enough recollection for the both of them. Sure some – maybe most — of what he remembered was pure fantasy of all that he wished she had been to him. But heck, here he was now, and she had become that fantasized lover, and more.

He didn't know where it would go from here, but he did know that he wasn't ready for it to be over yet, not by a long shot. He wasn't sure how things would've gone if the stalker hadn't shown up. It had certainly accelerated things and there was a sense of foreboding about the guy, particularly when he just appeared out of nowhere at Stout Grove and had scared the heck out of Meara.

But who was the guy? Cade tried to think about it logically. He still hadn't heard back from Witness Security. It could be they had no clue who the guy was either, but Cade's gut told him that the guy was connected to Reston.

Obviously, he was somehow connected to the whistleblowing incident. He said as much to Meara when he declared that it wasn't over, and there wasn't anything else that he could've been referring to. But Cade thought that the guy seemed way too young to be connected to the airlines and the drug running and all the rest. Cade admitted that he hadn't gotten a good look at the guy, but his impression was that he was maybe in his mid to late thirties, no older than that. The whistleblowing event took place in the mid-1980's, so that would make the guy...what? A little kid at the time. Not even a teenager, at best.

So what was the connection? He'd have to be intimately connected or why would he care this much? Why dig up the past like this and chase after Cade unless he had something at stake? He must have a huge revenge fantasy going on. But revenge of whom and for what?

"Cade?" Meara said in a soft voice, barely a whisper.

He opened his eyes and saw that Meara was up on one elbow looking at him. "Hey," he replied.

"You're obviously awake, but what are you thinking about so hard?" Meara asked, studying his face.

"It's the usual three a.m. jitters, I guess," he said with a sigh. "Don't you do that sometimes? Wake up at two or three in the morning and just think about your day or the past week or, I don't know, your life?"

She smiled, "Sure, sometimes. Usually I wake up in the middle of the night when I'm worrying about something." She paused. "Are you worried about anything?"

He reached out and put an arm around her, feeling the coolness of her shoulders in contrast to the warm silkiness of her skin where the duvet had covered her. "No, not worrying exactly; just thinking about Milan, and my meeting tomorrow, and thinking ahead about introducing you to my mother. That's about it." He smiled. "Nothing too earthshaking really."

"I'd like to meet your mother, Cade, but if you don't want me to, I'm OK with that, too. I mean, I understand that introducing me to her after you and I have only known each other for a little over a week and a half, well, I can see how she might get the wrong idea."

He grinned. "Oh, she is going to love getting the wrong idea. She lives for this kind of thing. Believe me. She has a rather diabolical sense of humor."

Meara smiled wryly. "I leave it up to you, then. I'm OK with whatever you want to do...or not do. Really."

"Hmmm, whatever I do or not do? Did you mean, like, now?"

She grinned. "You have a way of re-interpreting everything I say, don't you?"

"Well, I find that when I'm this close to you and you have no clothes on and I have no clothes on, well, my mind does seem to go on a single track."

"I've noticed that about you," Meara laughed. She leaned in and kissed him, her tongue pushing against his half opened lips.

They kissed and he swept his hands very slowly down her side over the curve of her ribs and the dip of her waist to the roundness of her hips. He knew he would be making love to her soon and it roused him to think that it could be this easy and that every time felt this good and new to him. He couldn't remember the last time sex had felt as exciting the second and third and tenth time as it did the first.

She lay on her back and looked up at him. He had maneuvered himself on top of her. They looked at each other in the dim light of the room.

She smiled, "What?" she asked softly.

"Nothing," he replied.

"Something," she responded watching him.

He looked deeply into her eyes. "Meara, I've never....God, this sounds dumb," he laughed softly. He looked back down at her to gain some courage. "It's just that I've never felt quite like this before."

"Huh?" she asked, chuckling.

He grinned. "I know. Sounds dumb when I try to put it into words." He paused and the room grew very quiet. "Meara, making love to you is different, that's all."

She held very still. "Different how?" she asked.

"I don't know if there are words for any of what I'm feeling. I've been with lots of women before, and sex is...was...well, always great, sure...sex is sex, you know? But with you, these past days, this past week...it's not just sex as usual. That's all."

"So what is it like for you, Cade?" she asked, seeming to really want an answer.

"It's like I've never done it before. It's like you and I tonight... every night...are just starting out on some new adventure. I never know what I'm going to feel or what you're going to do, and it's...I don't know...it's something, something worth hanging onto." He sighed. "I sound so inarticulate. Damn. That's not at all how I wanted it to come out."

She chuckled again. "I think I know what you mean, Cade. I've been feeling very differently about being with you, too."

"You have?"

She nodded. "I thought it was just because it'd been so long since I'd had sex. Maybe I was reacting so strongly to... you know, just having sex, not just you...I don't know. But I think it's you... and me, Cade. Somehow what we've got going on here is something special...different." She laughed suddenly. "God, now I've become as inarticulate as you."

"I really, really like being with you, Meara," Cade whispered finally.

He could hear her murmur. "I really, really like being with you, too, Cade."

He leaned in and kissed her long and softly and a conversation was going on between their mouths and tongues. As he slowly sank into her, he heard her groan of contentment and he knew he must've groaned in reply. He was where he knew he wanted to be.

Chapter 39   Never My Love

Meara lay in Cade's arms for a long time as the dawn arrived and the early morning sun rose and tried to shine through the heavy shutters covering the windows of the apartment. She didn't move. She didn't want to wake him. For now, she felt safely secure in his arms as he slept a deep sleep of contentment, and it felt good to just lay still and let her mind roam a bit. This was luxury – not to be up and doing, but only lying still and thinking.

She loved the feeling. For long minutes all she wished was that she could remain here forever, like a fairy tale character caught in some magic web. She couldn't remember ever feeling this contented in her life. Not when she was a pampered child overseas, not when she married Tony and thought her life would suddenly be perfect, not when she had children and thought, of course, that meant she was finally complete as a woman.

It was funny that the feeling would come over her now; now when she was middle aged, her childbearing years behind her, her children on the verge of having children of their own – giving her grandchildren, for goodness' sake! Why this sense of contentment now, she wondered? Why was it happening with this guy from her long ago past? Heck, not even someone she'd known or cared about in that past really. Why Cade? Why now? Was she fooling herself? Was this feeling even real, she wondered? Maybe it was just the hormonal after-effect of good sex. She smiled. There was that.

She felt him move, sliding his feet towards hers. He tucked his toes in around hers, and she heard him sigh, or at least, she thought he sighed. God, was she falling in love with him? Damn, she didn't want to be in love with him. She had so much baggage to work out in her life first, a mess to work through in her mind, before she thought she could bring someone new, someone important into her life.

After all, she didn't know what she wanted for her future really. Did she even WANT to be married again? She wasn't sure. Did she want to stay single, be the crazy grandma who traveled and did nutty spontaneous things with her grandkids? While it made her smile, she wasn't sure it was something she was cut out for. Did she want to live alone on the edge of a cliff overlooking the Pacific Ocean and just enjoy the solitude of being alone and cultivating some needed tranquility? She thought that might be closest to what she expected for herself, but was it what she really wanted? Eventually, wouldn't she feel lonely? Didn't it even sound a little pathetic? Like she was running away from life?

The truth was, she didn't know Cade well enough to know what a life with him would be like. Would it be trips like this, out of the blue, to Milan, Italy? Or would it be mostly a lot of hostessing for his law practice back in San Francisco? She couldn't guess, and that bothered her. She shouldn't be having fantasies about a person she didn't know that well, should she? And why the heck WAS she having fantasies anyway? It's not as if he'd indicated he wanted anything permanent with her. He still could be considered a "one-night stand" in many ways. They'd met on the plane, had a great first night in San Francisco, and then she'd gone to Oregon and a week later he showed up at her door; then they went back to San Francisco for another night and now they were in Milan. Geez, had it been just been a week or two? She felt like she'd known him for months, years, even.

Well, of course, she HAD known him years ago, when they were both teenagers in high school. He had a crush on her and she had noticed that he was a good-looking kid that was always hanging around. She found it sort of sweet at the time, but she hadn't let her mind imagine anything coming of it back then. He was two years behind her in school, after all; she had been on the eve of graduating and going back to the States for college. Where was the future in that?

Indeed. Here was the future in that, apparently. She smiled. Life was so strange...and wonderful...but, well, strange.

"What're you thinking about," Cade asked in a soft morning voice.

She adjusted her body up against his. "Just enjoying lying here. I don't tend to do this in my real life."

He chuckled, "Your real life? What is this if not your real life?"

"Don't you know? This is a fantasy, Cade. And I'd appreciate if you wouldn't wake me up from it just yet," she said turning to smile at him. "Anyway, I have a question for you about smells."

"Huh?" Cade's head rose a bit off the pillow as he looked at her.

"I know. Weird. But, I was wondering whether people smell differently over time. Like does a person smell differently when they're old than when they were young?"

She saw Cade's eyes squint as he looked at the ceiling. She was amused that he was actually considering it, or she thought he was anyway.

"First off, why are you wondering about it?" Cade finally asked.

She smiled, then her face turned serious. "After Tony had his prostate surgery, he smelled differently to me. I don't know if it was the surgery or if it was just that I hadn't noticed in a long time and then suddenly I did." She shrugged. "I was wondering about it because I was thinking how much I like the way you smell."

He chuckled. "The way I smell?"

She nodded. "I don't mean your after-shave or the soap you use or anything like that, Cade. I'm talking about your skin, the way your skin smells."

He stared at her for a second or two. "You're serious, aren't you?"

"Yes, I am, as a matter of fact," she nodded. "So, do you like the way I smell?"

He grinned. "I do."

Her nose crinkled. "I'm not talking about my perfume or anything like that, you know."

"I know," he nodded. "Although I must say when you sat next to me on the plane that first time, wow, I couldn't get enough of your shampoo. I wanted to wrap my arms around you and bury my nose in your hair."

She laughed. "There's an image."

He laughed, too. "So you think that prostate surgery changed your husband's smell, huh?"

"I do. I've been thinking that maybe it's the testosterone levels or something hormonal like that. His hormone levels probably changed after they took out his prostate, don't you think?"

He nodded. "Probably. But you noticed a difference in his smell?"

"Yes. And after the surgery, I discovered that sometimes I couldn't even stand the smell of the pillowcases he put his head on at night. It just reeked to me. Isn't that odd?"

He was quiet for a minute. "Meara? So have you found that I ever reek to you?"

She burst out laughing. "Come on. Do you think I'd be lying her talking about this if I thought you stunk?"

"Well, why are you talking about it?"

"I don't know. I guess because now I have someone to run these things by. I miss that about being married and having Tony around. I could think out loud with him. I haven't had anyone to do that with for quite a while now."

"Hmmm, even though he reeked, you still liked running things by him, huh?" Cade grinned.

"Well, it's not like I wanted to get rid of him. Anyway, it wasn't his fault that he didn't smell good to me anymore."

"But he did smell good to you once?"

"Oh, yeah, I remember when we first met. He'd hug me and I'd take a deep inhalation and...oh, boy...I could get off on just the manliness of the way he smelled."

"Seriously?"

"Sure. People are animals really. We all react to smells and touches and tastes. Why do you think the after-shave and cologne industry is so big? People love with all their senses."

He grinned. "I know about touches and tastes. I just never really thought about the smells."

"That's because you're a guy and 'smells' to a guy means farts, not something attractive or sexy."

"Hmmm, but you're right about my gender. We do like our fart jokes."

She shook her head, "I know. Why is that? It's maddening."

"And sometimes hilarious," he added.

"Never hilarious...it's completely juvenile."

"OK, we're not going to agree about that, but I will give you that women think differently about humor than men do."

"It's not humorous!"

He ignored her. "So your question was whether his change in smell was hormonal...or what? Aging?"

"Yeah."

"I'd say hormonal. Because if it was aging, it wouldn't have come on so suddenly. I mean, up to then, you hadn't noticed the change, right?"

"Well, maybe I had but I just didn't register it consciously. You know, like when you realize that you're not happy and you start looking around for reasons for why you're not happy."

"And you weren't happy?"

She shook her head. "No."

"Because of the surgery?"

"Way before then. The surgery was just the final straw, I think."

"Ah."

"It sucks that he died and I can't discuss all this with him."

"Just as well, I think."

"Really? Why?"

"Because you were going to tell him that he stinks, after he just got his prostate removed...sort of piling it on, if you know what I mean."

"So there's no discussing it, huh?"

"Listen, if I start to stink, maybe we should have some kind of code word or something, because I don't know if I'd want to hear that either."

"Really?"

"If I said that you didn't smell good to me, Meara, how would you feel?"

She paused. "Ah, yeah. I see what you mean."

He kissed her cheek lightly. "You don't, though."

"Don't what?"

"You smell really, really good to me."

She smiled. "I'm glad. You smell really good to me, too."

"I do?"

She nodded. "Maybe it's Italy, though. This is a really nice smelling place, you know."

"It is, isn't it?" He looked thoughtful for a minute, and then glanced over her shoulder at the digital clock on the bedside table. "Geez, it's only six-thirty...my meeting isn't until nine."

She smiled. "Ah, so you're saying we have time to kill, right?'

He grinned. "Not killing it exactly...I was thinking of using it wisely," he said as he reached for her.

Yes, she thought, this is definitely the way she wanted to wake up in the morning. No question about it.

Chapter 40   A Whiter Shade of Pale

Cade and Meara had coffee and a pastry at the cafe next door. It was a spectacular fall morning; the sun was shining brightly with deep blue skies and just a few wisps of airplane contrails marring an otherwise perfect blue sky. This was promising to be a perfect day for walking around and seeing the sights. Unfortunately, Cade had things to do, places to go, and people to meet. He supposed he could put it all off, but he'd made a pretty big deal to Meara about how important this trip was, so he knew he had to carry through with the pretense of a lawyer's meeting so she wouldn't begin to question the reason he had brought her to Milan. He wasn't sure how she'd take the idea that he was keeping her in the dark in the hopes of protecting her.

He was also anxious to meet with his uncle and cousin to figure out what to do about the stalker. Cade hadn't been to Italy for several months, so it would be good to see them again, even if the reason was to discuss what to do about this situation.

He was pretty sure the guy was in Milan and would eventually find them again. He even thought he glimpsed him at the airport in San Francisco and was pretty sure he saw him again in the transit area before getting on the connecting flight in London. So it wouldn't be a surprise to see him here soon.

But he was hoping that he could put off any encounter for a day or two so there would be time to prepare. He couldn't be certain how much the guy knew about him, his past, his family connection to Milan, or whether he knew where Cade might stay once here. In fact, he'd settled on the law office's apartment, so that the guy would have an easier time locating them.

He glanced around the cafe suddenly realizing the stalker might already be here. He studied the men sitting at the other tables – a businessman looking down at his mobile phone while sipping espresso; two younger men at the table near the street with their heads together chatting animatedly about yesterday's football match. He didn't see anyone that fit his stalker's build, even if he might be able to camouflage his American-ness to blend in.

It wasn't easy to disguise American clothing and style in Milan, the most cosmopolitan of Italian city. Young people were slightly better at it, Cade thought, wearing their uniform of jeans and t-shirts and beat-up jackets. But if you looked closely, you could generally pick out the Americans from the European kids. Maybe it had to do with attitude; but if nothing else, you only had to look at their footwear. There were no mistaking American and European shoes.

"This is so lovely!" Meara said. "I cannot believe a couple of days ago I was on a beach in Oregon and today I'm sitting at a cafe in Milan." She shook her head. Cade noticed the shine in her hair as it moved against her cheek and he smiled.

"Crazy, I know," he agreed. He glanced at his watch and signaled the waiter for the bill. This wasn't like the States where they expected you to eat and leave so they could make room for new customers in order to make more money on the turnover. Here, they would let you sit at a table all day, if you liked, and only brought the bill out when you asked for it.

Meara watched him. "Time to go, huh?"

He nodded. "I'll walk you over to the Duomo so you can check out the museum this morning. Here's a mobile phone so I can let you know when I'm done and we can meet up."

She looked surprised, "You have two phones?"

He chuckled, "Actually, I think I counted maybe three or four of them in the hall cabinet back at the apartment. The office maintains several mobile accounts here so when any of the attorneys are over here on business, the office can always reach them."

"Wow," Meara said.

"It's more for the convenience for the office than it is for the lawyers, but it's still a nice perk."

Cade guided her down the street, around the corner, and through the huge archway of the Galleria with its indoor shops and restaurants and its soaring neoclassical glass ceilings.

Meara stopped for a second and took in the scene. "I love this place," Meara exclaimed, raising her eyes naturally up to the ironwork and glass 154 feet above them.

The place was crowded with tourists as well as locals. The locals were moving through the space while the tourists, for the most part, were stopped with camera or phone poised and taking snapshots. They were either looking up at the soaring ceiling or they were looking down at the coat of arms mosaics displaying the three capitals of the Kingdom of Italy laid in the floor below the glass dome.

Today the restaurants and shops were only half full since it was still morning, but they would be overflowing with diners and shoppers in a few hours when the city workers took their long lunch breaks.

They emerged from under the grand arch that opened outside into the Piazza del Duomo. The cathedral, in all its Gothic magnificence rose up before them like a huge whitewashed wedding cake. Or at least, that's what Cade always thought. It was mesmerizing to look at, of course, so much intricate detail, hundreds of prickly pinnacles and spires, gargoyles and statues of saints, not to mention the flying buttresses.

Meara came to a stop at the edge of the square directly in front of the cathedral. She stood and just stared up at the Duomo, holding one hand above her eyes to shield them from the sunlight. Cade let her take it in without speaking. He remembered as a small boy seeing it for the first time. He remembered thinking that it looked like something from Disney, at the very least. He grinned thinking how as a child everything had been compared to Disneyland, his favorite place in the world. In fact, when his family had been living overseas, many times it was Disneyland that he thought of when they referred to anything "back in the States."

"Oh, Cade, I could never get tired of seeing this place," Meara said, reaching down and taking his hand.

He squeezed her hand. "It's something special, that's for sure," he replied. He pulled her gently across the square.

"Where are we going?" she asked.

"The Museo del Duomo is over there," he pointed. "It contains a huge collection of artifacts, sculptures, stained glass and paintings. They are the treasures of the cathedral and span about five or six centuries of art and history. It's really an amazing collection. I think you'll enjoy going on the tour."

"Sounds wonderful," Meara agreed.

"It'll take you about an hour and a half to two hours to go through it with the audio headsets as a guide. They do a pretty decent job."

He walked with her into the museum and stopped at the visitor's desk to buy a ticket for Meara to rent an audio device. He gave the woman the money and turned to Meara. He noticed with consternation that she was staring at him with her mouth slightly open.

"What?" He blinked and waited.

"You speak Italian," she said finally, as if he were a mute who suddenly spoke.

"Uh huh, so?" he squinted.

"I mean, you are fluent in Italian," she repeated.

He nodded. "Of course, I am. Have you forgotten that my mother is Italian and that I lived here for several years? I went to university here and got my degree here...all in Italian."

She stared at him for another moment then dropped her gaze. "Sorry, I guess I'm overreacting, Cade. It's just that I didn't know you spoke Italian so...uh...fluently. I feel a little foolish is all."

He chuckled. "You should've asked."

She looked up at him for several long seconds, and then smiled. "True. I should've realized, I suppose. I think it's wonderful, of course. I guess I feel silly and even a little jealous. I mean, I'm the one with the Italian last name, married to an Italian for thirty-plus years, and I can barely say 'hello' and 'thank you' in Italian, that's all."

He nodded and squeezed her hand. "It's no big deal, really. We Americans are way too impressed with Europeans and their multi-lingual skills."

She nodded. "That's true. But it doesn't make me feel less envious."

"I can teach you, if you'd like. It's a beautiful language."

"Thanks. I'd like that. For you to teach me a little Italian, I mean." She glanced up at him and he felt like she was sending some whole other message entirely.

He grinned. "I'd like that, too," he said and paused. "To teach you a few lines, I mean," he added.

He handed her the ticket and passed the audio device to her. "I'll be back for you, Meara. I'll call you when my meeting is over, OK?"

She nodded. "Sounds perfect."

He smiled and turned to leave. He knew she was watching him as he walked down the stairs towards the Duomo and the piazza. Waiting on the other side of the piazza was he car that would take him to the meeting that he hoped would help him figure out their immediate future.

Chapter 41   Eight Miles High

Meara wandered through the museum feeling like she was two people in one. On the surface, she was middle-aged Meara, the American woman visiting the museum, but she was also the other Meara who had been oddly transported to Milan with no agenda, no business to be transacted, and no dues to be paid. She was here with a man who was beginning to interest her, although she dared not think it through too carefully. Her desire for a "happy ending" was sometimes overwhelming and she knew from experience that it could overtake her good sense.

She had always been like that – even as a child with her circle of dolls she had wanted to give them each a happy ending to every story. Was that a "girl thing" or was it unique to her, she wondered? So now here she was in Europe with a man she was sleeping with, a man she was interested in knowing better, deeper, more intimately, and there was a part of her that desperately wanted it all to end with wedding bells and happily ever after. It was like a snowball gaining force as it tumbled down a hill and became what? A snowman or an avalanche? Whichever it turned out to be, it must be reckoned with.

But, the problem was she wasn't sure that she really believed in happily ever after anymore. She thought she'd had it with Tony, way back when. Boy, she had been ever the optimist.

Looking back, she knew that Tony had never been a romantic, but who cared? She was certain that he loved her; she knew he wanted their children almost more than she did, but where was the romance in that? His whole approach to romance had felt so much like a business transaction. He looked around to find a wife, she was available, and he married her. Deal done, marriage consummated.

For her part, she craved romance. Not having it, made her want it all the more. And the fact that it was missing popped up in subtle ways and that was where things got raw. For instance, he never complimented her. She knew that what she wanted didn't always make sense. For instance, she wanted him to say that she looked good...or that she turned him on...or that there was nothing he thought about all day but holding her close and dancing until dawn.

Meara grinned and shook her head. OK, maybe not that last one. But heck, even so, wouldn't that have been romantic? To say you want to hold someone you loved until dawn? Swaying to music....holding each other in a sexy embrace...? She could almost hear a saxophone wailing.

She looked at the religious paintings surrounding her on the walls of the museum room. The paintings depicted saints, angels, Jesus, the Madonna, devils and gargoyles. She sighed. There certainly wasn't much romance in religious paintings; plenty of devotion, of course, but not much magic. For herself, she wanted knights and ladies in waiting leaning out of tall towers, wearing long flowing gowns, and...uh, flowers in their hair.

Meara chuckled out loud. She really needed to get her head on straight. Where was she going with this line of thought anyway? What it came down to was that Tony wasn't romantic, and she was dearly hoping that Cade wouldn't prove to be the same kind of disappointment. She wanted to have a second chance at it. That was the crux of it. But more than that, she wanted it to be real this time around. She didn't want it all to just be happening in her head.

She heard a bustling behind her and thinking that she would soon be sharing the room with other museum goers, she stood in front of a sculpture of the Madonna and child and waited, hoping the other people would move on so she could continue to enjoy her solitude.

"He's not here with you, then?"

Meara spun around at the question and gasped. It was the man from Stout Grove. "Uh, pardon me?" she responded, feeling her limbs tucking in and her body stiffening slightly. It was an oddly physical reaction to a man who had scared her, she thought.

"Your friend," he said, his American accent undisguised. "Cade Chambers, right?" He smirked for some reason.

"Chandler. Cade Chandler," she corrected. "Do you know Cade?" she asked.

He smiled. "Chandler. Yeah, right. All that Witness Protection bullshit." He nodded. "Let's see. Do I know him? Actually, no, not personally. But let's just say, I know a lot about him. In fact, I could be his brother I know so much." There was a mirthless smile on his lips that didn't reach his eyes.

He took a step closer to her. He didn't touch her but she felt as if she shouldn't move.

"Is...Is there something...some message you want me to give him for you?" Meara asked in a surprisingly timid voice.

He eyed her for several long seconds. "No. What could I say now anyway? No, I think the time for messages is over. I think it's time to get down to business."

"What?" Meara asked in bewilderment. "I'm sorry but I really don't know what's going on. What's this all about? Who are you?"

He blinked. Then he glanced down at his shoes and then back up at her. His eyes bore into hers. Several seconds passed. "Meara? That's your name, right?"

She nodded. "Yes."

"Meara, your boyfriend, Cade, has done a terrible thing and I plan to make him rectify it. You're going to help me." He nodded.

"Help you?" Meara felt her stomach quake and wondered if she might faint or vomit. This was, by far, the strangest encounter she'd ever had and she was at a loss as to what to do. What would happen next? She had no idea. There was no precedent in her life that would give her a clue, just a lot of third-rate movie plots flashing through her head. How could she rely on them for guidance?

He watched her and seemed to wait patiently for her to mentally process what he had been saying. "Yes, I want your help. But first, you're right, I should introduce myself – you have to call me something, right?" he said with a chuckle. "My name is Brian... Brian Reston."

He said it like she should know the name, but it meant nothing to her. She didn't know whether she should pretend to know who he was, play along, or be honest and admit she hadn't a clue.

She went with the latter. She shook her head, as if to clear it. "Sorry, Brian, but I don't know who you are. Is it a name I should recognize?"

"Only if your boyfriend has been completely honest and above-board," he said with a cocky grin. He saw that she was totally perplexed. He grimaced. "Christ! He never mentioned anyone named Reston? Not even like maybe Joe Reston? Joseph P. Reston?"

Meara's eyes grew round and she shook her head. She could see that he was angry that she didn't recognize the name.

Behind them, a group of tourists entered the room, murmuring in German, their heads together as they paused before a statue of a kneeling saint, and then moved to the far wall to view a stain glass window.

Brian jerked his head around and looked at the group. There were two couples and a little girl, about seven or eight years old. He turned back to Meara. "We should go someplace else to discuss this. This museum is too public. Besides, I like the idea that Cade might think you're missing."

Missing. The word rattled around in Meara's brain. What in the world did he mean?

"Come on. Let's go," he said and took her elbow to lead her through to the center galley hallway that ran the length of the building.

They would have to go down two sets of heavy stone stairways to the front visitors area where she would turn in her audio headset. She noticed that he didn't have a set. Apparently, he hadn't planned to browse.

She let him lead her as she took in her surroundings and realized she was having an almost out-of-body experience. She felt like she could see herself walking stiffly beside this young man, as if she were his mother and they were on an outing together. It was a peculiar sensation.

She tried to figure out why it all felt out of sync and odd and she realized it was because in the movies he would be pushing and shoving her around, proving his dominance. But Brian wasn't doing any of that. He was leading her, it was true, but he wasn't being mean or brutal about it. In fact, she didn't feel threatened at all – a good thing.

She glanced at him and studied his profile. He didn't look like a bad guy. Heck, he looked like one of Paul's nerdy friends, or like the funny-looking kid that took Donna to her first prom. Of course, on the other hand, he might be mentally unbalanced. She decided she needed to engage him to figure him out.

"Brian, where are we going?" she asked, in an almost conversational voice, as she tucked the audio headset into its pouch getting it ready to turn in.

"Not too far. I know a place where we can talk."

She nodded and looked at her watch. Cade had left her an hour ago; she wouldn't expect a call from him for another half-hour to an hour, at the soonest.

When they got to the desk on the first floor a woman pointed to some bins along the wall where it was apparent Meara was to leave her audio set. The woman nodded and said something in Italian, but Meara couldn't understand. Brian looked at Meara and seemed to ascertain that she didn't speak the language. He grinned. "No comprendez, huh?" He shook his head. "Isn't your last name Cellini?"

"I was married to an Italian-American, but I'm Irish-American."

"Ah," he said. "Too bad for you. Cade speaks Italian pretty good, though, doesn't he?"

Meara nodded. "Yes, surprisingly well, I thought."

Brian shrugged. "I suppose. 'Course he lived here for a while. What a chump."

"Why do you call him a 'chump'?" Meara asked.

"The government screws everybody eventually. Even guys like Cade who played their game."

Meara blinked. "Which government? Played what game?" The questions swirled in her thoughts.

Brian paused as he pulled the heavy door open for her and nodded for her to go out. They stepped out into the sunshine and he glanced around squinting as his eyes adjusted to the brightness.

Then he glanced down at her. "Really? He's said nothing to you about Minneapolis? About working for Northwest Airlines? About the Feds getting him to lie in court?"

Meara's mouth fell open. "Cade Chandler?"

Brian snorted. "Well, Cade Chambers, actually. But apparently he hasn't mentioned his name change to you either." He shook his head. "What a jerk."

He took her elbow again. She pulled away for a second and they faced each other at the top of the steps. "Brian, why should I go anywhere with you? I don't even know you."

He blinked in surprise. After a moment, he nodded. "That's true. But you'd be nuts not to go with me."

"Really? Why?" Meara demanded, her arms folded protectively across her chest.

He studied her and then shrugged. "Look, I can call Cade and set up a meeting with him. Heck, I thought he'd be in the museum with you. I saw the two of you go in together."

"He wanted to get me set up with the headphones," Meara explained.

Brian nodded. "You should come with me because now I think you and I should have a talk first. About Cade."

Meara felt a confusing flood of conflicting thoughts and feelings. Cade never mentioned the name "Chambers," and now she was discovering that there was so much else he hadn't mentioned. Brian was making her feel like she should know all these things, but should she really? She had known Cade less than two weeks, after all. Maybe it made sense that she didn't know as much as she'd like. But she prided herself in being a good judge of people and that pride was now being shaken. Could she be totally wrong about Cade? Had she been blindsided by a good-looking charmer?

What pissed her off was the sense that he'd been holding back on her. How was she supposed to deal with this Brian fellow without the facts, without even a shred of an idea of what this was all about?

"OK, Brian. I agree that you and I need to talk. I have lots of questions," she said.

"I thought you might," he said with a smirking grin. "Look, my car's parked just up here in the next block." He pointed as they crossed the street. "I know a nice place not far from here that'll give us good coffee and a private place to talk."

Meara studied him for a second, again seeing the youthful naiveté in his face. Finally, she nodded. "OK, that sounds fine.

A few minutes later they arrived at his car, parked along the street but hidden between two larger vehicles. He opened the driver's side door and said, "Hang on, I'll unlock the passenger door."

Meara looked at the tiny car. It was one of those tiny two-person rental cars. It looked like a clown car from the circus. She couldn't stop from grinning. "This is your car?"

He glanced at her then at the car as he ducked his head and lowered himself in. "Sure," he said as he pushed her door open. "Why pay a lot for a big car that can't maneuver in these tiny streets? That's what I figured."

Meara climbed in and felt the compactness of the vehicle even more now that she was inside it. The windshield was barely an outstretched hands' length from her face. She could tap the back windshield with the back of her head. It was making her feel just a bit claustrophobic.

"Is this thing safe?" she asked.

He chuckled. "I'm sure if we get hit, we won't survive the accident, so no sense worrying about it."

She rolled her eyes.

He pulled out into the main thoroughfare and she shut her eyes for a second, waiting for the jolt of a collision, but it was fine. The car was so small that it nimbly maneuvered in the traffic. She let out her breath.

She looked over at Brian, whose shoulder was nearly rubbing against hers. She saw that he was totally focused on his driving. Well, that was probably a good thing, she thought. Perhaps she should refrain from talking or asking him any questions until they got to wherever they were going.

Instead, she looked out the window and marveled at the close-up view she was getting of Milan as she looked up at the cars around them and at the people on the sidewalks. She felt like she and Brian in this tiny toy-sized car must present something of a spectacle, but actually they were getting no reaction at all from the other drivers or from the people in the streets. This car was nothing special to them, Meara decided. Back in Boston, it would've caused some double takes and maybe even gotten honked at.

"Uh, Brian?" she said.

He grunted. "Yeah."

"First of all, where are we going?" she asked.

He pointed ahead. "I'm staying at a *pensione* about five or six blocks from here. We're going there. They have a little cafe in front and we'll talk. It's a nice day for sitting outside, don't you think?"

She nodded.

"Can your other questions wait?" he asked. "I need to focus on the traffic. These Italians are kind of nuts." He paused. "No offense, of course."

She shook her head. "None taken. I'm Irish-American, remember?"

He smiled. "Oh, yeah. It's your name that keeps throwing me."

She studied him as he maneuvered cautiously in the heavy traffic. He seemed like a self-assured grown-up, on the one hand; but at the same time like a naive teenager on the other.

They turned just after a non-descript building with a small outdoor cafe in front, with only a handful of tables. All were empty at the moment. Brian drove the car down the alley next to the building. It turned out there were a few parking spaces in the back. They walked back down the alley to the street and sat down at one of the outdoor tables that looked as if it had been set for them.

Meara was waiting for Brian to begin explaining. She looked over at him, in anticipation.

Just then, the waiter came out tucking a rag into his back pocket. "Buon Giorno."

Brian interrupted him, "We're American. Could you speak English?"

"Of course. What is it you would like to have?" he smiled proudly at his perfectly phrased question.

Meara smiled. "Cappuccino?"

"And you, Signore?" he said nodding to Brian.

"Same. I'll have a cappuccino, too."

"*Buono*. Uh, very good." He dipped his head and turned to go back into the cafe.

Brian looked across the table at Meara. "So?" he asked.

"Really?" she shook her head in wonder. "You are going to sit there and just say 'So?' – I don't believe you!" she said, as surprised as he was by the fury in her voice. She realized it must be her body reacting to the confusion she felt and the topsy-turvy way her morning had suddenly changed course.

He looked up at her in real surprise. "Hey! What do you want from me?"

"I want the truth....or some semblance of it."

"The truth?" He repeated, then with a snarky grin, said, "Well, the truth is that your boyfriend..."

She put up her hand. "First, stop referring to Cade that way, OK? He's not my boyfriend. He's 'Cade' or he's 'Cade Chandler.' I'm offended by you calling him 'my boyfriend' in that tone of voice."

"Hey, either he's your boyfriend or he isn't. That's your problem, I guess, isn't it?" Brian said.

"Look, Brian, I just want to know what's going on." She let a breath out. "What is it you think I should know?"

Brian took in a few deep breaths. "Let's see? Where to begin? It took a while for me to find him. They hid him pretty good, or at least, that's what I thought at the time. It turned out that he'd left the US entirely. Go figure. I lost track of him completely. But after my father died, I hired an investigator and he found Cade. By then, he had returned to the US, took over his brother's law practice and all the rest. I was following him when he went to Oregon and that led me to you. I thought he might disappear again and I didn't want to lose him. Then I got an idea that the surest way to keep track of him might be through you. So here we are," he said looking at her meaningfully.

Oh Jesus, she thought, this is never going to make sense. She had no idea what he was talking about and wasn't really certain where to begin asking.

He must have realized she was lost because he began again. "My dad..." he said in a softer voice, and looked at her for several long seconds. She instantly could see that this was the gist of it. "My dad's name was Joe Reston," Brian said. "He worked for Northwest Airlines...."

Meara listened and realized that he was revealing far more by his tone than in the information he was providing.

"My dad... He loved his job. He maintained the jets and made sure they were turned around in perfect shape and ready for service for as many hours of flying as the company needed."

Meara watched Brian and saw that a look of pride had come into his eyes as he talked about his father's service to the airline.

"My dad was the supervisor of the maintenance crew for the airline. Any jet that came into Minneapolis-St. Paul airport, my dad's people had it covered. And that was all fine, for about fifteen years. But then the government had it's own agenda. They came in one day and wanted my dad and his crew to help test out some cloud seeding chemicals. It was all hush-hush. Some big secret government project, you know? They told him that all his guys needed to do was to put the chemicals into the tanks underneath the belly of the plane and the stuff would spray out in the skies over America. They told him they were testing the capabilities of the chemicals to seed the clouds to produce weather."

Meara blinked. Did she hear him correctly?

He continued. "Cade was a maintenance guy, but he didn't work in my dad's area; not normally anyway. He came in and subbed for a guy on sick leave and instead of keeping his nose clean and just doing the job, he ended up getting everyone in trouble – they were all sent to prison. Thanks to Cade Chambers. My dad got life in prison, for God's sakes!"

"I'm sorry, Brian," Meara said. "But I'm lost in this story. I didn't know Cade then. You want me to give credence to something that I can't even begin to understand."

Brian bent over a second and nodded. "I know. He should've told you all this. Let's begin again."

She waited in silence as he pulled himself together.

"My dad," Brian looked up into her eyes for a second, "He'd worked for Northwest since the beginning, since he was a teenager, really. He loved his job." Brian nodded. "Then the government wanted to check out this new weather-making chemical, so they asked the commercial jet folks to test it for them."

That didn't sound so ominous.

"They filled the jets with chemicals that could be sprayed among the clouds as they traveled on their way across the country. Maybe it would result in rain or snow, maybe it would break up weather, stop the rain or snow...I don't know."

Meara looked at him. "Stop the rain or snow? Can they do that?"

Brian snorted, "Oh, lady, you have no idea what they can do. It'd blow your mind."

"So? How does Cade figure in this?" she asked.

"Cade was an innocent bystander. He worked in one of the other maintenance groups. Avionics or something. Someone screwed up and assigned him to sub for a guy who was out sick. It was one of my dad's guys. Cade wasn't in the waste management group normally – so you might say that he just happened upon the scene. He saw some things that he thought weren't kosher. So he immediately jumped to the wrong conclusion, and he called in the Feds."

He paused dramatically, his hands splayed in the air in front of him. "But once he spoke up, the government didn't know what to do but to play along. It's like one part of the government was dicking out another part. The weather guys didn't want anyone to know what they were doing, so basically they let my dad and his crew take the fall. They got busted for drug running."

"Drug running? I thought you said they were seeding the clouds with chemicals."

"Sure, that was the real job, but they had to cover it up with something else – so they packed in some cocaine. They made it look like a drug running operation. Pretty smart, huh?"

"Smart?" she snorted. "It sounds insane."

"It was just a front – they had a little coke that was being shipped around. But it wasn't what they were doing. That was the cover is all."

"Running illegal drugs was their 'cover'? You know that doesn't make any sense, right?"

"It does if these weather chemicals were actually something worse, wouldn't you say?"

"What do you mean? I don't understand."

"These chemicals could poison the water, ruin crops, kill off animals, and destroy whole towns. There's no limit. Heck, it'd be better to have a cocaine epidemic, believe me!"

The waiter returned with two steaming cups that he carefully set in front of each of them. He made eye contact with Meara and then with Brian, waiting for their reactions.

Meara smiled and nodded, "*Grazie*."

The waiter grinned. Then he glanced at Brian, but Brian was frowning. The waiter looked disgusted, then shrugged and left.

Brian lifted the cup and blew on it lightly. He took a sip of the hot liquid with a loud slurping sound.

Meara lifted her cup, too, and breathed in the rich coffee aroma. She took a very small sip and was glad that she didn't take a bigger one. The coffee was scalding hot. She set the cup back in the saucer. She glanced over at Brian. "I don't understand why you're upset with Cade. He came in and saw that his fellow mechanics were running drugs illegally and he turned them in. What's wrong with that?"

Brian was just bringing the cup to his lips again when he stopped and just stared at her for several long seconds. "You're not listening to me, are you? My dad and his men were working WITH the government. They weren't really running drugs. They weren't doing anything illegal. They were goddamn patriots really."

"They were running drugs, Brian. You admitted as much," Meara stated with finality. "They were running drugs and that is illegal in our country. I don't care if they were covering up a government program or whatever other excuse they might have. Cade saw that they were doing something illegal and he called them on it. Drug running IS illegal, Brian. You know that, don't you?"

Brian rolled his eyes. "I know drug running is illegal, Meara. Of course, I do." He closed his eyes for several seconds. "What I'm trying to get through to you is that the drug running was a cover. Just a cover."

"Since when does the US government cover up a secret program with an illegal activity?"

Brian snorted loudly. "Uh, just about every time it does anything these days."

Meara shook her head and sighed audibly. "That's not true, Brian, but I don't have the time or energy to prove it to you right now. I will give you that the government makes mistakes on occasion. But it's not the government's policy to front a secret activity with an illegal one, OK?"

He chuckled. "Yeah, right."

She was quiet for several seconds. "Regardless of how you feel about our government, I still don't understand what you want with Cade? I mean, even if everything you say is the absolute truth, didn't all this happen years go? What do you want from him now?"

"My dad died in prison about ten years ago. He was forty-six years old. They said it was a heart attack." Brian closed his eyes then opened them and looked at Meara. "He was only forty-six years old."

"I'm sorry for your loss, Brian." She was quiet for a minute then added, "I lost my dad in 1983. He was killed by a suicide bomber in Beirut, at the American Embassy."

He glanced at her in surprise. "Oh, I'm sorry, I didn't know. That's really awful." He gazed at her, and then shook his head. "Then you know what it means to lose your father," he said simply.

She nodded. "Yes, I know," she said softly.

They didn't talk for several minutes. Instead, they both sipped their cappuccinos and glanced out at the quiet street. Occasionally, a scooter buzzed by, and a taxi or two, but this wasn't a busy thoroughfare.

"I want Cade to get my father's name cleared. He wasn't a criminal and he didn't do anything wrong."

Meara opened her mouth to disagree, but shut it. She knew there was no sense in bringing up the illegality of drug running, particularly while using a commercial airline jet as your distribution vehicle. "What do you want me to do?" she asked.

"I want to meet with Cade. I want you to set it up. Tell him no Feds. Those sons-of-bitches need to stay far, far away from me," he said with deep loathing.

"What if he refuses?" she asked, having no idea at all how Cade would receive the request.

"I think there's a lot of incentive for him to listen to me. Besides, I'm sure he's plenty sick of me following him around. But you can tell him that I can mess up his life in a dozen different ways if he wants to play it that way."

Meara felt a coldness creep down her spine as Brian said it. She wasn't sure whether Brian had it in him to do something really awful to Cade, but she knew that people did lots of crazy things for revenge when their families were involved.

"So that's it? I talk to Cade and get him to agree to a meeting with you? OK. How do I get in touch with you?"

"Give me your mobile phone," he said holding his hand out.

She rummaged around in her purse and pulled it out. He took it and scrolled around and pressed keys on it for several seconds. He handed it back and glanced up at her. "I'll call you on this phone tomorrow morning, around nine a.m. OK?"

She nodded and then glanced around. "Can...Can I go now?"

He looked surprised. "Of course, you can go," he said. He stood up. "Do you need me to take you back to the Duomo? I could drop you off."

She shook her head. "No, no, that's OK. I think I'd like to walk a bit, then I'll grab a cab or take the subway." She stood up too.

Suddenly she felt a bit awkward. She thought she should shake his hand or do something to end the encounter, but nothing seemed quite right for the occasion. What did one do in a situation like this, after all? She smiled wryly. "Well, then. I guess I'll be talking to you tomorrow."

"Around nine," he repeated amiably.

"OK, Brian," she said with a nod as she backed away. "Until tomorrow." She turned, waved slightly, and walked away.

This has been the oddest morning of my life, she thought in wonder. But when she thought of Cade, she just wanted to kill him.

Chapter 42   Up Tight

Cade was driven out of Milan in the limo for the meeting with his uncle and two cousins. His cousins, Sergio and Pietro, and their father, Vincente, were waiting for him at their company's headquarters in the town of Como on the shores of Lake Como. The drive was only about forty minutes. Cade had forgotten how close Milan was to the lakes district.

Arturo stopped in front of the building and turned to Cade, "This is it?" he stated, but there was a question in his voice at the same time.

Cade smiled. It was so Italian to state something and be asking if it were true all in the same breath. He nodded. "*Si*. This is it."

He got out of the car and stretched. He felt good. He couldn't remember the last time he felt so good and full of energy. He felt younger than he'd felt in years. He was sure that Meara was the reason. Having a woman in his life again was invigorating. Of course, it had been a long time since he'd had so much sex and on such a regular basis. Normally, he'd be celibate for weeks, waking up with aching testicles from some very raunchy dreams. And then suddenly he'd get home to Emily or someone else and he'd be like a drunk on a weekend binge. He couldn't get enough.

But over the past two weeks, he was beginning to rediscover how nice it was to not have to think about it, to know that by the time the sun set and the evening came, he would have a desirable woman in his arms. He hadn't been in a committed relationship in at least two decades, so this felt fresh and new to him. He suddenly realized why the married guys in the office never talked about sex or ever seemed to think about it much – they didn't have to, they had it any time they wanted, those lucky sons-of-bitches. All they had to do was to turn over and there she was. OK, well, they had to keep up their end of the relationship. Sure. If they had kids, they had to be all-in on the sharing of chores and responsibilities. But heck, he did that when Vanessa was little even without the promise of any sexual reward from Jan. Imagine if he'd stayed married to her? He could've been one of those guys.

Well, OK, Jan was a bit over the top, even back then. She really had some very restrictive ideas of what was "right" and what was "wrong." She wasn't terribly fun or adventurous in bed, and she always had a killer list of things she needed him to do 'when he wasn't too busy.' To be honest, Cade had come to believe that their divorce had been a stroke of good luck.

But, the wife at home didn't have to be Jan; he could've married someone else, and had the sex and home-cooked meals and someone to listen to his stories of success and occasional failure. He'd missed out, he realized now. He could've had this all along.

He smiled as he opened the door and took the steps two at a time. He didn't bother to knock at the door at the top of the stairs. He knew they'd be waiting for him. When he opened the door he wasn't disappointed.

"Hey, Uncle Vincente!" Cade said with a grin as he took the older man into a bear hug. "Missed you, old man," he said in English.

His uncle's smile was so broad that his eyes disappeared behind the folds of his eyelids. "Ah, Nico, you are a sight!" Vincente said with a sigh and a laugh. He coughed and cleared his throat, and then he turned and hollered into the next room "Sergio? Pietro? Nico's here. Come."

In a little while Vincente's old secretary, Marta, brought in a tray of coffee. She'd poured it into delicate little espresso cups. 'The good china,' Cade thought with a smile.

Vincente glanced up at Marta with a frown, "What? We have no Anisette for Nico's coffee?"

Her face clouded for only a second, then she smiled, "*Si*," she said with a nod as she scurried away. She returned with a bottle of Anisette, the licorice smelling alcohol that the Giordano men liked in their espresso.

Each man took a satisfied sip from his cup before settling around the table, as they had done so many times in the past. They had things to discuss; manly things like stalkers, a new woman, the past, and the future.

Cade loved that he came from such a family. He felt cradled in its embrace, even when he was thousands of miles away. He knew that if there were something any of them could do for him, they would do it without a second's hesitation. And he knew that he would do the same for any of them. He understood to the very core of his being what it meant to be in and of this family.

Italians weren't the only nationality that raised the notion of family to such a level, but he was proud that Italians didn't skimp. If you were 'family,' nothing more needed to be said.

"So?" Vincente said to open the dialog after they had a few sips of their espresso and were relaxed back into their seats.

Cade leaned forward. "You all remember my difficulties in America, with the drug-runners and the long court case."

The three men nodded and eyed Cade, waiting.

"The boss, Joe Reston, died in prison of a heart attack a number of years ago. You remember? That was when I was able to return to the U.S."

They all nodded and agreed that they remembered.

"Well, recently, a man has been following me. I don't know who he is yet although I'm certain he's connected to Reston. He keeps turning up, and he's become a nuisance."

They each frowned as they waited for Cade to continue.

"I don't know what he wants. I doubt it's going to be anything good. I want to find out what he wants, why he's following me, and I want to make him stop."

Vincente listened and nodded. "OK, then we need to find this man and sit him down for a talk, agreed?"

Cade nodded. "I'd like to maybe scare him a little, so that he won't continue being a nuisance. But, more than that, I'd like to understand why he's bothering me at all. Why now? What's the connection?"

They talked about the man and what Cade had observed and very slowly they talked Cade through the several times he'd noticed the stalker. They wanted a minute description – what the guy looked liked, how old he was, what he was wearing, and so on. As they asked more questions and Cade talked, he thought he remembered more and more details.

They asked whether the WitSec people had any ideas and Cade told them that he still hadn't heard back from them. He wasn't sure if that meant they didn't know anything or no longer cared, or what.

Vincente nodded in thoughtful silence. He glanced up at Cade finally. "Let's make a plan then. Maybe if you can get the guy to follow you up here, we could take him out on the boat. That would be very private and a good opportunity to get your questions answered."

Cade nodded. "I'll see what I can do."

"So," Pietro said with a grin, as he nudged Cade, "Tell us about the new lady, huh? Nate called last night and he said that Vanessa told him...."

Cade rolled his eyes and interrupted, "Nate and Vanessa are spreading gossip. It's just the novelty..."

"Well," Sergio teased, "Vanessa likes her. She wants us to give her a big welcome."

Vincente chuckled at his nephew's discomfort, "So Nico, when is your mother going to meet the new lady? That's what I'd like to know. My sister is not going to let you get away without a look at the girlfriend."

The three men nudged each other and laughed at Cade's expense.

Cade smiled. "Yeah, I know. I'm going to call her this morning to tell her I'm in Milano. Maybe she'll invite us to dinner tonight, what do you think?"

They all laughed. Vincente agreed, "Better get it done soon. Otherwise, Maria will be hard to live with."

"She'll be building things up in her mind," Sergio added.

Pietro nodded, "She wants to know every detail of her children's lives."

Cade agreed, "All the women in this family are noisy and far too interested in our private lives, if you ask me."

"True, Giordano women are a force to be reckoned with," Vincente said.

"I'm surprised you think you have a private life, to be honest," Sergio grinned. "I know I have never had one. Ah, but perhaps you Americans are especially blessed..."

Cade nodded, "We are most definitely 'especially blessed,' he said with a salacious grin that made the other three men roar with laughter.

Marta returned and they muffled their humor. She looked at Cade, "A telephone call has come for you. It's your mamma," she said primly.

Cade looked around the table. "OK, which one of you told my mother that I'm here? It was going to be a surprise," he said. He shook his head in disgust. "What a family!" he muttered as he got up and followed Marta to the outer room where the telephone receiver was lying among the papers on her desk.

"Please, you can use my phone," she pointed at the desk. "Shall I leave?"

Cade shrugged, "No, it's fine. I have no personal life," he said loud enough so that the three men in the other room would be sure to hear him.

They responded with more laughter. Cade just shook his head.

"Buon Giorgno, Mamma," he said into the phone with a smile. For as much as she was a pain in the neck at times, he loved her despite her nosiness.

Cade chatted with his mother for a short while, long enough to explain that he was back in Milan to follow up on some business deals and that yes, he had brought a lady with him, but that she was just a friend, he emphasized. The sum of it was that his mother was expecting them for dinner at seven this evening. It was pretty much what he had expected. He just hoped that Meara would be amenable. Personally, he dreaded dragging anyone into a family dinner unprepared. Because she would be the first woman since Jan that they'd actually met, there was no doubt that they would assume there was some significance in that fact.

After hanging up, he returned to the men in the other room. They looked up at him with interest, as if they hadn't just listened in on every word he'd said.

"I assume all of you will be at dinner, as well?" Cade said as he eyed them.

Vincente broke into a huge grin, "Are you kidding? Who would miss this event?"

The three laughed again and Cade had to smile. What a family.

He called Arturo to pick him up and an hour later he was back in Milan. He looked at his watch and saw that it was twelve-thirty. No wonder he was so hungry. He dialed Meara's mobile phone.

"You done?" he asked.

She waited a beat. "I've had an interesting morning, Cade. You and I need to talk."

He could hear the coolness in her voice and it took him by surprise. What had happened in the couple of hours since he'd dropped her off, he wondered?

"Sure. Where are you? I'm in the car with Arturo, we can pick you up."

"Hang on, let me look at the street sign," she said and her voice was gone for several seconds. " OK, I'm on Foro Buonaparte. Do you know where that is?"

"Jesus! What are you doing over there?"

"It's a long story," Meara said. "One I think you're going to be very interested in hearing."

"Are you near the Cairoli Castello? It's a roundabout with surface trolley tracks running across it and a statue of a guy on a horse in the middle...."

"Yeah. I can see it just up ahead," Meara said.

"Good. There's an outdoor restaurant on the north corner. I'll meet you there."

"NORTH corner? How do I know which is 'north?'"

Cade grinned, "The horse's rump. That'll be the north corner, OK?"

"OK, see you at the horse's rump...." Meara repeated. He wasn't sure or not if there was a smile in her voice.

He was looking forward to seeing her.

Chapter 43   Runaway

Meara found the Largo Benedetto Caroli roundabout and noticed which way the horse and rider were facing and easily found the outdoor restaurant Cade had referred to. She was enchanted to look down the short street to see the front of Sforza Castle, as well. She knew that there were a number of museums housed at the castle, but even walking the grounds would be fun on a gorgeous afternoon like this.

It may very well take the whole afternoon to talk to Cade about Brian, his father, and all the history that made up Cade's past and that he hadn't thought important enough to tell her. She was hurt at his lack of trust, but mostly it pissed her off that he seemed to be treating her like a child.

She asked to be seated at a table facing the street to watch the passers-by and to keep an eye out for Cade. The waiter brought her a menu and with hand gestures, simple English and a few words of Italian, she made him understand that she was waiting for someone. She ordered a cappuccino, her third for the day and it was only lunchtime. But then, she was sure that jet lag and staying awake to fool around with Cade probably were to blame for her body's demand for caffeine.

She loved being in the middle of a busy city and getting the chance to just sit by the wayside and watch it flow by. Every person that walked by had a story, some business to transact, class to attend, or friend to meet. She liked trying to sort the people out and to give each a backstory. It passed the time and was a favorite form of entertainment from her childhood.

Her family had done a lot of traveling to exotic places, but that also meant a lot of time alone and a lot of time waiting. She got good at killing time, while waiting for airplanes to arrive or depart, for buses to stop or start, for people to be on time or be late. As a child, she didn't have any control over what was happening around her. She was simply pulled along in the wake of her father's career moves. But that was OK with her. Everyone had to be raised somewhere, or in her case, everywhere.

So she'd become good at making up games that she and her brothers and sister could play that would keep the younger ones entertained and out of her parents' hair. Mostly it would be some kind of word or guessing game, like this, where they'd have a go at guessing the backstory of the strangers around them. Sometimes the goal was the more absurd the story the better, but the best stories were always the ones that had a ring of truth. She remembered once her brother, Danny, guessed that a woman was waiting for her son to arrive, when not a minute or two later, a young boy did walk up to her and give her a hug. Danny couldn't have been prouder had he actually been a psychic.

She took a sip of her cappuccino and was startled to look up and see Cade taking the seat across from her. "Where did you come from? I've been watching for you!" she said.

He grinned, his dimple showing for just a second. "I had Arturo drop me off down the street a bit. There's a garage not far from here and I wanted to point him in the right direction." He looked up and the waiter appeared, seemingly out of nowhere. Cade nodded and chatted amiably in Italian with the young man.

Meara watched him, realizing that she was seeing him through new eyes after her meeting with Brian. Still, she noticed how he took an interest in the boy and joked with him and she couldn't help but admire his way with people. It made it hard to reconcile this man with the one Brian described, who was hiding some deep dark secrets from her. When the waiter left, she asked, "What did you say to him?"

He glanced at her and smiled, "Oh, I just commented that he was so fast coming to the table he must play football...uh, you know, soccer."

She nodded. "He obviously liked that compliment."

"He wanted to know if I'd seen the game against Torino yesterday. I said I hadn't, but I hoped that our great Milano team took care of business."

"And did they?" she asked.

"Apparently," he laughed. "It's a huge rivalry, as you can imagine."

She looked around. "It's funny how provincial we are in the U.S. – it's as if nothing happens anywhere else – we are so uninterested."

"True. It's very frustrating when you've been overseas and get back to the States, and even in the major cities, you can't get any international news – well, unless the U.S. has bombed someone, or there's been a huge natural disaster."

"We're very ethnocentric; more so than other countries, I think. It's odd cosidering America was founded by immigrants."

"Well, in Europe, it makes sense they are more tuned in because there are so many countries in a rather small area, and they are so interlinked. But even over here, you hear more on the news and in the newspapers about what's going on in Africa and Asia than we do in America."

Meara was quiet a moment, then said, "We need to talk, Cade..." She was interrupted by the return of the waiter.

He set a beer in front of Cade, who smiled his thanks. Cade looked at Meara quizzically. "You want to order some lunch before we get all serious and talk?"

She could tell he had no idea what she was planning to ask him about. Finally she nodded, "I'm starved. I was thinking about some pasta...maybe ravioli." She glanced at the menu then handed it to him. "Here, find me something good."

He grinned, "OK," he said as he glanced down the menu. He turned to the waiter and gave a rapid-fire order and the waiter nodded with a smile and said, "*Certo!*"

Meara smiled at the waiter. "Well, I understood that, at least," she said.

They watched the cars going by in the street for a minute or two, and then he squinted at her. "So how did you get over to this part of town anyway?"

Meara's good mood clouded over. "Do you want to eat first? I have a feeling you're going to be upset when I tell you about my morning."

He frowned. "Really? I can't imagine what I'd get upset about," he said.

She stared at him. "How about if I said that I met with the guy who was following us in Oregon?"

Cade's head jerked up. She knew that would get his attention. "What?" he exclaimed.

She continued, "He must've followed us to the museum this morning. After you left, he turned up in one of the rooms. Scared the shit out of me, as you can imagine."

Cade's mouth fell open. "You talked to him?"

"Oh, more than just talked. We got into his car and drove to another part of town and had a cappuccino together. Which, by the way, I've had three of now, and I'm starting to feel shaky from all the caffeine in my system." She pushed her cup away.

Cade was sitting up straight and leaning in towards her. "Are you...did he...are you OK? Jesus!"

She blinked and suddenly her anger returned. "Really? NOW you're worried about whether I'm OK? Wouldn't it have made more sense to warn me that someone was following us? At least, give me a heads-up?" Even she could hear the steel and biting sarcasm in her voice.

Cade jerked back a bit, as if she'd slapped him. "Meara, I...."

She shook her head. "No, Cade, just listen. I was a little hurt to discover how little you trusted me with your whole complicated life history, but now I'm just pissed at being treated like an imbecile... or a child." She looked at him pointedly. "That is what you were trying to do, isn't it? Trying to protect this poor defenseless little female?"

He breathed out heavily. "Meara, I didn't..."

"No, you didn't think about how it'd make me feel, did you? I am an adult, for God's sakes, Cade. Certainly you've noticed that. It is offensive that you'd hide information from me...heck, not to mention that you would bring me to Milan under false pretenses...I'm not some bimbo along for the ride, you get that, right?"

Cade's eyebrows rose in surprise. "I never said...I never thought..."

She held up her hand. She drew in a deep breath and then her voice turned somber and a little sad, "See? We should've eaten first...because now, I'm not hungry." She stood up and he immediately stood up, too, but she shook her head. "Sorry, Cade, I'm too angry to talk about this right now. I think I need to walk this off ... alone, OK?"

"But, Meara..."

She looked glumly at him. "No, Cade, believe me, you don't want to be around me for a little while."

She put the strap of her handbag over her shoulder. Then she lowered her head and stepped out into the stream of pedestrians and like a twig in a stream she let herself be carried along by the crowd of people down the street towards the castle.

After a few blocks, she took a deep breath. After a minute or two, she sighed long and low. Well, she'd screwed that up royally. Damn! She knew she didn't want to be walking away from him – the one guy who seemed to bring her to life again — but she couldn't go back now; she was too full of caffeine and pride to turn around. She'd just have to play this through.

Chapter 44   Bus Stop

Cade felt like he'd taken a body blow. What in the world had just happened? He stood watching the top of Meara's head as she melted into the crowds of tourists and other pedestrians heading towards the Sforza Castle. He'd follow her, of course, but he had to pay for their uneaten meal first. Damn, and he was hungry, too.

The waiter, Matteo, came out with the tray of food and stopped, looking confused and anxious. Cade gave him a shrug and half-smile. "She's gone," he said in Italian.

The boy glanced down the sidewalk then back at Cade and he grimaced, "*Mi dispiace* (I'm sorry)," the boy said quietly. He gestured at the food on the tray with a questioning look.

Cade took out his wallet and gave the boy money for the meal. "*Grazie*, Matteo," he said with a sigh. He glanced longingly at the tray of food, and at the last minute took a couple of slices of the bread that were tucked in a basket covered with a cloth. The bread was warm and smelled wonderfully. He bit into one of slices and wrapped the other two in a napkin and put them in his jacket pocket.

"*Grazie, signore*," the boy answered. "*Buona fortuna*! (Good luck!)," he called after Cade.

Cade waved over his shoulder without turning. He was intent on catching up to Meara, although as he strained to see ahead he wasn't sure the woman's head he was following was actually hers. But, he assumed she would continue on towards the castle and its grounds. And if she really was going to walk it off, as she said, that would be a good place to do it.

But why was she so angry, he wondered? What had the stalker told her? Heck, he knew he was at a real disadvantage since he still didn't know who the guy was or what he wanted. He sighed. Apparently, Meara did, though. And that was not a comforting thought.

She was right, of course, he should've told her everything right from the beginning. In his defense, he hadn't kept anything secret on purpose; there just never seemed to be an opportune time to bring it up, and where to start was always a problem. Well, of course, first he should've told her his real name was Cade Chambers, not Cade Chandler. God, he felt like such an idiot. For a lawyer trained to communicate, he was laughable.

As he crossed the Piazza Castello, the Sforza Castle stood before him with its huge fountain and clock tower just ahead. There was a long line of tour buses parked all the way down to the next intersection to his left. He thought he recognized Meara on the other side of the fountain heading towards the castle's drawbridge entrance. Good, he hadn't lost her.

Then his phone rang. Was it her? He automatically scanned the crowd for her but now he didn't see her. He frowned as he glanced down at his phone and saw it was a long distance call from the U.S.

"Hello?" he said, pausing near one of the benches surrounding the fountain and sticking a finger in his other ear to cut down on the distracting sounds around him.

"Hello?" he said again. There was static for a second then it cleared and he heard a man's voice. It only took a few seconds to realize it was a return call from WitSec. He looked around and quickly trotted away from the fountain and crowds of people, moving off the sidewalk towards a couple of trees where he hoped it would be quieter.

"Just listen," the voice said. "The guy is Joseph Reston's son, Brian Reston. He's thirty-three years old, a contract computer programmer. Belongs to a bunch of far-right conspiracy groups. We'd like to know what he's got going on, too. One of our guys will be in contact with you over there." The line went silent.

"Hey!" Cade said into the phone, but it was too late. The person had already hung up. He pulled the phone away from his ear and stared at it as he ended the call on his end. Conspiracy groups? Damn! What are we getting involved with here, he wondered?

The thought of "we" brought a jolting reminder of where he was. Jesus, Meara! He hurried back to the sidewalk and jogged around the edge of the fountain dodging groups of Asian tourists and young mothers pushing squirming babies in strollers. He needed to get into the castle grounds before he lost track of Meara completely. He had to talk to her. He had to find out what she knew about this Brian Reston fellow. His heart was racing now. Suddenly, this was all becoming too real and moving way too fast.

Chapter 45   Get Ready

Meara let the crowd move her through the thick stone entrance to the castle fortress. Inside was a large courtyard area, with segmented grassy areas and benches along the broad packed dirt walkways. It was all enclosed by the surrounding ramparts of the castle walls. Ahead was another gate leading into the Corte Ducale, which over the centuries had been one the duke's residences. Today the old buildings contain a number of civic museums, including a museum of ancient art, another of musical instruments, an archaeological museum, a furniture museum, and even an Egyptian Museum. Meara wished she were in the mood to wander through a museum – any museum – this afternoon. But she was just too upset.

She slowed her pace a bit. She thought slowing down might help to get her emotions and thoughts back under control. She knew from city maps she had studied as well as from previous trips to Milan, that there was a huge park on the other side of the castle. She would head in that direction.

To her right she noticed a temporary stage was being put together. She wondered what it was for. She assumed it was for some event to take place later that evening perhaps. She paused to watch the young men hollering instructions at each other as they worked together. There was a lot of chatter as one of them backed the truck into place that would be the foundation of the stage. She smiled as they laughed and joked with each other. You didn't need to know the language to understand what they were saying. They seemed to be having a great time.

One of the young men squatted down in front of the sound equipment and began fiddling with the controls. After a minute or two, music filled the air. Meara crossed her arms and leaned her head to one side as she listened. Well, go figure! It was music she recognized. The Beatles' "Here Comes the Sun." Now she recalled seeing the posters at the entrance about a special tribute event scheduled for the anniversary of the release of the Beatles' Abbey Road album.

It filled her with a familiar happiness. One of the young men glanced over and caught sight of her and put his hand in the air with a thumbs-up gesture, waiting for her reaction. She grinned and returned the thumbs-up to indicate she approved.

She used to hate the way Italian men responded to women, sometimes gesturing and making lewd comments. Well, she still did, but this was nice – just being acknowledged without any sexual overtones.

She moved to a bench nearby and sat down to listen and to watch the young people working. It was nice to have something happy and engaging to focus on after the fight – if she could even call it that – with Cade.

A minute or two passed and then Cade sat down on the bench next to her. She didn't even have to look up to know it was him. She realized she had been expecting him.

"Sorry," he said quietly. "I've been a jerk."

She turned her head to look at him. "You won't get a fight from me about that."

The edge of his mouth turned up but he suppressed the smile. "I should've told you everything from the start. I wanted to, but..." he stopped and sighed. "There just never seemed to be a right time."

She waited, but when he didn't say anything more, she looked at him more sharply. "Is that it?"

He looked nonplussed. "For my apology? What more did you want? I could get down on my knees...would that help?"

She smiled and closed her eyes for a second. "I don't care about your apology, Cade. I want to hear what it is you should've told me from the start."

"Really?" he said, looking around. "Now?"

"Is this not a good time for you?" she asked, knowing and not caring that she was being more bitchy than witty.

"Now's good. What do you want to know?" he asked.

She sat up, "Oh no you don't! It's not my job to drill you with questions. You TELL me what it is I should know about you, Cade. That's what I want."

He closed his eyes for a second. "All right. First of all, my real name is not Cade Chandler; it's Cade Chambers. But now that I've been using the Chandler name for two decades or more, it has become my "real" name, so maybe you shouldn't consider that a lie," he said looking at her for a response.

She didn't say anything, just waited for him to continue.

"Anyway, most of my background that you already know about is accurate. My dad was in the Air Force and I was a military brat until I went into the Army after high school. Then I was in Vietnam for two tours. I returned to the States just before I turned twenty-one and like most Vietnam vets, I came back a mess. After a couple of months of screwing around, my dad kicked me out of the house. I think it was his attempt at 'Tough Love.' Cade smiled without humor. "After that, I went to college for a year but didn't go back the next fall. I felt like I was a hundred years older than the other kids on campus and I couldn't stand being so out of sync with everything and everyone around me." He paused for a minute, not looking at her, but watching the group of kids huddled around the stage and the truck. Another Beatles tune wafted through the air, "If I Fell in Love With You." Listening to the lyrics, he shook his head slightly with a rueful smile.

She was watching the kids, too, and heard the song, one of her early favorites. She saw his smile and wondered what he was thinking. "What's funny?" she asked.

He glanced at her and shrugged. "Nothing. Uh, where was I?"

"Dropping out of college," she replied dryly.

He nodded. "Well, after leaving college, I bummed around for a while, then found a job in Minneapolis working for Northwest Airlines. It was their hub, where their maintenance facilities for all the aircraft were located. I'd done aviation mechanics in 'Nam and had the kind of experience they were looking for. It was a good union job and paid well. So, I stayed and worked there for just over ten years. It ended when I became a government whistleblower and then the next thing I knew the Witness Protection program, WitSec, took over my life."

She sat up, "WitSec? What's that?" she asked.

"Witness Security," he replied. "They are supposed to protect witnesses who might otherwise be in danger when going up against bad guys in court. The program started when the government was trying to find a way to get witnesses to take the stand against the Mafia. They realized that the only way it could be done was to make them disappear into some other part of the country with new names and a brand new life."

"Is that what happened to you?"

"Sort of. They gave me a new name and moved me to a new location; but then it got compromised by some of Reston's henchmen, and they had to move me again. By the third move, I decided I'd had enough and I dropped out of the program and moved here to Italy. By then, my dad was dead and my mother had moved back here. I had a large extended family over here. It was the perfect cover."

She was interested now. "So how long did you live here?"

"Eight or nine years, all told. At first, I worked at a small airport near Como, just north of here. Then my brother, Curt – Nate's father – talked me into going back to school and getting my law degree. It sounded like a good idea; something with a future, so I went to school here in Milan. At the time I figured I'd use the law degree here in Italy, maybe work at my uncle's company. But then, out of the blue, Reston died in prison. WitSec notified me, and Curt talked me into coming back to the States and working in his law practice. He was a partner by then and had a lot of pull. Of course, I had to take some law courses back in the States, but after that, I passed the bar and joined his firm. Curt died of a coronary four years later. That was back in 2000. So, that's my story, or the gist of it, anyway." He watched her for several seconds. Finally he asked, "So, Meara, how come you haven't asked me who Reston is?"

She jerked her head up, "What?"

"I've mentioned this guy Reston a couple of times and you haven't asked me who he was, which I have to assume means you already know who he is."

"Is that the lawyer in you that notices that kind of thing?" she asked.

"Probably. So?" he asked gently.

"Well, I told you I spent the morning with our friend from the redwoods. As it turns out, his name is Brian Reston. By the way, he told me HIS story right off the bat. And of course, he couldn't believe I'd never even heard yours." She looked at him pointedly.

He sighed. "And I'm sorry about that...again."

"He wants to meet with you," Meara said.

"He does?" Cade said in surprise. "Really? Because I'd like to meet with him, too."

"Good. Then maybe we can get this thing over with quickly, OK?" she said.

Cade put up his hands. "We just need to figure out where and when. Tell me something, Meara. Do you know what he wants from me?"

Meara blinked. She wasn't sure how she should respond. She knew Brian wanted his father's name cleared, but she thought maybe that was something he should discuss with Cade, one-on-one. She said, "He wants to meet with you. He wanted me to set it up."

But she felt a twinge of conscience that she should say more to Cade and tell him all that she knew. On the other hand, Cade hadn't been all that forthcoming with her, and Brian had, so she wasn't entirely sure where her loyalties lay, at the moment.

Cade nodded. "Good. Set it up. I'll meet with him."

Meara stood up. "Cade, I need to walk a bit. Think about all this." She stopped and then turned and looked at him. "You coming?"

He grinned with obvious relief. He obviously hadn't thought he'd be welcomed. "Yes. I'd like that." He reached for her hand and squeezed it for a second. He put his other hand into his pocket. "Oh," he said. He glanced at her. "You hungry, Meara? We left a pretty good lunch back there, you know."

She smiled ruefully. "Sorry about that. And yes, I'm starving, why?"

He pulled a couple of slices of bread wrapped in a napkin from his pocket. "Because I brought lunch." He grinned as he handed a slice to her.

She smiled at him. "Thanks, Cade. Nice of you to think ahead."

"I try to...on occasion," he added with a smile.

Chapter 46   Beyond the Sea

Cade held Meara's hand as they walked through the Sempione Park on the other side of the Castle. It was a huge park – one hundred and sixteen acres — with walkways crisscrossing from one end to the other. They passed a couple of groups of school children, a few couples strolling hand-in-hand, and a busload or two of tourists. There were also several people on bicycles.

"Meara," Cade said as he walked alongside her. "I met with my uncle and cousins this morning."

She glanced at him, "That must've been nice for you."

"Yeah, well, sure, it was great seeing them again. But while I was with them, uh, my mother called and invited us to dinner tonight."

"You and your cousins?" she asked.

Cade chuckled, "No, I meant, you and me."

Meara looked at him, "We're going to have dinner with your mother this evening?" she repeated, her eyes growing round.

He nodded. "Yeah, if it's OK with you."

She was quiet for a minute. "Well, sure, why not? I'd like to meet your mother actually. Besides, Vanessa said she's a real character. You know, a woman worth meeting."

He thought about that for a minute. He wasn't sure if Vanessa saying his mother – her grandmother! – was a real character was a particularly good reason to go ahead with this meeting.

"Yeah, well, no doubt she is a real character, but keep in mind that she's also my mother."

Meara smiled warmly and squeezed his hand. "It's OK, Cade, I promise I'll be nice, all right?"

He closed his eyes. "I didn't mean…"

She squeezed his hand again, "I know. I know. She's your mother, Cade. I get it."

He suddenly felt enormously unburdened. Meara would be fine with his mother. He wasn't so sure if the reverse was true. Both were formidable women. He was only just beginning to realize that in spades. But for now, he felt things would be fine. Still, he crossed his fingers.

They returned to the apartment late in the afternoon. He felt completely done in by the day, by his jet lag, and by the energy and strain it had taken to juggle the events of the day. It took everything in him to keep all the plates in the air, if not plates, then surely burning torches or chainsaws.

But, Meara, he noticed, was hyper-alert and alive as they entered the apartment. Why wasn't she as tired as he felt, he wondered?

"I'm thinking about a nap before we go to dinner," Cade said.

She grinned, "Really? You're up for that now?" she asked coyly.

Actually, he hadn't been thinking about sex at all. Which was certainly a first, but he'd honestly just been thinking about closing his eyes and resting. He smiled. "I'm beat, really, Meara."

She nodded, "Hmmm, me too. But, no, you go ahead, I think I'll give a call to Donna and Paul first. Check in with them, you know."

He glanced at her. Just over her shoulder he could see into the next room and the large bed with its soft duvet comforter tucked around the pillows. He longed to be there, his head resting between the mounds of pillows. God, even that sounded sexual.

He smiled and kissed her forehead tiredly as he passed her. "OK then, I'll get a little shut-eye. Wake me if I sleep too long, OK?"

She smiled and patted his shoulder. "Don't let the bedbugs bite."

He didn't bother to take his clothes off. He just kicked off his shoes before sinking into the thick duvet and was probably asleep before his head hit the pillow.

Chapter 47   In My Room

Meara was glad to see Cade fall into the bed. He did look tired. And she would love to join him, but she wanted to see if she could get in touch with Brian to let him know that Cade was open to a meeting with him. She pulled out the mobile phone, and scrolled through the contacts. There was no Brian Reston listed. What exactly had he done when he borrowed her phone earlier that day? She assumed it'd be easier to get a hold of him, not harder.

She sighed. Well, she'd just have to wait until nine the next morning, she supposed.

She turned and looked through the doorway to the large bed and Cade's prone body sprawled across it. What a strange day it had been for them. This morning they awoke in each other's arms, making love, happy together. Then he'd dropped her off at the Duomo museum, she'd met Brian, and her day had skittered off into a whole new direction.

She'd learned disturbing things about Cade and then met up with him again and it all fell apart and they seemed out of sorts with each other. They'd parted, and then come back together again. It was like some huge cosmic dance. Now she was back in the apartment with him and he was sound asleep in the bedroom while she was wide awake here in the living room. In another hour or two they'd be with his mother. How much weirder could things get, she wondered? Well, OK, she didn't see the sense in testing THAT.

She stood up and moved into the bedroom. She stood for a minute or two just looking at Cade as he slept. Men were so vulnerable looking when they were asleep. His arm was curled up like a child's next to his face; it reminded her of Paul when he was little; so sweet.

She kicked off her shoes and slowly removed her clothing until she was standing next to the bed naked. She climbed in next to Cade and cuddled up next to him. His arm came out almost automatically to pull her in and she smiled in contentment. He opened his eyes for a minute when he realized she was naked.

"Ah," he said groggily. "You're one move ahead of me, I see," he said into her hair. She burrowed into him feeling the heat from his body warm her cool skin.

"Yes, I am," she said softly. "No need to sound surprised."

Meara woke an hour later feeling rested and refreshed. It was a minute or two before she remembered that they were supposed to be at his mother's for dinner this evening. For a moment she didn't want to go, but she knew that she must make the effort. She really liked Cade and she knew meeting his mother and gaining her approval would be important, if not now, then perhaps for the future.

She turned into Cade's warm body. He groaned at her movement. "Cade," she said in a whisper. "We've got to get going if we're going to make it to your mother's for dinner."

He groaned again.

"I know. I'd like to stay here with you for the night too. But that's just our jetlag talking. We need to get up and get to dinner at your mother's. Come on."

He turned over. His eyes were slits as he looked at her. "You're serious, aren't you?" he said thickly.

"Hey, you were the one who invited us to your mother's for dinner. I'm just the innocent bystander in this," she replied with a laugh.

He smiled and sighed. "But I'm so tired."

She grinned. "Me too. You should not have said 'yes' to this dinner, my love," she said softly.

His eyes opened, "Really? I'm your love?" He grinned widely, like he'd caught her out.

"Hey! I'm just trying to get you moving, Cade. Don't take anything I say too seriously," she added with a laugh. "As IF I would say I loved you first! Really, AS IF!" she said defiantly.

He grinned with his eyes closed. "You will, darlin', you most certainly will," he said into the pillow.

He strained to stretch himself up. "Oh God, I really need to sleep," he murmured helplessly.

She chuckled, "I know just how you feel. I would love to lie here next to you and touch you, and...uh, caress you, and uh, you know, TOUCH you," she teased, now laughing as he reached for her. "Come on, Cade, we've got to get up and get ready to go. Arturo will be downstairs in a half-hour."

Cade groaned again. He turned his hand covering his eyes. He raised his head and looked at her. "Oh God, you look so good."

She grinned. "Yeah? You like the naked look?"

He nodded and groaned approvingly, "I do."

"Well, you'll like it lots better AFTER our dinner with your mother, OK?" she said. "Really, we have to get moving!" "

He sighed and let out a long breath. "Yup. You're right. But when we get back here in a couple of hours, you just look out!" He smiled.

She smiled too. "I'll be ready, don't you worry," she said, eyeing him. She got up and walked across the room to the bathroom. She knew he was watching her naked bottom as she moved and for the first time in years she didn't think it mattered. Her body wasn't as pert as her twenty year old self might've been, but it didn't matter because she was pretty sure she looked good to him.

Chapter 48   I Heard it through the Grapevine

Cade took a quick shower after Meara was done. While he was in the shower he could see her through the frosted shower door, drying her hair and applying makeup in front of the double mirrors. When she finished, he would shave. He knew his mother would notice any stubble and would comment. He didn't need any of her comments tonight. Just get me through this evening, he thought, his eyes lifting to the ceiling but praying to no one in particular.

Later, while he was shaving in front of the bathroom mirror, Meara came in half-dressed in an unbuttoned ivory colored blouse over her lacy bra and panties. She met his eyes in the mirror. "When did you want to meet up with Brian Reston?" she asked like a secretary getting ready to make an appointment.

"Huh?" he asked, pausing the razor just under his left sideburn, his cheek was sucked in, ready for the pull of the blade. He waited for her to explain.

"Well, he's going to call me in the morning and I just wanted to know what you want me to tell him."

"He's going to call you in the morning?" he repeated.

She nodded. "Nine o'clock."

He looked in the mirror and eyed her for a minute. "He's not your son, you know, Meara. You just met him less than twenty-four hours ago," Cade said. "You've got that motherly look in your eyes."

Meara stiffened slightly. "I don't think of him as a son," she said.

"You do...you seem to do that with any young man who is roughly around Paul's age."

"That's silly. Why do you say that?"

"Remember when we first met on the plane? Remember the kid standing in front of us, scared to death, as he proposed to his girlfriend? You looked up and you saw Paul – I know you did — and you empathized with that kid just as if it was Paul standing there. I can tell from your voice that you're starting to empathize with this Brian Reston," he said.

Meara blinked and thought back for a moment. "Brian told me about losing his father. I could tell how much it hurt him," she admitted finally. She sighed and she shrugged. "It's true. Ever since Paul was over in Afghanistan, I seem to have become overly sensitive to young men with burdens to bear." She felt tears fill her eyes but she chuckled. "You know what I did when Paul was in Afghanistan? I prayed to my dad that he'd especially watch over his grandson, Paul."

Cade grinned at her in the mirror, "You prayed to your FATHER?"

She nodded. "Well, come on, it wouldn't make sense to pray to God. I mean, let's face it, at least my father had a dog in the fight, so to speak."

"And you think God didn't?" he asked.

"Cade, ALL the dogs in the fight were God's. I couldn't expect him to play favorites, could I?" She shook her head and lifted her eyes to his again. "You know, I've never understood people praying that God will help their team win a game, or for their side to win a war. I mean, this is GOD they're talking about. He loves BOTH sides; how could they expect Him to choose?"

"So your God isn't a personal God, huh? Wait. That means you don't believe that God is Catholic?" Cade teased.

She smiled. "If one believes that there is only one God, then His church affiliation is irrelevant, isn't it? And even if He were affiliated with a church, it stands to reason that it'd be one of the earliest ones, wouldn't it? Christianity didn't come along until pretty late in the game, evolution-wise."

"I think I'd leave evolution out of the argument," he said with a smile. Then he stared at her for a second. "So when you pray, you call on your father to do all your spiritual dirty work, huh? What would you have done if you didn't have a father who had passed on?"

"Well, I do occasionally call on a few really fierce angels to provide special protection."

"A few really fierce angels? Seriously?"

"Sure! The truth is my dad wouldn't know what to do in a real war zone, so just to be sure, I used to also send a few really tough angels over there to hover around Paul." She grinned sheepishly. "Sounds silly, huh? But it worked for me...Paul came home safe and sound; and I was able to get to sleep on some pretty rough nights. I just left the worrying to my dad and my angels."

He smiled. "So, I should pray to my dad to ease the way with my mother tonight, huh?"

She glanced at him and met his eyes in the mirror. "Are you worried there's going to be a problem?"

He shrugged.

"Well, I would imagine if a prayer were needed, he'd definitely be the one to know how to handle your mom for you," she said with a grin.

He looked into her eyes, and then nodded. "True. And it couldn't hurt."

"And might help," she added.

He leaned over and kissed her. "Let's go, then."

They finished getting dressed in companionable silence and made their way down to the ground floor where Arturo was waiting. He flashed a huge smile when they stepped outside. He had the car ready and running next to the curb. Meara smiled as she noticed the car was glistening with droplets of water. Arturo had gotten the car washed for the occasion. She glanced at him and smiled widely.

"*La auto sembra buona,*" she said to Arturo, who smiled with pride.

"*La vettura,*" Cade corrected softly.

"Huh?" Meara looked at him.

"Sorry, we Americans say 'auto,' but they say '*vettura*.' Although it doesn't really matter since he knows exactly what you meant," Cade agreed with a smile as he helped her into the backseat.

"There's a lot I don't know about Italians," she said with a shake of her head.

"It's OK, I'm impressed that you're trying so hard," he said.

It took about a half-hour on the highway to get to the village that Cade's mother, Maria, once again called home. It had actually been the home village for the Giordano family for over a hundred and fifty years, although now Maria and her sister, Constanza, were the only ones who had houses in the village. Maria's siblings, aunts and uncles and nieces and nephews were spread across the entire region. Many were living in and around Milan and a few over in Turin, while Cade's uncle, Vincente, and his sons and families lived nearby just outside of Como, not far from their business.

Arturo pulled into the short driveway next to the house and glanced back at Cade for further instruction. Cade spoke to him quietly then nodded and got out, walked around the car, and opened the door for Meara. He reached in very gallantly and took her hand as she got out.

Meara glanced up at him, enchanted by the gesture, but he just smiled.

They walked arm in arm up to the door. A young man, who turned out to be one of Cade's cousins, opened it. He whooped when he saw Cade and behind him Meara noticed that the doorway led to an inner courtyard. This was indeed an old homestead.

His many little nieces and nephews swirled out the door and surrounded Cade. It was apparent that he was a favorite uncle, their American Uncle. He said hello and touched a face or high-fived each of the children around him. He moved like a swimmer going against the current in a stream. With one hand, he held Meara's hand, making certain not to lose her in the crush.

The whole group moved together into the kitchen where Meara spied several very lovely women standing off to the side chatting and looking over at her and Cade. After a moment or two, a tiny older woman stepped forward; it was Cade's mother, Maria.

Cade wrapped his arms around her and kissed her. He turned his eyes to Meara and pulled her near. "Mamma, I'd like you to meet a good friend of mine, Meara O'Connell."

Chapter 49   Happy Together

After being introduced as "O'Connell," Meara let the last name go. There was time enough to talk about her married name, her deceased husband, and her widow status. Instead, she reached out her hand to the small woman with the dark hair flecked with grey streaks. Meara was delighted by the welcoming warmth in her smile and the squeeze of her hand.

"Welcome, Meara," Maria said to her in unaccented English. "Vanessa has already told me how much she admires you. The praise comes highly valued."

Meara raised her eyebrows in delight. "Thank you. I was impressed with Vanessa, as well. She is a very special young woman."

Maria nodded and eyed Meara, "That she is." Meara could see that she was pleased with the compliment about her granddaughter.

Maria reached out and took Meara's hand. She squeezed it and then looked down noticing Meara's wedding band. She glanced up at Meara for just a second and then smiled and nodded, as if she understood more than was evident.

But Meara's heart sank as she wondered what the other woman was thinking. Perhaps she thought that she was still married and fooling around with Cade? God, she hoped she didn't think that. Once again she realized that she shouldn't be wearing the wedding ring. She should've taken it off.

Meara looked at Maria and she thought she saw something in her eyes, although she wasn't sure if it was understanding or merely acknowledgment.

Just then Cade came up behind Meara and told her that his Uncle Vincente wanted to meet her. She turned towards Cade and nodded, but when she'd turned back, Maria was gone. She felt disappointed.

She followed Cade out of the kitchen and into the courtyard area where his Uncle Vincente was chatting with several nephews circled around him. He looked up as Cade and Meara approached. As they drew closer he grinned and nodded a welcome.

He reached out and took her hand. He didn't notice the wedding band as his sister, Maria, had. Instead he gazed into Meara's face, into her eyes. She smiled at him. There was something about his open honest face that made her want to smile. She looked into his eyes and intuitively knew why Cade loved and respected him.

"So you are the one who has turned our Nico's head, eh?" Vincente said softly. "*Buono*," he nodded. "You are the one," he said with satisfaction.

Meara looked at him not quite understanding what he meant. Even so, she felt accepted and validated.

She felt Cade's arm wrap around her waist. She turned and smiled at him. He was so good at understanding how she might be feeling a little uncomfortable in the middle of this big, loving family.

"You look amazing," Cade whispered in her ear.

She looked at him and smiled. "You have a wonderful family, Cade," she said.

"I know," he replied, kissing her hair.

Meara turned and saw that his mother, Maria, was back in the kitchen with her cohorts. She was staring at Meara, but not unkindly, more out of curiosity and interest. Meara didn't feel disapproval in her look; only that she didn't understand. Meara knew that she would need to rectify that. Somehow.

The dinner was a slow progression through a lot of courses. Meara was fascinated with all of it. It was very much what she had grown used to with Tony's family dinners, except there was a subtle difference. Where Tony's family took everything as their due; Cade's relatives were more grateful and appreciative. When the appetizer was served, she heard the cousins commenting on the choice of mushrooms or the various cheeses. With the next course, a soup, there was a lively discussion on whether there should even BE a soup course. Meara loved that the family noticed the courses of the meal and appreciated what was being served. This was a family that seemed to pay attention and was mindful of even the tiniest details.

She also felt their warmth. Just being at the table seemed to extend an acceptance to her as one of them. Well, at least for the evening. They shared their food, and their camaraderie.

After the meal, the women got up to leave the table as the older children cleared the dishes. Cade's cousin, Sergio's wife, Drina, grabbed Meara's hand and invited her to come with the other women. It could've been an awkward moment − of course, she should go with the women, but if not invited, she would have had to stay with the menfolk. She'd have been fine with them, but she didn't think they would've been entirely comfortable with a female in their midst. She felt grateful to Drina, and Celia, Pietro's wife, for their thoughtfulness and sensitivity. She felt Maria was probably orchestrating it all in the background, but she couldn't be sure. Mind games, she thought with a laugh.

"So?" Celia said in accented but good English, "Tell us how you captured the heart of our good-looking cousin Nico?" she said with a grin. "He NEVER brings his girlfriends to meet the family. Never!"

Meara smiled, "I think it's just a strange circumstance that brought me here," she said trying to minimize the situation, but acknowledging that after all, she was here with Cade. "You see, Cade and I met in Bangkok, Thailand, when we were both in high school. He had a crush on me back then, I think. When we met again, well, we had a lot to talk about, as you can imagine. Thirty-some years' worth!" she added with a laugh.

Maria, Cade's mother, leaned forward then with interest. "You and Cade knew each other in Bangkok when you were teenagers?""

Meara nodded, "Yes, it was the oddest thing to run into him again. As a matter of fact, we've spent some time talking about how we've both grown and changed over the years."

Maria studied Meara's face. "*Buono*," she said finally with a nod. "I see."

"Wait!" Drina said, "I don't see. Cade has brought you to Milano from San Francisco, California, true?"

Meara nodded.

"And you are staying with him together at the company's apartment, true?"

Meara felt her cheeks grow pink, but she nodded, "Yes."

"Then, this is not just old friends catching up. This is...uh... something new!" she said with a smile. She reached for Meara's hand, "Truly, Meara, believe me, Nico likes you. He wouldn't bring you here to have dinner with us if that were not true."

Meara smiled, almost shyly. "Thank you. He is very special to me, too. But really, it's only been two weeks," she said with a shrug.

Maria nodded and looked down. She reached out to Meara and took her hand. She touched the wedding band. But said nothing, just looked questioningly at Meara.

Meara shrugged. "My husband died a little over a year ago, but I'm not ready to take it off."

Maria nodded, "I lost a husband, too," she said and rubbed the back of Meara's hand, then she patted it, as if to say "it's OK," or at least, that is what Meara thought she meant. She couldn't be entirely sure.

Suddenly, Meara felt tired; it's the tiredness of jetlag and lack of sleep and the days and nights getting all pushed together that can defeat a person. You struggle on and think you are wide awake and doing well, when suddenly you sit down for a minute to catch your breath and you almost can't get up again. That's the way she felt now.

As if he heard her weary sigh, Cade suddenly was there. His hand reached around her shoulder and she looked up.

"You look as tired as I feel," he said. "Are you ready to go home and get some sleep?"

She nodded and smiled weakly. "I think I'm crashing," she said with a shake of her head.

He grinned. "Me, too. Let's go," he said as he took her hand and pulled her to her feet. He looked at his mother warmly. "I'm taking her home now, Mamma. I'll call you tomorrow to thank you, OK? We'll get together again before we leave."

She reached out and squeezed his hand. "It's good to see you happy again, Nico," she said with an almost solemn nod.

He chuckled, "I've always been happy, Ma. I'm just happier now, that's all."

She smiled, "Yes, you are." She stood up and gave Cade a hug then turned to Meara. "Take care of my son, Meara O'Connell," she said and hugged Meara warmly.

Meara smiled. "Good night, Maria. Thank you for the wonderful dinner. I enjoyed meeting you and your family."

"And we, you," Maria responded.

Celia and Drina came to Maria's sides and they draped arms around the petite woman. It was apparent that they had very warm feelings towards her. The three of them walked arm in arm to the door to wave goodbye to Cade and Meara.

Arturo had the back door of the car open for them. Meara felt like royalty with Cade at her elbow and Arturo waving them into the car and Cade's family standing and giving their warm farewells from the doorstep.

Chapter 50   The First Cut is the Deepest

When they got back to the apartment, Cade felt exhausted but also exhilarated. The meeting with his family had gone well and now he and Meara were back at the apartment once again with a night together ahead of them. He couldn't have been happier or more excited by the prospects. He just hoped he could stay awake long enough to enjoy it as much as he wanted to.

Meara looked tired too. He studied her for several long seconds.

"What?" she asked with a frown.

He swallowed his smile and kept a straight face. "Well, I guess I was wondering how tired you are right now. Whether, for instance, you'd be up for some...uh...fooling around?"

She glanced up at him. "Really? 'Fooling around'?" she repeated. "Just exactly what would this fooling around entail?" she replied quite seriously.

For a second he wasn't certain if she was putting him on. But he smiled anyway and then immediately erased the smile from his face and voice, "I'm thinking it would involve possible nudity, some stimulation, and well, of course, sexual contact," he said, and added, "Lots of sexual contact, really."

She tried to keep a straight face, but as she looked at him she felt herself breaking into a huge smile. Then she laughed. "Uh...'lots of sexual contact'...I have to say that sounds promising."

They both burst out laughing and he hugged her. "Come on, that bed hasn't been laid in for at least a few hours. I don't know if we'll have the stamina to do much, but just being horizontal will be an improvement, don't you think?"

She nodded. "Oh, Cade, I've had such a good evening tonight!" she said.

He stopped and looked down at her, "Really? I wondered whether the whole situation with my family would just be too much."

She shook her head. "I loved them, Cade. Although, your mom did not like that I was still wearing my wedding ring."

"Oh, that was it!" he said. "I couldn't figure out what had dampened her ardor there at the beginning of the evening. So, it was the ring, was it?" he asked in delight.

Meara frowned. "You're happy about that?"

"Yeah, she didn't call for the priest to bless this union on the first meeting. I have to be honest; I couldn't understand why she backed off so quickly. It was so unlike her. But the ring...that was brilliant!"

"Cade," Meara laughed. "I didn't wear the ring on purpose to fend her off. I forgot that I was even wearing it, until she commented on it."

"I'd have asked you to wear it had I known how well it would keep her at bay."

Meara shook her head. "I felt awful about it. She looked so taken aback."

"You shouldn't have felt badly. She was at fault for jumping to conclusions so early in the game."

"I know. But I felt that the ring gave the impression that I was still married, and I realized that I shouldn't be communicating that message. It just isn't true anymore."

"Then why do you continue to wear it?" he asked quietly.

She blinked and looked at him. "I don't know. I guess I'm just not ready to give it up yet."

"It? Or him?" Cade asked.

Meara was quiet for several minutes. She shook her head. "I'd like to say that it's not him, but I don't know if that's true. So maybe I'm not ready to give up either of them just yet." She looked at Cade for a minute, and then added. "I'm sorry, Cade, it's probably not what you were hoping to hear, but I don't want to start lying to you now."

He took a deep breath and let it out slowly. "It's OK. But I have to admit it's not easy competing with a dead guy." He was silent for a second then glanced at her with a stricken look. "Jesus, you don't pray to HIM do you?"

"What?" Meara asked.

"You said you prayed to your father to protect your son Paul in Afghanistan...you don't pray to your husband to do stuff for you, do you?" He asked seeming to cringe.

Meara burst out laughing. She shook her head. "Oh my God, Cade, no, I don't pray to Tony to help me out. God! I can't imagine what he could do for me now worth praying to about!" After she said it aloud, she put her hand over her mouth. "Geez, that came out wrong. I meant...well, geez, I'm not sure what I meant! It's just that there's nothing he could help me with now, I guess." She looked down.

He smiled. "Thanks, Meara. That's exactly what I wanted to hear you say, whether it came out right or not."

He leaned down and kissed her gently.

Chapter 51   Time is on My Side

Meara stood entwined in his arms again after a very long day. She took a breath as she looked up at him. She could see the desire in his eyes. Suddenly, she wasn't feeling quite so tired any more. She was looking forward to being naked and in his arms again, and for a while, at least, not having to talk.

They should talk, though. There was a lot that needed to be said, she thought. His hands slid down her back and rested on her butt, his fingers spread out and moving, pulling her hips towards him. Yup, she should get him talking more about his past, about the Witness Protection program and the years he spent hidden away. Where was he then? How often did he see Vanessa? Was there a woman in his life? What about when he moved to Italy? She had a lot of questions; things she wanted to know.

His fingers were on the buttons of her blouse now. She felt him opening one button at a time, as his mouth was on hers. When the top button was open, she felt him lightly open it as he pulled away and his head ducked down to kiss the top of her breast above her bra. She felt her nipples pucker inside her bra. Oh, man, she knew there wasn't going to be any talking for a while. He reached around and unhooked her bra and she felt the weight of her breasts against the light material of her blouse. The straps were hanging loosely at her shoulders.

He leaned down and started kissing her lightly, his mouth moving lower on her breasts. OK, talking was definitely out, she decided. Besides, she didn't want to think about anything right now but what he was doing to her body and what he was making her feel. Talking was over-rated anyway. She leaned down and pulled him up and kissed him deeply, reaching for the buttons of his shirt. She reached in under his shirt and felt his skin, warm and inviting. She could feel the muscles in his back flex as he moved to pull her in close.

She realized after a second that she was already breathing hard and so was he. She smiled and pulled away so she could see his face. His eyes were pools of black arousal; his lids were lowered slightly as he gazed at her.

"Cade, I think we should get naked and get into the bed, what do you say?"

He groaned, "I want you so bad," he said with a half-laugh.

"I know," she replied as she unhooked her skirt and let it fall to the floor. She slid her half-slip and panties off in one motion, and with a shake of her shoulders her blouse and bra floated to the floor.

"Ah," Cade said closing his eyes to steel himself. He reached down and undid his belt and lowered the zipper of his slacks and let them fall to the floor. He stepped out of them as he shrugged out of his shirt and reached for her.

She slipped away from him and crawled over the top of the bed and sitting back on her knees, she pulled the duvet back. It was all crisp and white and clean smelling. She fell into it with a laugh. She looked over at him and reached towards him, "Come on, Cade. Quick. I need you."

He was there instantly, covering her with his body as his hands caressed her and his mouth kissed her. He pushed up for a second and just looked at her. She couldn't remember anyone ever looking at her body the way he looked at her. She was sure that Tony had taken her body for granted. For him it had always been about just having sex – the activity – but without any sense of wonder.

She reached down and caressed the side of Cade's face and he smiled so that she could touch the dimple in his cheek. Suddenly, she wanted to cry at her good luck to have this one more chance at making love to someone who enjoyed all of it as much as she did – the touching, tasting, sweating, moving together – beckoning the release of that all-encompassing orgasm as it drew nearer and nearer. They could sense its closeness in their quickening breath, in the driving need to be touched there, and there, and oh yes, there. And then it was on them. Cade driving harder and she was crying out, not wanting it to ever end, but pushing him to completion, just the same. Perfect.

She curled her arm around his neck and heard him sigh just before she fell into a very deep sleep.

Chapter 52   Uncle John's Band

The next morning the light was streaming through the room when Cade woke up. He must have forgotten to close the blackout curtains. Just as well since they would probably have slept half the day away, with their jetlag and crazy hours. Cade put the back of his hand over his eyes for a second. He needed to pull his thoughts together and prepare for the day. Today was going to be the day he would meet Brian, the Stalker.

He turned his head and looked over at Meara. "You awake?" he whispered.

Her eyes were closed but she said, "Sort of," and then she sighed sleepily. She stretched and turned towards him and he felt a warm leg slide up against his.

"What time is it?" she asked, her voice muffled slightly by the pillow.

He wouldn't think about the leg and how warm she felt or they'd never get out of here.

He needn't have worried, though, because just then her mobile phone started ringing from across the room.

"What's that?" she asked, her eyes opening.

"Your phone," he said, pulling back the covers to go and retrieve it for her.

"Oh! Is it nine?" she asked, sitting up suddenly.

"What?" he asked, turning back to her, in confusion.

She jumped out of the bed and hurried over to stuffed chair where it was apparent the ringing phone was hidden. She threw aside the blouse that was draped over the arm of the chair where she must have tossed it the night before. She dug around under it and found her purse underneath. She drew the phone out and put it to her ear just as it began to ring again. "Hello? Brian?" she said into the phone.

At the sound of the name, Cade reacted. He stood stock-still, watched Meara and listened, trying to make out Brian's end of the conversation.

Meara glanced at him, but she didn't seem to really see him. Her attention was riveted on what was being said in the phone. "Sure, I guess so," she replied carefully. "Do you want to speak with him?"

She pulled the phone away from her ear and looked at Cade. She held it out. "He wants to meet with you today. Do you want to talk with him to make the arrangements?"

Cade came over. He felt odd. This was the first business call he'd ever taken in the nude. It was an oddly vulnerable feeling, he realized. He took the phone from Meara's outstretched hand and put it to his ear. "Cade Chandler here," he said, trying to sound in charge and unfazed.

"Cade Chambers, don't you mean?" Brian said on the other end. Cade could hear him chuckle maliciously. "It's OK, Meara knows about the name even if you haven't gotten around to explaining everything to her yet."

"Don't worry. We talked," Cade replied bluntly. "Do you know where the town of Como is?" he asked, trying to put Brian at a disadvantage.

"That's a lake, I thought," Brian said.

"That's right, and there's a town called Como at one end of it. Meet us there. Let's say, one p.m. Is that enough time for you?"

"No problem for me. I've got a car."

"Yeah, I heard," Cade said, wanting to laugh, but at the same time not wanting to lose control of the call. "We'll take the ferry out on the lake from Como. Plenty of privacy. Be at the ferry terminal at one."

There was silence on the other end – he must be writing it down — and then Brian's voice came back on. "Fine. I'll meet you at the terminal. One o'clock." He hung up before Cade could ask any questions.

Cade looked down at the phone as he pressed the End button. He saved the number in Contacts in case they needed to get in touch with Brian Reston later.

Meara was sitting on the edge of the bed watching Cade. "What do you think?" she asked.

He shook his head. "I'm not sure." He would call his uncle and let him know and that would be that. He'd meet with Reston and settle this thing once and for all. He looked up and saw that Meara had gotten up and gone into the bathroom, probably to take a shower.

He sighed looking at the mussed up bed; too bad they couldn't just stay there for the day; sleep a little, make love a lot, and sleep some more. He didn't remember the last time he was on the same wavelength with a woman the way he was with Meara. She seemed to enjoy sex as much as he did, was always open to whatever he wanted to try next, and she had a very sexy earthy sense of humor. He smiled. He couldn't get enough of her.

His mobile phone with its clanging ringtone went off. He looked up and saw it blinking next to the clock on the bed stand. He went over to it, wondering for a second if it was Reston calling back, but when he picked it up and heard the second or two of silence on the other end, he knew intuitively that it was WitSec again.

"I'm your contact in Milan, Mr. Chandler. We will have Mr. Reston under surveillance shortly."

Cade broke in, "I just talked with him."

"You talked with him?" the man asked, in surprise.

"Yes," Cade said, wondering why it should be such a surprise.

"And did he tell you why he's been following you?" He sounded to Cade like he knew and just wanted to find out if Cade was successful in discovering it, too.

"No, not yet. I'm going to meet up with him later today to talk."

"That may not be wise. He's a bit of a nutcase, as I'm sure you've been told. We can handle it from here."

Cade felt a weird tingling sensation pass from his neck down his spine. This seemed suddenly so familiar. All those times they had moved him, how poorly they had seemed to plan things out, the small lies they had told him to cover up...well, he didn't know what they had been hiding, then or now. But he knew he never entirely trusted them. He had no intention of going down that road again. "That's OK, I've got this," he said into the phone.

"What? What do you mean?" the guy said. "My orders are to pick him up."

"That's not my problem," Cade responded. "I plan to find out what he wants with me. If you want him after that, fine by me."

"Listen, Chandler..."

"No, you listen," Cade said with as much conviction as he could muster. "I've been through enough, moved enough, had my life disrupted enough by you guys. I'm going to find out what this guy wants from me. What you do with him afterwards is your business."

There was silence on the other end of the line. "Where?"

"What?" Cade asked.

"Where are you meeting him?"

"Why do you need to know?" Cade asked suspiciously.

"Look, I can back you up if there's trouble, and I can take him in after you've had your little talk," the guy said reasonably.

Cade didn't feel reasonable. "If I need you I'll call you."

"From where?" the guy pressed.

Cade shrugged. What did it matter anyway? "Lake Como," Cade answered and ended the call.

He thought about the conversation for a second, and then placed a call to his uncle to make the arrangements. He felt much better after that. He heard the shower running in the bathroom and thought of Meara standing all soapy and wet under the showerhead. He grinned. He could think of something they could do to kill a little time before they had to leave for Como. He headed for the bathroom and was relieved to see that she'd left the door unlocked. A billowing cloud of steam escaped as he stepped inside. He could smell that familiar herbal scent of her shampoo. She was going to make him crazy. Very happy, but crazy.

Chapter 53   My Boyfriend's Back

Meara was excited and anxious about the impending meeting with Brian. She wanted it to go well, for the two of them to get along, but she didn't think either of them was particularly open to that possibility. She sighed. Men could be so difficult.

"You OK?" Cade said reaching across the seat for her hand.

The countryside flashed by as Arturo pushed the car to its limits. Glancing at him in the front seat of the car, Meara could see by the slight curl of his lips that he was enjoying driving the car fast, veering in and out of the sparse late morning traffic heading out of Milan. If it had been a Friday, the traffic would've been heavy and unforgiving. She remembered getting stuck in it with Tony once when they were driving north to Switzerland, just across the border.

She felt the squeeze of Cade's hand on hers and she looked over at him and smiled. "I'm fine," she said. "Cade? Why are we meeting with Brian on a ferry? Why not at a restaurant or even down here in Milan?"

He smiled. "Home field advantage," he replied smugly.

"What do you mean?" she asked.

"Uncle Vincente owns the private ferry boat that we're going to take. He has a tour group of Chinese senior citizens, but we'll have one of the meeting rooms to ourselves. It'll give us plenty of time and privacy to discuss whatever Mr. Reston wants to talk to me about."

"Vincente owns a ferry boat?" she asked in surprise.

He nodded. "Sure, I thought you knew that," he added. "He's been operating several boats out of Como for years. Summer's his high season, of course, with all the tourist business, but he's expanded into corporate events and parties in the fall and spring months now, too."

"He doesn't run the regular ferry service, though, does he?"

"No, tour companies are his bread-and-butter."

"How will Brian get a ticket then?"

"I called Vincente and he's expecting Brian to show up. Don't worry, he'll make sure he catches the right boat," Cade said reassuringly.

Meara frowned, "You don't think he'll feel trapped, though, do you?"

"Trapped?" Cade repeated. "Why would he feel trapped?"

She shook her head and shrugged. "I don't know. I just feel sort of weird about this whole thing, I guess." She squeezed his hand and let it go, resting her hand in her lap.

She did have an uncomfortable feeling about this meeting. After all the mystery and sense of danger Brian had made them feel when he was following them, it seemed almost anticlimactic now that everything should work out so smoothly. Instead it was like waiting for the other shoe to drop.

She didn't know why she felt the sense of foreboding. She should be happy knowing that within hours she and Cade would be free to begin their vacation together, for real, without any lingering sense of shadowy menace. She should feel that way, but she didn't. She glanced at Cade again and saw that he was looking out the window on the other side of the car. They were passing through an industrial area with lots of cramped buildings hardly brightened by the colorful signs and painted billboards on the highway-facing sides and along the edges of the roofs. The Milan area was the industrial center of the country with its automotive industry, as well as chemicals, textiles, and heavy machinery. This area wasn't scenic like Tuscany or Rome, but it spoke volumes about the wealth and productivity of the local economy.

She wondered if Cade would help Brian clear the name of his father. She couldn't discuss it with him since she didn't want him to know how much she knew about Brian's intentions. This was no way to start a relationship, she thought. Already they had secrets, and she realized that she didn't really know him well enough to predict how he'd react to any of it. She looked down and saw that she was fiddling with her wedding ring again, running her thumb back and forth along it's smooth surface. Damn, she'd meant to take it off. Well, she still didn't know what she'd do with it to keep it safe. It was easier to just leave it on until she figured it out, but she purposefully stopped touching it.

She looked out the window and up above the buildings at the blue sky. At least the weather was nice — warm, sunny, hardly a cloud in the sky, except for the crisscross pattern of jet entrails. They must be from all the airlines coming in and out of Milan's two big airports. They looked like those spidery cobwebs that you bought as decoration at Halloween.

"Cade, Brian told me that you were a government whistleblower and that you got his father in trouble. Is that true?" she asked.

He looked at her in surprise. "Really? What else did he tell you?" he asked, but without much emotion, as if he could imagine what might have been said.

"Well, that the government got you to lie in court," she began.

"I didn't lie in court. I told the truth, exactly what I saw and what I knew the maintenance crew was up to."

"Which was?"

"Smuggling cocaine and distributing it around the country. He didn't try to tell you they weren't doing that, did he?"

She shook her head. "He did mention some weather experiments, though. He told me that the drug running was just a cover for a secret government weather experiment."

"Meara, doesn't that sound a little paranoid to you? I mean even using the phrase 'secret government experiment' is a bit much. I think he's seen too many movies," Cade said with a shake of his head.

"So you don't believe it?"

He blinked. "Honestly? I don't know. I only know what I saw and that's what I was asked to testify about. Weather experiments didn't even come up in the case."

"Then how come you seem to know about them?" she asked, watching his face to see if there was a change in expression or some gauge as to what he really knew and believed.

"There were rumors, that's all. Pretty off-the-wall stuff, even back then."

"Rumors you heard while you were working for Northwest?" she pursued.

He nodded. "Sure. I didn't work with Reston's crew normally. They were a very tight group. But the thing was, they volunteered for the waste management detail and that seemed pretty odd to the rest of us, you know?" he stared off for a second before continuing. "I mean, no one wanted to work on the trucks that cleaned out the aircraft bathrooms, but those guys pretty much wouldn't let anyone else near them."

"And what were the rumors?" she persisted.

"That something wasn't quite kosher. Something was going on with that crew. They were just way too happy, doing too well – I don't know – it was just mistrust, and that sort of thing festers over time. People start trying to come up with reasons to explain it all."

Meara nodded. "I can see that happening. But were the rumors about the drugs or about the weather experiments?"

He smiled, "Both. But the drug running was easier to swallow." He chuckled.

"So he said you got called in to sub for someone who was out sick...," she said to get him back to the narrative.

"Yeah, the guy had an allergic reaction to a bee sting or something. I don't remember exactly. But the ambulance came to the hangar and took him to the hospital. All the groups were short-staffed at the time; people out with the flu, others on vacation – typical wintertime scheduling problems. I was working second shift and my boss told me that since the jet I was supposed to be working on wasn't in for service yet, he'd lent me to Reston's group for a couple of days. I was not happy about it."

"Really? Why was that?" Meara asked.

"First of all, I didn't want to work in waste management; no way, no how," he said with a smile. "Second, I felt devalued."

"Devalued?" she repeated in surprise.

He nodded and snorted. "I was pretty full of myself back then. I thought since I worked on avionics – the electronics, computers and all – I was too good to be driving a truck and emptying toilets." He grinned. "Plus, the idea that someone just offered me to another group, I don't know, it felt like I was a game piece and not a person, you know what I mean?"

She nodded. "Like a pawn without any control over your time or life."

"Exactly," he said. "So I went into it with a chip on my shoulder and a bad attitude."

"Did that color what you saw, do you think?"

He looked serious for a moment. "It may have. Certainly, I wasn't looking for things to be rosy and wonderful. But, on the third or fourth jet of the day, I drove the truck under a wing and I saw...I don't know...when I opened the undercarriage it didn't look quite right. There was a metal box or gears or something that I'd never seen before."

"No kidding. So what did you do?"

"I kept it to myself. Reston's guys were really wary of me and I sensed something was up. It was like that creepy feeling that people are whispering about you just out of earshot, if you know what I mean."

"How did you figure out what was going on?"

"I stayed late that night and got on to the maintenance computer where all the aircraft layouts and system diagrams were on file. I used them a lot with my avionics work so I knew where to look. I found that something had been added on to the wing and undercarriage, but when I did a search for the detail, the accompanying detail file was encrypted. I couldn't open it. So I went back to the plane – it was still in the hangar for servicing. I used the excuse that I'd left one of my tools in the hold, and when I opened that new metal piece, I found that it was loaded with packets of cocaine – it looked like cornstarch in little baggies. I opened one and took a couple of pinches of the stuff out and wrapped it in my handkerchief. I left and the next day I had a friend – a high school chem teacher – test it. It was pure cocaine."

Meara stared at him, her eyes wide. "Wow, just like in the movies, huh?"

"Tom, my teacher friend, was more than a little freaked out. He was certain we'd get arrested, he'd lose his job, and we'd both go to jail. He wanted nothing to do with any of it and pretty much threw me out of his house."

"What did you do? How'd you decide to get in touch with the government?"

"It took a few days for me to come to that decision. First, I went home and talked with Jan," he said with a grimace.

"What?" Meara asked.

"Her advice was for me to keep my mouth shut and try to get in on the money."

Meara looked stunned, "No. Really? Vanessa's mom?"

He nodded and sighed. "Well," he said with a shrug, "she'd been broke most of her life. I'm sure this seemed like winning the lottery to her. But for me, all I could think about was my dad, the Colonel, and I knew there was no way I was getting involved with drugs."

"Your dad was still alive then?"

He nodded. "He died the following year, but luckily he was gone before the court cases were done and I was put into Witness Protection. Having me change my name would not have gone over too well with him, so I'm glad he didn't live to see it."

"And your mom moved back to Italy?"

"Yeah, she left the States a month or so after my dad's funeral. When I think about it now, it was a real blessing that both of my parents were pretty much out of the way when the shit hit the fan."

Meara nodded. "Hard to think of that as a blessing, though, huh?"

He smiled. "True. But it would've been a whole lot more stressful if they'd been around and I had to worry about them, too. It was plenty stressful enough as it was."

Meara nodded again, "I can imagine. So, is that when Jan and Vanessa left?"

"Yes, I came home from work one day and all their stuff was gone. She'd been planning it for a while, but I was so focused on the FBI and the DEA and other government agencies questioning me, I just didn't give Jan a thought. It didn't occur to me that she'd actually leave me." He snorted and shook his head. "I was totally clueless."

"Sorry. That's a terrible way to find out."

"I know, I came home and walked in the front door and thought we'd been robbed." He laughed and shook his head again. "It was unbelievable."

"Wow," Meara agreed, not knowing what else to say.

They were both quiet for a minute or two. The car slowed down as Arturo turned off the highway following the signs for Como. They were in the mountains now and they could see villages clinging to the sides of the hills. They drove through a tunnel and when they came out they could see the dark blue-green of the lake and the orange roofs of the buildings in Como far down to their right.

"Oh, look! It's so lovely, isn't it?" Meara said.

Cade nodded. "It's a really nice little town."

"And look at the lake!" Meara exclaimed. "It's just gorgeous!"

Chapter 54   You Really Got Me

Cade knew he saw the place with a completely different perspective than Meara. He'd lived near here for several years, had worked on his uncle's boats on weekends, and had a deep connection to the people as well as the place. It wasn't "home" in the same way San Francisco was to him now, but he felt it was certainly a kind of home to him.

Besides, with his crazy mobile childhood he knew home didn't mean the same thing to him as it did to other people anyway. It took him years to realize that fact. He could always say the word "home" without getting choked up because home had always been wherever his parents were stationed, and while he loved his folks, he never felt anything special for the places they'd lived. The places – whether it was base housing or a house with a yard off base — were pretty interchangeable, he always thought.

When people would ask where he was from, where was his home, he was always a little disconcerted, trying to figure out what kind of answer they were looking for. Did they mean what physical place was he currently living? Or did they want to know where his family was living? Or was it a more cosmic and figurative question?

He knew it was odd to be stumped by such a simple question, but then he knew people who couldn't answer the question "What do you do for a living?" for a whole other set of reasons.

He leaned forward and told Arturo where to drop them off, down by the lakefront, and not in the company's offices where Arturo had taken him the day before.

Meara looked out the window and took in the quaint little town. As they got closer to the lakefront, she pointed out the town's Duomo with a smile.

"If we get a chance later, we should walk through it," Cade said with a smile.

She nodded. "I'd like that."

He reached over and took her hand. "Are you ready for this?"

She looked back at him and nodded. "I think so, Cade. Well, I hope so, anyway."

Arturo stopped the car and came around to open her door. Cade was already out of the car and waiting for her on the steps. He told Arturo to park the car and to wait for his call. It would probably be several hours.

Meara smiled when he returned to her. "What'd you tell him?"

"To enjoy himself because we won't need him until late this afternoon."

Cade looked over her shoulder and smiled to see his uncle and cousin Sergio coming towards them.

"Nico, your friend is already aboard," Vincente said into Cade's ear as he gave him a warm hug and patted his back.

"*Buono,*" Cade said quietly.

Meara smiled and hugged the two men warmly. "It's a beautiful day to be out on the water," she commented.

Vincente nodded, "True enough. The water is like glass today. See for yourself," he said spreading his arm wide to take in the lake behind him.

Sergio put out his arm for Meara to take his elbow. She did and he led her towards the boat docked close by.

Vincente fell back a pace and said to Cade quietly. "So who is the other fellow?"

Cade eyed him, "What other fellow?"

"There's another American trying very hard to blend in who asked for a ticket on the boat. I told him we are full. Unless you want me to put him on, as well?"

Cade frowned, "Is he around here now? Can you point him out?"

Vincente purposefully looked towards his own boat, but said, "Look at the tables outside the cafe to your right. He's at a table by himself."

Cade paused and looked, sweeping his eyes over the scene so it wouldn't be obvious that he was looking. "Not sure, but I assume it's the WitSec guy."

Vincente looked at him questioningly.

"Government," Cade answered.

Vincente nodded and grimaced. "Ah."

"Don't let him on. I told him I'd call him when I was done with our guest."

Vincente, "*Buono*. No problem."

They arrived at the gangway and Vincente nodded to Sergio. "You take this trip, Sergio. I'll stick around here for a while I think."

Sergio nodded and smiled, leading Meara onto the boat. When she and Cade had boarded, he signaled his crew to pull back the gangway and release the dock lines.

Cade watched as the WitSec guy stood up suddenly and hurried towards the departing boat. He ran over to the pier, but Vincente held him back speaking in furious Italian to the bemused man. Cade smiled and turned and he noticed Meara watching him.

"Who's that?" she asked nodding at the man with Vincente.

Cade shrugged. "Not sure. Probably not one of the Chinese senior citizens, though."

She eyed him. "You're not telling me something," she said.

"Let's go find our boy, Brian, huh?" he said, turning her away from the view of Como and towards the main galley. He knew that Sergio would probably have the smaller party room in the bow reserved for them. It would be far enough away from the tourists and their cameras to afford them some privacy.

Sergio nodded to Cade, "Mr. Reston is waiting for you in the Bellagio room. There is coffee and some pastries in the room now. Do you need anything else?" he asked solicitously.

Cade smiled, "Perfect. *Grazie*, Sergio. I know where the two-way box is in the room. I'll call if we need anything, but I think we'll be all set for now."

Sergio smiled and indicated the way with his arm.

Cade took Meara's arm. "Let's go," he said.

Chapter 55   Downtown

Meara suddenly felt very nervous about the meeting. She looked around and felt the warm breeze on her face as the boat picked up speed. It headed out beyond the marina and harbor buoys. She wished they could sit outside this afternoon and enjoy this magical summery weather.

The boat swayed slightly and she leaned against Cade to catch her balance. He grinned. "Forgot you're on a boat, eh? You'll get your sea legs soon enough. Luckily, it looks like it's going to be especially smooth ride this afternoon."

She smiled, "It is gorgeous out here," she said almost wistfully, taking in the mountains towering on all sides.

"I know," Cade said squeezing her hand. "With luck, you and I will get a chance to enjoy a little more of this."

He stopped before the door marked "Salon Bellagio." He opened the door and waited for Meara to go through in front of him. She blinked several times as her eyes adjusted to the relative darkness of the room compared to the bright sunshine outside.

Brian Reston stood up and came over to her. "Good to see you again, Meara," he said warmly taking her hand.

She smiled. "Hello, Brian." She stood back. "I don't know if the two of you have ever officially met. Brian, this is Cade Chandler... or Chambers, if you like," she said with a smile. "Cade, this is Brian Reston."

The two men eyed each other for a second and then shook hands without exchanging a word.

Brian turned and indicated they could sit at the two empty chairs at the table where he'd been sitting. His coffee cup sat in front of his place.

Meara went over to the tray on the table nearby and poured two cups of coffee for herself and Cade. She suddenly realized that although she'd had a number of coffees with him over the past weeks, she really wasn't positive how he liked his coffee. She turned to him, "Cade, just milk?" she asked.

He smiled, "Yes, thanks, Meara." She saw that he was looking at Brian with a fair amount of curiosity. She watched as Cade leaned towards Brian, "You look a bit like your father," he said.

Brian glanced at him sharply, probably trying to gauge whether Cade was being authentic. When he saw that Cade was making an honest observation, he visibly relaxed. "I've been told that."

Cade waited for Meara to come back and sit in the chair next to him. He glanced at her and nodded his thanks for the coffee she'd slid in front of him. He took a small sip then looked back at Brian. "So, let's get to it, shall we?" Cade said lightly. "You wanted this meeting, so tell me why you've been stalking me these past weeks."

Brian sat up, "Stalking? I wouldn't call it stalking. As a matter of fact, I had the devil of a time locating you. But soon everything added up: your brother's law firm, your stepdaughter in Palo Alto. I wished I'd known about your mother over here; I'd have found you years ago."

Cade frowned. "I've been back in the States for nearly twelve years, and not exactly living under a rock."

"I was eight when my father was sent to prison. I never thought about looking for you until a couple of years ago. When I did decide to find you, I had to do some digging. There weren't too many people I could ask about what happened. All my father's crew were in prison or gone, Northwest was kaput, other people who might know something died or retired. Plus, no one could tell me the real story; what was really going on."

Cade eyed him, "And what did you discover was the real story?" he asked calmly.

"That you were a whistleblower; that you got my father's whole team in trouble and they all ended up going to prison on drug charges."

Cade nodded. "That's all true."

"But it's not; not really."

"What do you mean?"

"My father and his crew were recruited to help with a government experiment to control the weather."

Cade snorted. "And I suppose the cocaine was how they got paid for their services?"

Brian sat up straight, anger straining the tendons of his neck. "The cocaine was a front to hide what was really going on."

"Why would your father and his team agree to something that crazy? That is, unless they saw it as an opportunity to make some money on the side," Cade said reasonably.

Brian slammed his fist on the tabletop and all the cups rattled. "He wasn't a drug runner and he didn't make a cent off the cocaine!"

"How do you know? You just said you were eight years old at the time."

"Don't you think he and my mother and our family would've been living a bit better off than we were if we had all this drug money flowing in? When my dad went to prison my mother had to go on food stamps. Believe me, he didn't leave a pile of dough."

Cade shrugged. "Look Brian, I don't know anything about this weather experiment, and I don't know what your father and his guys did with the money they made from the cocaine. Maybe they frittered it all away; maybe someone screwed them out of it. All I know is that it's over. Your dad did his time, and we've all moved on."

Brian lowered his head and looked Cade in the eye and asked, "Doesn't it bother you that you were used by them?"

"Used by whom?" Cade asked.

"The U.S. Government, that's who."

"How was I used by them?"

"OK, here's the scenario: Global warming has been proven to be inevitable. People are lazy and selfish; they are never going to stop it on their own until it's way too late. So what can a country do? Well, what if they had some geniuses that told them they could control the local weather. Give someone a drought; give another place a flood; or a tornado. That's real God power, don't you think?" Brian smiled as if waiting for Cade's agreement.

Cade just looked at him. "I'm listening," he said quietly.

"OK, they think they have the means but they need to test it; to prove it works. Problem is that there's no way they could ever get permission to seed the atmosphere with chemicals. No Senator or Congressman would vote for it; the President would have to be insane to give the go-ahead. What to do?" He paused as if waiting for Cade to supply a guess.

"They make it secret?" Cade asked.

"Exactly!" Brian said triumphantly, as if that proved everything.

"So where do I come in on this scenario?" Cade asked, lifting his cup and taking a long sip of his coffee and smiling with satisfaction.

"You diverted the attention from the weather modifications that were secretly taking place to drugs. My father and his crew were the scapegoat. You were the dupe."

Cade stared at Brian for several long moments. He shook his head. "Sorry, Brian, but I'm just not convinced. I saw what I saw."

"I'm not disputing what you saw. I'm saying that my dad got a bum rap. Maybe he shouldn't have agreed to help the government. I've read about the stuff those corporations are doing, seeding the clouds, creating persistent contrails that last up to a week or two. This isn't right. If it really wasn't harmful, why not let people know what's going on?"

Cade put his hands up. "Hold up. What are 'persistent contrails'?"

Meara leaned forward, too, interested.

Brian said, "They spray these chemicals out of planes – aerial spraying – by commercial jets and they create these contrails – some people call them 'chemtrails.' They can last as long as a week or two in the sky."

"And what does that do?"

"You've been in aviation, right? What is a contrail made up of?"

"Vapor," Cade answered.

"Exactly, water. Put enough contrails up there and you create clouds with rain, or maybe you shield the earth from sunlight, lowering the temperature slightly."

"Lowering the temperature of the earth?" Cade asked. "Seriously?"

"Oh, the science is there and it's been tested. Right after 9/11, all the airplanes over the U.S. were grounded; remember that?"

Cade nodded.

"The scientists did a study of the effects of suddenly no contrails at all and they measured the diurnal temperature range," he looked at Meara and then at Cade, "that's the difference of day and night temperatures. And do you know what they found?"

Cade and Meara both shook their heads.

"Without the contrails streaming all over the skies for three days, the diurnal temperature had gone up one degree Celsius, that's 1.8 degrees Fahrenheit. In other words, in just three days, the temperature rose nearly two degrees! Think about that," Brian said, shaking his head. "Oh, they are doing it, and we won't know a thing about it until it's way too late."

"But wouldn't that be a good thing? To lower the temperature, I mean. Reverse the effects of global warming," Cade said.

"Maybe," Brian agreed. "Except for the toxic chemicals that are drifting down on all of us, causing cancer, kidney problems, headaches, who knows what else. They are only beginning to study what the effects on human life might be, not to mention the effects on animals and plants. Like it or not, we're a part of a very intricate food chain. Mess with it, and you may be messing with the possibility of life not continuing on this planet."

Cade stared at him. "I assume you have the science behind all of this?"

"I can give you chapter and verse. I'm a computer guy; I spend my life on the Internet."

"That's not much of a recommendation, you know that, right?" Cade said with a short laugh.

Brian smiled, the first real smile he'd had for Cade. "Look, Cade, my dad may have been totally wrong to have helped these guys do this stuff and deceive the public, but I got to believe that he thought it was the right thing to do. He was a very patriotic guy, you know; he volunteered to go to Vietnam and the whole nine yards. The point is he shouldn't have ended up dying in prison as a drug trafficker. Maybe he didn't deserve a parade or commendation, but no way did he deserve to serve time for helping out his government."

It was quiet in the room for several long seconds. Cade was staring at Brian. Meara looked back and forth between the two of them. It was a compelling story, no question about it. She realized she believed Brian. He reminded her of Paul in his earnestness. But she felt overwhelmed by the information. Her father had been a patriot, too; but he worked for the government; what did this story say about him?

"I'm not an environmental lawyer, Brian. I can't fight that fight and win."

Brian shook his head. "No, no, you don't understand. I'm not asking you to fight the government about this whole weather modification program."

"Then what is you want from me? An apology?"

Brian chuckled. "Well, that'd be nice," he said, and then he turned serious again. "What I want is for you to get my father's name cleared, his record expunged."

Cade stared at him. "But...I...I'm not sure..." He looked at Brian and held up his hands. "Honestly, Brian? I'd need to really think it through, whether it'd even be possible, OK?"

Brian looked at him for a full second or two then he nodded. "OK. But you owe him, I think."

Cade smiled slightly. "Well, I don't think I do, but I concede that you've made a few good points, OK?" He stood up. "I'm going to take a walk on deck to clear my head. I'll be back."

Meara watched Cade leave and was a little surprised he didn't invite her to come along. She glanced at Brian who smiled at her. She returned the smile with reassuring warmth, realizing that she was beginning to like him.

"You think he'll help me?" he asked.

She lifted her eyebrows and shrugged. "Maybe. I hope so anyway, Brian."

"Thanks."

"Tell me something, Brian. How can you tell a regular contrail from these chemical ones? Is there a way?"

"Sure. A normal contrail is just water vapor and it dissipates literally in a few minutes. If you look up and see a contrail that just stays and stays, it's a chemical spray, you can be sure of it."

She breathed out. "I'll never look up at the sky in the same way again, will I?" she asked.

He gave her a crooked smile and just shook her head. "Changed me," he said. "Changes everyone that learns about it."

Chapter 56   Secret Agent Man

Cade stepped out and closed the door behind him. His mind was reeling with all that Brian had said. Could he get Brian's father's name restored? He'd have to prove that he didn't traffic in drugs, but there was no way he could do that. Heck, he was the one who had proved that he HAD been trafficking in cocaine.

Sergio came up beside him. "Everything OK, Nico?" he asked.

Cade smiled and nodded. "Fine. The guy isn't going to be a problem."

"Well, the other guy might be," Sergio said. "My father called a little while ago, said the guy has taken off in a rented speedboat."

Cade looked at him. "You're kidding," he said. "What a jackass. I told him I'd call him when I was done."

Cade thought about it, though. He didn't want to turn Brian over to the guy now. Who knows what they had in mind for him? Probably nothing good. Why the anxiety to follow him, he wondered?

"Sergio," Cade said. "Could we make a stop in Menaggio? Are we very far from there right now?" He looked over the side to try and gauge how far up the lake they were.

Sergio shook his head, "Not far. I can make a stop there, but it'll have to be quick because we have the Chinese group booked on a tour of Bellagio so we need to be there in time for that. What do you have in mind?"

"I want to get our guest off the boat and away from the other guy. From Menaggio he could either go back through Switzerland or around the lake. I'll meet up with the speedboat guy in Bellagio, I think."

He made the arrangements with Sergio and then returned to the Salon where Meara and Brian were having a lively discussion. He had an idea of what he needed to do next, but he'd have to get Brian to go along with it.

He sat back own at the table. "Brian, there's a guy following you. Do you have any idea of why that would be?"

Brian shot a look at Cade, "A guy? Where?"

"My cousin owns this boat. He and my uncle stopped a guy from getting a ticket, but apparently he's just rented a speedboat and is attempting to catch up with us."

Brian's eyes grew round. "You're kidding, right?"

Cade shook his head. "Are you in any other sort of trouble that we should know about?"

Brian shook his head. "Look, the truth is that when I started researching these weather modification programs, I attracted some government interest, especially when they realized who my father was." He shook his head in disbelief. "I'm a little surprised that they'd follow me over here. I mean, outside the U.S. and all."

Meara stared at Cade. "What's going on here, Cade? What aren't you telling us?"

He looked at her in surprise. "Me? The guy isn't following me."

"But you knew he'd be there, or at least, you weren't surprised when he turned up at the pier, were you?"

Cade blinked. "I don't know the guy, Meara." Which was technically true, but he still felt bad for the evasion.

"Is he connected to your Witness Protection thing? Did you call him?" her voice rose a bit as she realized that she knew that was what happened.

"Meara," Cade started to say, but she was up and moving away from him.

"Cade, how could you?" she asked plaintively.

"What about you?" Cade asked.

"What about me?" she replied her head rising.

"You knew what Brian was going to ask me but you never said a word to me. I don't think I'm the only one here with a few secrets."

She turned away. There was a clanking of bells out on the deck and they could hear the difference in the engine.

"Good," Cade said. "We're stopping in Menaggio. It's on the western side of the lake. You should be able to rent a car, Brian. There's a highway that will take you from Menaggio through the mountains and over to Lake Lugano in Switzerland. I'll make sure the guy doesn't follow you. We'll meet up in San Francisco, in a week, let's say."

Brian stood and eyed Cade. After a second, he nodded and put out his hand. "A week," he said solemnly, and they shook hands.

Meara looked from one to the other. "Brian, are you sure you can you get yourself to Lugano?"

Brian hesitated and looked sheepish for a second, then he shrugged. "I can probably figure it out."

Meara shook her head slightly and said to Cade, "I can't leave him here like this!" She turned to Brian, "I'm going with you."

Cade looked at her stunned. "You can't go with him," he said.

She looked at him coolly. "Oh really? Of course, I can. And I will."

Brian frowned. "You're welcome to come with me, Meara, but are you sure?"

She nodded. "It makes sense. I'm familiar with the area and heck, I was a travel agent for thirty years. I can get you to Lugano." She paused and smiled. "Besides, I don't think they'll do anything to you if I'm with you." She looked at Cade coolly and then added, "If I'd known Cade was going to tell the government agents, I'd never have let you get pulled into a meeting on this boat. I'm sorry, it's my fault."

"Meara," Cade said. "I can't let you do this."

She smiled at him without humor. "Sorry, Cade. You don't have a vote in the matter." She turned and nodded to Brian, "I think it's time to go," she said.

They walked past Cade and out the door.

Jesus! What just happened? Cade wondered.

Chapter 57 Good Vibrations

Meara was as surprised as Cade by the turn of events as she and Brian made their way off the boat. The gangway was pulled away almost as soon as they stepped ashore and when she turned around, she heard the engines reversing and the boat pulled away, picking up speed as it headed across the lake towards Bellagio. She could see Cade standing on the deck, his hand shielding his eyes and she had the urge to wave to him, but didn't. He might interpret it as a signal for help or something, and she knew that she and Brian needed to get away from the lake as quickly as possible.

Brian was quiet, watching her. "Ready?" he asked.

She nodded. "Yes. Let's go. We can ask at the ferry office where the nearest rental car office is located."

They got directions from the ticket seller window, although it took a little while since the attendant didn't speak English and neither Meara nor Brian knew enough Italian to make out what she was saying. Finally, a German gentleman, who was waiting to buy a ticket, stepped forward and offered to interpret. He leaned in towards the attendant and talked to her and the attendant answered with much pointing and arm waving. "Sehr gut," he said finally and turned to Meara and Brian. "She says there is no rental car office here in Menaggio; the closest would be in Lugano, across the border in Switzerland."

Meara looked at Brian. "Actually, we are trying to get to Lugano," she said to the German. "How do we get there from here?"

The German turned and asked the attendant, who had a short answer and pointed across the street. He nodded and turned back to Meara. "There is a bus service. The trip is about an hour." He took a notebook out of his breast pocket and wrote something and handed it to Meara. "Here is the bus number you'll need.

And I've written a note in Italian saying that you wish to go to Lugano, Switzerland. That way you can just point to it if you get into difficulties with the language."

Meara smiled. "That's very kind of you. Thank you. Uh, vielen danke," she said.

He smiled broadly. "Excellent. Sprechen sie Deutsch?"

She chuckled, "Nein, but I do like to use the few words I do know." She took the piece of paper and turned to Brian. "We'd better get going."

They walked back out into the street. "You're quite the capable woman, you know that?" Brian said in admiration.

Meara grinned. "Thanks, Brian. If there's one thing I can do it's navigating in foreign countries. I've been doing it most of my life."

"I'm glad you came along with me."

She glanced over at him and remembered Cade and the surprised look on his face when she said she was going with Brian. "I hope I don't regret it," she said, meaning it as a joke, but wondering if she would regret it.

It took about a half-hour to find the place that sold the bus tickets and then to get to the right bus stop. The bus was hourly, but with the vagaries of narrow roads, tunnels and traffic, they were given to understand that it could stretch to every other hour, on occasion. But luck was on their side because it arrived shortly after they did. They settled into their seats; Meara next to the window and Brian on the aisle.

"I'm sort of glad it worked out this way," Brian said. "I'm not sure I'd want to drive these mountain roads, to be honest."

Meara nodded. "Me, neither. When my husband and I were in this area, he drove the whole time and it was sometimes harrowing."

"Oh? You've been here before?" Brian asked.

"A few times. In fact, we stayed once in Bellagio, on the other side of Lake Como, and twice in Lugano."

"Lugano, the town we're heading to now?" Brian asked with interest.

"Yes, it's in Switzerland, but they speak Italian there. It's a lovely town right on the shore of Lake Lugano. There's some wonderful restaurants at the top of the mountains surrounding the lake. The one on Mount Bre is my favorite, and – oh my! – the sunsets are worth the trip!"

Brian smiled.

She sighed. "We won't have time to go up there, I'm afraid."

"So what's our plan?"

She looked at Brian. "Well, I thought that we should head back down to Milan, but you know, I think it might make more sense to get tickets back to the States from Lugano. We can connect through Zurich."

"But all my stuff is down in Milan," Brian said. "Yours, too, right?"

"I'm worried that the guy who was following you will assume you're going to return to Milan. That means that once he realizes he's lost you in Como, he will probably go back to Milan and wait for you to show up."

Brian looked down at his hands as he thought about what she had said. He nodded a few times.

"Brian, you have your passport with you, don't you?" Meara asked anxiously.

He grinned. "Sure. Of course! To be honest, I pretty much sleep with it when I'm outside the U.S."

She smiled. "Well, I don't think it's that precious, but it's good to have it with you. Anyway, we'll be stopping at the border pretty soon, so they'll probably ask to see it."

"The border?" he repeated, looking at her blankly.

"Sure. Switzerland isn't part of the EU – they have their own currency and they maintain their borders."

"Really? I didn't know that. I thought all of Europe used the Euro and was border-free."

She shook her head. "Not Switzerland. It has a thing about independence and non-alignment."

"Huh," Brian said. "Well, I'm glad I have my passport then."

After the border stop, Brian dozed most of the way to Lugano. Meara looked out the window taking in the scenery but also thinking about Cade and how suddenly they were once again on different paths. She wondered what he was doing right then? Was he in Bellagio? On his way back to Como? Had he met up with the WitSec guy, if the guy actually was from WitSec? She wondered when she'd see him again. Then she remembered him saying that he knew she'd kept her knowledge of Brian's intentions from him, just as she had known he was keeping some secrets from her. Maybe there was no future for this relationship, she thought bitterly. It seemed that Fate was striving to keep them apart, maybe for good reason.

Chapter 58   Get Off of My Cloud

Cade waited in the cafe across the street from the ferry wharf for the WitSec guy to appear. Sergio was lounging on the pier near his boat, within calling distance, should Cade need him.

Cade really didn't know what to do next. He never anticipated Meara leaving with Brian. And now he had to face this government agent with God-only-knew what agenda. He glanced up at the sound of a whistle. Sergio. It was a signal he and Sergio had developed back when they were kids, sneaking in and out of his uncle's house. He looked up and saw Sergio standing up and stretching broadly. OK, OK, cousin, I get it, Cade thought with a shake of his head. I'm on top of this.

He stood up so that Sergio would know he'd understood and to put a stop to his dramatic signaling gestures. Obviously, the WitSec guy was ashore.

Cade watched the wharf and then he saw the guy walking purposefully towards the boat. Cade eyed him for a second or two, but saw that he'd better intervene. Sergio would just deck the guy and that was no way to handle the situation. Cade stepped out onto the street and waited for the guy to turn in his direction. He did. Just like in the old Westerns, Cade thought. OK, now was the time to get that image out of his head. He nodded to the guy and saw that he had changed direction and was coming towards him. So far, so good, he thought.

Cade eyed the guy. Really, this was America's best? He closed his eyes for second.

"Cade Chandler?" the guy said.

"Or Chambers, whichever," Cade answered. "Come and sit. We need to talk," he said waving his hand towards the opposite chair.

The guy looked to his left and right, as if expecting foes to be descending all around, but he shrugged and sat. Cade had the urge to roll his eyes, but decided to try and take the guy seriously.

"Look, I know you were after Brian Reston," Cade started.

"So where is he?" the guy responded toughly.

"Really? You figured this would be that easy?" Cade responded with a laugh. "How long have you been in this job anyway?"

"You're Cade...uh...whatever, right?" the guy said eyeing Cade closely.

Cade nodded. "And you are?"

The guy looked at him for a full second, then wimped out. "John...John Streeter."

"Good, that's a start, John," Cade said. "So let's get this thing worked out, OK?"

John Streeter nodded. "Sure. Let's start with where Brian Reston is. That's what I want to know."

"Yeah, we'll get to that," Cade said, like an older brother schooling a younger one.

"Look," John said, "I was told to follow the guy and to bring him in."

"Yeah, well, that's out the window. Not on the table, OK? He's gone. You and I need to renegotiate the deal, capisce?"

"What deal?" John said with a frown.

"First off, who are you with?" Cade asked.

"With? What do you mean?"

"Who do you work for, John? That's what I mean," Cade repeated plainly.

"I work for the government. That's all you need to know," John said defiantly.

"No, that's not enough. Our government is deep and vast. I want to know whom you work for. WitSec?" Cade eyed him carefully.

"You aren't in charge here, Chandler," John said.

"Sure I am," Cade responded. "My cousin owns that boat there and his father, my uncle, has connections all along the lakefront," Cade said pointing to Sergio, the boat docked in front of them, and the lake beyond. He looked up at the agent and said with a shake of his head, "You, John Streeter, are the one who is not in charge here."

John Streeter looked around and suddenly noticed a group of Italian men surrounding Sergio that hadn't been there seconds before; they were all looking directly at him.

He squinted his eyes and glanced at Cade with a frown. "What are you pulling here, Chandler?"

Cade smiled. "Just want you to see the lay of the land, if you know what I mean."

John Streeter looked at him and then looked around at the men across the street. They weren't threatening, but they were plainly there, just the same.

"What do you want, Chandler?" he finally asked.

"I want you to get a message to your boss or bosses, OK?"

Streeter looked at him. "What?"

"We want Joseph Reston's conviction expunged...completely... as if it never happened."

John Streeter looked up at him sharply. "We can't do that!" he said.

"Sure you can. It's legal and it's actually done all the time. I'm a lawyer; I know these things," he said with a smile. "But, get one thing straight. This is not negotiable."

"Why should they agree to do it?" Streeter asked with disdain.

"Because they have a secret and I know what it is. If they don't do as I ask, I will make sure everyone knows their secret."

"You're as nuts as Brian Reston. Is this one of his stories?"

"Keep in mind that I was the key witness that put Joe Reston behind bars. If I were to recant my story, say that I know what was really going on with those Northwest jets. Heck, maybe I never saw any cocaine at all...just these...strange aerial spraying devices hooked onto the belly of a commercial aircraft."

"No one will believe you. You'll sound like just another crackpot." Streeter said dismissively.

"Maybe," Cade nodded. "But are they willing to chance it? I'm a lawyer and I've been trained to be convincing. After our government's history with secret projects, I really don't think it's going to be that hard to seem credible. And won't people just love to know about the chemicals that have been raining down on them for the past twenty years, huh?"

John Streeter stared at him for several long seconds. "I've got your number. I'll get back to you." He stood up abruptly.

Cade stood up, too, "When?"

"I don't know. Tonight? Maybe tomorrow. Probably won't be too long." He started to turn away and then looked back at Cade. "You're supposed to be a smart guy, but you're nuts if you side with Brian Reston. That guy's got a huge target on his back, believe me."

"What's that supposed to mean?" Cade asked.

"Let's just say that dying young might run in his family." He chuckled. "You can tell him to pay close attention. I would if I were him."

Cade stared as Streeter walked away.

His next thought was of Meara. She was with Brian. He had to find them.

Chapter 59   Satisfaction

Meara and Brian got off the bus at the main train station in downtown Lugano. She looked around and smiled. "Isn't it lovely? My husband and I spent three wonderful days here about four or five years ago. It doesn't look like it's changed a bit."

Brian glanced around. "Looks like Europe all right," he agreed. "Reminds me of Disney World."

Meara rolled her eyes, "What you mean to say is that Disney World reminds you of this place."

Brian looked at her and then slowly nodded, "Yeah, I know what you mean, but it can't remind me of something I hadn't seen before, can it? So I think I'm correct to say that this place reminds me of Disney World."

Meara laughed. "You're way too clever for your own good."

He grinned at the compliment. "So where do we go now?" he asked.

"I'm not sure. I wish we knew what happened with Cade and that guy who was following you, though."

"Why don't you call him?" Brian said.

"What?"

"Call him. You have a phone."

She shook her head. "The phone is dead. The battery must've run down."

"Want to use mine?" he asked, reaching into his pocket.

She looked a little sheepish. "I don't know his number," she admitted.

He snorted. "Well, that's romantic," he said and shook his head. "You guys are a very weird couple, that's all I can say."

Meara shrugged. He had a point.

"OK. What next?" Brain asked

"We need some information about flights and maybe train schedules. For that, we'll need the Internet."

"No problem," Brian said, taking his cell phone out of his pants pocket. "I have a map app that can give us the closest Internet cafe to our location. It's supposed to work anywhere in the world."

Meara looked dubious, "Really? Anywhere in the world? That's a pretty big claim."

Brian laughed. "Well, I agree that they probably do a better job in Western Europe than say South Sudan."

Maura smiled. "OK, let's try it out and see."

Brian scrolled to the app and tapped it a few times and then squinted at the image of the map. "Hmmm, looks like there's free WiFi at the McDonald's on Riva Albertolli and there's another place, not far from the McDonald's on the same street."

"Riva Albertolli runs along the Lugano waterfront. There should be lots of places to try along there, I would think."

It was about a ten-minute walk to the waterfront, all downhill, sometimes steeply with lots of stairs, and through twists and turns of the narrow lanes. There were lots of little shops and crowds of people, so it was an interesting and invigorating walk. They discovered that the Internet cafe and McDonald's expected you to bring your own computer, there were none available for rent, so in the end they went to one of the fancy hotels overlooking the lake because Meara knew they'd have a computer they could use in their business center. She remembered that Tony had used those types of business centers all the time.

When they got to the front desk, it turned out that in order to use the business center, which indeed did have computers that could be used, one had to be a guest at the hotel. Meara pulled out her American Express card and booked a room for one night.

"Kind of an expensive computer rental," Brian joked as they turned away from the desk.

"Well, who knows? We may need the room," she said brightly, tucking the key into her purse.

They found the business center to be a tiny room in the back of the hotel, just beyond the restrooms and right next to the freight elevator. On a positive note, they had the place to themselves. Any more than two people in that small room would've been claustrophobic, Meara thought. But it had everything they needed – a desktop computer and a fancy all-in-one laser printer/ scanner/fax machine.

Brian sat in front of the computer and Meara stood behind him looking over his shoulder at the screen.

"First check out the flights from Lugano," Meara said.

He glanced up at her expectantly, his fingers poised over the keyboard. "Any suggestions?"

"Try the Swiss airline first. I know they fly in here."

They tried several possible destinations from Lugano and discovered there were basically four flights a day to Zurich, two in the morning, one in the middle of the afternoon, and the last in the evening.

"OK, let's take a look at our choices and all the pros and cons, OK?" Meara said. "We can go back to Milan by train, we can fly to Zurich, or we could take a train there."

"The pros for going back to Milan are that all our stuff is still there and I have a car rental to turn back in," Brian said helpfully.

"But the biggest con is that the guy who was following you will probably be there waiting for you," Meara reminded him.

"We could fly to Zurich and then back to the States," Brian said looking up at Meara. "The biggest con is how much it will cost for a one way ticket to the States," he added, pointing to the fares listed on the screen.

Meara nodded. "But we would be far away from that guy," she said.

"True," he admitted. "But we don't really know what kind of trouble we're talking about, do we? I mean, maybe the guy was really after Cade, not me," he added speculatively.

Meara shook her head. "No. He called Cade. There would've been no need for someone to follow him."

"Well, I don't know why this government fellow would be after me; I mean, the people I pissed off weren't from the government, they were from a private company."

Meara stared at him. "You pissed someone off? You never told us that. Who was it? What was the name of the company?"

"AtmosTrace Inc."

Meara shook her head. "Never heard of them. Who are they?"

"They are a chemical engineering outfit up in Washington state, in a town called Puyallup, a bit south of Seattle. Monsanto tried to buy the company a few years ago, but the deal never got off the ground. They were offering millions, too. No one could understand why they didn't sell."

"Do a search on them," Meara suggested.

Brian shook his head, "I tried before. They are very hush-hush. No website, no information. I went through the business directories and all that, too. That's partly why I think they're the ones behind the chemtrails."

"And why is that?" Meara asked.

Brian looked her in the eye. "Well, the secrecy, of course, but also because my father had their business card."

Meara stared at him. "What?"

He let a breath out. "My mom had a box where she kept all my dad's personal stuff. You know, driver's license, social security card, passport, and lots of miscellaneous cards and things he'd had in his wallet. He couldn't keep anything in prison so she was saving it all for him for when he got out."

"How long was his sentence for?"

"Twenty years. He may have gotten out sooner for good behavior or whatever, but he'd only served half his sentence when he died."

"And he had a business card for this AtmosTrace?"

Brian nodded. "It's one of those crazy names that stuck with me." He smiled, "The phone number on the card still worked. I called it once."

She looked at him, thinking about the little boy he must have been when his father went to prison, and it made her sad. She sighed.

Before she could say anything more her phone rang. They both jumped and she could feel her heart thudding against her chest. She fumbled to get the phone out of her purse and looked at the number. It meant nothing to her. She pushed Talk. "Hello?"

"Jesus! Meara, where are you guys?"

She grinned. "Cade! We were trying to figure out how to contact you! I don't have your phone number. Well, I guess I do now, huh?" she said, realizing that she was babbling with relief at hearing his voice.

Thankfully, Cade interrupted her. "Meara, where are you?"

"Lugano," she responded, as if it were a lark.

"Switzerland." She could hear him let out a breath. "Good." There was a short pause. "Look, I'm back in Como, but I can be there in a half-hour or so. I'm going to take the train and send Arturo back to Milan in the car, just in case someone's following me."

Meara felt a thrill at the thought of seeing Cade again.

"OK, we have a lot to tell you."

"What? You're OK, aren't you?" he asked.

She laughed. "Oh, yeah, sure. We took the bus through the mountains and that was a little hair-raising, but otherwise, no problems. It's just that we think we know who's been following Brian...and it's not the government like we thought." There was silence on the other end of the line. "Cade? Are you still there?" she asked.

"Look, I don't think we should be talking like this on these phones. Don't say anything more, OK? We'll talk when I get there. Where will I find you?"

Meara felt a twinge of fear. If Cade was concerned, maybe she ought to be, too. "We're at..."

"No, hold on. Don't tell me that either, OK? I'll meet you...uh, let me think. How about at the ferry wharf? That's nice and public and easy to find."

She nodded, "OK. I know where it is. When?" she asked.

"In about forty-five minutes; let's say three p.m., OK?"

"Three o'clock, sure. We'll be there."

"And Meara," Cade said. "You guys will probably stick out as Americans, so find a place to lay low until I get there, all right?"

She was a little offended that he thought she'd "stick out as an American." She always believed that she blended pretty well wherever she was. But when she glanced at Brian, she had to smile. Cade was certainly right about Brian.

"OK. See you at three," she said.

"Meara?"

"Huh?"

He paused. "Uh, nothing. Just be safe, OK?"

"Sure. You, too," she said automatically. She wondered what he had meant to say, though. Something personal? Or was it just more advice? She wasn't sure.

"So Cade is coming here, huh?" Brian said.

Meara nodded. "He said to lay low until he gets here."

"Can we lay low in a restaurant? Because I'm starving," Brian said as he pushed back from the computer.

She smiled. "Good idea. I'm hungry, too. Let's go and find a cafe close to the ferry ticket office, then we can watch for him while we get something to eat."

"Now that's a plan!" Brian said happily. He logged off the computer and they were out of the hotel within minutes and heading down towards the Paradiso ferry stop to find a cafe nearby to eat.

Chapter 60   God Only Knows

Thirty-five minutes later, Cade got off the train at the Lugano station and was excited at the thought that Meara was here, that she was safe, and that he would be verifying those two facts in person shortly. It felt like it'd been years instead of hours since she had walked away from him with Brian in Menaggio. He shouldn't have let her go, but he didn't know what he could've said that would've convinced her to stay. It looked to him like she had practically adopted Brian and that he had become her substitute son. Why couldn't she see that?

And didn't she see how dangerous that kind of borrowed trust could be? He knew first hand because he'd done the same thing when he'd married Jan, Vanessa's mother. When he first met her he had felt sorry for her. She was struggling with a toddler, barely getting by, working at low-paying jobs to support herself and little Vanessa. Of course, Jan was pretty and sexy, too, and vivacious; she was the kind of woman who lit up a room when she entered it. And it was that quality about her that had reminded him of his sister, Terry, who was just a little bit older than Jan at the time and married, and who also had a little girl.

Because of the similarity in their personalities and situations, and maybe because he had been close to Terry and missed her, he mistakenly attributed lots of Terry's good qualities to Jan. The result was a disaster of a marriage. He was always expecting the best from Jan, and she was constantly disappointing him. But to be fair, he probably disappointed her just as much.

He thought Brian was a nice enough guy, if a little eccentric in his obsession with his father and everything surrounding his father's life, career and unfortunate end, but he didn't know him well enough to trust him. So why had Meara? Was it some crazy female thing? Or was it, as he believed, because she wasn't really seeing Brian; she was looking at him and seeing her son, Paul.

Leaving the train station, Cade hurried down the labyrinth of stairs and walkways leading down the hill through the town. He quickly arrived at the lakefront and looked out at the deep blue of the landlocked lake surrounded by tall mountains.

He crossed the street to walk along the wide promenade that bordered the lake. It was a beautiful little town surrounded by steep mountains; Mount Bre on one side and San Salvatore on the other. Both of these peaks had funiculars that took tourists to the top and he knew from previous visits that the views from up there were glorious. From up top, you looked down on the deep blue-green lake, with the colorful buildings and boats bobbing in the marinas of the town hugging the shore, and beyond along the far horizon were the jagged, snow-capped peaks of the Alps.

The lakefront promenade was a landscaped walkway with trees, flowers and lush foliage, and it was full of people walking their dogs, bicyclists gliding along, and women pushing baby strollers enjoying the warm afternoon. Cade was walking fast, dodging around the slower moving pedestrians. He could see the top of the ferry building not far up the way, just beyond the motorboat rentals.

He slowed down to a more normal pace and scanned the crowds. There were people sitting on benches and across the street at the outdoor cafe tables. He had arrived a couple minutes early and he hoped he'd catch sight of Meara and Brian before he got to the ferry terminal.

It was then that he recognized her sitting at a table along the outer edge of the cafe across the street. She was laughing at something that Brian had said, her head thrown back and her face animated and happy. He stared for a second or two. She was an attractive woman. And because of that, people would take notice of her. They shouldn't be out in public, he thought, looking around him. Still, it was so good to see her again.

His phone rang and broke his attention. He pulled it quickly from his pocket. For a second, he wanted it to be her, but could see from across the street that it wasn't. Damn! It was the WitSec guy, John Streeter again. "Mr. Reston is in Lugano," he said without preamble. "Are you?"

Cade felt his blood go cold. How did the guy know? But wait, he didn't seem to know where Cade was. "Lugano? Switzerland? I think you got your coordinates wrong, John," he said, as he watched Meara and Brian from across the street.

"Your car arrived empty in Milano, Cade," Streeter said coolly.

"Maybe I'm getting a haircut, or stopped to visit a friend," Cade said dryly. "So? What did your boss say, Streeter? That's what we should be focusing on here, right?"

"He said, 'No deal'."

Cade paused a second. "OK, I guess I'll have them pretty me up for my media shots when I tell my story to the press. I should be back in the States in a day or two."

"You're bluffing."

"Yeah, you just keep thinking that, Jack."

"John."

"You tell your bosses, they're making a mistake. There's no way they'd know this, but I look pretty good on TV," Cade said with a humorless laugh.

"Chandler, you got nothing to offer them."

"Hey, I'm fine with this. Looking forward to the fight, actually. To be honest, my regular accounts have been kind of boring lately."

"Like I say, you're bluffing."

"Like I say, your boss will probably be sorry," Cade said lightly and hit the End button.

He looked down at the phone. Damn, he'd wanted that to work out. He glanced up and saw Meara and Brian coming across the street towards the ferry terminal. He watched them for a second as he thought about how the WitSec folks knew where they were. He was sure they hadn't followed them; he'd have known it back in Menaggio. It had to be Brian, he decided. Maybe Brian had some kind of tracking device on him. How else could they know exactly where he was?

He hurried towards them. Meara looked up and when she caught sight of him he could tell she was really happy to see him. He let go of a breath he hadn't realized he'd been holding. He took her in his arms and kissed her soundly. "Geez, it's good to see you again," he said grinning.

She smiled back at him. "It's good to see you, too."

Cade looked at Brian and said bluntly, "I'm pretty sure they're tracking you, bud. Any idea how?"

Brian looked confused and he patted his pockets thoughtfully as if the answer was something he could feel. "You sure?"

Cade nodded. "The guy, John Streeter, just called me. Said he knew you were here in Lugano, but wanted to know if I was here too. Sounds like he's got a tracker on you, but not me, and probably not Meara. What are you carrying?"

Brian shook his head. Then he looked down at the mobile phone in his hand like it was some alien thing. "Damn! It's got to be my phone. I brought it with me from the States."

Cade stared at it. "Any new apps? Has it ever been out of your sight?"

Brian shrugged. "Since when? Who knows how long they've been tracking me with it. But it's probably the source. It has GPS and would be an easy way of following someone. Damn it! I've been so stupid."

"You need to get rid of it," Cade said.

"Hey! I've got lots of stuff on this phone. Pictures, contacts, all sorts of important stuff!"

Cade shook his head. "If you want to get away from these goons, you'll have to lose the tracking device," Cade said reasonably.

Brian frowned then finally nodded. "OK, but hang on a few minutes while I back my stuff up to the cloud, then you can get rid of the phone."

Cade stared at him for a second and shook his head. Even though he understood what Brian meant, he had to admit that he sounded like a kook when he said things like that.

"How do we get rid of it?" Meara asked. "Throw it into the lake, do you think?"

Cade nodded thoughtfully. "Well, that would certainly destroy the phone, but it'd be better if it was active for a while, to give

Brian a chance of getting far away first." He looked around and then smiled. "How about we give it a ride on the ferry. It'd take a while before they'd know you weren't on it."

Meara looked at the ferry now docked at the pier and noticed the passengers lining up to board. She glanced at Cade and nodded her approval. "How about sticking it in one of their bags?" she said, indicating the luggage on the ground next to the passengers.

Cade smiled. He put his hand out to Brian who gave him the phone.

"Cade, find someone who doesn't look like they'll steal my identity once they have the phone, OK?" Brian said morosely.

Cade smiled. "Will do." He walked over to the passengers and engaged a few of them in banter, probably asking about the ferry and times and so on. He went down on a knee, to check the laces of his boots and while he was there he nonchalantly tucked the phone into the side pocket of the bag beside his foot. He glanced up, and satisfied that no one saw what he'd done, he stood up and sauntered back to Meara and Brian.

"Let's go," he said, taking Meara's arm and nodding to Brian.

The three of them headed down the promenade back towards the downtown.

"I think you should get back to the States, Brian," Cade said.

"That's what we thought. Next flight is at seven tonight to Zurich," he said. "But what about my stuff down in Milan? I have a car rental and a room at the penzione..."

Cade nodded. "Give me the information and I'll take care of it for you. We'll bring your suitcase back with us."

Meara looked at him sharply. "Wait, I'm going back with Brian," she said to Cade.

Cade pulled Meara to a stop. He looked at Brian and nodded. "Could you give us a moment, Brian?"

Brian's eyebrows raised but he nodded and moved away.

Cade looked down at Meara. "Let's get one thing straight here. Brian is not your son, Meara. You just met him for the first time yesterday, OK? You're not responsible for him."

"Cade, he needs me," Meara said. "He's not as comfortable traveling internationally as you or me."

Cade was already shaking his head. "No, Meara. He got himself out here, and he can get himself home just fine. You need to separate your motherly feelings for all the helpless young men in the world. The reality is that you don't know Brian well enough to feel this responsible for him, OK?"

"Cade, you don't understand. If something happens to him before he gets back to the States, I'll feel like it's my fault."

Cade snorted. "You won't even know about it, honey."

Meara eyes narrowed, "What do you mean?"

He shook his head. "Meara, you aren't his next of kin. If anything happens to Brian, you wouldn't be notified. How would you even find out about it? You think it'll be in the news?"

She looked nonplused, and then her shoulders fell. She breathed out. "You're right." She shook her head and then she looked at him again. "Which is exactly why I should travel back with him."

Cade looked at her. He sighed. "That's nuts, but to be honest, I would feel better if you were out of harm's way, too, so fine, you can go with him."

She narrowed her eyes, and said coolly, "You are giving me permission?" Her voice rose with the last word.

Cade swore under his breath. "Of course not. All I'm saying is that I think it's a good idea."

The three of them got into a taxi that Brian managed to hail at the curb while Cade and Meara were rolling their eyes at each other.

Brian looked from one to the other and noted the stony expressions. "Cade, did Meara tell you about AtmosTrace?"

Meara looked at Brian in surprise and then excitement. She turned to Cade grabbing his arm, instantly over her hissy fit. "Oh my God, I forgot to tell you. It's not WitSec that's tracking Brian; it's a company, AtmosTrace. Have you heard of them?"

Cade leaned forward. "How do you know it's not WitSec?"

"Well, who knows?" Brian shrugged, "They may be working together, for all I know. But the people who have been giving me a lot of trouble is a company called AtmosTrace. It's located in Puyallup, Washington."

"Have you heard of them, Cade?" Meara asked again.

Cade shook his head and tried to think through how this news might change things. It was possible that it wasn't WitSec who'd called him; he'd made the assumption, but Streeter only said he worked vaguely for the government; he never specified. That could be a sort of secrecy-speak for any of the agencies or even a government contractor, when he thought about it.

He looked up at Brian, "So tell me about the company. Why would they be after you?"

"Well, like I told Meara earlier, my dad had their business card and...."

"What? Your father had their business card?"

Meara nodded, "I know I reacted the same way, but apparently Brian's mother kept all of her husband's personal effects in a box while he was in prison, and this business card was among his stuff. Brian even called the number," she said glancing at Brian.

Brian nodded. "It is a very security conscious place. They don't have a website, and don't advertise. They're supposed to be an engineering consulting group. At least, that's what they told me."

"When was this?"

"Maybe two years ago. I actually went to Puyallup to see the place for myself last year. I pissed them off while I was there. I started asking lots of questions around the area. Who they were? What business are they in? You know, that sort of thing."

"What happened?" Cade asked.

"One of them snuck into my hotel room in the middle of the night. Scary as shit to wake up with someone sitting on the bed right next to you, believe me!"

Meara shivered at the thought.

Cade stared at him. "Jesus! What did you do?"

"Asked him what he wanted and prayed I wasn't going to be killed or robbed or both."

"And?"

"And the guy very quietly told me that I was to go away and stop asking questions about AtmosTrace or I would regret it." Brian looked from one to the other. "And after that, he left; just sort of disappeared into the darkness. As you can imagine, I turned on all the lights and didn't go back to sleep. Morning couldn't have come soon enough for me."

"You did what he said, though, right?" Meara asked. "You went away and stopped asking questions about them?"

"Well, I definitely left the next morning. But I've been trying to find out more about them ever since. Not much to tell, though. The company is listed as having less than fifty employees, and the owner isn't an actual person it's another corporation with an offshore address. I think it was listed in the Cayman Islands."

"Interesting," Cade said nodding. "So you think maybe they're behind the aerial spraying?"

"Could be," Brian said. "I've always thought so because why else would my dad have their card, you know?"

The cab was turning into the airport and soon Cade was sorting through the currency in his wallet for Swiss Francs to pay the driver. He asked him to wait because he wanted to make sure that Meara and Brian were all set and to get their flight numbers and departure and connecting times.

The three of them went into the terminal. There were only a few people milling around. It was several hours before the next flight would depart and the plane hadn't even arrived from Zurich yet.

Cade walked up to the counter and started talking to the agent in very fast Italian. Meara and Brian watched him, impressed.

He shook his head a few times and he pointed at the computer screen once and they talked some more. Finally, he turned to Meara and Cade, "No luck. The next flight is full with a tour group and there's even a waiting list of non-group passengers. So I made reservations for you for tomorrow morning first thing. It's a really good connection in Zurich to San Francisco. You would've had to spend the night in Zurich anyway, since there was nothing going to San Fran tonight, so I guess it's not a big deal. Give me your passports so she can put all the information in and we can get your tickets."

They did as he asked and he turned back to the agent. Within fifteen or twenty minutes they were back out in the parking lot and the taxi driver was coming around to pick them up. He was all smiles, happily predicting a good fare coming his way.

Cade looked at Meara and said, "We'll have to find a place to stay for tonight."

Meara grinned, "No problem. I had to book a room at the hotel so we could get access to their computer with Internet. But, we'll have to get a second room for Brian," she said with a smile.

Cade grinned. "I like a lady who plans ahead," he said.

"Depends on the plan, though, huh?" she countered.

Cade was thinking that the evening was already looking better and better.

Chapter 61   Louie, Louie

Meara and Cade booked a single for Brian and gave him his key.

"Sort of like having a grown son who still lives with you, huh?" Cade said to Meara as they took the elevator up to their own room. Cade had upgraded their room to one on the front side of the building overlooking the lake.

Meara looked around, "I wish I had my suitcase and clothes," she said.

"Why? You look wonderful," Cade said. "Besides, this can't be the first time you've had to wear the same clothes two days in a row, is it?"

She chuckled, "Hardly, I grew up in the Sixties, you know," she replied and added. "But that doesn't mean I look forward to it now."

"Hey, come on, we got these awesome little toiletry kits," Cade said holding up the small bags they had been handed at the desk.

She had to admit that the front desk clerk had been very cool, to the point where Meara had wanted to burst out with suppressed laughter. The guy took in that they had no luggage, that she had a different man with her, and that they were now asking for toiletry kits, but still, he never let on that there was anything in any way odd about the situation or the request.

"Hmmm," Cade said pulling things out of the little toiletry bag. "No condoms." He looked up. "Do you think that's judgmental of them or just an oversight?"

She giggled. "Well, it is Switzerland...and this is the Italian canton..." she shrugged as if that said it all.

He grinned. "Well, no problem, I'm sure I have one in my wallet."

"It's not as if I could get pregnant," she said with a laugh.

"You need to take your health precautions more seriously, Meara," he said with a shake of his head. "Condoms aren't just for preventing pregnancy; they're also for preventing STD's."

"God, I hope you aren't trying to tell me something here," she said with raised eyebrows.

He smiled. "No, I'm clean. And I haven't been with anyone else since last night. But, I'm trying to tell you that you need to be more proactive about these things; that's all I'm saying. The world has changed since the last time you were single."

She chuckled, "Thanks, Cade," she said and he came over next to her. Arm in arm, they walked out on the small deck off the room and took in the late afternoon sun over the lake. They could see a few boats bobbing at their moorings, and one or two motorboats with their wakes cutting white across the otherwise glassy surface. There was a stillness to the lake, too; an unexpected silence just beyond the hum of the traffic going by and the scattered voices of people talking on the sidewalk below.

"It's really lovely, isn't it?" she said softly.

He put his arm around her shoulders. "This part of Europe is spectacular – the deep lakes, surrounded by high mountains, the peaks of the Alps on the horizon. It's really a view I never get tired of."

"Me, either," she agreed. She leaned in and he kissed her. She felt something release within her, some stress or worry was melting away. She put her hand on his chest, just resting it there. She could feel his heart beating beneath her fingertips. She looked up into his eyes and she could see that he was getting aroused, and that knowledge affected her like a switch. She felt the warmth of her own desire traveling through her body. "I thought maybe we'd eat first," she said, in response, as if he'd spoken.

"We could," he agreed, his fingers brushing her collarbone as he nuzzled into her neck, "if you want."

She took a breath in and then out. She looked at him again, "You know I want you. God, Cade! You touch me and I want you," she said softly.

"Let's take a shower together before we go to dinner, OK?" he whispered into her hair.

She looked at him and knew she wasn't going to be able to resist his offer. She finally shrugged and grinned and took his hand, "All right. Let's go."

He let her lead him to the bathroom, surprised at how easily she acquiesced, but getting more excited by the minute.

They stepped into the small bathroom with its tiny white tiled floor and walls. It was a small intimate space. Meara unsnapped and unzipped her pants and let them fall to the floor. She glanced down as she quickly unbuttoned the tiny pearl buttons on her deep purple blouse. She saw that Cade was unzipping and unbuttoning his own clothes as fast as he could. He looked up at her but his eyes immediately dropped to her open blouse billowing out as she reached around to unhook her bra. He watched mesmerized as the bra loosened and her breasts fell. She arched her back and shrugged, letting the bra and blouse float to the floor. She looked up at him and smiled.

He grinned back at her as he opened his shirt and stepped out of his pants. He hopped for a second as he removed his socks. His underwear was last. But he had no modesty; most men didn't. He dropped his pants and stepped out and kicked them into the pile of clothes at his feet.

He reached out and hooked his thumbs on the edge of her panties – all that she was wearing now – and slowly lowered them as he sat down on the closed toilet seat. Free of the panties, she straddled him and then it was just one long ride. They were both groaning and straining towards the final release and when it came, they held each other tightly and moved together as one.

When they were done, they sat wrapped in each other, waiting for their breathing to go back to normal.

As they remained in their embrace, they heard a knock at the outer door. She closed her eyes, and then snorted. "Must be our son," she said.

"YOUR son," Cade replied crossly, as he lifted her off him, then got up, stepped into his slacks and pulled them up. He zipped them closed before opening the bathroom door and striding over to the room's door.

He opened it and it was, indeed, Brian.

"Hey, Cade! Man, I'm getting hungry. Are we going to go have dinner or something?" he asked, looking over Cade's shoulder searching for Meara.

Cade blocked his view. "Sure, Brian. Wait in the lobby. We'll be down in a few minutes."

Brian eyed him for a second, then nodded. "OK, I'll see you guys in...what?...Ten minutes, do you think?"

"Sure, Brian. Ten minutes," Cade agreed.

He shut the door just as Meara came out of the bathroom wrapped in a bathrobe. Cade looked at her and smiled. "You know, I think Brian is here because of you, not me. So if we take him to dinner, I think you should pay the bill," he teased.

She smiled as she walked over to him. "Fine, but I'll expect to be repaid, you know," she said in a low voice.

He made eye contact with her for one long second, "My pleasure," he said with a nod of his head.

She put her arms around him and added, "Ummm, mine, too."

Cade already knew where they would go for dinner. When he mentioned Mount Bre, Brian remembered Meara talking about the restaurant at the top of mountain and he was all for the idea. They took a cab to the funicular station not far from downtown Lugano and in the late afternoon's waning sunlight they soon were rising up the side of the mountain. They could see the lights along the streets and in the buildings of Lugano begin to go on, and the town grew smaller and smaller the higher the funicular car went.

Meara sat next to Cade and held his hand as she looked out and marveled at the scenery. Brian, on the other hand, was pacing from one side of the car to the other looking out and snapping pictures with his phone He seemed to be enjoying himself, in an attention-deficit sort of way. It was just like having a teenager along, Meara thought with a smile. She had to admit it was hard to believe he was in his mid-thirties. There was something about this younger generation though; they seemed like teenagers, well into their thirties. She wondered why that was?

She believed that her generation, by contrast, always seemed older and more mature than they actually were. Oh, sure, they did lots of dumb things and got way more into drugs than was good for them, but overall they had a world consciousness and maturity that the younger generations that followed hadn't seemed to develop yet. Well, she had to admit that she admired other things about them — their openness to differences and lack of race consciousness. Her generation tended make too much of racial blindness and sometimes their eagerness to be accepting ended up becoming ingratiating and false.

The Millennials also seemed to be less enamored with making a good living and being well off than her generation. Even though the Sixties generation spent their twenties demonstrating against conformity and trying to live up to the whole Free Love reputation, in the end, she believed her generation wanted what their parents had had and more. That's why it was a particular sick irony that many of them now watched that dream pass them by as the economy soured and their 401K accounts shrank with the shrinking economy.

She watched Brian for a few more minutes and then got drawn back to the panorama of the lake below her.

Cade squeezed her hand, "Pretty, huh?" he said softly.

She smiled and squeezed his hand back, "It's breathtaking."

Brian tinkered with his phone as he took pictures.

"He should just enjoy the scenery instead of trying to capture it," Cade commented dryly.

Meara thought about that for several seconds. "That's so true, isn't it? We miss a lot when we try to hold on to it."

Chapter 62   Light My Fire

Cade had made the reservations for the three of them at the restaurant on the top of Mount Bre. But he really wished it had just been the two of them — him and Meara — without the third wheel, Brian. Oh, sure, he liked the guy well enough, but Brian seemed to have only a few focused interests – chemtrails, his father, and the intricacies of computer programming on the Internet. None of these topics were especially interesting to Cade, and he doubted Meara cared much about them either, although she seemed to encourage Brian more than Cade thought she should.

They arrived at the top and Cade led Meara down the path towards the restaurant. Brian lumbered next to them, sometimes next to Meara and then after a few long steps, he'd be walking next to Cade, as if he couldn't figure out where he belonged. Truth was, Cade thought, he was like a lost puppy following whoever patted his head.

The sky was starting to turn orange with rays of purple behind the peaks of the Alps in the distance. It was going to be a spectacular sunset, Cade saw. He was glad to be here with Meara for something this good.

Even though it was getting cool, they asked to sit outside on the patio under the stars and the twinkling strings of lights circling the tables. The restaurant had set up portable propane heaters that threw off a lot of heat and it was cozy and warm on the side closest to the heater. Meara had remembered to bring her sweater along.

Cade engaged the server in Italian; discussing the specials and what would be good for appetizers and which wine would be good. Merlot was a local specialty; many of the area vineyards provided the house wines so Cade agreed that they would try a bottle. When their glasses were filled and bread and a little dipping dish of basil olive oil was set out, the three of them toasted the sunset and sat back in the chairs and relaxed.

It was early for dinner in Europe. It wasn't like in the States where people might have dinner even in the late afternoon, depending on the region and the age of the diners. Cade and Meara would've been satisfied to sit and talk for an hour or so, sipping wine and tasting an appetizer or two. But Brian was antsy and apparently hungry, so they went ahead and ordered their entrees.

Cade was quietly hoping that their meals would be delayed a bit, though. He wasn't ready to rush headlong into a heavy meal after the day they'd had. He really wanted an hour or so to catch his breath and register where he was and who he was with. He glanced at Meara and smiled. He was happy that things had worked out for them so far. There had been so many twists and turns since they arrived in Milan that it was staggering to review it in his head, much less realize that they'd actually done it all in just the past two days: Milan, his mother's dinner, the cruise on Lake Como, Meara and Brian's bus trip to Lugano, his train trip from Como to Lugano, their trip to the airport, and the taxi trip back to Lugano to the hotel, and now here on this peak overlooking the twinkling lights of Lugano on the lakeshore below. It was breathtaking.

"Hey!" Brian said, swatting at the air.

Cade glanced at him with a half-smile. "What's up?" he asked.

"Hey!" Brian repeated. "It's some kind of bumblebee or something!" Brian said with an edge to his voice. He was swatting at the air around his head.

Cade chuckled. "Can't be a bee this time of year and not at this altitude...." he said as he watched Brian waving his arms at his invisible enemy. But then he saw it, too. It was tiny but there was the unmistakable glint of metal, maybe reflecting off the candlelight on the table or perhaps from the fire of the propane burner.

Cade sat up, "What the...!" he swore.

The thing was hovering in the air between them. It seemed to be some kind of the metal device and Cade thought he saw it spray something into the air. He frowned and squinted to get a better look at it, but it was buzzing and weaving too quickly.

Suddenly a guy came up behind Cade and in one swift motion, he reached over and snatched the thing from the air. "Got it!" he said triumphantly. Just as quickly, he turned and vanished into the darkness beyond the lights of the patio.

Meara looked at Cade in shock. "Who was that?" Then she noticed the look on Cade's face. She saw that he wasn't looking into the dark where the guy had disappeared; he was looking at Brian. "What is it, Cade?" Then she glanced over at Brian, too.

"Jesus!" Cade breathed out. He could see something was very, very wrong.

Brian was bent forward holding his throat and his face was turning purple.

Cade jumped up and raced to Brian's side. "What is it, man?" he asked, touching Brian's arm.

"Can't....breathe..."Brian choked out.

"Is he having a heart attack?" Meara asked, as she stood up to come to his aid.

"Heart attack?" Cade repeated. He looked more closely at Brian. Maybe. But he was in his thirties, he thought. He did seem to be having trouble breathing, and he had his hand over his heart as if in pain. Then Cade glanced down at Brian's hands. The backs of his hands were covered in an angry reddish rash. Hives.

"Jesus!" Cade exclaimed again. "Not a heart attack. He's allergic...he's having a reaction to something." He loosened Brian's collar, and the top buttons popped off. "Brian? Brian! What are you allergic to?" he asked. "Come on, man, focus! Tell me what you're allergic to!"

In the meantime, Meara grabbed the waiter and told him to "dial 911" which, of course, didn't mean anything to him, but then she said "Doctor!" and pointed at Brian, who was obviously struggling to breath, his face crimson and his eyes bulging. The server quickly got the message and ran for help.

Cade got Brian to the ground. He could see that Brian's lips and face was swelling. When Brian opened his mouth to try to draw a breath, Cade could see his tongue was also swollen and probably beginning to block his airways.

Cade leaned over and asked earnestly again, "What are you allergic to, Brian?"

Brian didn't respond. He was choking and gasping, trying to force a breath in through the tightening circle of his throat.

Cade leaned in closer and focused his eyes on Brian's one more time. "Come on, man, tell me what you're allergic to!"

Brian coughed and gagged. His eyes spun in their sockets, then focused for a second onto Cade's face. He reached out to Cade and gripped his hand. "Latex," he whispered.

Cade frowned. "Latex? Did you say 'Latex'? Brian? Latex?" he repeated.

Brian closed his eyes and seemed to nod.

Cade looked at Meara. "He's allergic to Latex. He's allergic to God-damned rubber!" he said, looking around. "What the hell?"

When the emergency responders finally arrived, Cade told them in rapid Italian that Brian was having an allergic reaction and needed a shot of adrenaline and some kind of antihistamine. Meara took Brian's hand and stayed with him, as he was loaded onto the ambulance. The medical EMT's worked on him in the back while the ambulance made it's way down the winding road that ran down that backside of the mountain and would take them to the hospital on this side of Lugano.

Cade paid for the dinner that they never got a chance to eat and took the funicular down. At the base of the peak, he caught a taxi to the hospital to meet up with Meara and find out how Brian was doing. He thought back to the dinner and Brian's sudden symptoms. What the hell was that bumblebee thing? A tiny drone? He felt an icy fear creep down his spine. What in the world were they dealing with here?

When he got to the hospital, Brian had already been taken to a room. Meara was sitting on a chair outside in the hall. She glanced up as Cade got off the elevator and watched him come towards her. She stood up and he folded her into his arms.

"You OK?" he asked softly. He pulled her away from him and looked down at her to gauge her emotional state.

She sniffed, but didn't look like she'd been crying. "What happened?" she asked. "I tried to ask the doctor, but he doesn't speak any English."

Cade closed his eyes for a second. "I'm not sure, but he seems to have had an allergic reaction."

"But you said he's allergic to latex. Was it in our food?" she asked, with a look of disgust.

"I don't think it was in the food," he said shaking his head. "You didn't see that thing flying around us? The bumblebee? The thing that guy grabbed out of the air?"

Her eyes grew round and she looked stunned and she nodded. "What? What are you saying?"

"I don't know what I'm saying," he said shaking his head again. "But I think someone obviously knew about his severe allergy to latex and figured out a way to deliver it to him."

"You think someone made him have that allergic reaction? But he could've died!" Then her look changed as she repeated more slowly, "He could've died." She closed her eyes for a second. "Oh, my God."

Cade held her against him. "Look, Meara. I called Angie on the way over here. I've asked her to arrange for a private jet to fly him back to the States to a good hospital in San Francisco. The plane should be at the Lugano airport in a couple of hours. I've also asked her to contact his mother, to let her know what's happened. We'll fly her in from Minneapolis and get her to the hospital."

Meara looked at him and nodded but he wasn't sure she actually understood what he was saying. She looked shell-shocked.

"I want to go in and talk to him for a minute, if he's awake, to let him know what's going to happen now."

Meara let go of him and sat back down in the chair. She closed her eyes for a long minute and lowered her head, although he didn't know if it was sheer exhaustion or if she was praying. She looked completely spent.

Cade went into the room. Brian was in a private room and was hooked up to all sorts of medical paraphernalia. Cade walked slowly to the bed. As he drew next to it, he saw that Brian's eyes moved behind the swollen mounds that were now his eyelids.

There was a breathing tube down his throat so he couldn't speak, but Cade saw that he was following Cade's movements.

"Brian, we're flying you home, back to the States, in a couple of hours. You can just rest for now."

Brian blinked, although it was hard to tell.

Cade took his hand. "I want to ask you a few things, man. Squeeze my hand once if the answer is 'yes' and twice if it's 'no', all right?"

Cade felt a strong squeeze to his hand. He noticed that Brian's hands were clammy and swollen, but his grip was surprisingly strong.

"Did you see the bumblebee thing?" Cade asked.

Brian squeezed his hand once.

"I think it was a tiny drone. Do you agree?"

Brian paused for a second then squeezed Cade's hand once.

"I'm guessing here, Brian, but I think this was meant to be a message, not a hit. I don't think they will try again."

Meara's voice cut into the room, "Why do you think that?"

Cade turned to her. "Because if they wanted him dead, he'd be dead. They delivered the allergen in a device that could easily have been knocked out of the air or not worked, or not delivered the spray correctly. Too many things could've gone wrong. Plus, it was in a public place with plenty of people around to help him. If they wanted him dead, like I said, he'd be dead." He felt Brian squeeze his hand and when Cade looked down at him, he felt badly for being so blunt. But Brian seemed to agree with his assessment; at least, Cade hoped so.

Chapter 63   Stand By Me

Meara stood beside the bed and gently squeezed Brian's other arm. "You just try to get better, Brian. Don't worry. We'll take care of everything. OK?" She smiled down at him with almost motherly concern.

When she turned she saw that the Swiss nurse had come in and was talking quietly in Italian to Cade.

"We've got to go," Cade said when he saw that Meara was looking at him. "They want Brian to rest, especially since he'll have a big trip ahead of him later tonight."

She came to him and he took her arm and led her out into the hall. She wasn't sure what they would do while they waited for the plane to arrive and for the arrangements to fall into place. But she was determined to accompany Brian back to the States – she felt that she had to — but she hated the thought of leaving Cade.

Suddenly, she felt Cade tense up beside her. She looked up in time to see a guy step forward.

"Cade Chandler?" he asked, looking directly at Cade.

Cade stared at him for several seconds. And then suddenly he dropped Meara's arm and took two steps towards the guy and slammed his fist into the guy's cheek.

Meara gasped in shock and jumped instinctively back out of the way. She couldn't remember ever seeing two grown men in a fistfight except in the movies. It was surreal.

"You, bastard!" Cade said savagely, bent over and breathing hard.

The other guy, obviously taken completely by surprise, had fallen backward against the opposite wall. In an instant, though, he was crouched, his arms out, ready. His quick reflexes made it quite apparent even to Meara that he was trained in hand-to-hand combat and was more than ready to respond if Cade were to throw a second punch.

"What the hell, man?" the guy said fiercely. "I'm here to help you, you asshole."

"Help me? By nearly killing that kid in there?" Cade replied just as fiercely. Meara saw that Cade was cradling his fist with his other hand. She wondered if he'd broken something when he punched the guy.

"What kid? What're you talking about?"

Meara and Cade exchanged glances and looked at him in surprise.

"You're with WitSec, right?" Cade asked.

The guy eyed him for a second, but then nodded. "Yeah. So?"

"The kid in there is Brian Reston. Does that name ring a bell?"

Recognition came into the guy's eyes and he nodded. "Sure. Joseph Reston's son. He's the one you told me was stalking you, right? We've been checking him out."

"And you followed him to Como..." Cade started to say.

The guy put his hands up and shook his head. "No, we haven't been following him at all. Heck, until this afternoon, we weren't even sure he was in Milan." He gradually stood up out of his crouched position, feeling a little surer that Cade wasn't going to hit him again.

Cade stared at him. "I don't get it," he said with a shake of his head. "Hold on. Do you know a guy named John Streeter? Does he work for you guys?"

The guy shook his head again. "Streeter? No, I know all the guys working this detail. There's no John Streeter. Why? Who is he?"

"Well, he's a guy I met this afternoon in Bellagio after he'd tailed Brian from Milan to Como. He implied that he worked for WitSec."

The guy frowned. "He said that?"

"Well, not exactly. What he said was that he 'worked for the government.' After I talked to you the other day, I assumed he was sent out by you guys to contact me."

The guy's lips curled into a smile, "No, that would be me." He stared at the wall above Cade's head for a second, thinking, then he looked at Cade. "So do you know who he really is?"

Cade sighed. "Well, if he isn't with you guys, then I'm guessing he must be with AtmosTrace like Brian thought." He glanced at Meara for confirmation.

She nodded.

"AtmosTrace? Why would they be after Reston?"

"So you know who AtmosTrace is then?"

"Sure," the guy nodded. "They're a government contractor. They did a lot of work for NOAA."

Meara took a breath, NOAA, the National Oceanic and Atmospheric Administration. That would definitely be the federal agency involved in anything to do with the aerial spraying, if what Brian said was true.

"That figures," Cade said, mirroring her thoughts. His brows furrowed. "So does that mean that these chemtrails are a real thing then?" he asked.

"Chemtrails?" the guy looked at Cade in surprise. "Where did you hear about chemtrails?"

Cade nodded to the room behind him, "From our boy, Brian." Cade looked at him searchingly. "So how much do you know about that bumblebee drone thing?"

The guy eyed Cade. "How'd you know it was a drone?"

"It was a guess. Especially after Brian started breaking out in hives."

"We've been investigating AtmosTrace for a while now. We've got them by the balls with that thing. I want to thank you for leading us to it."

"Huh?"

The guy glanced around. "Listen. Maybe we should take this discussion to someplace more private, all right?"

Cade smiled. "Fine by me. I'm starving. Let's find a place to eat. We can talk over food." Cade nodded at Meara. "We haven't had dinner yet."

The guy looked at Meara and smiled. He put his hand out. "James Starling, ma'am."

She shook his hand "Meara Cellini."

"Cellini? Hmmm. You don't look Italian," he said with a smile.

Damn, she thought, he's flirting with me. She suspected Cade realized it too because he immediately stepped forward next to her.

"Obviously you know my name already, James, but it's nice to finally find out yours. In fact, it would've made things a whole lot simpler had I known it before Streeter came along, and you could've saved me a sore fist if you had introduced yourself at the restaurant on Mount Bre."

James turned to him. "Sorry about that, Cade, but it's 'need to know' in this business." He shrugged and rubbed at his jaw. "Nice cross punch. You ever take boxing?"

Cade nodded, "High school. I took Karate too, but I doubt I could throw a kick in these clothes."

The two men chuckled like old buddies.

Meara felt like she was in a small rowboat being tossed around. She'd spent the whole day – heck, maybe the whole week – following Cade's lead. Now she really needed some time to think.

"Cade?" she said stopping before they got as far as the elevator. "Why don't you and James go and have your talk. I think I'd rather stay here with Brian. I hate to leave him right now."

"But, honey, aren't you hungry?" Cade said with concern.

She shook her head. "I feel like I've swallowed a brick, to be honest. If you want, why don't you just bring me back a couple of pieces of bread and maybe something to drink, OK?"

He looked worried and frowned, but he noticed that James had pushed the elevator button and almost immediately they heard the ping of the elevator arriving. He nodded to Meara. "If you're sure...?"

She smiled wanly. "I'm positive. Really. I'd rather keep an eye on Brian right now. He's all alone here."

The elevator doors opened and James walked on. Cade nodded again. "OK, I promise I'll be back right after I hear what he has to say. I'll bring you back something."

Meara nodded and quickly turned and walked back to Brian's room before Cade could change his mind. The nurse nodded to her, indicating she could go back in to see Brian. She smiled at the tiny woman and went in, feeling a sense of relief to have something definite to do – make Brian feel less alone.

Chapter 64   My Generation

Cade and James stepped out into the cool evening air. It was apparent that the warm summer evenings were a thing of the past, Cade thought. The autumn air felt bracing but it was a nice change from the stale closed-up smell of the hospital.

There were several cafes near the hospital, so it was a question of finding one that had a table open. They stopped at two cafes before they reached the larger one on the corner. It looked full but Cade chatted with the maître d' and managed to snag a table inside. It was a tiny round table covered with a crisp white linen tablecloth. There were only two chairs and Cade decided it was probably just as well that Meara hadn't come with them.

He and James got settled, ordered a bottle of the local merlot, and enjoyed the fat slices of Italian bread in the basket that was immediately set on the table next to a small saucer of olive oil sprinkled with basil. Cade glanced up at James who was watching and imitating him as he broke off a piece of the bread and dipped it hungrily into the saucer. Cade grinned. "When in Rome...eh?" he commented companionably.

James smiled sheepishly. "I admit that you Italians have this food and wine thing down pat," he agreed with a laugh.

Cade felt complimented but realized that it was rare for someone to identify him as an Italian since his last name certainly wouldn't indicate anything but Anglo-Saxon heritage. But then he remembered that James was with WitSec and probably knew more about him than he knew about himself. Well, close to, anyway.

James leaned back in his chair, brushing crusty breadcrumbs from his lap. "So? What do you know about AtmosTrace?"

Cade eyed him. "Actually, I'd like to ask you the same question," he said. "Because the truth is I don't know that much." He proceeded to tell James everything that he'd learned from Brian.

James nodded and then took out a small notebook and scribbled a few things down. "That pretty much confirms what we know, too, but I think I can fill in a little more of the background for you at least." He took a sip of his wine and swallowed with apparent satisfaction. "I wasn't around when you and Brian's father were involved in the court case about the drug-running operation, but from what I've been able to piece together, there was a lot more to it than just trafficking. I would say it was really a case of a company that was given an inch and that took a mile."

Cade frowned. "What does that mean?"

"First, keep in mind that AtmosTrace was a legit government contractor. They bid and won contracts on some very hush-hush work, one of the projects being experimental aerial spraying. That project was overseen by NOAA through the OAR."

"OAR?" Cade interrupted.

"Office of Oceanic and Atmospheric Research. They are sort of NOAA's R&D department."

Cade nodded.

"Well, as near as I can tell, the project ended right after Reston was put into prison and you ran away to join the Witness Protection circus." He paused and smiled at his joke. "At least as far as NOAA was concerned, it ended. Apparently, though, AtmosTrace didn't actually stop working on it."

"How could they afford to continue it? That had to cost a lot of money. Where were they getting the funds?"

James shook his head. "No idea, although my personal guess is that the drug running operation was paying for the project. I'm sure there was a ton of money being thrown off from selling the cocaine. But that's just a guess on my part; I really have no facts to back it up. For all we know, there may even be other players involved who were funding them."

Cade nodded. "And what happened to the research? Were the results published or a report ever written?"

James shook his head. "Don't know. It was a secret project, so it could be nothing was ever officially going to be published. Anyway, for AtmosTrace it wasn't research."

"Huh?" Cade questioned, leaning forward. "What do you mean?"

"At some point it stopped being hypothetical; I think they were actually doing it."

"Doing what exactly?"

"Weather modification, man. What did you think it was all about?"

Cade shook his head. "I thought it was about drugs...at least, that's what I thought originally. Now I just don't know. Brian has a crazy story about chemtrails and shit like that...Is that what they were doing? Was the drug-running just a front for controlling the weather?"

Their food arrived and James and Cade just exchanged glances while the waiter laid out their plates and took away the olive oil saucer and then asked if they wanted more bread. Cade remembered Meara and nodded, telling the waiter that he wanted to order some warm slices to take back with him when they were done. The waiter smiled and said he'd take care of it.

James looked from Cade to the waiter. "Must be nice being fluent in another language. I picked up a little Arabic and Kurdish when I was in Iraq, but it was pretty basic 'hello-how-are-you-please-don't-shoot-me' kind of phrases that they taught us."

Cade smiled. "I was lucky. My mother spoke to us kids in Italian all the time when we were growing up. It was interchangeable with English to me. I was in second or third grade before I realized that my classmates couldn't understand Italian too." He chuckled.

James nodded and lifted his glass of wine. He took a long slow sip and then eyed Cade again. He lowered his voice. "Tell me about the bumblebee drone. I got there late. How did it seem to work?" He took a second sip of the merlot as he looked at Cade.

"Not much to tell. This tiny metal thing buzzed around our table and immediately seemed to zero in on Brian. Then it sprayed something into the air. The whole thing was over in seconds."

"Was there any smell to the stuff it sprayed?"

"I don't think so. It was like a liquid or steam being sprayed. There was a small hissing sound, I think, but no aroma at all."

James nodded. "And then Brian had an allergic reaction to it?"

"Yeah. It turns out he's allergic to latex – and he's not allergic to anything else – just latex. So I think that's what was being sprayed in his face. They obviously knew about his sensitivity and targeted him specifically."

James nodded in agreement. "Sounds like it from your description of his toxic reaction."

"Jesus! You have no idea!" Cade said shaking his head. "He nearly died in my arms. His face swelled up so fast, you could literally see his eyes bulging and his throat closing. It was horrible to watch. I can't imagine how excruciating it must have been for him!"

James let out a long breath. "Yeah."

"So what do we do? I mean, I'll get Brian back to the States, but what happens next?"

"My bosses think that it's time to go after AtmosTrace. This killer drone thing really crossed the line. If you're willing, we could use your help."

Cade glanced at James in surprise. "In what way?"

"Brian's out of the picture now, but we need some way of getting AtmosTrace to step out of the shadows. We know about some of their activities but we don't have a person to link it to. You talked to this Streeter fellow, right? Do you think you can contact him? Get him to meet you again?"

Cade stared at James as he thought about it. "Maybe. I mean he may call me again, probably either tonight or tomorrow. I don't know if this business with Brian changes that, though," he said thoughtfully. He looked up at James and continued, "I made a demand that he was supposed to pass along to his bosses. I'm assuming he'll get back to me about that."

"A demand?" James repeated with a slow smile of amusement.

"Sure. Remember, I thought he was with you guys. I told him I wanted Joseph Reston's record expunged as if it never happened.

It's what Brian asked me to do, and I didn't have a problem with it. His father's dead and it's all water under the bridge, as far as I'm concerned."

James' eyebrows shot up. "And what did Streeter say to that demand?"

"He passed it along to his bosses and they said 'no,' but I don't think that's a final 'no.'

"Why not?"

"I told him to tell his bosses that I'd expose them to the media if they don't agree. I assume he'll take that message to them."

"So if we can get Reston's record expunged you'll agree to help us get AtmosTrace?"

Cade looked up at James. They eyed each other for several seconds. Finally Cade nodded. "Fair trade. Sure."

"OK, then. I'll see what can be done. Reston is dead, so it's not like we have to let him out of prison, after all."

"Expunging records is done all the time," Cade responded, watching James carefully.

James looked at him, "Well, I doubt that, but I'm sure it probably can be done. I'll pass it along. I think in exchange for your help, something could be arranged."

Cade felt a well of satisfaction growing in the pit of his stomach. He was thinking about how grateful Meara might be if he were able to get Reston's record expunged. He wanted to turn things around with her. She was beginning to look at him like he was in her rear-view mirror, and that was not where he wanted to be with her.

Chapter 65   House of the Rising Sun

Meara was again sitting outside of Brian's room when she saw Cade get off the elevator. James wasn't with him, but she didn't find that particularly surprising.

"Hey," he said as he came up close. He sat down in the chair next to her and reached for her hand. "You OK?" he asked softly.

She nodded and smiled weakly. "I'm beat, Cade," she said letting her breath out.

"Got just the thing for you, then," he said with a smile and handed her a carefully wrapped package.

She looked at him questioningly as she took the package. She could feel the warmth emanating from it. Then she remembered and smiled. "Bread?"

He nodded. He pulled a half-full bottle of wine from his jacket pocket. "Bread and wine...an excellent local merlot, I might add," he said. "Sorry, I couldn't steal a wine glass, but I figured we could get a cup of some kind for you here somewhere."

She took the bottle and pried the cork out. She tipped it to her mouth and took a sip. "Hmmm, you're right, an excellent local merlot," she said approvingly with a smile. She opened the package and sighed at the several slices of bread. "Perfect," she said with a shake of her head. She looked at him. "Thank you."

He nodded. "The least I could do."

"So? What did James have to say?" she asked biting into the slice of warm bread. It tasted heavenly.

He smiled. "I'll tell you all about it, but first things first. The plane for Brian will arrive in an hour and a half. I have arranged for an ambulance service to take him out to the airport and they will fly him to Zurich. In Zurich, he'll be transferred to a private jet that will take him back to the States, directly to San Francisco. Angie's arranging for him to be transported from the airport to San Francisco General once he arrives. She's also been in touch with his mother and is making the arrangements to fly her out to San Francisco some time tomorrow."

Meara looked at him wide-eyed. "You did all that while you were at dinner?"

"Before, during, and then on the walk back over here afterwards. Meara, it's no big deal. All I'm doing is making phone calls; Angie's the one doing the real grunt work."

"How do you have the energy for any of this, Cade?" she asked shaking her head. She felt a thousand years old. It was all she could do to find the energy to direct her hand to bring the slice of bread to her mouth. Biting and chewing were another story requiring focused thought and motivation.

"I don't know. I've always been like this. When an emergency situation happens, I kick into overdrive, I guess," he said patting her hand. "How's our boy doing?" he asked nodding at the door.

"I think he's asleep. They gave him a sedative a little while ago because apparently the swelling, especially in his mouth and throat, can cause panic."

Cade nodded. "It would for me, that's for certain."

Meara sighed. "Me, too." She chewed slowly, enjoying the aroma and taste of the warm bread. She swallowed and remembering something, she looked at Cade. "Can I borrow your phone?" she asked. "Mine is dead; it must need to be recharged. I'd like to call Paul to let him know that I'll be coming home."

Cade pulled his cell phone from his pocket and handed it to her. She handed him her phone. "You may as well keep this one since it belongs to the Milan apartment."

"I'll see if I can find you a cup for your wine," he said, sliding the cell phone into his pocket. "Go ahead and make your call." He got up and walked down the hall towards the nurse's station.

Meara dialed the phone and waited. No answer. Paul must be in class or studying, she figured. Those were the only times he didn't answer his phone. After several rings, Paul's voice came on directing her to leave a message. "Hi, Paul. It's Mom. Sorry I missed you, but I just wanted to let you know that I'm heading back to the States tonight. I'll call you when I get to Oregon and we can chat then. Bye, honey. I love you." She clicked off.

Cade was standing in front of her with the small plastic cup. "You're leaving to go back tonight?" he asked in surprise.

Meara took the cup and poured a small amount of wine into it and set the bottle on the floor next to her chair. She glanced up at Cade. "Of course. I thought you assumed that I'd be going back with Brian. I can't leave him to travel alone," she said matter-of-factly.

"Why not?" Cade asked. "A medic will be going with him, and he'll probably sleep the entire trip anyway."

Meara nodded. "I know, Cade, but if he wakes up he won't know where he is or who those people are. It might frighten him. If I'm there, I can reassure him."

Cade just looked at her. "He's not your son, Meara," he said in a soft voice. "His mother is going to be meeting him at the hospital."

"I know that," Meara snapped. "I'm not confusing him with Paul, Cade. I just feel responsible for having brought him here to Lugano. Maybe none of this would've happened if..."

"Stop!" Cade said, putting up his hands. "None of this is your fault or has anything to do with you, Meara. And you don't have to feel responsible for him. He's a grown man," he paused and tried to lighten his voice as he added with a laugh, "even if he does act like a bloody teenager."

Meara looked at Cade, then she shook her head. "I understand what you're saying, Cade, but my mind's made up. I just feel it's the right thing to do. Tomorrow when we arrive in San Francisco, I'll turn him over to his mother and reassure her that he's going to be fine. Believe me, I know she'd do the same thing for me if the situation was reversed and I know I would appreciate it."

Cade shook his head, but didn't say anything more. She could tell that he'd given up trying to convince her. He stepped away and stuck his head into Brian's room. A nurse came out and he took her aside to ask about Brian.

Meara finished the three slices of bread that were in the package Cade had brought and had several small cups of wine. She did feel surprisingly revived. Probably, she thought, it was the wine that was giving her a second wind.

She saw the gurney being wheeled off the elevator and rolled towards her. She stood up and brushed off the crumbs from her lap and carried the empty wine bottle to the receptacle a little way down the hallway. When she came back she saw Cade's phone sitting next to her purse on the chair and she absently slid it in the outside pocket so she could give it back to him.

She stuck her head into the room and saw that the nurse and medical EMT were already carefully moving Brian from the bed to the gurney. Cade was talking to the both of them in Italian, giving them additional information, she assumed.

He saw her and waved her in. "This is Henri Duprey. He's the flight paramedic that will be traveling with you on the plane." He turned to the EMT and he introduced Meara.

Henri nodded and smiled at Meara. "*Bonjour, Signora* Cellini. You are American, no?"

"Yes," she replied with a warm smile. She noted his French accent and remembered that Switzerland had four official languages, French, being one of them, along with German, Italian, and Romansh, a local language only spoken in the southeast of the country and parts of northeastern Italy.

Cade took her arm and led her out of the room, just ahead of the gurney and Henri, who was now fiddling with the IV saline bag attached to the gurney. "Are you sure you want to go back with him? He'll be just fine, you know," he said.

Meara looked at him. "I know, Cade. And yes, I'm sure." She touched his arm. "Thanks."

The elevator pinged and opened and Arturo stepped out. He looked around and then caught sight of Cade and Meara. He grinned in recognition.

He stepped forward and said something in Italian to Cade, which seemed to get his attention. He asked a few questions, and Arturo answered, looking serious and professional.

"What is it?" Meara asked.

"I asked him to check us out of the hotel since I'll be returning to Milan tonight. He said that the desk clerk told him that someone had been asking after Brian earlier in the evening."

Cade asked Arturo a few more questions and nodded. He turned to Meara. "I'm going to have to return to Milan right away. Apparently, Arturo has James waiting in the car downstairs already. Is it alright if I don't go out to the airport with you? Henri knows that you will be traveling back with Brian, so he'll take care of getting you and Brian through Swiss Customs. You shouldn't have any problems."

Meara nodded and took Cade's hand. "We'll be fine, Cade. Really."

He looked her in the eye for one long second. "I know. But I'm going to miss you...tonight," he said softly as he leaned in to kiss her goodbye.

She smiled. "I'll miss you, too. We'll catch up when we're both back in the States," she added.

"We will," he nodded, taking her in again. He took a deep breath and turned away, stepping into the elevator with Arturo. He turned and looked at her with a deep penetrating look.

Meara returned the look and maintained the eye contact until the doors had closed between them. She felt a momentary plunging sense of loss, like her world had collapsed just a little, and her eyes welled for a second. But then she blinked the tears away and took a deep breath and squared her shoulders. The gurney rolled in next to her and when she turned and looked down at Brian, he seemed to be completely out. Just as well, she thought, his face looked pretty horrible, bloated and blotchy, almost like his face was covered with a huge red bruise. Poor kid, she thought, patting the sheet under which his arm lay. She lifted her eyes and saw Henri watching her. She smiled and he returned the smile.

The elevator pinged and opened behind her.

"D'Accord," Henri said with a nod of his head indicating that she should get onto the elevator first.

She did and then he pushed the gurney on. The nurse followed them with her eyes trained on Brian.

Once they got Brian and the gurney loaded onto the ambulance, the trip to the airport was short. They didn't use the siren; it was nearly nine o'clock on a weeknight so there wasn't much traffic on the roads. When they arrived at the Lugano airport, they stopped at a gate where a security guard had a short conversation with Henri and the driver. The guard bent over and pointed his flashlight at each of their faces and looked at all of them, and then he asked for their passports. Henri had Brian's, and Meara took hers out of her purse and leaned forward to pass it to the guard. He took the passports and paperwork and left for a few minutes and then returned, handing back their passports and tickets and other paperwork. He nodded them through and the driver drove them across the tarmac right next to the small jet parked just outside the private aviation hangar. It was next to the commercial airport facility, which was pretty quiet now. No flights were scheduled to be coming in or leaving until morning, with the exception of this medical flight.

Meara found all of the travel details interesting. She'd never flown on a private jet, although she'd certainly been on small propeller planes before. She got out of the ambulance and stood by to watch as they used a special lift to raise the gurney, with its legs now shortened, and gently lifted it so it could be rolled into the plane.

Suddenly her purse began to vibrate. For several seconds, she was confused, wondering if the plane or the lift was causing something in her purse to vibrate. But when she stuck her hand into the side pocket she immediately felt the source of the vibration. Cade's phone! Oh, no! Immediately, she wondered if Cade was calling? She pulled the phone out but the number didn't look familiar, not that she'd have any idea of what phone number he might be calling from — Arturo's, perhaps? Or maybe James' phone?

"Hello?" she said after pressing Talk.

But the voice on the other end wasn't Cade's. "Who is this?"

the male voice asked. American, she thought, definitely American.

"Who is this?" she asked in return.

"You've answered Cade Chandler's phone so I'm guessing you're a friend of his. Could I speak to him?" he asked curtly.

"Yes this is Cade's phone, but he isn't here, at the moment. Could I leave him a message?"

"He isn't 'here'? Where is here?" the man asked.

"Never mind that. Do you want me to give him a message or not?" Meara asked politely.

"Tell him John Streeter would like to meet with him. In Milan. In the lobby of the Park Hyatt Hotel. Cade will know the place."

Meara was going to ask about the time and more details, but he had already clicked off. "But..." she said into the dead phone. She looked around. Now what?

She went over to Henri who was waiting for her at the foot of the small stairs. "I can't leave," she said bluntly.

Henri looked at her in surprise. "Has something happened?" he asked in heavily accented English.

"I just received a phone call for Cade...an important phone call. But I have no way to give him the message. I must go to Milan and speak to him."

Henri's eyes grew round. "You won't be flying with us tonight?"

She shook her head. "No, I'm sorry, I can't. I must get down to Milan...somehow," she said with a worried frown.

He nodded to the ambulance driver. "Perhaps he could drive you to the train station? Shall I ask him for you? It should be no problem."

Meara smiled in relief. "Oh could you? That would be fantastic!"

In her head, she was already calculating what she must do. First, get her passport back from Henri, and then get a ticket on the next train to Milan. Then when she arrived in Milan, she'd go to the apartment and hope that Cade was there. Or should she go straight to the Hyatt and meet this John Streeter? But then, suddenly, she knew precisely what she would do. She smiled.

Chapter 66   Yesterday Once More

Arturo dropped Cade off at the apartment and then left to take James to his hotel. They agreed that Cade would call James if he heard from Streeter tonight, otherwise they would get together the next morning. Cade was hoping to be on a plane back to the States by the afternoon, at the latest. He was already regretting Meara speeding away from him, and he wasn't sure if he would ever be able to get her back into his orbit if he lost track of her now.

He looked into the bedroom and saw Meara's bottle of perfume on top of the dresser and a few of her slacks and dresses hanging in the closet. He sighed. He'd have to pack everything to get it ready to go, too, he realized. And tomorrow he would have to go over to Brian's hotel, pack his stuff and turn in his rental car. He wondered idly if he could get Arturo to do that for him?

He was tired. Maybe he'd take a shower and just go to bed. He pulled the cell phone from his pocket and pushed the button. Nothing happened. He frowned. And then suddenly he realized that it wasn't his phone; all in a rush, he realized it was Meara's dead phone. But then, where was his phone? He thought back, remembered her handing him her phone and taking his to call her son. Had she given it back to him? Damn! She must still have his phone. An icy chill went down his spine. What if Streeter called her and she answered? But she was in the air by now; how could it matter? Probably he wouldn't even get through. He relaxed a little. But how would Streeter get a hold of him then? Streeter had called him on his phone, so he would need that phone to dial back the number.

He called James at his hotel. He answered on the first ring. "What number is this your calling from?" was his first question.

Cade told him about his cell phone being with Meara and that he was now using one of the extra mobile phones from the apartment.

"Jesus Christ!" James said in disgust. "Do you think the guy will try and find you then? Or will he just give up?"

Cade thought about it. "Probably will give up. I would in his shoes," Cade added.

"So are you going home tomorrow?" James asked.

"Yeah, I have to go clean up after Brian first and get his stuff out of his hotel and get someone to drive his rental car back from Como. I want to say goodbye to my family, too. Then I'll catch a flight, maybe in the afternoon."

"OK. I'll check in with you in the morning just to see where we are. This really sucks, man," James said as he hung up.

"Yeah," Cade agreed as he clicked the End button.

He looked at his watch and saw that it was already a quarter to eleven. He yawned and decided to take a hot shower before going to bed. He felt dirty as well as exhausted, but the bed looked crisp and inviting.

After his shower, Cade wrapped the towel around his waist and went over to the sink to brush his teeth. He looked into the mirror and really stared into his eyes. He saw an aging version of himself. He had this picture of himself at about thirty or thirty-five and that's pretty much who he'd imagined himself to be, the guy he would look like forever. He suspected that if there was a Heaven that's the age he'd be there, too – a really good-looking thirty or thirty-five. He smiled at the thought. Then he heard a click from the next room. What the hell? There was no maid service in the evenings at this apartment; he was pretty sure about that.

Before he could think further about it, the door opened and Meara was standing there, out of breath and looking tired but, oh, so good.

He stared at her for a number of stunned seconds. "Meara?" It was as if he had conjured her up.

She grinned. "Well, I guess I should be glad to find you alone," she said.

He smiled. "What else? But what are you doing here?"

She bit her lip. "Sorry. I had your phone. I forgot to give it back to you."

"So you missed your flight to give me back my phone?" he asked incredulously.

She shook her head. "I wouldn't have done that, except that it rang." She looked at him significantly.

"Streeter?" he asked.

"Streeter," she confirmed with a nod. "He wants to meet you at the Hyatt."

"When?"

"Now, I guess."

"Now?"

She nodded. "I think so. He didn't actually state a time. Just said he'd be in the lobby and that you'd know where the hotel was."

"Damn."

"What?"

"You walk in looking like a dream come true. I'm naked. And I'm pretty sure I could probably get you naked pretty quickly. And now you tell me I have to get my pants back on and go out? Damn."

Meara smiled. "That must be why they pay you the big bucks."

He looked at her and opened his arms. She curled into him. "I am so glad you are here," he said softly, kissing the tip of her nose and then honing in to her lips.

She let a breath out. "I'm so glad you're glad, because I thought you'd be upset."

"Upset to see you?" Are you kidding? You're the best thing that's ever happened to me."

She stared at him. "You mean that, don't you?" she said in disbelief.

He nodded.

"Oh," she said. "I don't know if I can live up to that, Cade. I don't know if I'm ready for that...that kind of...relationship."

He looked at her. "I'm not going anywhere, Meara. I've wanted you since I was sixteen; I can wait as long as you need me to."

She just looked at him. Her fingers were twirling her wedding ring around and around on her finger. He looked down at it and watched her. She glanced down and suddenly realized what she was doing. "Sorry," she said, and stopped twirling the ring around. "Stupid nervous habit."

He nodded. "Yeah." He turned and opened the bathroom door. "I guess I need to get dressed, huh?"

"I'm coming with you to meet him," she said to his back.

He turned. "No, you're not," he replied.

"Well, but I am," she said. There was steel in her voice.

He pulled on his underwear and then sat down on the bed to put on socks. He looked up at her then. "Why would you want to come?" he asked.

"I feel like I should see this thing through."

"But why?"

"OK, it's stupid. I know it makes no sense..." she said slowly. "You see, my father died in a crazy terrorist attack. I had nothing to do with any of it personally. I wasn't there. But there was no one to help him. Maybe no one could have stopped it, but the truth is, no one even tried." She paused and shrugged. "I know, Cade, this doesn't make sense. But I need to go, to see this thing through. Brian's alive because you saved him. I was two steps behind and if it were left up to me, he'd have died at the restaurant. But then, Streeter called me on your phone, so that put me back in the game again and I don't want to bail on you. I don't want to drop the ball. Besides, I can't sit here in this apartment not knowing what is happening. That's all."

"That's the dumbest thing I've ever heard," Cade said. "You realize that makes no sense." He stood up with a grin on his face as he pulled his pants up and zipped the zipper. He walked over to her and put his arms around her. "Meara, that is ridiculous logic. Tell me that you know that, right?" He pulled her head down and kissed her forehead. "I can't believe that you brought your father and his horrible and unfair death into this. That's a play for unearned sympathy. Yikes, you are one scary fighter." He looked her in the eyes. "That last part about not being able to sit here waiting. That, by the way, I believe. So, you can come, and we will attempt to ferret out the bad guys and make all things right with the world, if we can."

"Have you been drinking, Cade?" Meara asked with a frown.

He shook his head grinning. "No, that's the beauty of it. This is all just straight up crazy."

He called James and alerted him that Streeter was probably in the lobby at the Hyatt. He hoped that he, at least, might be more prepared than they were.

With that, they left the apartment for the short walk to the Hyatt hotel.

Chapter 67   Nights in White Satin

When they walked into the lobby of the Hyatt, it was nearly empty. A few people were sitting in the comfortable cushioned divans in the far back area near the elevators, but most of the seats were empty. It was off-season, a weeknight, and getting late.

Meara looked around. She glanced at Cade who nodded at the one seat that was occupied. He shrugged.

She looked closer. Although she didn't know what the guy would look like, she supposed it could be him.

She took a breath then boldly walked up to him, "Hello, I'm Meara Cellini, a friend of Cade Chandler's." She left the rest unsaid, hoping he would say something.

He did. He leaned forward, looked at her and nodded. "Yes. We talked on the phone. So is Mr. Chandler here?" he replied softly.

She nodded, and Cade stepped forward.

"I'm Cade Chandler," he said. "But you aren't John Streeter."

The man studied him for several long seconds. "Yes, I can see it is you. And you're right. I'm not John Streeter. The name is Levitt."

He gestured for Cade to sit in the seat across from him. He ignored Meara entirely. She rolled her eyes wanting to cuff him in the side of his head for his rudeness, but she turned and moved to the couch across the way, where she could hear what was said.

"So? Where is our Mr. Reston then, Mr. Chandler?" the man asked without preamble.

Cade looked at him. "He's resting comfortably, no thanks to you folks." He stared at the man waiting for a reaction.

The man chuckled. "Didn't like the flavor of our spray I take it?" he said, catching his breath. "What? You're shocked, Mr. Chandler? That we could target him with his specific allergy, huh? I'd say it showed some impressive expertise. Pretty cool, even."

Cade continued to stare at this guy, Levitt.

"Well, I can see you need some laugh pills. Taking life too seriously, are we, Mr. Chandler? Heck, it's only an allergy," he said with a broad smirk.

Cade cringed. There was something elementally evil about this guy that gave him the creeps.

He could feel Meara looking at him and he felt that he needed to man up. "You're with AtmosTrace, right?" Cade asked. He was pleased to see the surprise in the guy's eyes. "Yeah, I figured it out. You're not with WitSec, and neither is John Streeter. That means you guys play for the other team."

"We were all on the same team once, don't forget," Levitt responded smoothly.

"The good ole days, huh?" Cade said with a sarcastic smile. "OK, let's get to it. What do you want from me?" Cade asked. "After all, you called me, remember?"

"Thought we might come to some arrangement with you is all. You told Mr. Streeter that you wanted Mr. Reston's conviction and prison record expunged. Apparently you've figured out that since we're no longer working with the government, we can't go around expunging criminal records." He chuckled. He grew serious then. "But we would like to get young Reston off our backs, so I'll just leave you with a threat instead."

Cade frowned. "A threat?"

"Sure. If Brian Reston continues harassing my company, you'll be reading about his fatal asthma attack in the news. And should you suddenly feel the urge to come after us, personally or professionally, I'm sure we can find a few of your weak spots as well." He glanced meaningfully at Meara who was sitting stiffly on the couch closer to the door.

Cade felt his anger rise. This Levitt guy was an asshole and he wished he could wipe the smug look off his face. But he promised James he wouldn't do anything but keep the guy occupied. Cade saw Meara glance up at something behind him and he saw a shadow of movement in his peripheral vision. He hoped it was James.

Levitt must have felt the change in the atmosphere, too, because he looked up sharply and squinted his eyes. "What's going on here?" he asked Cade roughly. Levitt didn't wait for an answer. He stood up and started moving towards the main doors. Then he paused and nodded, which must've been some kind of signal, Cade thought, because just then a dark figure came bounding through the door. Levitt pointed at Cade and said dryly, "Streeter, shoot them."

Cade sprang up and took the three steps to where Meara was sitting and tackled her, covering her with his body as two shots rang out. At the same moment, James ran in through the doors and leaped over a set of loveseats, and in an instant Levitt was sprawled on the floor.

Cade looked up and realized that the dark figure in the doorway wasn't Streeter at all; it was his cousin, Sergio. Sergio flicked the black hood of his jacket off his head and grinned at Cade. "Good times, Nico!" he said. "Salut!"

"Jesus, Sergio! You could've been killed."

"No, no. I met your man, James Starling, in front of the hotel. He took care of the other guy – Streeter – who was waiting outside for the signal to come in and get you."

"But," Cade shook his head in confusion. "I don't get it. What are YOU doing here?"

Meara sat up. "I called him, Cade. I got the call on your cell phone from Streeter saying he wanted to meet you at the Hyatt. I didn't have a number to call you, so I called your uncle. I knew his number would be in your phone."

Cade looked at her and smiled. "Smart thinking."

James and Uncle Vincente and a hotel employee dragged Levitt out the back door and into a waiting vehicle.

Cade nodded after them. "What are they going to do with Levitt's body?"

"He's not dead," Sergio said knowledgeably. "James just put him to sleep."

James came back in and explained the rest. "He'll wake up back in the U.S. in time to do some explaining. He tried to kill Brian Reston and you, and he tried to kill me, an American federal agent. He's got some explaining to do. Then there's the whole miniature drone device business. We've got Streeter outside."

"So who was this guy, Levitt?" Meara asked finally.

"Carlton Levitt, one of the founding partners of AtmosTrace Incorporated."

Chapter 68   Tuesday Afternoon

Cade and Meara walked slowly back to the apartment. "Do you think Arturo could drive me back to Lugano to catch that flight tomorrow morning?" Meara asked.

"There's no rush now. We can go back together tomorrow evening, or even stay another day, if you want," Cade said. He could see that she looked troubled.

Meara shook her head. "No, I need to get back to my real life, Cade." She sighed.

"OK, what are you trying to say to me here?" he asked softly.

Meara stopped walking and paused for several seconds before saying, "Cade, this is not for me." She looked around. "I don't mean Milan; I mean all this craziness." She shook her head again, and then looked up to meet his eyes. "Cade, I could've been killed back there." She waited a moment for it to sink in and then she dropped her gaze. "I have two children who lost a parent a year ago. I shouldn't be taking chances like this." She paused and shrugged. "Besides, I'm not cut out for this kind of drama."

"It's all done now, Meara. The drama is over, OK?" he said, knowing that he was desperately trying to negotiate a temporary truce, or at least, he hoped so.

She shook her head again. "No, Cade. There's no guarantee that the other guys you put in prison won't get out or that they don't have sons who want some retribution. How could I ever be sure?" She frowned. "I can't live like this. I'm not an edgy person. I like the quiet life. I liked having a husband who might've been a little boring at times, but who always came home at the same time every evening, with the same smile and enthusiasm for our life together." She looked at Cade. "But it's not just all this drama," she gestured in the air. "The truth is I'm not over that previous life yet, Cade. I'm not ready to leave it behind and start a new one yet." She dropped her eyes.

He took her hand and they continued on to the apartment in silence. There wasn't much he could say or wanted to say. Except, heck, when he looked at her, he knew that he loved her; maybe he'd always loved her. The one thing he was certain of was that he didn't want to be without her now that he'd found her again. But looking at her and seeing her resolve and the grim determined look on her face, he realized that he'd probably already lost her.

"Meara," he said.

She stopped and looked at him. She reached up and touched the side of his face. "Oh Cade, I wish you had come along when I was in my twenties before I met Tony," she said with a sad smile.

"I'm here now, Meara. I'm here now," he said softly. But he could see she wasn't listening, and his words simply evaporated into the air around them.

Chapter 69   In the Midnight Hour

When Meara finally made it back to Brookings, she found that all she wanted to do was to sleep. She'd flown from Lugano to Zurich and then on to San Francisco, a very long flight that she'd dozed through, but never really fell into a deep sleep. Arriving in San Francisco for an overnight before her puddle-jumper flight to Crescent City, she dragged herself like a zombie through the airport to the baggage area to collect her suitcase.

"Meara?"

Hearing her name, Meara turned to find Vanessa standing there, like an apparition in the baggage area.

Meara smiled, reached out and hugged the younger woman warmly. But when Vanessa tried to convince her to stay at Cade's apartment and to wait for him to arrive in a day or two, she declined. She was anxious to get back to the condo in Brookings, to think and to regroup, and it would've been anticlimactic to see him again now, she thought. There was nothing more to say.

Vanessa finally gave up and drove Meara to the Embassy Suites near the airport and they had a drink together.

"So my dad blew it, huh?" Vanessa said taking a sip of her red wine.

Meara smiled, "He didn't blow it, Vanessa. I think your dad's a really good guy. The problem was me. I thought I was ready for a real relationship and I guess I just wasn't. I should've given myself more time before I jumped back into all that again."

"What happened in Milan?" Vanessa asked quietly.

Meara got a far away look in her eyes and then shook her head as if to brush the thoughts away. "I'm not really sure. We got mixed up in some very strange..." she sighed, "Honestly, I don't know what was going on over there. Let's just say, we'll know more in the coming weeks when everything plays out." She lifted her glass of wine. "But for me, I want to take some time and get my head on straight."

"What does that mean?" Vanessa asked studying Meara's face as she answered.

Meara looked down at her wedding ring and she held her hand up. "See this? I'm still wearing my wedding ring and my husband's been gone for over a year." She shrugged. "Apparently, I haven't been ready to give it up. Maria, your grandmother, noticed that I was still wearing it and commented on it. And, you know something, Vanessa? I realized that she was right. I need to be able to take it off and put it away before I get involved in another relationship." She shook her head. "It's not fair to Cade."

Chapter 70   I Got The Feelin'

Cade came home to no fanfare and very little notice. Angie called to give him an update on Brian Reston, that he was doing fine in the hospital and that Brian's mother was with him.

He also got a call from Vanessa. "Hey, Dad. Just wanted to check in..." she said hesitantly. "How are you?"

"Hi, honey. I'm tired. I got in last night but I still need another eight hours of sleep to clear away the cobwebs in my brain," he said with a dry laugh.

"Just so you know, I had a drink with Meara the other night," Vanessa said quickly and added, "before she headed back to Oregon." She waited for his reaction.

"How is she?" he responded immediately, his interest apparent.

"She's fine. She was tired, too, but said she needed time to... uh...you know, to think about all that's happened."

There was a pause, and then he said tiredly, "Yeah, I know. We all need time. Me, too."

"Dad?" Vanessa interrupted.

"Yeah?"

"What happened in Milan?"

There was a silence for several seconds. She thought maybe he'd never answer. But then he cleared his throat. "Hard to say, honey. It was...I don't know...it was...maybe it's too soon to say what it was?" he chuckled. "When I know, I'll let you know."

"Dad?"

"Yeah?"

"Whatever it turns out to be. I'm sure you gave it your all, OK? Sometimes things just don't work out."

He hesitated, and then she heard him let his breath out in a whoosh. "Yeah, honey. I know. But to be honest, I really wanted this to work out, you know?" There was a pained wistfulness in his voice.

Chapter 71   Reach Out of the Darkness

Meara was in Brookings, but she also wasn't in Brookings. Her body was there, but her mind was a thousand miles away, well, probably more like four hundred miles away. She wondered about Cade's trip back to the States. She thought about where he was at that particular moment and wondered if he was thinking about her, too? She couldn't help herself, even though she was certain that it was over, there was a part of her that speculated nonetheless.

It wasn't as if Cade was all she thought about, of course. She wondered about Brian's recovery, too, hoping that he was fine. And she wondered how long it would take to finally readjust to her new life.

There had been so many changes — starting with Tony's death and becoming suddenly single. Then she had gone through months of dealing with the fallout of his death - reassuring his family, closing out his estate, dealing with the emotional needs of her kids. She'd escaped to Oregon to gain some perspective.

Then she met Cade, as if the fates had predestined it. How could they have ended up on the same plane, in seats next to each other? It boggled her mind. Maybe that was the reason it had all moved so fast...too fast, she reminded herself. She should've realized she wasn't ready. She needed time to just live through the transition, slowly and serenely; not at some breakneck speed.

Even though she spent a lot of time brooding, she wasn't cut off from everything. She still had her family and Jill and other friends who checked in with her, and her children called pretty regularly. She should be happy to feel so loved and needed, but she also wished she could put them all on pause for a while. She didn't want anyone but herself to have a say in how she lived her life from now on.

"Mom?" Donna asked on the phone. "When are you going to come to Colorado and see our new apartment?"

And Paul called, "Mom, I'd like to come out to Oregon to spend some time with you. Is next week OK?"

They were her children and it was her job to be there for them, wasn't it?

"Honey," she had said to Donna with a sigh, "maybe on my way back to Boston, I'll stop by for a day or two. You know that I'd love to see your apartment."

And to Paul, she said, "Sure, next week's as good a time as any. Are you sure you can take the time off, though?"

Meara didn't feel that she could fill the void for them that their father's death had left in their hearts and lives. In fact, she felt a little bereft herself, like they should be comforting her instead. But as usual, she assumed her default "everything's-OK" mode. She carried on, a smile on her lips and a perky voice on the phone, so that they wouldn't know how torn and confused she felt right now.

Was she in love with Cade? Or was she just grabbing at straws, a last chance at love and romance and a relationship? It felt over; completely over. She'd left him in Milan. How could she expect anything more from him?

She'd salve her wounds in time — that was all she needed – time. If only enough time would go by, she'd be all set. Eventually, she'd be able to resign herself to losing Cade. She'd learn to gear her life to a solo adventure headed into eventual retirement and being viewed as an older woman, past her prime.

Damn! She hated getting old. She wanted, particularly now that she was single, to be in the game again. She got a taste of being a part of life again with Cade. She wasn't in the game now; not any more. She was a middle-aged has-been, side-lined. No fair, was all she could think. No damn fair! Don't I get another shot? I'm not old! I still have a lot of life in me; I'm smart, I'm healthy; I shouldn't be sidelined like this. Not now. Heck, not ever!

But, she wouldn't call him. And that was her failing. She was sure that he was waiting for her to make a move. But she couldn't.

Chapter 72   People Get Ready

Cade walked down the beach, his sandals swinging from his hand. He could see her sitting on the sand facing out towards the water. He saw that she wasn't alone; but he wasn't surprised because he knew her son was in from Boston visiting her. He knew that because two weeks ago he'd called Paul; an awkward conversation if ever there was one.

It took some time but eventually he realized that Meara had her pride and she wasn't going to contact him. He'd be damned if he'd lose her again. So he swallowed his pride and called Paul to ask if he could meet with him when he was in Boston on business the following week.

Paul was hesitant, but also very curious. His mother was tightlipped about her private life and completely glossed over the short trip to Milan, which had baffled him. She was a woman who liked to travel and enjoyed recounting her adventures. So after only a moment's hesitation, he agreed to meet this mystery man, Cade.

They went out for drinks in Boston's North End and Cade told Paul the story about meeting Meara in Bangkok when they were teenagers, running into each other on the plane to San Francisco, and eventually making the trip to Milan. He didn't mention Brian or AtmosTrace and naturally, veered away from discussing the sleeping arrangements. Paul was her son, after all.

"So, Cade? What is it you want from me?" Paul had asked finally, eyeing Cade over the top of his glass of beer.

Cade had leaned back and let out his breath. "Your mom cares what you and your sister think. I guess I'm hoping to get your blessing."

"My blessing?" Paul repeated with a grin.

Cade looked flustered for a second, then he leaned forward and said, "Look, Paul. I come from a large Italian family that's filled with busybodies, and it's a real pain in the ass at times. But when it's not a pain, I've learned a few things about the right way to start a relationship. And that is if you want someone to be a part of your life, you have to reach out and bring in the families."

Paul blinked and finally nodded. "Makes sense. Although I'm afraid you may have a fight from my sister. She's barely able to admit my dad is gone, much less that mom might want to date someone."

"Well, to be honest, I'm not positive she still wants to date me anymore, but I'm not giving up just yet," Cade said with a smile. And that led into Cade telling Paul about the Witness Protection years, his name change, and how he was now kicking himself for not being as open and honest with Meara from the beginning.

By the end of the evening, Paul had agreed to serve as go-between. "I'm going out to Oregon to see Mom next week," Paul said. "I should be able to find out whether there's any hope for you or not. I have to warn you that she can be a very stubborn woman."

Cade nodded and chuckled. "You don't have to tell me that." He paused and looked seriously at Paul. "Thanks. I'd really appreciate your help."

* * *

The sand was warm beneath Cade's feet as he walked slowly towards her. She was facing away from him, watching Paul jog down the beach. His phone vibrated in his pocket, but he didn't want to talk to anyone on the phone right now; he only wanted to talk to her. He smiled at the thought of talking to her again.

Chapter 73   Magic Carpet Ride

The sun was bright and warm and there was only the slightest of sea breezes. Meara could hear the seabirds squawking above the sea stacks off shore. Paul had just jogged off down the beach, but his words had stayed with her.

"You should call him, Mom," Paul had said. "At least, talk to him. I know you really liked him. You wouldn't have gone to Milan with him if you didn't." Paul had kicked off his sandals as he said, "It's not like you to give up on something you care about... especially someone you care about." Then he jogged off before she could respond.

She watched him for a few minutes thinking about what he had said; thinking about Cade. Then she shrugged and felt for her phone in her pocket. He was right; she wasn't the sort to give up on something...or someone who was important to her. His number was in her contacts. She took a deep breath and smiled as she made the call.

She heard the phone ring, and then ring several more times before going to voice mail. She panicked and ended the call. What would she say? What excuse would she use for calling?

She was looking down at her phone when she noticed the shadow on the sand in front of her. She looked up and saw Cade standing there. She blinked a couple of times, wondering if she had conjured him up. Then she smiled as a new warmth filled her. "You came," she said, blocking the glare of the sun with her hand in order to see him better.

"I did," Cade replied.

"I just tried to call you," she said, indicating her phone.

He grinned and pulled out his phone and saw her number in his Missed Call listing. "I should've answered it."

Paul came jogging up and Meara smiled.

"Cade, I understand that you've met my son, Paul," she said.

"Paul?" Cade repeated with a nod and then looked down at Meara and grinned, "Named him 'Paul,' eh?"

Paul glanced from one to the other. "Oh, Jesus, Mom!" he said in exasperation. He looked at Cade, "Don't tell me she told you the story about naming me after Paul McCartney?" He shook his head in mock disgust.

Cade nodded and chuckled. "Hey, there are worse people to be named after...it could've been Paul Revere and the Raiders..."

Meara grinned, "What Cade? You didn't like Paul Revere and the Raiders? Really? Not even 'Louie, Louie'?" And she laughed at the look of confusion on her son's face.

Paul rolled his eyes, "You two are made for each other." He picked up his sandals. "I'll leave you two to figure things out. I'm going up to take a shower. Nice to see you, Cade. We can talk more about Sixties rock groups later..." he added dryly then paused and said, "that is, if she lets you stay." He grinned maliciously at Cade, then turned and headed towards the trail up to the condo..

Cade looked after him for a few seconds then glanced down at Meara. "Nice kid. And he has a good point. So...do I get to stay?"

She looked up at him, squinting against the bright sunshine again. "Probably shouldn't let you," she sighed, "but I have to admit that you sure know how to answer a phone call."

He sat down next to her and nuzzled his shoulder against hers until she looked at him. "I can be very entertaining. I have a million stories that you haven't heard yet."

"True stories?" She laughed and rested her head on his shoulder for a second. He reached down and took her hand in his and gently squeezed it, then laced his fingers in hers. A second passed and then his brow furrowed. He lifted her hand still linked in his and saw that her wedding ring was gone. He looked at her questioningly and she just shrugged. "I still have it; I just decided it was time to stop wearing it."

Cade smiled and they were quiet for several minutes.

"By the way," he said, "I ran into Mr. Pierson on my way down."

Meara grinned.

He shook his head. "I can't believe you slept with that guy."

She jabbed him lightly in the ribs. "You needed to be brought down a notch, as I recall. Besides, he's a sweet old guy."

"I'm keeping my eye on him, just the same," Cade said.

The waves gently curled into the shore and gulls continued to circle the sea stack a hundred yards out. Meara broke the silence, "Have you seen Brian?"

Cade nodded but continued watching the gulls. "He's out of the hospital and the last time I talked to him he was desperately trying to get his mother to return to Minneapolis."

Meara smiled. "Good, I'm glad he's OK."

Cade squeezed her hand and she glanced at him. "I told him I'm looking into his father's case."

Meara squinted, "Do you think you can do anything for him, Cade?"

"About his father? Sure. Not so sure I can do much about AtmosTrace, but I've got one of our associates digging up whatever information is available. We'll see."

Meara nodded and enjoyed the feeling of her hand in his as they sat quietly watching the gulls and the rolling surf. She took a deep breath and let it out slowly. This pausing and savoring moments in her life was something she had come to realize was important after Tony's death. So many days and weeks and months of their life together had gone by in the routine of daily living, and even though they were content in that life, it was a blur with few markers of cherished memories.

The truth is that we only remember moments. And this was one of those moments that she wanted to store away: her sitting next to Cade, shoulder to shoulder and hands clasped on this empty beach in Oregon on an unseasonably warm September afternoon. She closed her eyes for a second and when she opened them, she glanced up at the blue sky and saw that it, like her new view of her future, was completely clear; blue and cloudless all the way to the horizon.

About the Author - M.H. Sullivan

Prior to moving to New Hampshire in 1977, the author spent most of the previous 20+ years living overseas. As the daughter of a U.S. State Department diplomat, she lived in Korea, Taiwan, the Philippines, Thailand, and Ethiopia.

After graduating from Boston University, she worked in Washington, D.C. as a travel agent and then as a staff aide on Capitol Hill. She moved to NH in 1977 and got married in 1978 and has lived in NH ever since. She has two daughters.

Maureen has written travel articles, poetry, and fiction, and was the publisher of the *Southern NH Children's Directory* and related publications from 1994 to 1999. In 2008, she published her first novel, *Travel Magic: Lost in Crawford Notch*, and in 2010, she published a memoir, *The Sullivan Saga: Memories of an Overseas Childhood*.

Books by M.H. Sullivan:

Trail Magic: Lost in Crawford Notch
   (ISBN#978-1-891486-09-8)

The Sullivan Saga: Memories of an Overseas Childhood
   (ISBN#978-1-891486-13-5)

Jet Trails: Looking for Blue Skies
   (ISBN#978-1-891486-01-2)